LOVE IN THE LIMELIGHT

LIMELIGHT

VOLUME ONE

NEW YORK TIMES BESTSELLING AUTHOR

BRENDA JACKSON

A.C. ARTHUR

LOVE IN THE LIMELIGHT

VOLUME ONE

HARLEQUIN® KIMANI ARABESQUE®

Love in the Limelight Volume One
ISBN-13: 978-0-373-09163-8

Copyright © 2014 by Harlequin Books S.A.

This edition published October 2014

Recycling programs
for this product may
not exist in your area.

The publisher acknowledges the copyright
holders of the individual works as follows:

Star of His Heart
Copyright © 2010 by Brenda Streater Jackson

Sing Your Pleasure
Copyright © 2010 by Artist Arthur

Printed in U.S.A.

CONTENTS

Dear Reader,

Love in the Limelight Volume One presents a pair of wonderfully inspired stories that will take you on an exciting journey of romance into the world of fantasy, fortune and fame.

New York Times bestselling author Brenda Jackson introduces Rachel Wellesley in *Star of His Heart*, a woman who is afraid to fall for any man. But when Ethan Chambers comes along, he is determined to heal her heart.

In A.C. Arthur's *Sing Your Pleasure*, Charlene Quinn and Akil Hutton's love for music has the potential to set the stage for a *real* love that could ultimately save them both....

We hope you will enjoy *Love in the Limelight Volume One*, and look out for *Love in the Limelight Volume Two*, available next month.

All the very best,

The Harlequin Kimani Editors

STAR OF HIS HEART
Brenda Jackson

To my Heavenly Father. How Great Thou Art.

A good name is to be chosen rather than great riches,
loving favor rather than silver and gold.
—*Proverbs* 22:1

Chapter 1

"Quiet on the set!

"Take one!

"Action!"

The director's voice blared from the bullhorn and the words sent a pleasurable thrill up Rachel Wellesley's spine. She had known before she'd uttered her first words as a child that she had an overabundance of artsy bones in her body.

The only problem was that as she got older, her choice of an artistic career would change from week to week. First she had wanted to become a painter, then a writer. Later on she had considered becoming a fashion stylist. But at the fine arts college she'd attended, after she took theory and practicum classes on beauty, she had finally decided on a career as a makeup artist and wardrobe designer. This was the life she lived for and what she enjoyed—being on the set of a movie. Or in this case, the TV set that was taping the popular prime-time medical drama *Paging the Doctor*.

It was day one of shooting for the second season. All the cast members from last season had returned except for Eric Woods, who'd played Dr. Myles Bridgestone. No one had been surprised to hear his contract was not renewed, especially with all his personal drama last season. The well-known Hollywood movie star had evidently felt it beneath him to do TV and to play a role other than a leading one. But the ratings of his last few movies had plummeted. Everyone who worked with him last season had been aware of his constant complaints. Eric was an egomaniac and a director's worst nightmare.

Rachel had managed to get along with Eric, but she couldn't say the same for others who considered him a pain in the rear end. But then, her older sister Sofia claimed Rachel could get along with just about anybody, and she would have to agree. It took a lot to rock her boat. She was easygoing by nature and was an all-around nice person. She figured some things just weren't worth the hassle of getting high blood pressure and stress.

A slight movement out of the corner of her eye made her shift her focus to the actor she'd heard would be added to the show this season in the role of Dr. Tyrell Perry. His name was Ethan Chambers.

He had been in Hollywood only a couple of years and already, at twenty-eight, he had taken the town by storm. And most noticeably, over the past few months, he and his playboy behavior had become quite the talk in the tabloids and gossip columns.

She gave him an appreciative glance. The only thing she had to say was that if the producer added Ethan to the show to boost the ratings, then he had hit the mark. Ethan was definitely eye candy of the most delicious kind. There was no doubt in her mind he would stir the interest of their female viewers, young and old, single or married.

And she couldn't help noticing he had already stirred the interest of several of the females on the set. He seemed oblivious to the open stares as he talked to a man she assumed was his agent. Although she found Ethan extremely attractive, she was too much of a professional to mix her private life with her professional one. And the one thing she detested above all else was being in the spotlight, which was something he evidently enjoyed since he'd managed to garner a lot of publicity lately.

She thought that his flashing white smile was as sexy as they came and figured he would be perfect for any toothpaste commercial. He was tall, probably six foot two, and powerfully built with broad shoulders, muscled arms and a masculine chest. He did a whole lot for those scrubs he was wearing. The company that manufactured the medical attire should be grateful, since he practically turned them into a fashion statement.

And last but not least was his cocoa-colored face with those striking blue-gray eyes—a potentially distracting pair for any woman fool enough to gaze into them too long—and his ultrasexy dimpled jaw. She had to hand it to him, he was as handsome as any male could get in her book, hands down.

A soft smile lifted the corners of her lips as she thought that this was bound to be an interesting season. Already a number of the women on the set were vying for his attention. The show's director, Frasier Glenn, would just love that.

"Cut! Good scene, everyone. Let's move on!"

Frasier's words had Rachel moving quickly toward the producer, John Gleason, and Livia Blake, a model and budding actress who would be guest-starring on the show for a few episodes as Dr. Sonja Duncan. The scene they had just filmed was an emotional one in which Dr. Duncan had broken the news to a devoted husband that his wife had died of cardiac arrest.

Livia would be in the next scene as well and it was Rachel's job to refresh her hair and makeup. And since Rachel was also the wardrobe designer for the show, she needed to verify John's request for a change in the outfit Livia would be wearing in the scene they would be shooting later today.

Rachel flashed a look back to Ethan Chambers, and her gaze raked over him once again. The man by his side was doing all the talking, and for a quick moment she detected a jumpy tension surrounding Ethan. She had been around enough actors on their first day on the set to tell he was nervous. That surprised her. If anything, she would think a man with his looks would be brimming over with self-confidence, even arrogance. If he wasn't, than he was different from Eric Woods in more ways than one.

Ethan Chambers took another sip from the water bottle, wishing it was a cold beer instead. He couldn't believe he had finally gotten his lucky break and was here, on the set of *Paging the Doctor,* playing the role of a neurosurgeon. He wasn't a hospital maintenance man or a victim who needed medical care but a doctor. He had landed the role of a lifetime on what was one of the most top-rated shows.

He would even go so far as to pinch himself if there weren't so many people around, and if his agent, Curtis Fairgate, wasn't standing right next to him, smiling, gloating and taking it all in. And of course, Curtis was ready to take credit for the whole thing, as if Ethan hadn't worked his tail off to get where he was now.

He thought about the three years he had studied acting abroad while doing some well-received but small theater gigs. He could finally say he was now building an acting career. Even his older brother, Hunter, who had tried pressuring him to stay in the family business, was happy for him now. And that meant a lot.

"You do know your lines, don't you?"

Ethan lifted a brow, not believing Curtis would ask such a thing. "Of course. I might be nervous but I'm not stupid. I'm not about to screw up my big break."

"Good."

Ethan pulled in a slow breath, wondering how he and Curtis had managed to survive each other for the past two years. Hollywood agents were known to be pushy, cynical and, in some cases, downright rude. Curtis was all three and then some. Ethan only kept him around because they had a fairly decent working relationship, and Curtis *had* managed to land him a spot on this show by talking to the right people. But Curtis probably would not have managed that if the sister of one of Ethan's former girlfriends hadn't been the current lover of one of the show's writers.

Curtis began talking, rambling on about something Ethan had no desire to listen to, so he glanced around, fascinated at how things were going and what people were doing. He had been on the set of a television show several times, but this was his first time on one that Frasier Glenn directed, and he couldn't help but admire how smoothly things were running. The word around Hollywood was that Frasier was a hard man to work for, a stickler for structure, but he was highly respected in the industry.

Ethan was about to pull his concentration back to the conversation he was supposed to be having with Curtis when his gaze settled on a gorgeous petite woman wearing a cute baby-doll top and a pair of wide-leg jeans. She was gorgeous in a restrained sort of way. He figured she was an actress on the show and wondered what role she played.

She couldn't be any taller than five foot two, but he thought she was a sexy little thing with her short dark hair and exotic looks. And she was smiling, which was a change of pace since everyone else seemed to look so doggone serious.

"Ethan!"

Curtis snapped his fingers in Ethan's face, cutting into his thoughts. "Don't even think it, Ethan," the man warned.

Ethan blinked, and an annoyed expression showed on his face as he met Curtis's gaze. "Think what?"

"About getting involved with anyone on this set, especially that hot little number over there. I know that look."

Ethan frowned. He liked women. He enjoyed sex. He did short-term affairs better than anyone he knew. The women he was involved with weren't looking for long-term any more than he was. "Why?" he finally asked.

"Frasier usually frowns on that sort of thing on his set, that's why."

Ethan took another sip of his water before asking, "Are you saying that he has a fraternization policy?"

"No, but a workplace romance isn't anything he gets thrilled about, trust me. It can cause unnecessary drama, and Frasier doesn't like drama since it can take away from a good day's work."

Ethan didn't say anything as his gaze found the object of his interest once again. For some reason, he had a feeling she would be worth any damn drama that got stirred. He shook his head, thinking he needed to put his player's mentality in check for a while, at least until the end of the season. Making his mark on this show was his goal, and now that he was in the driver's seat and pursuing his dream, the most important thing was for him to stay focused.

Although the urge to hit on the sexy pixie was strong, he would keep those longings in check. Besides, she probably wasn't even his type.

"I have a feeling you're going to be a big hit this season, Ethan."

Ethan glanced over at the woman who had introduced herself earlier as Paige Stiles, one of the production assistants. "Thanks."

"And like I said, if you ever need help with your lines after hours, just let me know. I will make myself available."

"I appreciate that, Paige." The offer seemed friendly enough, but he recognized it for what it was. The woman had been coming on to him ever since they had met earlier that day. She wasn't bad looking, in fact he thought her rather attractive; but she hadn't stirred his fire the same way the sexy pixie had.

Once the show had begun taping one scene after another, the petite brunette had all but disappeared. If she was an actress on the show then her segment was evidently being shot later. He was tempted to ask Paige who she was but thought better of it. The one thing a man didn't do was ask a woman who was interested in him about another woman.

"So where are we headed?" he asked as they moved away from the set toward an exit door.

"To the makeup trailer. That's also where wardrobe is located since the same person handles both."

He lifted a brow. "Is there a reason for that?" he asked, since that wasn't the norm, especially for a show of this magnitude. It was a lot of responsibility for one person.

"None other than that she wanted to do both, and Frasier obliged her. But he would since her last name happens to be Wellesley."

Ethan immediately recognized the last name. The Wellesleys were the brilliant minds behind Limelight Entertainment Management, one of the top talent agencies in the world. Their clientele consisted of some of the best in Hollywood, although in recent years they had expanded to represent more than actors. The firm now represented an assortment of talent that included big-name singers, set designers, costume designers, writers and makeup artists.

"Wellesley?" he asked.

"Yes, the high-and-mighty."

Ethan had the ability to read people, women in particular, and had easily detected the scorn in her voice. And because he knew about women in particular, he decided to change the subject. "How long have you worked for *Paging the Doctor?*"

She began talking and just as he'd done to Curtis earlier, he nodded while he tuned her out. His thoughts drifted back to the woman he'd seen earlier and he wondered if and when their paths would cross again and they would finally meet.

Finally a break, Rachel thought, sliding into a chair that was now empty. She had been in the trailer for the past five hours or so. She had sent one of her assistants out on the set to do those second-by-second touch-ups as needed while she hung out in the makeup/wardrobe trailer, making sure those actors shooting their scenes for the first time that day went through their initial makeup routine.

A couple of the scenes being shot today showed the doctors out of the hospital and in a more relaxed atmosphere either at home or out on dates, which called for a change from medical garments to casual wear.

John had approved her choice of outfits, and she felt good about that, especially since the outfit she'd selected for Livia hadn't been on John's preapproved list. And some of the artwork being used as props were her own creations. Other than Frasier and John, few people knew that when she left here at night she became Raquel, the anonymous canvas artist whose work was showcased in a number of galleries.

Her sister was worried that with being a makeup artist and wardrobe designer by day and a painter at night, Rachel had no time for a love life. But that was the least of Rachel's concerns. She was only twenty-six and wasn't ready for a serious involvement with any man.

In her early twenties she'd dated a lot, but to this day she couldn't admit to ever falling in love. She would like to believe such a thing could happen for her. Her aunt and uncle had a loving relationship, and she'd been told her parents had had one, too. Regrettably, they had been killed in a plane accident before her second birthday.

Rachel eased out of her chair when she heard conversation outside her door and glanced at the schedule posted on the wall. She wasn't supposed to work on anyone for another hour or so. Who could be infringing on her free time?

There was a knock on the trailer door, followed by a turn of the knob. Rachel fought to keep the frown off her face when Paige stuck her head in. The twenty-four-year-old woman had gotten hired during the middle of the first season. For some reason they had rubbed each other the wrong way that first day and things hadn't improved since. Rachel still didn't know the reason Paige disliked her, but figured it had to do with Rachel's amicable relationship with Frasier and John.

"So you're here," Paige said in a voice that for some reason gave Rachel the feeling Paige wished she wasn't.

Determined to present a friendly facade despite Paige's funky attitude, she smiled and said, "Yes, I'm here. Was there something you wanted?"

"Frasier wants to go ahead and shoot the next scene as soon as lunch is over, which means you need to get started on this guy right away."

Paige came inside the trailer, followed by the hunky and sexy Ethan Chambers. The moment Rachel's gaze clashed with those blue-gray eyes of his, she knew for the first time in her life how it felt to be totally mesmerized. And nothing could have prepared her for her hormones suddenly igniting into something akin to mind-blowing lust.

Chapter 2

So this was where his sexy pixie had gone to, Ethan thought, entering the trailer and glancing around. He pretended interest in everything inside the trailer except for the woman who'd been in the back of his mind since he'd first seen her that morning. And now here she was.

"Rachel, this is Ethan Chambers and starting this season he'll be a regular on the show as Dr. Tyrell Perry. Ethan, this is Rachel Wellesley, the makeup artist for the show. She's the wardrobe designer as well."

Again Ethan picked up a bit of scorn in Paige's voice, although she had a smile plastered on her face. But then it was evident her smile was only for him.

He crossed the room and extended his hand. "Nice meeting you, Rachel."

"Ditto, Ethan. Welcome to *Paging the Doctor*."

The moment she placed her hand in his he was tempted to bring it to his lips, something he had gotten used to doing while living abroad in France. And when she smiled up at him the temptation increased. She had such a pretty smile.

"John wants him ready for his scene in thirty minutes. I'll be back to get him, so make sure he's on time."

Both Ethan and Rachel glanced over at Paige and

watched as she exited the trailer, leaving them alone. Ethan returned his gaze to Rachel once again and couldn't help asking, "What's got her panties in a wad?"

Rachel couldn't help the laughter that flowed from her mouth, and when he joined in, she knew immediately she was going to like this guy. But then, what wasn't there to like?

Up close, Ethan Chambers was even more handsome than he had been across the room earlier. With him on the show, this would be a pretty good season. She couldn't wait to see them shoot his scene.

She finally answered him. "I have no idea," she said. "But we won't worry ourselves about it. My job is to get you ready for your scene."

"But what about your lunch? Shouldn't you be eating something?"

"I should be asking you the same thing, but to answer your question, usually I bring lunch from home and eat while taking care of business matters," she said, thinking about the order she had downloaded off her iPhone. *Libby's,* an art gallery in Atlanta, had just requested several of her paintings to display.

He nodded. "I'm too nervous to eat so I asked if I could go ahead and get the makeup part taken care of. I apologize if I'm infringing on your time."

She waved off his words. "You're not, so just go ahead and take the chair while I pull your file."

"My file?"

"Yes. Sorry, I can be anal when it comes to being organized, but there's no other way to work with Frasier and John. I have a file of all the scenes you'll be doing today, what you'll need to wear and the extent of lighting needed for that particular shot, although the latter is definitely changeable on the set. That gives me an idea of what kind of makeup I need to apply."

She tried not to notice how he slid into the chair; specifically, how his muscular thighs straddled it before his perfectly shaped backside came in contact with the cushioned seat. She grabbed the folder off the rack and tried to ignore the dark hair that dusted his muscular arms. However, something caught her attention. A tattoo of a cluster of purple grapes draped above his wrist.

"Grapes?" she asked, meeting his gaze and finding it difficult to breathe while looking into his eyes.

"Yes. It's there to remind me of home."

"Home?" she echoed, breaking eye contact to reach over and hand him a smock to put on.

"Yes. Napa Valley."

She recalled the time she'd visited the area years ago as part of a high school field trip. "I've been to Napa Valley once. It's beautiful."

"Yes, it is. I hated leaving it," he said after putting on the smock.

She glanced over and met those killer eyes again. "Then why did you?"

He would be justified to tell her it wasn't her business, she quickly thought, but for some reason she knew he wouldn't do that. They had met just moments ago, but she felt she knew him, or knew men like him. No, she corrected herself. She didn't know any man like him, and how she could say that with such certainty, she wasn't sure.

"I left to pursue my dream. Unfortunately, it wasn't connected to my family business," he said.

Now that she understood. Her sister and uncle always

thought she would join them in the family business, but she hadn't. Limelight Entertainment Management had been founded by her father, John Wellesley, and his brother Jacob. It had been the dream they shared and made into reality, with the purpose of representing and building the careers of African American actors during a time when there were many prejudices in Hollywood. Today the company was still very highly respected and had helped many well-known stars jump-start their careers.

"It's a nice tattoo, but I'll need to use some cream to completely cover it for the shoot. Dr. Perry doesn't have a tattoo," she explained, pressing a button that eased the chair into a reclining position

"That's no problem. Do whatever you have to do, Rachel."

It wasn't what he'd said but how he'd said it that sent sensuous chills coursing through her. For a timeless moment, they stared at each other as heat flooded her in a way it never had before. As the flames of awareness licked at her body, somehow a part of her—the sensible part—remained unscathed. In a nagging voice it reminded her that she needed to get back on track and prep Ethan for his scene.

She swallowed and broke eye contact with him again as she turned to reach for her makeup kit. "Comfortable?"

"Yes."

"Then why are you so nervous?" she decided to ask him while checking different tubes of makeup cream for one that would work with his complexion and skin type. It was August, and although the air conditioner on the set would be on full blast, all the lighting being used would generate heat. She needed to prevent any facial shiny spots from showing up on camera.

He shifted in his seat and she glanced over at him. "This is the first day on the job of what I see as my big break," he said, straightening in the chair. "This is what I've worked my ass off for since the day I decided acting was what I wanted to do. I've done small parts in theater and guest spots on a couple of shows and was even an extra on *Avatar,* but being here, getting this opportunity, is a dream come true."

She nodded, knowing just how he felt. She had wanted to step out on her own without any help from her family's name. She had submitted her résumé to Glenn Productions and had gotten called in for an interview with both Frasier and John. Although Frasier had been a friend of her father's, and both men were well acquainted with Sofia since she was Uncle Jacob's partner in the family business, Rachel was convinced she had been given the job on her own merits and hadn't been given any preferential treatment.

This was her second season on the show and she worked doubly hard to make sure Frasier and John never regretted their decision to give her a chance. So, yes, she knew all about dreams coming true.

The first thing she thought as she applied a light brush to Ethan's face was that he had flawless skin with a healthy glow. He had perfect bone structure and his lips were shapely and full. She bent toward him to gently brush his brows and was glad he had closed his eyes since crazy things were going on in the pit of her stomach. A tightness was there that had never been there before. She drew in a deep breath to relieve the pressure. His aftershave smelled good. Almost too good for her peace of mind.

"So tell me, Rachel, what's your dream?"

She smiled. "What makes you think I have one?"

"All women do."

She chuckled. "Sounds like you think you know us pretty well."

"I wouldn't say that, but I would think everyone has at least one dream they would love to see come true."

"I agree, and this is mine—being a makeup artist and wardrobe designer."

"You're good at it. Very professional."

He opened his eyes to meet hers and she was aroused in a way that just wasn't acceptable, especially for a woman who made it her motto never to mix business with pleasure.

"Thanks," she said, taking a step back and reaching over to grab a hand mirror to give to him. "You didn't need much. I don't believe in being heavy-handed with makeup."

"I can appreciate that."

She had made up enough men in her day to know if they had a choice they would gladly skip this part in preparing for their scene. "Now for that tattoo. I have just the thing to blend in with your skin tone that won't rub off. And later you can wash it off."

"Okay."

He held out his arm and she began applying the cream. Against her fingertips, his skin felt warm, slowly sending her body into meltdown. She could feel his eyes on her but refused to glance up and look at him for fear that he would know what touching him was doing to her. Instead she tried concentrating on what she was doing. This time, though, she was too distracted by other things, such as the feel of his strong veins beneath her fingers and the rapid beat of his pulse. Her body responded with a raging flood of desire that seeped into her bones.

Not being able to resist temptation any longer, she looked over at him. For a long, achingly seductive moment, they stared at each other. She wanted to look away but it was as if he controlled the movement of her neck and it refused to budge. She swallowed the panic she felt lodged in her throat as she slowly released his hand. So much for being a firm believer in the separation of business and pleasure. For a moment, no matter how brief, thoughts had filled her mind about how it would be to take her hand and rub it down his chest and then move her hand even lower to—

There was a quick knock at the door before it opened and Paige walked in. And for the first time ever, Rachel was glad to see the woman.

Chapter 3

"If he's as hot as you say he is, then maybe you should let him know you might be interested, Rachel."

Rachel wiped paint from her hands as she glared at the phone. If her best friend since elementary school wasn't there in person to see her frown, transmitting it through the speakerphone was the next best thing. "I'm not interested."

And because she knew Charlene would belabor the point, she went on the defensive and said, "Look, Cha, I thought you of all people would understand. You know I don't like mixing business with pleasure. Besides, I have plenty of work to do."

Charlene laughed. "You always have plenty of work to do. If becoming involved with a man is a way to slow you down, then I'm all for it. It's time you started having fun."

Rachel rolled her eyes. "I could say the same for you."

"Face it. Men aren't drawn to me like they are to you."

Rachel pulled in a deep breath knowing there was no use telling Charlene just how wrong she was. Her words would go in one ear and out the other. For once she wished Charlene would be the one to face it and see that she was beautiful and sexy.

Charlene had to be the kindest and sweetest person Rachel knew, but she always slid to the background when it came to dating and romance. Rachel blamed Charlene's parents, since they always thought their older daughter, Candis, was the "pretty one" and had always put her in the limelight. As far as Rachel was concerned, Charlene had a lot going for her, including a beautiful singing voice.

"I'm in no mood to argue with you, Cha. You know how mad I get when you put yourself down."

"I'm not putting myself down. I'm just stating facts."

"Then let me state a few of my own," Rachel said. "I'm the one on set every day surrounded by gorgeous men. The only problem is that those men are checking out the tall, slender actresses, not me."

When Charlene didn't say anything, Rachel had a feeling there was more going on with her friend. "Okay, Cha, what's wrong?"

There was another long moment before Charlene replied, "I talked to Mom today."

Rachel slumped down into a chair. Mrs. Quinn was the mom from hell, and that was putting it kindly. She'd always managed to boost one daughter up while at the same time tearing the other one down. "And?"

"And she wanted me to know that Candis made the cut for the *Sports Illustrated* swimsuit edition next year and will be staying in Paris for a while."

"That's great, and I'm sure you're happy for her." Rachel knew she could say that because deep down she knew Charlene was. Candis and Charlene had a rather good relationship despite the competitive atmosphere created by their mother.

"Yes, of course I'm happy for her."

"And?"

"And what?" Charlene asked.

Rachel pulled in a deep breath; her patience was wearing thin. "And what else did Mrs. Quinn say?"

"Just the usual about she still doesn't understand how Candis could be so pretty and me so plain when we had the same parents. She ended the call by even suggesting that maybe she and Dad got the wrong baby from the hospital. She said it in a joking way but I knew she was dead serious."

Rachel bet the woman had been dead serious as well, but she would never tell Charlene that. That was the kind of garbage she'd had to put up with all her life. "She wasn't serious, Cha. You and your mother look too much alike for you to be anyone's baby but hers."

Evidently Mrs. Quinn never took the time to notice the similarity. Or maybe she *had* noticed and since she'd never been happy with her own looks, she was passing her insecurities on to Charlene.

Rachel thought about her own situation. She had been raised by her uncle Jacob and her aunt Lily after her parents had been killed. Rachel had been only one year old and Sofia had been ten. Her aunt and uncle were wonderful and had raised her and Sofia as their own children, since unfortunately they'd never had any. The one thing Uncle Jacob and Aunt Lily didn't do was play her and Sofia against each other. Everyone knew that Sofia wanted to follow in their father's footsteps and take his place with Uncle Jacob at Limelight.

Although her uncle and sister would have loved for

her to join them in the family business, Rachel had never been pressured to do so. She chuckled, thinking it was enough to have Sofia as her agent.

"Hey, let's do a movie this weekend," she suggested, thinking her best friend needed some chilling time.

"Sounds super, but don't you have a lot to do?"

Rachel laughed. "I always have a lot to do, but I need a break to have fun, and it sounds like you do, too."

A short while later, Rachel made her way to the kitchen, hungry after missing lunch. On the way home she had stopped by a restaurant owned by one of the cameramen's parents. She considered Jack Botticello her buddy, and his parents were truly a godsend. Whenever she dropped by their Italian restaurant, Botticello's Place, for takeout, they always gave her more food than she could possibly eat in one sitting. There would definitely be enough lasagna left for tomorrow's dinner.

As she sat down at the table to enjoy her meal, she recalled everything that had happened on the set that day, especially the scenes that included Ethan Chambers. She couldn't help but remember the moment he had walked into a patient's hospital room. To say he swaggered into the room would probably be more accurate. And when he began speaking in what was supposed to be a northern accent, all eyes and ears were on him. There was no doubt in her mind he was a gifted actor. It was as if the part of Dr. Tyrell Perry had been created just for him.

She couldn't wait for the airing of the show in a few weeks to see how he would be received by the viewing audience. It would probably be no different than the way he'd been received on the set. Women were all but falling at his feet, doing just about anything to get his attention.

He had mentioned to a member of the camera crew in between scenes that he was going to get a cup of coffee. The three women who'd overheard him had all but broken their necks racing across the room to the coffee cart to get it for him. She could tell he'd actually gotten embarrassed by their antics. That surprised her. Most men would be gloating about all the attention. But then, this had been his first day on the job. There was no doubt in her mind that eventually his media-hungry playboy tendencies would come out. It was only a matter of time.

Unbidden, the memories surfaced of what had happened during their makeup session that day. Had he deliberately tried to unnerve her? Break down her defenses so she would behave the way Tina, Cindy and Nina had done today with the coffee incident? It wouldn't surprise her to discover he was just as superficial as all the other playboys in Hollywood. And to think for a short while today she'd actually been attracted to him. But with his make-you-drool looks, the attraction couldn't be helped. It had a way of vamping your senses the first time around.

And his family had money. He'd mentioned his roots were in Napa Valley, but it was only later that day when she'd overheard some of the camera crew talking about how wealthy he already was that she realized he was one of *those* Chamberses. There were two African American families whose roots and vast financial empires were in Napa Valley. The Russells and the Chamberses. Both families' vineyards were known to produce some of wine tasters' finest.

So, okay, she had let her guard down and let herself be affected by him. But tomorrow would be better. She had gotten used to him and would be more in control.

With that resolved, she proceeded to finish her meal.

"Do you promise, Uncle Ethan?"

Ethan couldn't help but smile. "Yes, I promise."

"Truly?"

"Yes, truly."

His six-year-old niece, Kendra, had him wrapped around her finger and probably knew it, he thought. When his parents had mentioned to her that Los Angeles was close to Disneyland, she had begun asking him questions. Mainly she wanted to know if he'd seen any princesses.

Just to hear her voice was a sheer delight because Kendra hadn't done much talking since her mother had died three years ago in a car accident. She had pretty much been withdrawn and quiet much of the time. But she would always talk to her Uncle Ethan.

"Daddy wants to talk to you, Uncle Ethan."

"Okay, sweetheart, and always remember you're Uncle Ethan's cupcake."

"I remember. Nighty-night."

He then heard her hand the phone over to his brother, Hunter, after telling her daddy nighty-night, too and after exchanging an "I love you" and an "I love you back." It was only then that Hunter placed the phone to his ear. "What's going on, kid?"

Ethan couldn't help but chuckle. There was an eight year difference in their ages, and Hunter never let him forget it. But even with that big variation, they'd always gotten along. Like all brothers, they'd had their disagreements, but they'd never lasted more than a few hours. Except for that one time a few years ago when Hunter had tried pressuring him into staying in the family business and getting all those ideas out of his head about making it big in Hollywood.

Ethan had left home anyway to pursue his dream. It was only after the fatal car accident that claimed Hunter's wife's life—an accident that Hunter and Kendra had survived—that Hunter had understood why Ethan had to do what he did. He'd learned that life was too precious and fleeting to take for granted. Tomorrow wasn't promised to anyone.

"Nothing much is going on. Kendra talked a lot tonight," he said.

"Only because it's you. She loves her uncle Ethan. Besides, she wanted to ask you all about princesses."

Ethan grinned. "Yeah, I noticed. What's up with that?"

"*The Princess and the Frog.* She's seen it five times already. I should blame you since you're the one who got her the DVD as soon as it went on sale."

"Hey, there's nothing I wouldn't do for my cupcake," he said, meaning it.

He talked to Hunter for a few minutes longer before his brother passed the phone to their folks. In addition to the winery, Hunter and his parents ran a small four-star bed-and-breakfast on the property. It was always good to call home because he truly missed everyone, and updates were priceless.

"And you're eating properly, Ethan?"

He cringed at his mother's question, knowing he would have to tell her a little white lie, especially when at that very moment the timer went off to let him know his microwave dinner was ready. He had a beer to drink and his dessert would be a bag of peanut M&M's he'd grabbed out of the vending machine when he'd left the studio today. Paige had invited him to her place for dinner but he had declined.

He removed his dinner from the microwave and said, "Yes, Mom, I'm eating properly."

"Met any nice girls you want to bring home?"

She has to be kidding. The last few girls he dated weren't any he would dare bring home for his parents, brother and niece to meet. But then the face of his sexy pixie flashed across his mind and he couldn't help but think that she would work. For some reason he liked her, and the sexual vibes between them hadn't gone unnoticed, although it was evident she'd tried ignoring them.

Besides, he didn't have time to meet girls—nice or any other kind. He had lines to study every night, especially tonight. Frasier had been impressed with him today and had added another scene to his schedule for tomorrow.

"No, Mom, so don't go planning a wedding for me yet."

Later that night when he slid into bed, he couldn't help but think just how blessed he was. Both of his parents were alive and in good health. As the oldest son, Hunter had taken on his role with ease and was the perfect businessman to manage the family's vast wealth. And Hunter had had the insight to utilize the property surrounding the winery to build the bed-and-breakfast, which was doing extremely well. The reservation list was always filled up a year in advance.

As much as he'd loved Napa Valley, Ethan had known it wasn't in his blood to the extent it had been in Hunter's. After college, he returned home and tried working alongside Hunter and his parents, but he hadn't been happy. Hunter had said it was wanderlust and that eventually he would get over it, but he never did. A year later he had made up his mind to pursue his dream.

So here he was, living in a nice place in L.A. and building the career he'd always wanted. Money was no object, thanks to a trust fund that had been set up by his grandparents as well as the financial standing of the winery, in which he was a stockholder. Of course, every once in a while some smart-ass reporter would ask him why an independently wealthy person would want to work. He was sure Anderson Cooper was asked the same question often enough, too. Ethan wasn't privy to Anderson's response, but his was simply, "Wealthy or poor, everyone has dreams, and there *is* such a thing as continued money growth."

He reached over to turn off the lamp light, thinking that things had gone better than he'd expected on the set today. His lines had flowed easily, and for a while he had stepped into the role of Dr. Tyrell Perry. To prepare, he had watched medical movies and had volunteered his time at a hospital for ninety days. He had come away with an even greater respect for those in the medical industry.

As he stared up at the ceiling his thoughts shifted to the woman he'd met that day, Rachel Wellesley. There had been something about her that pulled her to him like a magnet. Something about her that he found totally adorable. Even among the sea of model-type women on the set, she had somehow stood out.

And when she had leaned over him to apply whatever it was she brushed on his face, he had inhaled her scent. With his eyes closed, he had breathed it all in while imagining all sorts of things. It was a soft scent, yet it had been hot enough to enflame his senses.

So he had sat there, letting her have her way with his face while he imagined all kind of things, especially the image of her naked.

More than once during the shoot, he had had to remind himself that he didn't really know her and that it would be crazy to lose focus. But he would be the first to admit that he hadn't counted on being bowled over by a woman who had to tilt her head all the way back just to look up at him. He smiled, remembering the many times they had looked at each other and the number of times they had tried not to do so. And nothing could erase from his mind the sight of the soft smile that had touched her lips when she'd seen his tattoo and when he'd told her why he had it. If he had been trying to impress her, he would definitely have garnered brownie points. But he wasn't trying to impress her.

He shifted in bed, knowing he had to stay focused and not let a pretty face get him off track. All that sounded easy enough, but he had a feeling it would be the hardest thing he'd ever had to do.

Chapter 4

"Quiet on the set!

"Take four!

"Action!"

Rachel sat quietly in a chair and watched the scene that was being shot. When she heard two women, Paige and another actress on the set named Tae'Shawna Miller, whispering about how handsome and fine Ethan was, she had to press her lips together to keep from turning around and reminding them about the no-talking-during-a-take policy. But that would make her guilty of breaking the rule, too.

So she sat there and tried tuning them out and hoped sooner or later they would close their mouths. It didn't help matters to know that Paige was one of the women. Rachel figured she of all people should know better.

Rachel turned her attention back to the scene being filmed and couldn't help but admire the way Ethan was delivering his lines. He was doing a brilliant job portraying Dr. Tyrell Perry, the sexy doctor with a gruff demeanor that could only be softened by his patients. And from the looks of things, a new twist was about to unravel on the show with Dr. Perry being given a love interest—another new doctor on the hospital staff, the widowed Dr. Sonja Duncan.

Rachel had been on the set talking to one of the cameramen when Ethan arrived that morning, swaggering in and exuding rugged masculinity all over the place. The number of flirtatious smiles that were cast his way the moment he said good morning had only made her shake her head. Some of the women were probably still wiping the drool from their mouths.

Why did women get so silly at the sight of a good-looking man? She would admit she had been attracted to him yesterday like everyone else, after all she was a woman, but there was no reason to get downright foolish about it.

"Freeze! No talking on the set!"

Frasier was looking straight at Paige and Tae'Shawna and frowning. He knew exactly who the noisemakers were, and to be called out by the director wasn't good. They had caused time to be wasted, and everyone knew Frasier didn't like that.

"Unfreeze!"

This time around, everyone was quiet while the shooting of the scene continued. In this scene, Dr. Tyrell Perry and Dr. Sonja Duncan were discussing the seriousness of a patient's condition. It was obvious in this scene that the two were attracted to each other. The television viewers would already know through the use of flashbacks that Sonja's late husband, also a doctor, had gotten killed when an L.A. gang, intent on killing a man being treated in the hospital, burst into the E.R. and opened fire, killing everyone, including the doctor, a nurse and a few others waiting to be treated.

Rachel figured since Livia was only a temporary

member of the cast, there would not be too much of a budding romance between the two doctors, although it wasn't known just how Livia's exit would be handled. Frasier was known to leave the viewers hanging from scene to scene, so it would be anyone's guess what he had in mind. She couldn't help but wonder if the chemistry the two generated on the set would extend beyond filming.

She hadn't gotten a chance to get to know Livia. During the makeup and wardrobe sessions there hadn't been much conversation between them. Her initial impression was that Livia was just as shallow and self-absorbed as the other Hollywood types Rachel had met. She'd seen no reason for that impression to change. Livia had a reputation of being a party girl and as much the tabloid princess as Ethan was the tabloid king. So it would stand to reason the two would be attracted to each other both on and off the set.

"Cut! Good scene! Let's enjoy lunch. Everyone take an additional hour and be back to start again on time."

Rachel smiled, grateful for the extra time. It seemed a number of people were in a hurry to take advantage of Frasier's generosity...in more ways than one, she thought, when out of the corner of her eye she noticed several women bustling over in Ethan's direction. She rolled her eyes. My goodness, did they have no shame? Interestingly, Livia walked away in another direction, as if the attention given to Ethan didn't concern her one bit.

Shaking her head, Rachel walked back to her trailer to grab her purse. She had a few errands to do before lunch was over.

Ethan watched Rachel leave before forcing his attention back to the two women standing in front of him.

Tae'Shawna had all but invited him over tonight to go skinny-dipping in her pool. Of course he had turned her down. Paige had offered to come over to his place to help him go over his lines. He turned her down as well. For some reason, he wasn't feeling these two. If truth be told, he wasn't feeling any woman right now. Except for the one who'd just headed off toward her trailer.

"So what are you doing for lunch, Ethan? We would love for you to join us," Paige invited, interrupting his thoughts.

"Thanks, but I have a few errands I need to take care of," he said, knowing it was a lie as he said it. But in this case, he felt it was justified.

"No problem. Maybe we can help with your errands and—"

"Thanks again, but that's not necessary," he said, pulling his keys out of his back pocket. He had planned to wait until the weekend to shop for Kendra's gift, but now was just as good a time since these two were beginning to make a nuisance of themselves.

"I'll see you ladies later. I need to leave so I can be back on time."

For a second Paige looked like she was going to invite herself along. Instead she said, "Then I guess we'll see you when you return."

He only smiled, refusing to make any promises as he headed toward the exit. He was grateful for the additional hour and planned on making good use of it. Moving quickly, he reached for the door at the same time someone else did. The moment their hands touched he knew the identity of that person. Her scent gave her away.

"Excuse me."

"Excuse me as well," he said, taking a step back, opening the door and holding it for her to pass through. "You're taking advantage of the extra hour, I see."

Rachel smiled up at him. "I think everyone is." She glanced back over his shoulder. "Where's your fan club?"

His gaze scanned over her face and he saw a cute little mole near the corner of her lip. How could he have missed it yesterday? "My fan club?"

"Yes."

They were walking together as they headed toward the parking lot. "Trust me, there are some fans you can do without."

"And you want me to believe you're not flattered?" she teased, speaking in a low tone when a crew member passed them on the sidewalk.

He slowed his pace as they got closer to where the cars were parked in the studio lot. "Yes, that's exactly what I want you to believe."

She stopped walking and so did he. "Why? Why does it matter what I think?"

Ethan thought she had asked a good question. Why did it matter what she thought? He knew the answer before he could pull in his next breath. He liked her, and if he had the time he would try to get something going with her. The thing was he didn't have the time. He had to stay focused and doubted he would have time to pursue a relationship, serious or otherwise, with any woman anytime soon. He kept reminding himself that this was his big break, and he wasn't about to mess it up by trying to get between any woman's legs. He had gone without for six months, and he could go another six months or more if he had to.

But that didn't mean that he and Rachel couldn't be just friends, did it? It would be nice to have someone who wasn't interested in anything more than friendship. The little attraction that had passed between them yesterday couldn't be helped. After all, she was a nice-looking woman and he was a hot-blooded man. But as long as they kept things under control, being just friends would be fine.

"It matters because I like you and I'd like for us to be friends," he said.

She pushed a wayward strand of hair from her face as she looked at him. "And why would you want us to become friends?"

Providing an answer to that question was easy enough. "The one thing I noticed yesterday was that you're genuinely a nice person." He chuckled then added, "Hey, you didn't rag on me about being nervous. And it's obvious everyone on the set likes you, from the maintenance man all the way up to the big-wigs. I figure with that kind of popularity, you can't be all bad. Besides, you and Livia are the only two females on the set that I feel pretty comfortable around."

She lifted a brow. "Livia?"

"Yes."

She tilted her head back as if to give him her full attention. "Not that it is any of my business, but I thought that maybe something was going on between the two of you."

He smiled. "There is, on the show. But it's all acting. She's supposed to be my new love interest for the next few episodes."

She nodded. "Your scenes earlier were pretty convincing."

He chuckled. "We're actors. They were meant to be convincing."

Ethan glanced at his watch. "I'd better get going. I want to pick up something for my six-year-old niece from the Disney Store. After watching *The Princess and the Frog* she's into princesses, so I thought I'd pick her up a Princess Tiana doll."

A smile touched the corners of her lips. "You have a niece?"

"Yes, Kendra. She's my older brother's little girl and, I hate to say it, but she's perfect."

She chuckled. "I believe you. And there's a store in walking distance on Hollywood Boulevard. I'm headed that way myself to pick up something from the art supply shop."

He turned the idea over in his mind only once before asking, "Mind if I tag along?"

He did his best not to watch the way her lips were tugged up in a smile when she said, "Sure, you can tag along, as long as we don't talk about work. We need to give our brains a break."

He jammed his keys in his pocket as he resumed walking by her side. It was a beautiful August day, and he had a beautiful woman strolling alongside him. Things couldn't get any better than that. "So what do we talk about?" he decided to ask her.

She slanted her head to look at him. "You."

"Me?"

"Yes."

"Hey, we talked about me yesterday."

Her mouth twitched in a grin. "Yes, but all I know is that you're from Napa Valley and you have a niece." She chuckled. "I guess I could go by what I've heard and—"

"Read in the tabloids," he said, finishing the statement for her.

"No, I don't do tabloids. It would be nice if others didn't do them either, then they would go out of business."

He glanced over at her and laughed. "You don't like the right of free speech?"

She laughed back at him. "More like the right of sleazy speech. Ninety percent of what they print isn't true, but then I guess that's the price of being a star."

He smiled, liking the way the sunlight was bouncing off her hair, making it appear even more lustrous. He liked the short cut on her. "Yes, it's one of the detriments, that's for sure. I just go with the flow. As long as I know what's true about me and what's not, I don't lose any sleep."

She didn't say anything for a while, and then replied, "I hate being in the spotlight."

She kept looking ahead, but he'd heard what she said. Clearly. If that was true, he wondered how she managed it, being a Wellesley. The company her family owned was so connected with this industry, and had been for close to thirty years, they were practically an icon in Hollywood.

He had researched information on Limelight when he'd returned to the States from abroad. He had even considered contacting them to handle his affairs before he'd chosen Curtis, who'd been a friend of a friend to whom he'd owed a favor. But he wouldn't hesitate to consider them again when his contract with Curtis ended. Lately, he'd begun feeling as if he was making his own contacts. Everyone he knew handled by Limelight was pleased with its services. Not once had they ever been made to feel like they were a passenger instead of a driver.

"Being in the spotlight doesn't bother me," he decided to say. "It comes with the territory. But then, my family is well-known in Napa Valley, so I got used to having a mike shoved in my face, only to be quoted incorrectly." He could recall a number of times when he'd been referred to as "the playboy Chambers" while Hunter had always been considered the one with a level head. The responsibly acting Chambers.

"And it doesn't bother you?" she asked.

He met her gaze. "A distortion of the truth will bother most people, and I'm no different. However, I don't lose sleep over it," he said, shifting his gaze to study her features.

But he had a feeling she would.

There had to be a reason, and the question rested on the tip of his tongue.

But he had no right to pry. This woman owed him nothing, had no reason to divulge her deep, dark secrets and innermost feelings. Not to him. They weren't husband and wife. They weren't even lovers. Nor would they ever be.

No, he reminded himself, he was trying out the friendship thing.

Chapter 5

Rachel could feel the power of Ethan as he walked beside her. And although it sounded strange, she could feel his strength. Not only did she feel it, she was drawing from it.

The very thought that such a thing was possible should be disconcerting, but instead the knowledge seemed to wrap her in some sort of warm embrace. That in itself was kind of weird since they'd decided to just be friends. She was fine with that decision. In fact, she refused to have things any other way. She didn't mix business with pleasure and she had too much on her plate to become involved in a serious relationship.

The last guy she had gone out with that she'd truly liked had been Theo Lovett. That had been a couple of years ago. They had dated for almost six months before she'd found out the only reason he'd been interested in her was as a way into her family's business. Luckily, she'd overheard him bragging to a friend on the phone when he'd thought she was in the shower and out of hearing range. Theo's explanation that he'd only been joking with his friend hadn't made her change her mind when she had kicked him out that day.

She stepped out of her memory and into the present.

Apparently she'd missed some of what Ethan had said while she'd been daydreaming, because he'd changed the subject and was talking about his family.

"My older brother's name is Hunter. There is an eight year difference in our ages."

She glanced over at him. Despite the fact he was a lot taller than she, walking side by side they seemed to fit, and their steps appeared to be perfectly synchronized. How was that possible with his long legs and her short ones? He'd evidently adjusted his steps to stay in sync with hers. It was a perfectly measured pace.

"There is a nine year difference in me and my sister's ages," she said.

"Really? Was your sibling as overprotective as mine while you were growing up?"

Rachel made a face. "Boy, was she ever. She was ten when our parents were killed in a plane crash, and I was one. Our aunt and uncle became our legal guardians, but somewhere along the way my sister, Sofia, thought I became her responsibility. It was only when she left for college that I got some breathing space."

"Are the two of you close now?"

"Yes, very. What about you and your brother? Are the two of you close?"

"Yes, although I would be the first to admit he was somewhat of a pain in the ass while we were growing up. But I can appreciate it now since he covered for me a lot with my parents."

She could imagine someone having to do that for him. She had a feeling he'd probably been a handful. "Was your family upset when you decided not to enter the family business but to forge a path in a different direction?"

The corners of his lips lifted in a wry smile. "Let's just say they weren't thrilled with the idea. But I think it bothered Hunter more than it did them," he said. "The Chamberses have been in the wine business for generations, and I was the first to pull out and try doing something else. He lay on the pressure for me to stay for a while but then he backed off."

He placed his hand at the center of her back when others, walking at a swifter pace than they, moved to pass them. She could feel the warmth of his touch through her blouse. She breathed in deeply at the feeling of butterflies flapping around in her stomach.

"What about your family?" he inquired, not realizing the effect of his touch on her.

"Once I explained things to Uncle Jacob and Aunt Lily, they were fine with it. They wanted me to do whatever made me happy. But Sofia felt it was part of our father's legacy, that I owed it to him to join her and Uncle Jacob at Limelight. I had made up my mind on how I wanted to do things with my future, so instead of letting there be this bone of contention between us, she backed off and eventually gave me her blessings to do whatever I wanted to do with my life."

She chuckled. "As a concession, I am letting Limelight Entertainment handle my career. I'm one of their clients."

They paused a moment when they reached the security gate. They had deliberately walked the expanse of the studio lot to avoid running into the paparazzi that made the place their regular beat. Now that they were no longer in safe and protected territory, she noticed Ethan had slid on a pair of sunglasses. He had kept on his medical scrubs and had a stethoscope around his neck, and she wondered if anyone seeing him would assume he was a bona fide doctor walking the strip on lunch break.

She pulled her sunglasses out of her bag, too, although it had been years since she'd had the paparazzi on her tail. When she was younger, they'd seemed to enjoy keeping up with the two Wellesley heirs. She'd always found the media's actions intrusive and an invasion of her privacy. She could recall all the photographs of her as a child that had appeared in the tabloids. That was the main reason she much preferred not being the focus of their attention again.

She glanced over at Ethan when his hand went to the center of her back again. It was time for them to cross the street, and he was evidently trying to hurry her along before traffic started up again. Her pulse began fluttering, caused by the heat generated from his touch.

They increased their pace to make it across the street. She checked him out from the corner of her eye and saw how sexy the scrubs looked on him. They had agreed to be just friends, she reminded herself. And it meant absolutely nothing that they had a few things in common. Like the fact that they were both renegades. That they were both members of well-known families. That they both had siblings who'd chosen to go into the family business. Overprotective, older siblings who meant well but if given the chance would run their lives.

Rachel inconspicuously scanned the area around them and breathed a sigh of relief when she saw the paparazzi was nowhere in sight. But then they were known to bounce out from just about any place. Hopefully she and Ethan looked like a regular couple out on a stroll during their lunch hour.

A couple who were just friends, which was something she could not forget.

"You are such a good uncle."

Ethan glanced at Rachel while accepting his change from the girl behind the counter at the Disney Store. Had he used his charge card his cover would have been blown. Even through his sunglasses, he could see the woman was looking at him, trying to figure out if he was a doctor or someone she should know.

He smiled at Rachel. "I'd like to think so, especially since I doubt very seriously that Hunter will have any more children," he said, accepting the bag the cashier was handing him.

"Why is that?"

"He lost his wife in a car accident," he explained as they headed for the exit. "He took Annette's death hard and hasn't been in a serious relationship since. It's been three years now."

"Oh, how sad."

"Yes, it was. Hunter and Kendra were in the car at the time of the accident and survived with minor injuries," he said. He paused a moment and then added, "Kendra was three at the time and very close to her mother. She felt the loss immediately and withdrew into her own world and stopped talking."

The eyes that stared into his were full of sorrow and compassion. "She doesn't talk?"

He released his breath in a long and slow sigh, wondering why he was sharing this information about his family with anyone, especially to a woman he'd only met yesterday. But there was something about Rachel that was different from most women he'd met. For one, she wasn't trying to come on to him or jump his bones. It was as if she saw him as a person and not some sex symbol, and he appreciated that.

"She talks now, but not as much as she should for a child her age," he responded. "And she talks more with some people than with others. I happen to be one of those she will talk to most of the time. But it took me a while to gain that much ground again after the accident." He recalled the time he had come home from France to give his brother and niece his support. "But a part of Kendra is still withdrawn and so far no one has been able to fully bring her back. She's been seen by the best psychologists money can hire. They practically all said the same thing. Kendra suffered a traumatic loss, and until she's convinced in her mind that she can love someone again, become attached to that person without losing them all over again, she will continue to withdraw into her own little world."

He checked his watch and figured they needed to head on back. Prior to stopping at the store, they had stopped by an art supply place and picked up some new brushes. She'd told him that she liked dabbling with paints on canvas every once in a while and had promised to show him some of her work one day.

As they began retracing their steps back toward the studio lot, he had to admit he had enjoyed his time with her and knew that he was going to enjoy having her as a friend. An odd thought suddenly burned in his brain. What if they became more than just friends? He quickly forced the notion out of his head. The fact of the matter was they were just friends, or at least they were trying to be.

He glanced at her and saw her scan the surrounding area. He could tell she was nervous about the possibility of being seen by the paparazzi. So was he, but only because it bothered her. Despite the fact that only minutes ago he'd vowed not to pry, he couldn't stop the question now.

"Why do you avoid the spotlight, Rachel?" He could tell his question surprised her and suspected her reasons were deep-seated.

"I just do," she said.

She tried to act calm, like his question wasn't a big deal, but he sensed that it was. "Why?"

She frowned up at him, and the first thing he thought was that he'd made her mad. He hadn't meant to, but a part of him wanted to push her for an answer.

"Well?" he asked.

She didn't say anything as they kept walking. She had stopped glaring at him and was staring straight ahead. He'd almost given up hope for a reply when she began speaking. "I told you my parents were killed before my second birthday. Since my uncle and aunt who adopted us couldn't have any kids of their own, my sister and I became known as the Limelight heirs. For some reason we made news, and the paparazzi followed us practically everywhere we went—school, church, grocery stores…you name it, they were there. I couldn't tell you how many times when I was a little girl that I got a mike shoved in my face or my braid pulled by a reporter to get my attention. It was…scary.

"Things only got better when I went away to college. By the time I returned, the media interest was on someone else, thank goodness. But every once in a while someone tries to connect the dots to see what Sofia and

I are up to. She doesn't mind being in the spotlight and uses it to her advantage."

Ethan took in what she said. The thought of someone harassing a child to get a story angered him, and knowing the child had been Rachel angered him even more. It was interesting that he felt such protective instincts for her.

A flicker of some sort of alarm flashed through his brain but he chose to ignore it. No matter what his mind thought, there was no way he would get in too deep with Rachel.

Chapter 6

Rachel stood by the window in her uncle's study and gazed out at the ocean. The sun was going down and she enjoyed watching it. Just like she had enjoyed being on the set the past two weeks.

Frasier and John were pleased with the tempo of the series. Ethan was working out perfectly as Dr. Perry, and the blossoming on-the-air love affair between the gruff doctor and the resistant Dr. Duncan had pretty much heated up. They had shot a love scene yesterday that had pushed the temperature on the set up as hot as it could get for prime-time programming.

She could definitely say she was pleased with this assignment and looked forward to going into work each day. The more time she and Ethan spent together during filming, the more they talked and bonded as friends. She found him fun to be around, and the two of them would laugh together about some of the actresses' hot pursuit of him. A few had tried some outlandish things to get his attention. Like the time Jasmine Crowder summoned him to her trailer to help rehang a photo that had fallen off the wall. Instead of going, Ethan had sent one of the cameramen, Omar Minton, in his place. Poor Omar had walked into the trailer to be met by a half-naked Jasmine draped across the sofa.

That had been just one of many times during the past week that Ethan had had to foil seduction plots. Just the fact that he'd done so impressed Rachel, and she would be the first to admit that she was seeing him not as the superficial playboy she'd originally thought he was but as a focused, hardworking actor. That was another thing they had in common. They believed in professionalism on the job.

"Lily said I'd probably find you in here."

Rachel turned at the sound of her uncle's deep voice and smiled. Since she'd been only one year old when her parents had gotten killed, she didn't have a solid memory of them the way Sofia did. But what she did remember was her aunt and uncle being there for them, raising her and Sofia as their own. Rachel appreciated having been part of a family in which she'd always known she was loved and always been encouraged to use her talents in whatever way she wanted to do.

She'd learned from her aunt and uncle that her mother was a successful artist, and several of Vivian Wellesley's paintings were on the walls in this house as well as in a number of art galleries across the country. Vivian had passed down her talent and love of painting; Rachel really enjoyed the time she spent putting color to canvas. She was definitely her mother's daughter.

And Sofia was definitely her father's. She had stepped into the role of the savvy and successful businessman that he'd been. And because Sofia had been the only child for almost nine years, she had been the pride of her parents' life and definitely the apple of her father's eye. Sofia had worshipped the ground their father had walked on and was still doing that same thing even though their parents had been dead for twenty-five years. Sofia thought John Wellesley was the most amazing person to have ever lived.

The man standing before Rachel was John's identical twin.

"Uncle Jacob," Rachel greeted, crossing the room to give her uncle a hug. She'd seen pictures of the brothers from years past, and to see one was to see the other. That said, she knew if her father had lived he would have matured into a rather handsome man. And at fifty-five, her uncle was definitely that, with a charm and charisma that should be patented. Ethan had told her about the close relationship he had with his niece, and she had fully understood because such a relationship existed between her and her uncle.

"And what honor has been bestowed upon me for this visit?" he asked, leaning back and scanning her from head to toe. "Hmm, I don't see anything broken or in need of repair, although I still keep plenty of bandages around."

Rachel could only laugh. While growing up she had been a handful, a tomboy in her earlier years. And anytime she got hurt, she would run to her uncle to fix her boo-boo.

"C'mon, Uncle Jacob, it's not like I never come to visit," she defended herself, laughing.

"No, but since you've moved to the other side of town we barely see you these days."

Rachel nibbled on her bottom lip. In addition to the enormous mansion her aunt and uncle owned in Beverly Hills, they also had this place, a luxurious oceanfront hideaway on Malibu Beach. A few months ago she had purchased a condo in the gated community of Friar Gate that was located on the outskirts of Hollywood. Before moving, she had lived in a condo that had been within walking distance of Rodeo Drive. It was fine until one of the Jonas Brothers had moved into the complex. There was no peace with the paparazzi, and she'd figured it was just a matter of time before they added others to their list to harass.

"I needed more space," she said and knew her uncle would understand. It was no secret she didn't like being in the spotlight.

He nodded. "And when will I get invited to your new place for dinner?"

She threw her head back and laughed again, knowing that was a joke since she didn't cook. The few times she'd tried, she had made a complete mess of things and decided there were too many restaurants serving good, tasty food to put herself through the agony of following some recipe.

"Just as soon as I get everything in its proper place. I still have a few boxes left to unpack, but I've been so busy on the set. And then there's that painting I want to finish before the gallery hosts that charity event next month."

"I understand," Jacob Wellesley said, leading her to the nearest sofa so they could sit down. "You are a very busy lady, just like your mother was. We would try and convince her there were but so many hours in the day, but she was always determined to stretch them anyway."

Rachel couldn't help but smile. She always liked hearing the stories her uncle and aunt would share about her parents.

"And how are things going for you at work? Frasier isn't working you too hard, is he?" he asked.

Frasier Glenn was not only an old friend of her father's but he'd been close to her uncle as well and had been one of Limelight's first clients. When she'd interviewed for the position of makeup artist and wardrobe designer for *Paging the Doctor,* Frasier had been upfront and let her know it was her own merit and work ethic, not the long-standing friendship he had with her family, that had gotten her the job. She had appreciated that.

"No, both Frasier and John are wonderful, and I'm learning so much from them," she said, leaning back against the sofa's cushions.

"Good. I understand Eric Woods's contract didn't get renewed."

"No, but we were expecting it with his behavior last season. I hear he's mouthing off to the tabloids that he had no idea he was getting the ax."

Jacob shook his head. "Oh, I'm sure he knew. Frasier doesn't work that way. When he makes a decision to let you go, you know why. Eric's just trying to save face. Everyone in the industry knows his last few movies bombed out, and because of his temperament, it's hard to find a director in Hollywood with the patience to take him on."

Rachel nodded. "This season is going to have a new twist. They brought in a new doctor and I think his appearance will boost ratings."

"Really? Who is he?"

"Ethan Chambers."

A slow smile touched Uncle Jacob's lips. "I've never met Chambers but I've heard of him. Word's out that he's an actor who's going places. He received good reviews from the guest spot he did on *CSI* that one time last year. And there was that rumor earlier this year that he was being considered for *People's* Sexiest Man of the Year. That didn't hurt. There hasn't been an African American male to get that honor since Denzel and that was close to fifteen years ago."

Rachel could see Ethan being considered. He was definitely a hot contender in her book.

"And how is Chambers working out?"

"I think he's doing a great job. It is difficult, though, to get the females on the set to concentrate on what they are supposed to do instead of on him. He has a way of grabbing your attention and holding it."

"Mmm, does he now?"

She smiled, knowing what her uncle was probably thinking. "Okay, I admit he's hot, but I'm beyond fawning over any man, Uncle Jacob. Besides, Ethan Chambers comes with something I could never tolerate."

Jacob Wellesley lifted a thick brow. "What?"

"The spotlight."

Later that night, after spending time in front of the canvas for a good part of the evening, Rachel's phone rang. She reached out and picked it up without checking caller ID, thinking it was either Charlene or Sofia.

"Hello?"

"Save me."

She blinked upon hearing the sound of the ultrasexy, masculine voice. "Ethan?"

"Yes, it's me."

She was surprised. They had known each other for two weeks now, considered themselves friends and had even exchanged phone numbers one day on the set, but he'd never called her before and she'd never had a reason to call him. And what was his reason for calling her now? Had he said something about saving him?

"What on earth is going on with you?" she asked, putting him on speakerphone while she dried her hands.

"I need a place to crash for the night. I came home and found the place swarming with paparazzi. Luckily they didn't see me, and I made a U-turn and headed in another direction. So, will you have pity on me and put me up for the night?"

She tossed the hand towel aside as she leaned against the kitchen counter. "Ethan, you know how I detest being—"

"In the spotlight. Yes, I know," he said interrupting her. "And that's the reason I hesitated calling you, but I need this favor, Rachel. I've been driving around for a few hours now and have periodically checked my rearview mirror to make sure no one is following me. They're probably still parked out front waiting for me to come home. They wouldn't think of looking for me at your place."

That was an understatement, Rachel thought. They probably figured he was somewhere warming some starlet's bed. He was single, sexy and a man who probably had needs that any woman would love filling. In that case, why couldn't he go back to his lady friend's place instead of putting her privacy at risk?

She began nibbling on her bottom lip. Tomorrow was Sunday and they were due back on the set Monday morning at eight. All she needed was for someone to get wind that Ethan had stayed overnight at her place, no matter how innocent it might be, and make a big deal of it.

Everyone on the set knew the two of them had become friends, but no one thought anything of it since she was friendly with just about everyone…except for Paige, who still had her panties in a wad for some reason. Besides, no one would assume something was going on between them because she wasn't the type of woman Ethan would be interested in. She was definitely not model material.

But still, she didn't want anyone assuming anything or, even worse, the paparazzi hunting him down at her place. Jeez, she didn't want to even think of that happening. One good thing was that she had a two-car garage, so his car wouldn't be seen parked in front of her place. And her gated community was known for its privacy and security.

"Rachel?"

She drew in a deep breath. "Fine, but if anyone from the media gets wind of this and starts harassing me, Ethan, you're dead meat."

She heard him laugh. "I don't want to be dead meat, Rachel."

She folded her arms across her chest and tapped her foot. "Well?"

"All right, I'll take my chances."

"With the paparazzi?"

"Heck no," he said. "I'll take my chances with you. I'm hoping our budding friendship will keep you from actually killing me. Besides, I've been around you enough to know that you do have a soft heart."

She either had a soft heart or a foolish mind, Rachel thought an hour later when she opened her door to Ethan. She also had a bunch of erratic hormones. The tingle started in the pit of her stomach when she looked at him, and it took a full minute to catch her breath. Not only did Ethan look good but he smelled good enough to eat.

She was caught off guard by her reaction to him. They'd agreed to just be friends, but at the moment friendship was the last thing on her mind. She couldn't stop her gaze from roaming all over him. He was leaning in the doorway in a sexy stance, wearing jeans and a button-down shirt with the top four buttons undone. She glimpsed his chest beneath, poking out like a temptation being dangled in front of her. If this was the way he showed up at his woman's home, no wonder he was in such high demand. And no wonder a rush of adrenaline jolted through her.

"And you're sure you weren't followed?" she asked, taking a step back to let him in. She figured conversation between them would distract her long enough to get her mind and body back under control.

He gave her a wry smile as he entered, moving over the threshold and filling the room the same way he'd filled the doorway…with dominating sexiness. "I'm positive. I drove around an additional twenty minutes or so to be sure. Those were good directions you gave me, by the way. I found this place without any trouble."

She nodded as she closed the door. That was when she noticed the shopping bag in his hand. When she gave him a questioning look, he said, "I made a pit stop at a store to pick up a few toiletries."

"And you weren't recognized?" she asked, moving away from the door.

"No. I had my disguise on," he said, pulling a baseball cap and a fake mustache out of the pocket of his jacket.

Rachel lifted a brow while fighting back a smile. "That's the best you can do?"

He gave her a flirty smile. "Depends on what we're talking about."

He was flirting with her.

On a few occasions over the last couple of weeks, he'd turned on the charm and flashed his devilish smile that lit up his blue-gray eyes. But she'd just rolled her eyes at him. Tonight was different. Tonight she couldn't help her body's reaction to his flirting.

As much for herself as for him, she said, "We're talking about your disguise, Ethan."

"Oh." He glanced down at the items he held in his hand. "There's nothing wrong with my disguise. It served its purpose."

With a suddenly sweaty palm, she pushed her hair behind her ear and met his gaze. "We can only hope."

Then he flashed that devilish grin that she'd tried so hard to avoid. And something slammed into her. Awareness. Attraction.

Uh-oh, said the one remaining rational part of her brain. *You've made a big mistake.*

She had to agree. Letting Ethan stay overnight just might be the biggest mistake she'd ever made.

Chapter 7

Ethan gave Rachel a hot look because there wasn't any other type of look he could give her. He was totally taken with seeing her again. Had it been just yesterday when they'd last seen each other? Just yesterday when he had been alone with her in her trailer, reclining in the chair while she applied his makeup?

She had leaned over him and her scent had almost driven him crazy. They had agreed to be just friends, and God knows he'd tried keeping his desires under control with her on the set. But at night, alone in his bed, his dreams had been another matter. She was his friend by day and his dream lover at night. And the things that went on inside those dreams were enough to make a man stiff just thinking about them.

No woman had ever dominated his thoughts like she had.

As he'd told her, he had driven around a couple of hours before finally deciding to call her. There were a number of women he could have called, but she was the one he knew he could contact and not worry about anything getting leaked to the tabloids. But now he had to be honest with himself and admit the real reason he had sought her out. He had wanted to see her.

He pulled in a deep breath, and instead of standing there staring at her like she was a nice juicy steak he couldn't wait to eat, he glanced around, needing a distraction as much as he needed a cold beer. He saw several boxes and then recalled her saying she'd only been living in this place a few months. Obviously she hadn't finished unpacking yet. But it was a nice place, large and spacious and her choice of furnishings hit the mark. "Your place is tight, Rachel."

"Thanks. You want to see the bedroom?"

At his raised brow, she said, "I mean the one you'll use tonight. The guest room."

He'd known what she meant but thought she looked cute when she blushed. He liked seeing her get all flustered. "Sure. But you didn't ask if I wanted something to drink, and I'm thirsty."

She rolled her eyes. "Are you going to be a pesky houseguest?"

"I'll try hard not to be but I do have another confession to make. I'm hungry, too."

Rachel shook her head, chuckling. "Then you're at the wrong place. I can give you something to drink, but for a meal you're out of luck."

"Why is that?"

"I can't cook, and before you ask, my aunt and uncle always had live-in cooks and I never had a desire to learn."

He chuckled. "No problem. I know my way around a kitchen."

She laughed. "That's all nice but there's still a problem."

"What?" he asked.

"I don't have any groceries."

He lifted a brow. "Nothing?"

"Well, my best friend did feel sorry for my refrigerator and went to the store last week and picked up a few items like eggs, butter and bread. The basics."

A smile touched his lips. "That's all I need. Just lead me to your kitchen."

"That was simply amazing," Rachel said, leaning back in her chair. "If I hadn't seen it, I would not have believed it."

Ethan leaned back in his chair as well and laughed. "It was just an egg sandwich on toast, Rachel. No big deal."

"Hey, I beg to differ. I never got the hang of cooking an egg. Or anything else for that matter."

"Why would your friend buy eggs if you can't cook them?" he asked, taking a swig of his beer. He'd found several bottles behind all the art supplies she kept in her refrigerator.

"They can be boiled, you know," she said, taking a sip of her own beer, right from the bottle. "And I know it was just a sandwich but it was still good. I hadn't realized I'd gotten hungry."

"Hadn't you eaten dinner?" he asked, getting up and grabbing their plates off the table. They had used paper plates and plastic utensils so all they had to do was trash them. No dishes to wash. How convenient. That had been a good idea on her part.

"I had lunch with my aunt and uncle earlier in the day and when I got home, I started painting and lost track of the time." She got up from the table as well. "If you hadn't called, I probably would have ordered out for a pizza or something eventually."

He watched her stride across the floor to the sink to rinse out her beer bottle before tossing it into a recycle bin. She was wearing a pair of shorts and a top and looked pretty in them. He glanced down and thought she even had cute bare feet with polished toes.

"My uncle knows you or at least he's heard of you," she said, causing him to shift his gaze to her face. "He was very complimentary."

"Was he?"

"Yes. He believes you're a person who's going places."

A broad smile touched his lips. "That means a lot coming from the likes of Jacob Wellesley," he said before finishing off his beer.

He joined her at the sink and she slid over to give him room when he proceeded to rinse out his own beer bottle. She smelled good, he thought, pulling in a whiff of her scent through his nostrils. She smelled better than good. She smelled like a woman he wanted.

He smiled over at her and she glared at him. "What's wrong?" he asked, moving to place the beer bottle in the recycle bin. "I assured you that no one followed me over here."

"That's not what's bothering me, Ethan."

He leaned back against the sink. "Then what is bothering you, Rachel?" He had an idea but wanted her to tell him.

She had moved back to the table and stood with her arms crossed over her chest. "I think we need to reiterate a few things, like the fact that two weeks ago we decided to be friends and nothing more."

"I thought we were."

"I thought so, too," she replied. "But…"

He lifted a brow and tried looking baffled. "But what?"

"I'm getting these vibes."

"Really? What kind of vibes?"

When she didn't say anything, he crossed the room to her. "Rachel, just what kind of vibes are you getting?"

He was staring at her and those gorgeous eyes of his were probably seeing a lot more than she wanted them to. A lot more than she needed them to see. And that put her on the defensive.

"None. Forget I said that," she said.

"Not sure I can do that now," he said, eyeing her up and down the way he'd done the first day they'd met. Before they'd decided all they wanted between them was friendship. Her mind scrambled as she tried to recall that day. It had been his second day on the set. Had it really been two weeks ago already? They had walked to the Disney Store and Art World. He had purchased a Princess Tiana doll for his niece, and she had picked up some art supplies.

They'd both agreed they were not involved in serious relationships and wanted to keep things that way. Besides, she had painstakingly explained to him that she didn't mix business with pleasure. He had understood and said the same rule applied to him. That should have settled things...so why didn't it?

Why was he looking at her now in a way that made her so aware of her sensuality while at the same time reminded her that it had been a long time since she'd been with a man? Nearly two years, to be exact, and even then it hadn't been anything to brag about.

"You have no choice, Ethan," she heard herself say.

"I don't?"

At the shake of her head, he said, "And what if I told you I'm getting those same vibes, and that if we don't at least share a kiss, there will always be curiosity between us?"

Heat circled around in her stomach at his admission and his suggestion. "Maybe for you, but not for me," she said, lifting her chin.

He took a step closer. "And you want me to believe that you aren't curious?"

Of course she was curious. What woman wouldn't be when there were lips that looked like his? "No, not in the least," she lied while looking him straight in the eye.

Unfortunately, those eyes were staring right back at her, as if seeing straight into her. Heat crawled all over her skin and her heart thumped faster. And when the corners of his mouth eased into a sexy smile, she inhaled sharply.

She broke eye contact with him, not liking the look on his face. It was taunting her and tempting her, all at the same time. She nervously licked her tongue across her top lip as a sudden case of panic gripped her.

God, how he'd love to try out that tongue.

Thrumming heat raced through his gut. Funny the difference a couple of weeks could make. His first days on the set, he was ready to push everything aside to focus on his role on *Paging the Doctor*. But now that he felt comfortable playing Dr. Tyrell Perry, he no longer went to bed with his lines infused into his brain. Instead something else—or should he say someone else—occupied his thoughts. And that person was standing right in front of him.

"You know what I think, Ethan?" she asked, interrupting his thoughts.

"No, what do you think?"

"You being here, claiming you needed a place to crash for the night, is part of some manipulating scheme." He could hear the sharpness in her tone and could see the fire in her eyes.

"Not true. I called you for the reason I told you. I didn't have anyone else to call."

"C'mon, Ethan. Do you honestly expect me to believe that? Of all the women you've been linked to, do you really assume I'm that gullible enough to think none of them would have let you stay overnight at their place?"

"I imagine one of them would." He paused a moment and then said, "Let me rephrase what I said earlier. There are others I *could* have called but you are the only one I *wanted* to call." Boy, if only she knew how true that was.

She got silent and he knew she was thinking, trying to make heads or tails of what he'd said. Then she simply asked, "Why, Ethan? Why was I the only one you wanted to call?"

He saw the frustrated expression on her face. But it was what he saw in her eyes that captivated him. Desire. Although she might wish it wasn't there, it was and it was just as deep as what he was feeling.

But Rachel was a logical person who would not accept anything less than a logical and straightforward answer, so he said, "Because you are the only one I want."

Chapter 8

Speechless, Rachel could only stare at him while all the sexual desires she'd had for him since day one came tumbling back. Why was he trying to make things so difficult? Why was he forcing her to admit the one thing she had tried to deny? She was attracted to him something awful.

It would be so easy to let her guard down and walk across the room, wrap her arms around his neck and give in to temptation and indulge in a heated kiss. A kiss that would probably curl her toes and then some.

But she had to think logically. He threatened something she couldn't risk losing—her privacy. Any woman he was involved with would become just as much news as he was. The paparazzi would make sure of that. He was a man who spent his life, both personal and otherwise, in front of the camera, a place she tried to avoid.

She shook her head. Things were going all wrong. They had decided they wouldn't go down this road, so why were they? They were friends and that's all they would ever be. He knew it and she knew it, as well. If he refused to do what was best, then she would.

Rachel backed up and nervously tugged at the hem of her T-shirt. "C'mon, let me show you where you'll sleep tonight. I think you'll like this room since it has its own private bath."

He held her gaze and, for a moment, she felt a weakening she didn't want to feel. Those eyes were the reason and she understood what was happening. Ethan had invaded her space, both mentally and creatively. And she couldn't deal with it.

Instead of saying anything else, she walked off and drew in a deep breath when she heard him falling in step behind her.

Walking behind her had its advantages, Ethan thought, watching the sway of Rachel's curvy hips and the lushness of her backside in her shorts. She probably hadn't figured out yet that he was enjoying the back view, and it was just as well since he definitely needed to think.

Contrary to what she thought, when he had shown up tonight it hadn't been with the intent of jumping her bones, although he found such a possibility a very enticing prospect.

He followed her up the stairs and once they reached the landing, he glanced around. The second floor was just as large and spacious as the first. There were a number of hung paintings and he couldn't help but admire them.

"Are these your creations?" he asked when she turned around after noticing he had slowed down.

She followed his gaze from wall to wall and smiled. "Some of them." She pointed out those that were. "The others are my mother's. She was a successful painter. A few of her pieces are on display at the L.A. Museum and various others."

"They're all beautiful. You inherited her gift and it shows in your work."

"Thanks."

They began walking again and as before, he followed. When she paused by a door he moved ahead and glanced inside. It was a huge room with a small bed. But it was a bed and tonight he wasn't picky, although he would much prefer hers.

"This is it," she said, entering the room. "The bath is to your left and there are plenty of towels and washcloths. Everything you need for your overnight stay."

He didn't miss her emphasis on "overnight." She intended for him to be gone in the morning. "Thanks, I appreciate it, and no matter what you think, Rachel, I didn't have an ulterior motive for coming here tonight."

Instead of saying she believed him like he'd hoped, she merely nodded, turned and walked away. Instinctively, his gaze went to her backside, and a sizzling heat began building inside of him. Hell, he was a man and tonight he was reminded of just how horny he was.

A few hours later, Rachel curled up in her favorite spot in her king-size bed. Ethan had been in her home only a few hours and already her house smelled of man. And as much as she hated admitting it, she liked the scent.

She couldn't help but notice it after rechecking the doors for the night and walking up the stairs to get ready for bed. She had heard the sound of the shower and the fragrance of his aftershave had floated through the air. Immediately, tremors of desire had rippled through her, and upon reaching the landing she had quickly hurried to her room and closed the door.

While getting dressed for bed, she had heard him moving around. The sound of someone else in her house felt strange because other than Charlene or Sofia, she rarely had houseguests.

All was quiet, so she could only assume Ethan had settled in for the night. That was just great. He was probably sleeping like a baby, and here she was, wide awake and thinking about him and the fact that he'd wanted to kiss her. She could now admit to herself— although she would never admit such a thing to him— that she had wanted to kiss him as well and that she *was* curious. However, being curious wouldn't benefit either one of them. It would serve no purpose.

Yes, it would...if it didn't lead anywhere.

Rachel rolled her eyes. *Not lead anywhere? Yeah, right.* There was no doubt in her mind that kissing Ethan would probably lead right here to her bedroom. And they had agreed to be nothing more than friends, she reminded herself.

But since he seemed quick to break the rules, why couldn't she break a few of her own? As long as the kiss and anything that followed after the kiss was all there could ever be and they knew where they stood with each other, would it really hurt for them to indulge in something that her body was telling her she both needed and wanted?

Her ears perked up when she heard the sound of Ethan moving around. A smile touched her lips. It was two in the morning and she felt grateful he couldn't sleep any more than she could.

She sat up in bed when she heard his bedroom door opening and then picked up the sound of him going downstairs. Being hungry at this hour would serve him no purpose since she didn't have any food in the house, unless he was planning to make another egg sandwich.

Before she could get cold feet, she eased out of bed, deciding if a kiss was what he wanted, then a kiss was what he was going to get.

With a deep sigh, Ethan closed the refrigerator door after pulling out a bottle of beer. He was hot and needed to cool off. He'd tried to get some sleep only to be awakened with dreams of him and Rachel together in some of the most explicit sexual positions possible. If those dreams kept coming, they could possibly ruin him for future relationships—at least until he discovered how close his dreams were to the real thing.

After screwing off the beer bottle top, he took a huge swig, appreciating how the cold liquid flowed down his throat and hoping some would keep moving straight to his groin.

"I see you couldn't sleep either."

Ethan spun around. Rachel was the last person he expected to see. After showing him the guest room, she had made herself scarce, basically hiding out in her bedroom.

She crossed the room toward the coffeepot, and he wished he could ignore the tantalizing view of her bare legs and curvy backside in a pajama set that consisted of clingy shorts and a spaghetti strap tank top.

"No, I couldn't sleep," he answered, before taking a final swig of beer while wishing it had been something stronger.

"Why?"

He looked over at her after placing his empty beer bottle on the counter. "Why what?"

"Why couldn't you sleep?" Her expression grew troubled, showed her concern. "Isn't the bed comfortable enough?"

For a moment he thought about telling her the real deal, then decided she probably couldn't handle it if he did. "The bed is fine."

"Then what's your problem?"

He crossed his arms over his chest. "What's yours?"

Ethan hadn't meant for his tone to sound so gruff. Nor had he meant for his eyes to shift from her face to slide down to her thighs. But they did. Heat settled in his gut before he returned his gaze to her face. Just in time to see the corners of her lips lift in a wry smile. "Something amusing, Rachel?"

"You tell me." She began walking toward him and her scent—lush, exotic, jasmine and womanly—preceded her. He watched her as a sharp, tingling hunger swept through his groin, and suddenly, memories of the dream that had awakened him had his skin feeling like it was being licked with tongues of fire.

He never took her for a tease and hoped that wasn't her intent because he was not in a teasing mood. It wouldn't take much to push him over the edge right now. When she came to a stop directly in front of him, he inhaled and filled his lungs with her scent. And his testosterone level shot sky-high.

"Remember earlier when you asked me about those vibes, Ethan?" she asked.

"I remember," he said while thinking her mouth was almost too luscious for any woman's face.

"Well…"

He refused to let her get all nervous on him now. "Well what, Rachel?"

Ethan watched her take a long, slow breath. "You were right about that curiosity thing."

He didn't intend to make it easy for her. "What curiosity thing is that?"

She cleared her throat. "That curiosity thing about kissing."

He nodded slowly. "So are you admitting to being curious?"

"Umm, just a little," she said.

He went silent, deciding to let her think about what she'd said and, more important, what she planned to do about it.

Standing there facing Ethan, not all in his face but probably less than two feet away, Rachel concluded she had never felt anything close to the stomach-churning heat that had taken over the lower part of her body. It didn't help matters that he was shirtless with his jeans riding low on his hips. His muscular physique dominated her kitchen and reminded her that she was very much alone with a very sexy man.

And apparently he was a man who didn't forget anything, especially her evasiveness from earlier when she'd refused to elaborate on these vibes she was sensing. She was smart enough to know Ethan had no intention of letting her off the hook and was making her work for anything she got. That was fine with her, since she'd always considered herself a working girl.

He was a man who knew women. So he had to know she wanted him to kiss her. She hadn't been ready earlier tonight and hadn't been accepting. Now she was both ready and accepting. Nothing would change between them with one kiss. She was convinced of that now. Why would it? She wasn't his type and he definitely wasn't hers. Sharing a kiss wouldn't produce a marriage license or any document that said they would have to take things further than that. Monday, on the set, they would go back to being just friends. Nothing more. Nothing less.

"You think too damn hard."

She blinked upon hearing Ethan's blunt words and had to agree that she did think too hard. But then she'd always been the type of person to weigh the pros and cons before she acted. This was one of those times she had to really consider whether the pros outweighed the cons.

She quickly concluded that they did.

A smile touched her mouth when she took a couple steps closer to him, fascinated by the blue-gray eyes watching her. Now she *was* all in his face and decided it was time to do something about it. Granted, she wasn't the typical kind of woman he became involved with; however, she intended to show him that good things could come in small packages. With a pounding heart, she stood on tiptoe, reached out and placed her arms around his neck.

"Now, are we in accord?" Ethan asked, placing his hands at her waist, drawing her closer and lowering his mouth toward hers, hovering mere inches from her lips.

She drew in a deep, unsteady breath, barely able to contain the heated passion taking over her body, filling her with all kinds of sensations. She had never responded to a man this way. Had never been this affected and bold. "Yes, we're in accord."

Fueled by a degree of desire she'd never felt before, she leaned farther up on tiptoes and whispered against his lips, "So, let's go for broke."

Chapter 9

Nothing could have prepared Ethan for the need that took over his body at that moment. Unable to hold back, he captured her mouth with a possession that fueled his fire in a way it had never been with another woman. He wanted to devour Rachel alive.

A part of him couldn't believe that she was in his arms and that he was taking her mouth like it was the only feminine one left on earth. For now, for him, it was.

For some reason, he couldn't control the rush of physical hunger consuming him. His tongue tangled with hers with a voracity that sent pleasure spiking throughout his body. He was kissing her hungrily, as if he was seeking out some forbidden treat and was determined to find it.

Moments later, only because they needed to breathe, he released her mouth and stared into her stunned gaze. Refusing to allow her time to think again, he lowered his mouth once more and at the same time, he swept her off her feet and into his arms. Before the night was over, his touch would be imprinted on every inch of her skin.

Somehow he managed to get them up the stairs. Upon reaching the landing, he moved quickly toward her bedroom. She wanted to get it on and he was determined not to let anything stop them. Though he had wanted her from the first moment he'd laid eyes on her, he'd thought he would be satisfied with them just being friends. Well, he'd been proven wrong.

The moment he placed her on the bed, he joined her there, wanting to keep her in his arms, needing his lips to remain plastered to hers with his tongue inside her mouth and doing things so wicked it made his skin shiver. The kiss really had gotten ridiculously out of hand because never in his life had he been so damn greedy. So hard up to make love to a woman.

In an unexpected move, she pulled back, breaking off the kiss and drawing in a ragged breath. Her gaze latched on to the mouth that had just thoroughly kissed her, and he felt his rod pulsate when she took her tongue, that same tongue he'd tried to devour, and licked her top lip before saying, "I think we should get out of our clothes, Ethan."

He couldn't help but smile as he pulled up on his haunches. "I think you're right." He moved away from the bed to pull the jeans down his legs while flames of desire tore through him. He pulled a condom pack out of his wallet and ripped it open with his teeth. Sheathing his aroused member was an exercise in torture.

Without wasting any time, he returned to her. With a ravenous growl and a need he didn't want to question, he reached out and began removing the clothes from her body. The moment she was completely naked, the lusciousness of her feminine scent filled his nostrils and further stimulated every nerve in his body, making his protruding erection that much harder. He intended to stake a claim on every inch of her body. Beginning now.

He lowered his head and captured her mouth at the

same time his hands reached around and began caressing her back and pulling her closer to the fit of him, his hard arousal pressing into her stomach.

He broke off the kiss and his mouth trailed lower, planting kisses over the soft swell of her breasts before taking a nipple into his mouth and sucking it with an intensity that made her groan.

Without losing contact with her nipple, he tilted his head and gazed up at her, saw the heated desire flaming her pupils. Returning his attention to her breasts he began kneading the other while continuing to torment the one in his mouth. He liked the feel and the taste of her and realized his desire for her was intrinsically raw.

"Ethan…"

He liked the sound of his name from her lips, and his erection throbbed mercilessly in response. "Tell me what you want, Rachel," he coaxed softly, planting kisses across her chest while his hands remained on her breasts. "Tell me what you like."

When she didn't say anything but let out a tortured groan, he blew his breath across a moist nipple. "You like that?"

She didn't hesitate, responding, "Yes."

"What about this?" he rasped in her ear before shifting, letting his wet, hot and greedy mouth slide down her body. She arched her hips the moment his mouth settled between her legs, and he could taste the honeyed sweetness of her desire on his tongue.

Her eyes were closed, her breathing was heavy. He knew she was feeling every bit of what his mouth was doing to her. With his hands he widened the opening of her legs as her taste consumed him and made him want to delve deeper into her womanly core. Her unique and sensuous flavor drove him to sample as much of her as he could get.

But he wanted to do more than that. He wouldn't be satisfied until he shattered her control the same way she had shattered his.

When he felt her body tremble beneath his mouth, he released her and pulled his body up and then over hers, easing between her legs and caging her hips with the firmness of his thighs just moments before thrusting into her. The force alone made her scream out her orgasm mere seconds before he released his.

A pulsing and fiery explosion rocked his body, which subsequently rocked hers. He leaned down and captured her mouth and knew what it felt to truly want a woman in every sense of the word.

Next time around they would go slow. And there would be a next time. He would make sure of it.

An aftermath of sensations consumed Rachel as she lay there, unable to move. Ethan excused himself to go to the bathroom, and she could barely nod in acknowledgment of what he'd said. Nor did she have the strength to turn over off her stomach and onto her back. She felt completely drained. And it wasn't because it was her first orgasm in two years. It was all about the man who'd given it to her.

Moments later, she heard him return and opened her eyes, only to see his naked body walking out of the bathroom. The dim light from the bedside lamp didn't miss his engorged erection. How could he be hard again so soon when she could barely catch her breath? And she couldn't help noticing he had on another condom.

He couldn't possibly assume she had strength for another round.

The bed dipped beneath his weight as he slid in next to her. His hands began gently caressing the center of her back and the rounded curves of her buttocks. She closed her eyes again, enjoying the feel of being touched by him. When he replaced his fingers with the tip of his tongue and licked up and down her spine, a moan of pleasure escaped her lips.

Now she understood how desire could get stirred all over again so soon and gave herself up to the pure joy of it in his hands and mouth. She drew in a deep breath and then breathed out slowly, reveling in the passion building in every part of her body. It was a primitive force she didn't want to yield to again so quickly. She wanted to prolong the enjoyment.

"Turn over, baby."

She pulled in another deep breath and whispered, "Can't. Too weak."

"Then let me help you."

She heard his soft chuckle moments before he gently eased her onto her back. She stared up into his gaze, and the look in his eyes stroked something she hadn't counted on—intense desire even in her weakened state. Desire she couldn't resist or deny. She'd never wanted a man this much, so this was a first for her. And when he leaned down and claimed her mouth in a way no man had ever done before, a shiver of intense heat rode up her spine, renewing energy she didn't think she had. Her heart began pounding in her chest. At the same time, her body started shuddering with sensations she felt all the way to her toes.

With a burst of vigor that was rejuvenating every part

of her, she lifted her arms and wrapped them around his neck while his mouth continued to mate with hers in a kiss that progressed from hot to scalding with a stroke of his tongue.

When he finally released her mouth it was only to shift his body between her thighs. She moaned, knowing he was about to soothe the ache at the juncture of her legs.

He reached out, cupped her bottom, lifted her hips and thrust deep inside of her. For a moment he didn't move. It was as if he needed to savor the feel of his erection planted so profoundly inside of her, pulsing, thickening and growing even larger while her inner muscles clamped down on him tightly.

Then, finally, he began moving in and out at a rhythm and pace that had every cell in her body humming, trembling and shuddering in pleasure. The muscles in his shoulders bunched beneath her fingers when he lowered his head to breathe against her mouth. Her breath hitched in her throat and then her lungs cleared in a precipitated slam.

"Ethan…"

He tasted her lips with his tongue as he drove into her. His hard thrusts made her bed shake, the springs squeak and the headboard hit against the wall. Not only was he drawing out a need and desire within her, he was fulfilling it to a degree that had her meeting him, thrust for thrust.

With one final thrust into the depth of her, her body spun into an orgasm of gigantic proportion. As she reveled in her climax, he kissed her with an intensity that elicited moans from deep in her throat.

At that moment, there was only one thing she could think of. So much for them being just friends.

Ethan eased from the bed and slipped into his jeans. Once he had snapped them up, he glanced back over his shoulder at the woman asleep in the bed. Never had any one woman touched him the way she had, in and out of bed.

And that was the crux of his problem.

He pulled in a deep breath and leaned down to brush a kiss against her temple and then quickly pulled away when he breathed in the scent of her, which had the power to render him helpless.

He rubbed a hand down his face. What the hell had he gotten himself into? Rachel had made it clear, exceedingly so and on more than one occasion, that she had no intention of getting involved with anyone she considered to be in the spotlight, anyone who would put the media on her tail. If she became involved with him, she ran the risk of that happening. He knew if there was any ounce of decency within him, he would grab his stuff and leave and when he saw her tomorrow he would pretend last night never happened.

Easier said than done.

He couldn't do that.

Something was forcing him to not only acknowledge that it happened but to do whatever he could to make sure it happened again.

He shook his head in dismay as he left the bedroom, closing the door behind him. Wasn't it just a little over two weeks ago that he'd made the vow to focus on his career more than anything else, certainly more than any woman? But there was something about Rachel that called out to him at every turn.

He had gone back into the bedroom he should have been occupying to freshen up when his cell phone on the nightstand rang. He released a deep, annoyed breath when the caller ID indicated it was his agent.

"Yes, Curtis?"

"Ethan, where are you?"

He rolled his eyes. "Is there something you need, Curtis?"

"The paparazzi can't find you."

"That's too bad," he murmured with agitation clearly in his voice. "And how did you know they were looking for me?"

His agent paused a second before saying. "It's my job to know everything that's going on with you."

Ethan frowned. Was Curtis somehow responsible for the media hounds hanging around outside of his house last night? It wouldn't surprise Ethan, since his agent liked keeping him in the news. In the spotlight, as Rachel termed it. The thought that Curtis could be connected didn't sit well with him. "Your job is to advance my career, not fabricate lies about me and my love life."

"It's never bothered you before," his agent countered.

The man was right. It hadn't bothered him before. "It does now, and it would behoove you to remember that. Talk to you later, Curtis."

Ethan then disconnected the call.

The sound of a ringing telephone worked its way into the deep recesses of Rachel's sleep-shrouded mind. Without lifting her head from the pillow, she reached out and grabbed her cell phone off the bedside table. "Hello," she said in a drowsy voice.

"I can't believe you're still in bed."

Rachel forced one eye open upon hearing her sister's voice. "What time is it?"

"Almost noon. You weren't at church today, and Aunt Lily wanted to make sure you were okay since it's not like you to miss service."

Rachel moaned, which was followed by a deep yawn. "I'm fine, Sofia." *Am I really?* "I overslept." That wasn't a lie.

She slowly pulled herself up in bed, surprised she had the energy to do so. Taking part in lovemaking marathons wasn't something she did often, and thanks to Ethan, her muscles had gotten one heck of a workout.

Ethan...

She glanced at the rumpled spot beside her in the bed. It hadn't been a figment of her imagination. He had been there. His masculine scent was still in her bedcovers. And she could hear him moving around downstairs, which meant he was still there.

She closed her eyes as memories of their lovemaking flowed through her mind. There were the memories of his hands all over her body, his tongue licking her nipple, his head between her legs, his—

"Rachel?"

She snapped her eyes back open. "Yes?"

"I asked if you wanted to do a movie later."

Sofia was a workaholic and any other time Rachel would have jumped at the chance to do something fun with her sister, but not today. But she knew better than to tell her sister the real reason. "Can I get a rain check?

I want to finish this painting so it can be ready for the gallery's opening day."

"Sure, just let me know when."

They talked for a few more minutes and then Sofia had to take another call. Rachel disconnected the call and stretched her body in bed, thinking that as much as she had enjoyed making love with Ethan, it couldn't happen again.

She eased out of bed, knowing they needed to talk.

Few people knew that cooking was one of Ethan's favorite pastimes, so he wasn't taken aback by the look of surprise on Rachel's face when she walked into her kitchen. Her sexy-pixie expression was priceless.

Something else that was priceless was the way she was dressed. She had showered and was wearing a printed sundress with spaghetti straps at the shoulders and a cute pair of sandals on her feet. On anyone else the simple outfit would have been so-so, but not on her. It gave her an "at-home" look that couldn't be captured any day on the set.

There were a number of reasons for him to make that conclusion. Heading the list was the fact that this was the first time he'd seen her out of bed since they'd made love, so in his book she could have worn a gunnysack and she still would have looked good to him.

"Ethan, what are you doing?" she asked, glancing around her kitchen.

"I'm preparing brunch. I figured you'd be hungry when you finally woke up." He didn't have to say why he'd expected her to sleep late. Last night had been quite a night for them. He doubted either of them had gotten a full hour's sleep.

"But where did you find the stuff to prepare this spread?"

He smiled. "I went to that grocery store on the corner, and before you ask, no, I wasn't recognized. I wore my disguise and quickly went in and out."

"But your car…"

"I drove yours." At the lift of her brow he said, "I left a note just in case you woke up while I was gone."

"Oh." The thought of his male scent infusing the interior of her car was almost too much to think about. Now she would drive her car and think about him.

"You like cooking, I gather," she said moving across the room to the coffeepot. The coffee smelled good but she smelled even better. There was a sensuality to her fragrance that could reach him on a masculine level each and every time he took a whiff of her.

He chuckled. "You gathered right, although I didn't get an interest until college. It was a quick and easy way to get a girl up to your dorm room."

She glanced at him over her shoulder. "I'm sure getting a girl up to your room wasn't hard, Ethan."

A grin formed on his lips. "Should I take that as a compliment?"

"You should take it for whatever you want. I know it to be true. Most women would find you simply irresistible."

He tilted his head and looked at her. She was reaching up to open one of the cabinet doors, which was an almost impossible feat for her without stretching and standing on tiptoes. What flashed through his mind at that moment was a reminder of a position they had used last night when they'd made love standing up. Those same feet had been wrapped around him, locking him inside her body. "Do you find me irresistible, Rachel?"

She turned around to face him, leaning back against the kitchen counter as she did so. Her gaze roamed over him, up and down, before coming to settle on his face, where she gave him her full attention. His stomach tightened at her perusal since it seemed as intimate as any physical caress could get. She pushed a few strands of hair behind her ear before a smile touched her lips. It was tantalizing in one sense but frightening in another.

"Yes, but not the same way that other women do."

Her words, spoken both seriously and honestly, had a profound effect because a part of him knew they were true. She had a way of seeing beyond what the media described as the "killer-watt" smile, past the persona of a jaw-dropping Hollywood leading man. In the two weeks they'd known each other, she'd shown him that she had the ability to get to know the real Ethan Chambers. She knew that what you saw was not always what you got.

And that made *her* irresistible.

Needing to touch her, wanting to kiss her, especially at that moment, he moved toward her and pulled her into his arms. She came willingly, without preamble, filled with all the grace and refinement that most women didn't possess. She had the ability to change the physical to the sensual the moment her lips locked with his. She also had the intuition to know that when it came to an attraction between them, he needed more.

And more importantly, she was willing to give it.

He pulled her closer, wanting to seal every inch of space between them. She leaned up, wrapped her arms around his neck and tilted her head back automatically to meet his mouth that came swooping down on hers. He needed her in the way a man needed a woman.

A woman he was beginning to think of as his.

Nobody kisses like Ethan Chambers, Rachel concluded when she could manage to think again. She loved being held captive in his strong grip, loved being the recipient of his lusty and marauding tongue. And she loved the feel of her breasts pressed against the hard and firm lines of his chest. The same chest she had kissed every inch of last night. Even then she had felt the strength of it beneath her lips. Ethan had a body that was an artist's dream, and she would love to paint him one day, capture the essence of all his masculine beauty on canvas.

"Brunch has to wait."

Those words were barely out of his mouth before he swept her off her feet and into his arms. Once again she had managed to drive him out of control and she enjoyed every single moment of doing so. It was only last night that she had discovered her ability as a woman and the pleasure-filled places that skill could take her.

It might have been his intent to take her back to bed, but somewhere between the kitchen and living room he decided they couldn't make it that far. He headed for her sofa.

Her heart began beating rapidly because with Ethan she had discovered you never knew what you would get, but the one thing you could expect was the most intense pleasure any man could deliver. And that knowledge caused an intense ache between her legs that only he could appease.

She caught her breath when she felt the sofa cush-

ion touch her back, and he spread her out as if she was
a sampling for his enjoyment. He would soon discover
that he was also one for hers. His musky and ultrasexy
scent was devouring all common sense in her body
and replacing it with a spine-tingling need that had her
moaning out his name.

"I'm right here, baby," he whispered while quickly
removing the clothes from her body and then from his.
When he stood over her naked, fully aroused and looking as handsome as any man had a right to look, she
was filled with a craving that had her moving upward,
launching herself at him and toppling them both to the
floor.

He cushioned their fall, and they ended up with their
legs entangled and her stretched out over him. Just the
way she wanted. Some deep, dark emotion, an intense
hunger he had tapped into last night, consumed her and
she began licking him all over, starting with his broad
shoulders and working her way downward.

Moving past his tight abs, she cupped his erection
in her hands before lowering her head and taking him
fully, needing the taste, texture and total length of him
between her lips and as deep in her mouth as he could
go.

"Rachel!"

His palms bracketed her head, his fingers dug into
her scalp and his moan became music to her ears while
she proceeded to torture him. She felt his shaft swell
deep inside her mouth and she stretched to accommo-
date its size.

"I'm coming, baby."

And he did.

She appeased every deep craving she ever had, using

her throat to prolong his orgasm. He seemed lost, powerless as he gave himself over to the magic she created. And she reveled in the control as she never had before.

When he could draw another breath, he pulled a condom pack from his jeans, sheathed himself and entered her. Quick work but thorough.

He began moving in and out of her, thrusting hard and deep, taking her to the brink where she'd led him moments ago. No matter what would come tomorrow, she knew she would have these memories of their lovemaking. Memories that would comfort her and tear at her heart long after he was no longer a part of her life.

But for now, for today, he was and because of that, she was satisfied.

It was time for him to leave.

After making love on her living room floor, they had returned to the kitchen and eaten the brunch he had prepared before going back up to her bedroom and making love some more. When they were spent, they had showered together, returned downstairs to devour the apple tarts he'd made for dessert, then he'd gone upstairs to gather his few belongings.

"Do you think the paparazzi have gone now?" she asked, walking him to the kitchen door that led to her garage, where his car was parked beside hers.

"Yes. I spoke with the manager of my condo complex and she apologized profusely. The one thing I was assured of when I moved in was that my privacy would be protected. She doesn't understand what could have happened." He paused. "I think I do."

She lifted a brow. "What?"

"My agent. He thinks one of the ways to build my

career is for me to stay in the spotlight, to keep my name in the news."

He could tell her mind was at work. Making that statement had made her remember her one argument as to why there could never be anything but friendship between them. For that reason, he was not surprised by her next statement.

"I refuse to think of this weekend as a mistake, Ethan, but it's something we can't allow to happen again. You are who you are and I am who I am. We live different lives and reside in basically different worlds."

"It doesn't have to be that way, Rachel."

"Yes, it does. I could never ask you to give up your dream for me, like you can't expect me to do the same for you."

He paused for a moment and then asked, "So where do we go from here?"

A sad smile touched her lips. "Nowhere. Let's chalk it up as nothing more than a one-night stand. This weekend is our secret. And it's up to us to know it was just one of those things that can't happen again."

He glanced down as if studying the floor and then he looked back at her. "What if I said I don't agree? That there has to be a way?"

A bittersweet smile touched her lips. "Then I'd say don't waste your time trying to figure one out. It doesn't exist. We are as different as day and night."

Ethan pulled in a deep breath and felt a tightening in his gut because he knew, in a way, she was right. Becoming a successful Hollywood actor was his dream, and it was a dream that didn't mesh with hers.

He leaned down and kissed her hard and deep. Only

one thought pierced his mind then and again moments later when he walked out her door. How on earth was he going to give her up?

Chapter 10

"Quiet on the set!

"Take three!

"Action!"

Rachel could hear the sound of Frasier's booming voice carrying all the way into her trailer. Today they would be shooting mostly medical scenes, and several doctors from an area hospital were on the set to make sure that aspect of the show was done correctly.

She had arrived at work early, mainly to have herself together by the time Ethan got there. Like she'd told him yesterday, although she hadn't regretted any of it, their time together could not be repeated. For twenty-four hours she had let herself go and had made love to a man who had pleasured her body in ways probably not known to most men. All women should be made love to the way Ethan had done to her. Memories of their time together still made her skin hot whenever she thought about it.

When he had arrived this morning, he had not given her any more of his time and attention than he always had. There was no way anyone seeing them interact together would suspect they'd spent practically the entire weekend behind closed doors. There had been so much red-hot chemistry between them and they had taken advantage of it time and time again.

Although no one on the set had a clue, each and every time he glanced her way or gave her a smile, heat would begin simmering in the pit of her stomach. One look into Ethan's eyes had the power to send a rush of desire spiking through her. That was why she was letting Theresa work out on the set today, brushing up the actors during shooting, while she remained in her trailer applying the makeup for those in the next scene.

"You're quiet today."

Rachel blinked, remembering where she was and what she was doing. There never had been a time when thoughts of a man had interfered with her job. She looked down at Tae'Shawna Miller, the model-turned-actress from last season who played a nurse on the show. Tae'Shawna was known to be moody and self-centered and, not surprisingly, months ago she'd begun hanging around Paige.

Rachel wasn't sure what Paige might have told her, but lately Tae'Shawna had been acting even moodier where she was concerned. She'd even gone to John saying Rachel had applied her makeup too heavily last season and that she wanted to bring in her own makeup artist. John had denied her request.

"It's Monday," Rachel said, hoping that would end things. It was a joke on the set that although Wednesday was considered hump day, Monday was pretty low-key with everyone trying to recover from the weekend.

"I hear you, girl. I could barely pull myself out of bed. If it wasn't for Ethan calling to wake me up this morning, I probably would have been late coming in today."

Trying to keep her hands steady and acting as nonchalant as she could, Rachel continued applying Tae'Shawna's makeup and asked in a casual tone, "Ethan Chambers?"

A smile touched the woman's lips. "None other. We spent some time together this weekend. I'm only mentioning this to you because I know you're the soul of discretion. Ethan would be upset if he knew I told anyone. He wants to keep things quiet since we're both working on the show."

The woman gave a naughty smile before adding, "Needless to say, I had to all but force him to leave last night."

Rachel managed to remain calm as she dissected the woman's words, hoping what Tae'Shawna was saying was more wishful thinking than gospel truth, especially since Ethan had been with *her* from Saturday night to late yesterday afternoon.

But she couldn't help wondering if he had left her bed and gone directly to Tae'Shawna's. And where had he been before coming to her place on Saturday night? She'd felt it hadn't been her place to ask. However, now the woman in her couldn't help wondering if Ethan had shared his weekend with her *and* Tae'Shawna.

That question was still on her mind hours later. For the moment, her trailer was empty and she slid into the chair to take a breather, trying to fight the green-eyed monster of jealousy consuming her. She pulled in a deep breath, wondering why the thought of Ethan being involved with Tae'Shawna bothered her and how she could get beyond it.

The odds had been high when he'd shown up at her place Saturday night that he would probably spend some of his weekend with another woman. It would have made perfect sense that he did. After all, he was a known playboy around town. It really shouldn't concern her since they had used protection every time they'd made love, so she wasn't at risk. But still…

It disappointed her that, on the set, Ethan portrayed himself as a man not giving any of the women who came on to him the time of day. Although he was always friendly to them, she'd had no reason to assume that things had been any different after hours. Was it only an act? Was he involved not only with Tae'Shawna but others as well, possibly even Paige?

She eased from the chair and began pacing. She told herself she should not be bothered if he was also seeing other women. They hadn't set any rules or guidelines regarding their relationship. A frown deepened her brow when she reminded herself they didn't have a relationship. What happened this weekend was just a one-time deal. She had made that clear to Ethan. But why had he bothered to make it seem as if he hadn't had sex for a while, certainly not that same day? Men!

She knew when it came to sex, men would get as much of it as came their way and still want more. A part of her couldn't help feeling somewhat disappointed to discover he was one of those men and wasn't different at all.

"Looks like you're thinking too hard again."

She spun around to find the object of her deepest and most disappointing thoughts leaning against the trailer door. She hadn't heard him enter the trailer.

"And what's it to you?" she asked in a tone that sounded pretty snippy to even her own ears.

He shrugged. "With that attitude, nothing, I guess.

Frasier gave everyone an additional hour for lunch again, and I was wondering if you'd like to take a walk over to—"

"No." And then because she knew there was no reason for her to have an attitude, she said, "Thanks for asking, but I have a lot to do here."

He nodded slowly as he continued to look at her. She wished he wouldn't do that. And she wished it didn't bother her, didn't make her feel those vibes again, especially when he probably looked at Tae'Shawna the same way. Not only Tae'Shawna but all the other women with whom he was probably involved.

"Is that why you haven't been out on the set today?"

"You could say that."

Avoiding his gaze, she moved around the trailer, picking up items to repack in her various makeup kits, as well as hanging up items of clothing that cast members had discarded.

"Is something wrong, Rachel?"

She glanced over at him. "No. What gives you that idea?" She then returned to what she was doing, basically presenting her back to him.

Moving away from the door, Ethan strode through the space separating them and came to stand in front of her, forcing her to look up and meet his gaze. "Hey, I knew yesterday you were serious about continuing this 'friends only' thing and, although I prefer more between us, I will respect your wishes."

"Do you?"

He had a confused look on his face. "Do I what?" His tone was low, gruff, with more than a hint of agitation.

"Do you prefer more between us?"

He released a frustrated sigh. "I told you I did."

She nodded slowly. "And what did you tell Tae'Shawna?" The moment the words left her lips, she wished she could take them back. She probably sounded like a jealous shrew. And she had no right to be that way, considering she had told Ethan there would be nothing between them. Ever.

She stared up at him to see even more confusion settle in his features when he asked, "Is this supposed to be a trick question or something?"

"Not a trick question, Ethan, just a curious one."

He crossed his arms over his chest. "And what does Tae'Shawna have to do with us?"

A shiver ran through her when he said the word *us.* Although when it came to them there was no "us," just hearing him say it did something crazy to her. "By 'us,' you mean you and Tae'Shawna?" she asked.

A smile that didn't quite reach his eyes touched his lips. "Was that question supposed to be a joke, Rachel?"

"What do you think?" She made a move to walk away but he reached out and gripped her arm, not too tight, but enough that the heat of his hand felt like a flame licking her skin. *Amazing,* she thought. Even when she wasn't happy with him, he had the ability to make her want him.

"Explain what you meant by that," he said. She thought she heard somewhat of a growl in his tone.

He was staring at her, and she returned his stare with no intention of breaking it. And she had no problem explaining what she'd said as well as elaborating on what she'd meant. "When I worked on Tae'Shawna's makeup earlier today, she took me into her confidence and shared information about you and her."

His expression seemed thoughtful. "Me and her?"

"Yes."

"And what did she say?"

She shrugged and then said, "Nothing more than that the two of you spent part of the weekend together and that you didn't leave her place until late last night and that you were her wake-up call this morning. I know you were with me from Saturday night until yesterday afternoon, but—"

"You're not sure about the time I wasn't with you?" he said, finishing her statement for her.

"Yes, but it really doesn't matter. Saturday night just happened between us. And it's not like I didn't know about your reputation."

He nodded as he held her gaze. "My reputation that you know about from a tabloid you *don't* read. Right?"

It was easy to see his expression had gone from thoughtful to rigid, as if he was struggling to contain the anger she could actually feel radiating from him. She was smart enough to take a step back when he took one forward, and she noticed the eyes staring at her had turned a stormy gray. Not a good sign.

She took another step backward only to have her spine hit a wall. He caged her in when he leaned forward, bracing his hands against the wall on both sides of her face. If his aim was to get her attention, he had it.

She lifted her chin and met his glare with one of her own. "What is this about, Ethan?"

"You tell me, Rachel."

"I told you. And I also told you that you don't owe me an explanation about Tae'Shawna because—"

"I wouldn't repeat it if I were you," he interrupted in a tone gruff enough to make her heed his warning.

He didn't say anything for a moment. He just stared

at her. Then finally he said, "First of all, when I made love to you Saturday night, it was the first time I had been intimate with a woman in over six months."

She couldn't stop her mouth from dropping open. Nor could she disguise the flicker of surprise in her eyes. Both were probably what made him continue on to say, "This weekend I needed to get away, so I got up early Saturday morning and drove across the border to Tijuana. Alone. When I got back later that night, I discovered the paparazzi camped out at my place and called you. When I left your apartment Sunday afternoon, I went straight home. I don't know what make-believe game Tae'Shawna is playing but, unfortunately, it's not the first time and probably won't be the last time that some woman claimed we were together or involved in an affair when we weren't. That's how those tabloids you *don't* read are sold."

"Ethan, I—"

His sharp tone interrupted her. "The only thing I want to know from you now is whether you believe me or Tae'Shawna."

She frowned. "Does it matter?"

"To me it does."

She took a deep, uneven breath as she stared into his eyes, still jarred by his admission that their night together had been his first time in over six months. Her heart was pounding because he indicated what she believed mattered to him. And although she didn't quite understand why, she was glad that it did.

As odd as it might seem, she didn't want him to be involved with women like Tae'Shawna, women who would go so far as to invent a relationship with a man.

Or even worse, women like Paige who would try anything to get him into their beds.

There was one thing that was actually making her feel somewhat warm inside—the fact that he hadn't wanted any of the model types. He had wanted her. And the strangest thing of all was that she didn't want any of those other women to have him either.

She couldn't explain the thought processes that supported her reasons, especially not to him when they were still somewhat foggy to her. But what she could do was give him the answer he was still waiting for. "I don't believe you're involved with Tae'Shawna, Ethan."

Ethan hadn't realized he was holding his breath until he released it after Rachel had spoken. Why what she believed mattered so much he wasn't sure, but it did. It might have everything to do with that bond he felt with her. A bond he'd never felt with any other woman. That bond had strengthened when they'd made love. He wondered if she realized it. If she didn't comprehend it now, he was certain she would later.

Needing to kiss her, he reached out and pulled her into his arms and captured her mouth with his. All the reasons this weekend had meant so much to him came roaring back to life like a living thing with a mind of its own. It had the ability to push him closer to her even when she wanted to keep him at a distance.

He tried to steady his heart rate and had almost succeeded until she wrapped her arms around his neck and pressed her body closer to his while returning his kiss with equal fervor. Her response was what he had hoped for and definitely what he was enjoying. It wouldn't take much for him to take her like this, standing up against the wall. He fought the temptation. Instead, he continued to make love to her mouth with a hunger that seemed relentless. The feel of her hardened nipples pressing against his chest was sweet agony, as was the rough texture of her denim jeans rubbing against his hard erection. He continued to fight the temptation, knowing what his body wanted would only lead to trouble.

That fight was taken out of his hands when they heard the sound of conversation right outside the trailer door and they quickly ended the kiss. He took a deep breath while forcing his body to cool down, which seemed nearly impossible to do.

He reached out and flicked the pad of his thumb across her bottom lip. "I know what you said last night, but I think we'll be doing each other an injustice not to explore what could be, Rachel. There will be risks but I intend to convince you they will be worth it."

He leaned down and swiped a quick kiss across her lips before moving toward the door.

Chapter 11

"Let me make sure I got this right." Wide-eyed, Charlene spoke in a low tone of voice as she leaned across the table while they waited in Roscoe's for their food to be served. Lower still, she said, "You spent the weekend with Mr. Drop-Dead Gorgeous himself? Ethan Chambers?"

At least Charlene hadn't blurted it out in a loud voice, Rachel thought, grateful for that, although it was evident Charlene was stunned. "Only *part* of the weekend," she quickly clarified. "He arrived around eight Saturday night and left Sunday afternoon around five. That's not even a full twenty-four hours." What she didn't have to say, and what Charlene could figure out on her own, was that a lot had happened during that period of time.

"Wow!" Charlene said, still clearly stunned. "Two weeks ago you said the two of you were nothing more than friends. What happened?"

Rachel drew in a deep breath, wondering how she was going to explain to her best friend that lust happened. The man was simply irresistible, both in and out of bed. "Well, it happened like this…"

Charlene leaned even farther over the table. Not only were her ears perked but her eyes were bright with curiosity. Rachel figured she was more than ready to take in all the hot-tamale details. "Yes?"

When Rachel didn't say anything, Charlene lifted a brow. "Well?"

A smile touched Rachel's lips. "Well what?"

Charlene gave her a don't-you-dare-play-with-me-like-that look. "Tell me what happened."

"Whatever you can imagine probably did happen, Cha. The man knew positions that are probably outlawed in most states, and he has more staying power in bed than Peyton Manning has on a football field."

A huge grin lit Charlene's face as she sat back in her chair. She exclaimed proudly as she looked at her with envy, "What a woman."

Rachel shook her head as she recalled the past weekend. "No, what a man."

And she seriously meant that. Ethan had her considering taking risks she normally would not take. He said he would make it worth her while and, considering this past weekend, she had no reason not to believe him. After that incident in the trailer a few days ago, she had been trying to keep a level head around the set and handle things decently and in order. In other words, although she didn't try to avoid him, she didn't do anything to seek him out either. But she was well aware that he was waiting for her to make the next move.

She glanced over at Charlene. "What have I gotten myself into?"

Charlene smiled naughtily. "His pants, for starters."

"Girl, be serious," Rachel protested.

"I am."

Rachel chuckled. Yes, her friend was serious and also right. She had gotten into his pants and was looking forward to getting into them again. How shameful was that?

"It doesn't make sense," she said. "You know what a private person I am and how I hate being in the spotlight. Anyone involved with Ethan will have their face plastered all over the tabloids. There's no way to get around that unless we sneak around."

"And how do you feel about doing something like that?"

That was a good question and one she needed to think about. Were earth-shattering, toe-curling orgasms worth all of that?

"You know what's wrong with you, don't you?" Charlene asked, smothering a giggle.

Rachel took a sip of her iced tea. "I don't have a clue."

"You went without a hot male body too long. Trust me, I know how it feels."

Rachel hated to admit that Charlene was probably right. In the past, she'd always had enough on her plate to keep her mind occupied so she didn't think about sex. She was just as busy now as she was before, so what was there about Ethan that made her want to make him a top priority on her "to do" list? It wasn't like she wasn't routinely surrounded on the set by gorgeous, sexy men. Why had her body decided Ethan was the one?

Before she could offer any more input to the conversation, her cell phone began vibrating. Caller ID indicated an unknown number. Normally she refused to answer those kinds of calls, but she felt a warm sensation in the pit of her stomach. She excused herself from the table and quickly headed toward the ladies' room.

"Yes?"

"This is Ethan. I want to see you."

So much for him waiting for her to make the next move.

The sound of his voice plunged her into a sea of desire so deep she felt herself going under. "Why? Do I need to save you again?"

"No, but I do need you to make love to me like you did last weekend."

If she hadn't been drowning before, she was certainly drowning now and there was no one around to throw her a life jacket.

"Ethan, I think—"

"You do too much of that."

For a moment she struggled with the possibility that maybe he was right. "One of us needs to."

"No, we don't. Just consider it something we both deserve. We work hard, so we should get to play harder."

He did have a point. Didn't he?

She drew in a deep breath, wondering where her logical mind was when she needed it the most. It had probably taken a flying leap with that first orgasm Saturday night. "We're risking the chance of you being followed."

"I have everything under control."

Including her, she thought, when she tried summoning the gumption to deny what he was asking. But then all she had to do was to remember Saturday night or the kiss they'd shared in her trailer earlier in the week. His lips had teased her mercilessly, and his tongue had nearly made her short-circuit.

"Rachel?"

"Yes?"

"Will you meet me?"

She nervously licked her lips. "Where?"

He rattled off an address that was followed by a brief set of instructions. "Do you need directions?"

"No, I'll use my GPS," she said, tucking the piece of paper she'd written on back in her purse.

Moments later, she hung up the phone with her heart pounding in her chest. Emotions she refused to put a name to stirred in her stomach, and she knew she was falling deeper and deeper into lust.

Slow down, buddy. The last thing you need is a ticket while racing across town for a night of hot and heavy sex.

Ethan flinched at the thought of that because he knew his meeting with Rachel was more than that. She was different and not just because she wasn't a woman anxious to blast their affair to all who'd listen.

And they were involved in an affair because neither of them was looking for any sort of heavy-duty relationship right now. He was satisfied to keep things under wraps as much she was, especially since he knew how she felt about the matter.

He had actually been followed for a short while after leaving his place. He had driven his car to the private parking garage of condos owned by a friend of Hunter's from college. If the person tailing him thought he was smart, Ethan intended to show he was smarter.

Ethan had parked his car in a designated spot and had donned his disguise before getting out of his car and getting into another vehicle—one owned by that same friend of Hunter's, who was presently out of the country for the next month or so.

He had smiled upon leaving the garage and bypass-ing the photographer who was parked across the street, waiting for Ethan to come out. No doubt, the man would be there for some time while trying to determine what woman and at what address Ethan was visiting at this particular condo complex.

Ethan couldn't ever recall going through this much hassle to keep his interest in a woman hidden. If he wasn't so concerned about Rachel's feelings, he truly wouldn't give a damn.

But he needed tonight. He needed her. This had been one hell of a week, with Frasier in rare form, demanding more than perfection from everyone. The rumor floating around the set was that the man and his partner were having problems. Although Frasier's policy demanded all of them leave any and all personal matters at the door and not bring them on the set, evidently that rule didn't apply to Frasier.

Luckily, so far none of Frasier's tirades had been leveled at him but at a number of others, including Tae'Shawna when she had messed up her lines. After the lie she'd told to Rachel, the woman hadn't gotten any pity from Ethan.

He had come close to confronting Tae'Shawna on more than one occasion about the lie she had told. However, Rachel had asked him not to say anything. She worried that Tae'Shawna would resent her for breaking a confidence and possibly even retaliate in some way.

Ethan exited off the interstate and noted a lot of cars on the road for a Thursday night. He was in Industry, a city in the San Gabriel Valley section of Los Angeles. His destination was an old warehouse owned by Chambers Winery that was used to store bottled wine shipped from the vineyard. In other words, it used to be their off-site wine cellar. More than once he had considered the idea of fixing up at least part of the place as a possible hideaway when he needed peace from the media's scrutiny. This week he had acted on that idea, and after a few phone calls and explicit instructions, he had received word that the place was good to go. He couldn't imagine not bringing Rachel here to help christen the place.

More than once during the drive over, he had glanced back in his rearview mirror to make sure he was not being followed. Satisfied that he had not been, he pulled into the drive and around the side of the building that was away from the street.

Grabbing the pair of wineglasses off the seat beside him, he got out of the car and closed the door behind him. It was a beautiful August night with bright stars lighting the sky. The perfect night for a romantic rendezvous.

He had made good time, intentionally arriving ahead of Rachel. As he headed for the entrance with the wineglasses in his hands, he smiled. So far so good. His evening was going according to his plans.

Rachel pulled into the parking lot of the huge vacant building to park next to the vehicle already there. Her heart began pounding and her hand on the steering wheel began trembling somewhat.

She glanced around through her windshield. She had followed Ethan's instructions to the letter, and the huge building looming before her appeared dark and scary. But she knew somewhere inside, Ethan was waiting for her.

She opened the car door and glanced around as she

got out. It had been hard for her to consume her dinner knowing what her plans were for afterward.

If Charlene suspected anything was amiss, she hadn't let on. Rachel would give her best friend all the details later. But for now, the plan for tonight was something she hadn't wanted to share. She didn't want to take the risk of anyone talking her out of doing something she really wanted to do. She didn't want anyone to knock the craziness out of her and force her to go back to being her logical self.

She pushed the door and, to her intense relief, it opened, just like Ethan had said it would. The moment she stepped over the threshold, the smell of vintage wine consumed her nostrils. She could probably get intoxicated just from the scent alone.

The place was dark. The only light was a bit of moonlight shining in through one of the windows. She'd never been afraid of the dark but there was something eerie about this place. Her heart rate increased, and she fought back a nervousness that was about to consume her as she took a step back and bumped against the hard, solid wall of a masculine chest.

She gasped when a pair of strong, muscular arms reached around to enclose her within a powerful embrace. The familiar scent of him surrounded her and she breathed it in and relaxed against him. She could feel his hot breath at her neck, close to ear, when he whispered, "Welcome to my lair."

Her heart rate steadied when another type of response took control—not fear of the unknown but apprehension of the known. She knew why she was here, why he had asked her to come and how tonight would end up.

She released her breath with a shaky sigh when he turned her to face him and leaned forward to give her a more physical display of welcome, one she had no problem receiving.

His tongue tangled hotly with hers while his hands seemed to roam all over her, finding her bare skin not covered by her short skirt. And he was caressing her backside in a way that only he could execute. When he finally pulled back, she was grateful for his hands around her waist because her knees seemed to buckle beneath her, and she felt herself swaying against him.

He held her tight as he continued to rain kisses all over her face while his hands gently massaged her back. They stood that way for a while as their heartbeats and breathing returned to normal. But she was completely aware of the way her hard nipples pressed against the hard wall of his chest.

"Come on, let me show you around," he whispered against her temple.

He took her hand in his, and using a flashlight that he pulled from his pocket, he led the way. She glanced from side to side and saw rows and rows of wine bottles and immediately knew this was a place his family owned.

"There's usually a security guard around," he said. "Clyde has worked for us at this place for years, making sure no one runs off with anything. I thought I'd give him the rest of the night off."

Instead of saying anything, Rachel nodded and merely followed him through another door and up a flight of stairs. She tried pushing back the question rushing through her mind. Why was she here and not at home in her own bed getting a good night's sleep?

After all, it was Thursday and tomorrow was a workday for the both of them. But she knew the reason. Ethan had called and said he wanted them to make love again. She wanted them to make love again as well. For what other reason would she be here?

She knew getting involved with him, secretly or otherwise, was probably not a good idea, but then she could do casual dating just like the next man or woman. She wasn't looking for everlasting love. She liked her life just fine the way it was.

He used a key to open another door and it was only then that he put the flashlight away and flipped on a switch. She nearly closed her eyes at the brightness but not before she saw the immaculate-looking office.

She continued to glance around when he locked the door behind them. And when she gave him a questioning look, he smiled before taking her hand again and leading her through another set of doors.

She gasped when she saw what was in front of her. It was the most beautifully decorated room she could imagine, one designed as a lovers' hideaway, complete with a king-size bed and all the other matching furnishings. There was even an expensive throw rug on the floor and several beautiful paintings on the wall, lit candles around the room and a vase of roses sitting on a dresser.

She lowered her head when an errant thought hit her. Was this where Ethan brought all his conquests when he needed privacy? She glanced over at him and apparently the question was there, looming in her gaze, because he said, "I called and had this place renovated just a few days ago. I'm pleased with what they've done in such a short period of time."

And then in a voice that had thickened, taken on a rough edge in an ultrasexy sort of way, he said, "And let me go on record as saying that you're the only woman I've ever brought here, Rachel. I consider this place as ours."

Her breath caught in her throat as she took in all he said and all he meant. He had created this place for them? Did he assume there would be many more secret rendezvous for them? So many that they would need a place to slip away to and be together without prying eyes or stalking photographers hell-bent on fueling the tabloid frenzy?

The thought of such an idea—Ethan being so into her—was ludicrous. She could see him taking advantage of her willingness to engage in no-strings-attached sex a couple of times, but did he honestly think it would become a long-term affair? No, he probably knew that it wouldn't be and would be satisfied with the here and now. When she ceased being his flavor of the hour, he would replace her with someone else, someone more his style. More than likely it would be one of those leggy models his name was usually hooked up with. A woman who enjoyed being in the spotlight just as much as he did.

She fought the thick lump blocking her throat. Not wanting to put a damper on the mood he'd set for them tonight, she let her eyes roam around the room. The decor was simply beautiful in the warm glow of candlelight. Then her eyes lit on the glasses and the bottle of wine on a nightstand beside the bed.

"That's Chambers Winery's finest," he leaned over and whispered close to her ear. She glanced up into the depths of his eyes, saw all the desire embedded deep within them, and an unfamiliar sensation overtook her. It ran through her like a burning ball of heat and settled in the pit of her stomach as if it belonged there and had no intention of going away.

Mentally she weighed her options. She could take tonight and accept it for what it was—a night two sexually charged individuals wanted to enjoy each other. Or she could go along for the ride as long as it lasted and as long as they took all the measures necessary not to get caught—providing it was all enjoyment and no emotion. There *had* to be a no-emotional-attachment policy.

Deciding which option she would go with, she eased closer to him and said, "I can't wait to have a glass."

The tips of her nipples were beginning to heat up, and she intentionally rubbed against him to bring her breasts in contact with his chest. The hitch in his breath let her know she'd made a hit. It seemed Hollywood's newest heartthrob wasn't immune to her charms. Just the thought that she had enough to hold his interest made her heart pound and her entire body begin to tremble inside.

The look in his eyes told her that he knew exactly what she was doing and was willing to let her take the lead for now.

"And there's something else I can't wait to have," she said, tilting her head back to meet his gaze.

"What else do you want, Rachel?"

The huskiness of his voice made a shiver ripple through her. She lowered her gaze to his chest and then lower still to his crotch. She'd never been fascinated with the makings of an aroused man before, but now she couldn't help marveling at what a fine specimen of a man he was. His erection nearly burst through the zipper of his jeans, and she felt proud of herself that she had caused his intense arousal.

"I want this," she said, reaching out and groping that part of him. She heard his low growl and glanced up. His eyes could not hide the desire she saw in them.

"Sweetheart, I'm going to make sure you get everything you want." And then he swept her off her feet and into his arms and carried her over to the bed.

There was something about Rachel's scent that got to him every time. It was an intimate fragrance that seemed to beckon him on a primitive level that even now had every muscle in his body rippling in a way he found tormenting.

He undressed her and then undressed himself. He had seen the way she blushed when he tossed several condom packets on the nightstand and took a step away from the bed to put one on. She watched him sheath himself and the thought that she was doing so sent a rush of blood to his loins.

Silence dominated the room and for a heartfelt moment he wished some type of music was playing to set the mood. Too late now. But next time…

And there would be a next time. He was going to make sure of it. Like he told her, this was *their* place. When he'd made the arrangements on Monday, it had been with her and only her in mind. He hadn't wanted any other woman in that bed with him.

He flinched at the thought, like he always did when his mind would begin thinking of more than sex between them. During those times, he would do whatever was needed to get his thoughts back in check. The only reason he and Rachel were drawn to each other was their intense sexual chemistry. And they were well aware that the attraction could never go beyond what they were sharing now. Neither of them had plans of ever falling in love.

He moved back toward the bed and she shifted on her haunches and met him, reaching out and taking hold of his throbbing erection. She tilted her head back and stared into his eyes for a long moment. Something was passing between them, and he felt it in the hands holding him as well as in the eyes locked with his.

"Tomorrow will we be able to pretend tonight didn't happen?"

Her question broke the silence. "Yes, it's going to be hard but we'll manage it."

She leaned up and licked the side of his face. "You think so?"

"Hell, I hope so, but I'll be the first to admit, every time I see you on the set, I want to tear your clothes off."

He heard her snort at that. "You would have a hard time convincing me of that with that love scene you did today."

He lifted a brow. Love scenes were staged and she was well aware of that. Surely she didn't think any part of them meant anything to him. He was simply following the script. Did he hear a bit of jealousy in her voice?

"Then I need to do whatever it takes to erase that scene from your mind," he said, and for emphasis he reached out and pulled her closer toward him.

He felt the shiver that passed through her and, in response, a slew of emotions flowed through him, nearly taking his breath away. A need for her filled him to capacity, and for a moment he could imagine her with him even when he was in his eighties.

At the thought, he went momentarily still. Where had that come from? He knew there was no way he could consider anything with her beyond this affair.

He reminded himself of that again as he captured her mouth with his and lowered her body to the bed.

There was something about being pressed into the mattress by the man you wanted. A man who was holding her gaze as he entered her slowly, as if he was savoring the journey.

The last time they'd made love he had taken her hard and fast, and now the slowness was driving her mad. She could only ask, "Why?"

He knew what she was asking and said throatily, "There's no rush. We have plenty of time and I want to take things slow, draw it out and make you scream. A lot of times."

She could feel the hardness of him grow inside of her and knew he intended to make some point. Being the skilled lover he was, he'd succeed in making all his wishes come true.

Chapter 12

"Quiet on the set!

"Take one!

"Action!"

Rachel fought back the rush of jealousy as she watched yet another love scene being shot between Dr. Tyrell Perry and Dr. Sonja Duncan. Did Ethan have to appear to be enjoying it so much?

Usually she stayed in the trailer working with the actors, but today she decided to venture out and would be the first to admit a part of her had wanted to see Ethan. More than once he had accused her of hiding out in the trailer, so today she had decided to be seen.

Although, she thought as a smile touched her lips, hiding out in the trailer hadn't stopped him from seeking her out on occasion and making the find worth his while. He had introduced her to quickies. She didn't want to think about the risk they took of someone discovering their secret. So far no one had, and she was thankful for that.

It had been a week since that night when they'd started their secret rendezvous. Most of the time they would meet up at their hideaway haven but on occasion he would come to her place. So far he was still outsmarting the paparazzi.

She smiled, thinking about how Ethan had bought her a disguise—a honey-blond wig and green contacts. And because she was a makeup artist, it hadn't been difficult to add her own camouflage to make herself unrecognizable when they'd made a decision to branch out beyond the bedroom to grab something to eat. They had even risked going to a movie together.

On more than one occasion she had found herself thinking just how a normal relationship with him would be, one where they wouldn't have to sneak around to be together. But she knew such a thing wasn't possible.

"Cut!"

The production crew rushed around trying to get the props changed for another taping, and it was then that Ethan glanced over at her. When he winked and smiled, she couldn't help smiling back. Last night they had spent the night together at *their* place, and he had surprised her by having an easel with art supplies waiting for her when she had arrived. After having made love, he reclined on the bed while she painted him, something he had surprised her by agreeing to do. It would be her own personal painting of him in all his naked splendor to be shared with no one.

She had returned to the trailer when her cell phone went off. Caller ID indicated it was Charlene. "Yes, Cha?"

"I know you don't read the tabloids so I feel I should give you the scoop."

She raised a brow. "About what?"

"Ethan. He's driving the paparazzi crazy by eluding them every chance he gets. They've begun wondering what's going on with him and who the woman he's intent on hiding is."

Rachel felt a knot in her stomach. "Do they have any idea? Did they mention a name?"

"No, but they have vowed to find out, so you might want to cool things with him for a while."

Rachel began nibbling on her bottom lip. Yes, that would be best, but it would be hard to do.

"The media can be relentless when they want to find out something," Charlene added.

Rachel knew that to be true. "Thanks for keeping me in the loop. I appreciate it."

"What are you going to do?"

Rachel drew in a deep breath. She had few options and knew there was only one thing that she could do. Regardless of whether she liked it or whether she was ready for it to happen, their affair had run its course. "I'm going to talk to him."

"And if the two of you meet up somewhere to have this talk, you might want to be looking over your shoulder. Disguise or no disguise, the two of you will have the media hounds on your heels for sure."

Ethan glanced in his rearview mirror. He was being followed. A deep frown set into his features. He'd been trying to elude the guy now for a full hour without any success.

He was to meet Rachel at *their* place and he couldn't do so as long as this reporter was still on his tail. Even switching cars and donning his disguise hadn't helped. This guy was on to him and seemed intent on letting him know it.

When his cell phone rang, he almost snatched it off

his belt and his frown deepened when he saw the caller was Curtis. He had been trying to avoid his agent for a week or so now. "Yes, Curtis?"

"Damn, Ethan, are you trying to mess up a good thing?"

Ethan glanced into his rearview mirror, getting more agitated by the minute. He needed to get rid of this reporter so he could hook up with Rachel at their scheduled time. "What are you talking about?"

"The tabloids. You've become elusive over the past few weeks, annoying the hell out of several tabloid reporters who even claim you've purposely given them the slip."

Ethan rolled his eyes. "And?"

"And they are wondering why and just who you're trying to hide. Someone has connected you to a nameless married woman and has vowed to uncover her identity."

Ethan's hand tightened on the steering wheel. That was not what he wanted to hear. He of all people knew how tabloid reporters could make a pest of themselves more so than usual when they thought they were on to a story.

"I'd like to see them try to uncover anything," he said, almost in a growl, knowing he would do whatever it took to protect Rachel's identity.

"So you're admitting to being involved with a married woman?"

"I'm not admitting to anything, but if I were, it would be my damn business," he responded.

"Not here in Hollywood, Ethan, and not while we're trying to build your career. You were doing a great job wining and dining the ladies, causing others to take notice and earning the title of this town's newest heart-throb. All of that is what we need to continue to build your image the way we want. I know how important that is to you."

Ethan pulled in a deep breath. Yes, it had been important to him at one time, but now…

"And in that same vein, I have a suggestion for a date for you on Saturday night."

Curtis's words pulled Ethan's concentration back into the conversation. "Excuse me?"

"I said that I have a suggestion for a date for you on Saturday."

Ethan frowned. "What are you talking about, Curtis?"

"I'm talking about Faith Pride. I got a call from her agent, who suggested it might be a good idea if the two of you attended the event together."

"I know nothing about an event next Saturday night."

"Sure you do," Curtis insisted. "I sent you the invitation with a mailing confirmation so I know you got it."

He might have gotten it but, like the rest of his mail, he hadn't opened it. His time and the majority of his attention had been given to his sexy pixie, with no regrets. He looked back in his rearview mirror. The man was still there. Damn.

"I'm not going anywhere Saturday night, Curtis."

"What? You can't be serious, Ethan. You have to go. You're hot news and expected to be there. If I didn't know better I'd think you didn't give a damn about your career anymore. I assume you still want one, right?"

"Of course I do!"

"Good, but it sounds like you have a distraction and that isn't good. Get rid of her."

"Come again?"

"I said get rid of her, Ethan. I don't know who she is and frankly I don't care. She's interfering with your life in a negative way. Your actions in keeping her a secret mean she isn't someone you want to be seen with." Curtis paused a moment then said, "Oh, hell, please tell me the person is a she and not a he."

Ethan fought the urge to tell his agent just where he could go. Instead he said, "Bye, Curtis."

"Hey, you didn't answer me."

"And I don't intend to. If you don't know the answer to that then it's time I start looking for another agent."

"Wait, Ethan, I think we—"

Angrily Ethan clicked off the phone. He then glanced back in his rearview mirror and saw the bastard was still on his tail. Deciding he'd had enough, he figured it was time to seriously lose this guy. Increasing his speed, he darted in and out of traffic before making a quick exit off the interstate, only to make a quick right and then a quick left into the parking lot of a car wash.

He smiled, thinking it was his lucky day since there weren't many cars around and immediately drove around the side of the bay. A glance in his rearview mirror showed his stalker speeding by. Backing up, Ethan quickly pulled out and headed back toward the interstate, satisfied for the time being that he'd lost his tail.

Rachel continued to pace the bedroom floor. Ethan had called to say he was on his way but would be late due to "unforeseen circumstances." He hadn't elaborated.

She paused by the bed and drew in a deep breath, remembering her conversation with Charlene. Rachel's common sense was basically telling her that continuing to take risks at this point would be acting irresponsibly. She was an intelligent woman and Ethan was an intelligent man. They had enjoyed each other's companionship but both fully understood that they could not have a future together of any kind. And that was where their similarities ended. Their connection over the past three weeks had only been physical. He didn't love her and she didn't love him.

Then why was the thought of not being with him, not sharing stolen moments any longer, causing her heart to ache?

She began moving again, pacing the floor. He would know something was bothering her the moment he saw her. For one thing, she still had her clothes on, and usually if she was the first to arrive, she would be naked in the bed waiting on him.

She turned when she heard the sound of footsteps and felt the fluttering in her chest when the door slowly opened. She couldn't deny the excitement and joy she felt when her gaze met his blue-gray eyes. It was the same moment of elation she felt whenever she saw him.

He closed the door and leaned against it, holding her gaze for a moment, and then he began slowly unbuttoning his shirt. She knew she should stop him, tell him what she'd heard and that they needed to talk about it.

But she couldn't now.

Her hands automatically went to her skirt and undid the zipper, then slowly shimmied out of it before pulling her blouse over her head. She then kicked off her sandals and by the time they met next to the bed they were both completely naked.

As they tumbled together on the bed, one thought ran through her mind. *So much for talking.*

Chapter 13

An hour or so later, a very satiated Ethan was stretched out in the bed with Rachel in his arms and their legs still entwined. Mentally he was ordering his heart rate to slow down, but it wasn't listening. And his brain cells, which had gotten scrambled after a couple of back-to-back orgasms, were still a jumbled mess. But he didn't mind. In fact, he couldn't imagine it any other way. He was precisely where he wanted to be and was with the one person he wanted to share his time.

He raised her hand to his lips to kiss it and in response she snuggled even closer to him. Her body felt warm all over, and he liked the feel of spooning her backside, cradling her hips.

"So tell me," he leaned down and whispered close to her ear. "Why were you still wearing clothes when I got here?"

He noticed the exact moment her body stiffened and he tightened his arms around her. Only a man who had been a lover to this woman could detect at that moment she was bothered by something. He shifted his weight, turned her in his arms to face him and his eyes met hers. "What's wrong, Rachel?"

For a moment he wasn't sure she would answer him,

and then in a soft voice she said, "My friend Charlene called today."

He was sure there was more. "And?"

"You were in the tabloids. It seems reporters are trying to figure out who's your flavor of the month."

"They wouldn't have to try and figure it out since I'd be glad to tell them, if you would let me."

She stared at him through long lashes, surprise showing in her eyes, and he understood why. This was the first time he'd ever suggested they take their affair public. The only reason he'd never done so was because he knew her feelings on the matter.

"Ethan," she breathed out in a regretful tone. "I can't."

In other words, you won't, he thought and fought back the frustration he felt. He thought about the party and knew he didn't want to take any other woman but her. He pulled in a deep breath, wondering at what point he had decided he wanted more than a fling with her. When had sneaking around with Rachel become something he did only because that was the way she wanted it?

"Okay, you can't," he said, trying to keep the sting from his voice. "What does a tabloid reporter have to do with you having your clothes on when I got here?"

She turned her head to look at the painting of him that she had done and hung on the wall. It was a good thing they were the only ones with keys to this room in the building. He would hate for anyone to ever walk in and see that painting of him. She called it art; he thought of it as borderline X-rated. The only thing keeping him from being completely nude was the very thin piece of cloth that covered a certain part of his body at the juncture of his legs.

"Rachel, you're thinking too much again."

She returned her gaze to his. "Tabloid reporters are trying to figure out who you're spending your time with. You and I know if they keep snooping then it's only a matter of time before they find out, and I can't let that happen, Ethan. I can't risk being placed in the spotlight ever again. And then there's my career I have to think about. I've worked too hard building myself as a professional in the industry to risk losing everything."

He pulled in a deep breath. Those damn reporters had definitely done a job on her when she was a kid for her to have this intense fear. He could just imagine the hell she went through. He pulled her tighter to him, trying to imagine life without her. He would still see her on the set but he had begun thinking of these interludes with her as their time. He looked forward to them. In a way, he needed them. They had stopped being just sexual escapades a while ago. There were those times like these where he would hold her in his arms and savor what they shared, both the physical and the emotional.

"You won't lose anything, Rachel. I told you our secret is safe. No one knows about us or this place."

"For now, but how long will it be before they—"

"Once they see I'm no longer worth their time and effort, they will leave me alone," he interrupted her. "Hmm, as much as I don't want to attend that function Saturday night, maybe I should."

Rachel lifted a brow. "What function?"

"Some charity function Curtis wants me to attend with a date to calm the waters with the tabloids. Maybe if they see I'm a boring person who's gotten so absorbed in my career and nothing more, they will move on to someone else."

He could tell by the look in her eyes that she was confused. "But I thought you wanted to court the media, build your career that way as a playboy."

He studied her features. *I thought so, too,* he said to himself. And instead of trying to determine why he'd had a change of heart, he said, "There are other ways."

He pulled her closer into his arms. "Come on, we've talked enough. Let's get some sleep."

She pulled back. "Sleep?"

He smiled. "Yes, but if you prefer that we didn't…" He leaned over and kissed her in a way that had her body quivering. And when she responded by returning the kiss he proceeded to deepen it.

This was what he wanted and what he needed. Tabloids or no tabloids he intended to keep her by his side, even if they had to continue to sneak around to do it.

Rachel wrapped the sheet around her as she sank into the chair across from the bed. She needed to think and she couldn't do so wrapped in Ethan's arms. She had to have distance.

She closed her eyes and could clearly recall how it felt to be accosted by a crowd of reporters shoving mikes in your face, pulling on your hair to get your attention and all but screaming questions at you. She would try hiding behind her aunt and uncle, and later behind Sofia, but they would get relentless, their questions more demanding, the hordes of reporters even bigger. Then there was the period where she'd had nightmares about them and how they would all enjoy making her life unbearable.

And it had kept up that way until after she'd finished high school and then decided to travel abroad for a while. When she returned home, all the attention had shifted to other heiresses and up-and-coming starlets and actors. They forgot about her, practically left her alone, except for those times when the Wellesley family appeared together at a social function.

Over the years she had worked so hard to avoid that, as well as strived to be taken seriously in the industry as a makeup artist and wardrobe designer. To land a job on one of the most popular television shows was definitely a feather in her cap, one she refused to lose.

But she didn't want to lose Ethan either. She glanced at him, asleep in the bed. She enjoyed these times with him when she could be herself. Although they made love, they spent time talking as well. He had become her lover but he was still her friend, a very good friend. And it was a friendship that she cherished.

"Rachel?"

She heard the sound of her name and glanced toward the bed again. Ethan had awoken and had stretched his hand out to her. Without a moment's hesitation, she eased from the chair, dropped the sheet and went to him.

He gathered her into his arms and whispered, "You're thinking again and that's not a good thing."

She pulled back and looked up at him and smiled. "It's not?"

"No."

"Well, then, can you come up with a better pastime?"

He rubbed his nose against her neck. "Um, I think I can," he said throatily before capturing her mouth.

He released her mouth and eased her down on the

bed. "Yes," she managed hoarsely, as her body began shivering in a need only he could satisfy, "I believe you can."

A few days later Rachel looked down into the face of the actress reclining in her makeup chair and smiled before handing the woman the mirror. "There you go. Your makeup looks good on you, as always."

Livia studied her features in the mirror and smiled. "And, as always, you did a wonderful job, Rachel. You certainly know your stuff."

Rachel thanked her. Livia Blake was always giving her compliments about her work. Unlike Tae'Shawna Miller. The woman was still living in a fantasy world, still weaving the story of a secret affair with Ethan. Rachel figured she was the only one the woman had probably shared her lie with, probably because she figured Rachel was the only person gullible enough to believe her.

"You're one of the few people I'm going to miss when I leave the show," Livia said, easing up in her chair and handing the mirror back to Rachel.

Rachel knew she was going to miss Livia as well. Over the past weeks, she'd discovered her earlier assumptions about the woman had been all false, especially when she'd taken time to compare her to Tae'Shawna. Both were beautiful women who turned men's heads without much effort. But their attitudes and the way they treated people were totally different. Livia wasn't shallow or self-absorbed at all. Tae'Shawna took all those honors.

"You know how directors are. They may decide to rewrite the script and keep you on."

Livia shook her head sadly. "I doubt that will happen, although it would be wonderful. I'm thirty and nearing the end of my modeling career and although it's been a good one, it's time I moved on, although I haven't figured out to where just yet. *Paging the Doctor* has been a stepping-stone in the right direction. I've met some good people on the set, and—" she threw her head back and chuckled "—a few not so good ones."

Rachel smiled. Livia didn't have to tell her who the "not so good ones" were. Everyone had figured out by now there were several women on the set who were jealous of Livia's beauty, with Tae'Shawna heading the list.

"Well, I wish you the best," Rachel said sincerely.

"And I wish you the best, as well." Livia paused and then said, "Can I offer you some advice, though?"

Rachel raised a brow. "Advice about what?"

"Not what, but who. Ethan Chambers."

With effort, Rachel kept her features expressionless as she continued to pack away her cosmetics. "Ethan?" she asked, fighting to keep her voice steady. "And what kind of advice do you want to offer me about him?"

Livia paused, as if trying to choose her words carefully, and then she said, "I know the two of you are fiercely attracted to each other and…"

When Rachel began shaking her head, trying to deny it, Livia waved her off. "Hey, I felt the vibes between the two of you, even during his hot and heavy love scenes with me."

"But I—"

"Want to deny it," Livia said, smiling. "I don't know why you would want to when you're both beautiful people. Look, I'm sorry if mentioning it got you all flustered. That wasn't my intent. I just don't know why the two of you are keeping it a secret."

Rachel dropped down in the nearest chair, totally outdone. She and Ethan had worked so hard not to give anything away on the set, yet Livia had picked up on it. She met Livia's curious gaze. "Do you think others noticed?"

Livia shrugged. "Probably not. I'm just good at reading people and picking up vibes. I doubt Tae'Shawna noticed, since she's under the illusion he's all into her, and Paige isn't any better. Those are the only two still hanging on, hoping he'll give them some attention. I think the other women on the set have decided he's truly not interested."

Rachel didn't say anything for a moment, and then asked, "What did we do to give ourselves away?"

Livia chuckled. "The way the two of you look at each other when you think no one else is noticing, and I'm sure no one else is noticing but me, only because I have a tendency to notice everything. But I still don't understand why the two of you are keeping it a secret."

Rachel nibbled at her bottom lip. "It's complicated. I prefer not being in the limelight and he's a person who can't help but be there, dead center."

"Well, I hope things work out for the two of you because I think you're a good match, and you and Ethan truly deserve each other. Since I've gotten to know the both of you, I can easily see you're good people."

Livia glanced down at her watch. "It's time for me to get ready for my next scene. I'm not sure how they plan to write in my exit from the show since I'm supposedly Dr. Perry's love interest with emotional baggage. I think I'm supposed to pack up and leave when things between us get hot and heavy because I haven't gotten over my husband's death."

Rachel nodded. It was either that or killing Dr. Duncan off, but she couldn't see them doing that. Still, on the set, you never knew how things would go.

"Ethan, can I see you for a moment?"

Ethan kept the annoyance out of his face as he turned around. "Yes, Tae'Shawna, what is it?"

She smiled up at him. "I have tickets to the premier of *Saturday's Hussle*. Would you like to go with me tonight?"

Ethan knew just where he planned to be tonight, and Rachel's arms were far better than any movie premier. Even if he and Rachel hadn't made plans to meet up later, Tae'Shawna would be the last woman he'd go out with. "Thanks, but I have plans already."

"Oh. Maybe next time."

He doubted it. In fact, he knew for certain there wouldn't be a first time or a next time. "I'll see you later," he said, turning to leave.

"Umm, you don't know how I wish on that one, Ethan."

He kept walking, refusing to turn back around and respond to her flirty comment. His workday had ended, and for him, the fun was about to begin with the woman he wanted.

Chapter 14

Rachel glanced over at Charlene as they got out of the car. They were at a karaoke bar for a girls' night out. It was Saturday night and Ethan had decided to go to the charity event solo, against his agent's wishes. He'd insisted he would not take a date.

"Are you ready to have some fun?" she asked her friend. Rachel knew she needed to cheer Charlene up since her mother had hit again, calling her and telling her younger daughter all the reasons why she couldn't get a man.

"Yes, although you should have let me spend the weekend alone getting wasted."

Rachel laughed. "Neither one of us can handle too much booze and we both know it. Come on, let's enjoy ourselves."

A few hours later they were doing just that. Rachel was trying to talk Charlene into competing in the singing contest to win the five-hundred-dollar prize. Everyone knew what a beautiful voice she had.

"You really think I should?" Charlene asked.

Rachel smiled. Charlene had a dynamite voice but she'd always had this thing about singing in public. She much preferred staying behind the scenes, working as a voice coach at one of the local schools. "Hey, so far I haven't been impressed by the others I've heard. The sound of your voice has spoiled me. Personally, I think you have a good shot at winning. Just think of what you could do with the money." And Rachel could see from her best friend's expression that she was thinking the same thing.

"I don't know, Rachel."

"Well, I do, so just think about it. You have time to make up your mind. We're going to be here for a while."

And she meant it. She wasn't ready to go home to sit around or go to bed wondering if Ethan was having a good time at that event without her. No doubt there would be plenty of women there throwing themselves at him. She pulled in a deep breath. By mutual agreement, they were in an exclusive relationship. She knew she hadn't dated anyone else since they'd begun sleeping together and he'd said he hadn't either.

"Okay, I'm going to do it!"

Charlene's exclamation interrupted Rachel's thoughts and she smiled over at her friend. "Good. I have a feeling that you won't regret it."

The hounds were on Ethan the minute he got out of his car.

"Chambers? Where have you been hiding?" a reporter asked as a mike was shoved in Ethan's face and cameras went off from all directions.

Stepping into his role, he smiled for the cameras. "I haven't been hiding."

That began a series of other questions and he answered every last one of them with the intent of diffusing their curiosity and getting them interested in his role in *Paging the Doctor* instead. After a while it worked, although there were still a couple of reporters who seemed determined to dig into his personal life. Years of being one of the heirs to the Chambers Winery had taught him how to handle that kind.

"No date, Ethan?" one of the two resilient reporters asked.

"No, no date. Is there anything wrong with a man coming alone?"

"Not when he doesn't have to," was the other resilient reporter's quick comeback.

Ethan smiled. "I call it freedom of choice."

He answered a few more questions before bidding the reporters good-night. He knew he would be tailed when he left the event, but he figured eventually they would reach the conclusion he was no longer newsworthy and go find someone else to harass.

"I can't believe I won!"

Rachel smiled brightly over at Charlene, who was holding a bottle of champagne in one hand and a check for five hundred dollars in the other. "I told you that you would. I keep telling you that you have a beautiful voice. Maybe one day you'll finally believe me." Charlene had done a beautiful rendition of "Bridge Over Troubled Water" and brought everyone out of their seats. "You sounded like a young Aretha."

Charlene waved off her words. "You're my best friend, so of course you'd think so, and you know how much I love me some Aretha."

Yes, Rachel did know, but no matter what Charlene thought, she was dead serious.

"Excuse me, ladies."

Both Rachel and Charlene glanced at the man standing by their table. "Yes?" Charlene asked.

"I hate interrupting, but I wanted to congratulate you, Ms. Quinn. You did an outstanding job. And I want to introduce myself. I'm Jason Burke, a talent scout," he said, handing Charlene his card. "Please call me. I would like to discuss a few things with you. The company I represent would love to bring you on board."

Rachel could tell from the look on Charlene's face that she wasn't taking the man seriously. Playing along with him, Charlene slid his card into her pocket and said, "Sure, I'd love to contact you. Will next week be soon enough?"

The man smiled brightly. "Yes, and I'll look forward to that call." He then walked away and out of the club.

Charlene rolled her eyes. "Does he really think I'm going to call him?"

Rachel took a sip of her drink. "You said that you would."

"That was to get rid of him. Please. I can sing but not that good. And he's probably not who he's claiming to be."

"Let me see his business card." Rachel waited while Charlene dug it out of the pocket of her jeans.

Rachel studied the card. "I think you should call Sofia and let her check him out to see if he's legit. If he is, I would follow up with him if I were you."

Charlene waved off her words. "Whatever. Hey, let's forget about Jason Burke and have a good time. We need to get on the dance floor and celebrate my win."

Rachel laughed as she followed Charlene onto the floor to shake their booties for a while.

* * *

It was past three in the morning by the time Rachel had showered and slid between the sheets. She was about to turn off the lamp when her cell phone rang. Thinking it was Charlene still on a high from that night's win, she answered the phone saying, "Hey, haven't you gotten enough already?"

"Of you? Never."

Her body immediately began throbbing at the sound of the deep, husky voice. Her eyes clouded over in desire just from hearing it. "Hey, lover boy, haven't you heard it's not nice to call a girl after midnight?"

His soft chuckle came through the phone and touched her in places she'd rather leave untouched. But since he was going there, she might as well let him finish. "I prefer being there in person but some ass is parked outside the complex, waiting for me to leave. So I guess I'll stay in and engage in some sex talk with you."

She chuckled. "Sounds like a winner to me. Speaking of wins, Charlene won a singing contest at the club tonight. A whopping five hundred dollars and a bottle of champagne. And a talent scout approached her afterwards."

"I'm happy for her."

Although Ethan and Charlene had never officially met, they knew a lot about each other thanks to Rachel. "I'll tell her you are." There was a pause, and then she asked, "And how was your night?"

"Boring."

"Did you change your mind about taking a date with you?"

"No."

Rachel tried not to feel giddy at that one single word

but couldn't help it. She had convinced herself that she could handle it if he'd decided to take a date. After all, they were nothing more to each other than occasional bed partners. She drew in a deep breath, not wanting to think about it or how depressed she'd get when she did.

"So what are you wearing?"

His question made her smile. "What makes you think I'm wearing anything?"

He chuckled. "You only sleep naked when you're with me."

"Says who?"

"Says me. The man who has made love to you a lot of times."

"Hmm, how many?" she asked in what she hoped was a sexy, low tone. And he was right. He had made love to her a lot of times.

"Was I supposed to be counting?"

"I was."

He laughed. "Okay, then how many?"

"Tally up your own numbers, Chambers."

"If I were there, I would tickle it out of you."

"If you were here, Ethan, I'd make sure you put your hands to more productive use."

When Rachel hung up the phone an hour later she drew in a deep breath. Ethan's smooth, hot talk had almost made her come several times, it definitely had made her consider leaving her house and meeting him somewhere. But luckily her common sense held tight. They had agreed to throw the paparazzi off their scent by not meeting at their place anytime during the coming week. That meant when they did get back together for some bed time, they would have a whole lot of making up to do.

* * *

Ethan left his home on Sunday morning to go to the diner for some coffee and a roll. When he walked out with his purchase, he noticed one of the reporters from last night was waiting on him, braced against Ethan's car. The man was Joe Connors and he was known to be as tenacious as they came.

Since he was wearing the same clothes as he'd worn yesterday when he'd followed him, Joe had apparently slept in his car. And because Ethan considered himself a good guy, while buying breakfast for himself he'd also grabbed something for Joe.

"Looks like you could use this as much as I can," Ethan said, handing the man the extra breakfast sack he had in his hand. "All the creamers, sugars and artificial sweeteners you'll ever need are in that bag," he added.

The man accepted the offering. He then took a sip of the coffee, drinking it black. "Good stuff. Thanks."

"You're welcome." Ethan took a sip of his own coffee and asked, "Now, why don't you be a nice guy and leave me alone."

Joe chuckled as he shook his head. "No can do. I have to make a living."

"Don't we all?" was Ethan's dry response.

The man eyed him curiously. "Since you're in a giving mood, Chambers, how about an interview?"

Ethan shook his head. "I gave you an interview last night. You asked your questions and I answered them."

"Yes, but you refused to talk about your love life."

Ethan smiled. "What makes you think I have a love life?"

The man shrugged. "I just figured you did. This time last year you were dating anything in a skirt, and now for the past month you've been cooling your heels, so to speak, which can only mean you've been caught."

"Caught?"

"Yes. Some woman's got your heart. Is she married?"

Ethan threw his head back and laughed. "What is this obsession that I'm involved with a married woman?"

"What other reason would make you go to great pains to hide her?"

Ethan fought back the temptation to respond by saying he wasn't trying to hide Rachel. He would be perfectly happy if they made their affair public but...

"Um, look's like you started to say something and then changed your mind. Did I get close to the truth or something?"

"No."

"You sure?"

"Positive."

Joe looked at him for the longest time. "Then what was that funny look about?"

"Nothing. Eat your food, Joe. It's getting cold."

After pulling a warm croissant from the bag, Joe tilted his head and looked at Ethan. He grinned and said, "Hey man, you're not such a bad guy."

Chapter 15

"Have a nice evening, Rachel."

Rachel smiled over at one of her assistants. "You do the same, Loraine."

"And don't hang around here too late. They start killing the lights around seven," Loraine advised.

"Thanks for letting me know that."

There were only a few more weeks of filming left before the final shoot of the season. A wrap party was already being planned and Frasier was going all out to make it a monumental affair.

As she thought about the season ending, Rachel was happy that Livia's character was not killed off. It left the door open for a possible return next season. Just as she had predicted, Dr. Duncan was not emotionally ready for a hot and heavy love affair with Dr. Perry so soon after her husband's death. The season would end with her asking to be transferred to another hospital in Florida. That meant Dr. Perry would be free to pursue another love interest next season.

Livia would be joining her and Charlene for dinner over the weekend. Ever since Livia had mentioned that she was aware of her affair with Ethan, the two of them had become friends. Rachel appreciated Livia not gossiping about her and Ethan; apparently somebody in Hollywood could keep a secret.

Rachel's cell phone went off and she pulled it out of the pocket of her smock. "Yes?"

"Whooo, Rachel, you'll never guess what happened to me!"

Rachel couldn't help but hear the excitement in Charlene's voice. "And what has happened to you?"

"That guy Jason Burke is legit. Sofia checked him out. He works in A&R for the big music company that distributes Playascape."

Rachel lifted a brow. Playascape was a well-known recording company. One of the biggies. "Are you sure?"

"Sofia verified everything."

Then that settled it. Sofia knew just about everyone in the music, movie and television industry through Limelight Entertainment.

"And guess what?"

"What?"

"They want me to come in and meet with them."

Rachel couldn't help but be ecstatic as well. "Wow, Cha, that's fantastic."

"I think so, too, and Sofia suggested I send them a copy of that demo tape I did a while back."

"That's a smart move."

"Sofia's managing everything for me."

Rachel's smile widened. She knew her sister's abilities when it came to working deals. "Then you're in good hands."

Rachel heard a sound and turned around. Her breath caught in her throat when she saw Ethan. He had entered the trailer and was leaning against the closed door.

Their eyes met and she watched as he reached behind him and locked it. The click sounded loud.

"Cha, that's good news but I need to call you back later."

"You okay?"

Evidently Charlene had heard the change in her voice. "Yes, I'm fine. I'll call you when I get home." She then clicked off the phone.

"Ethan, what are you doing here? I thought you'd left hours ago."

He crossed his arms over his chest. Instead of answering her, he had a question of his own. "And why are you still here?"

"I had some paperwork to do."

He checked his watch. "It's late."

"I know but I'm fine. The security guard patrolling the studio lot is still here."

He was still leaning against the door, but now his hands were tucked into the pockets of his jeans. Although they saw each other every day on the set, they hadn't been together intimately for over a week thanks to that tabloid reporter dogging Ethan's heels. But they did talk on the phone every night and had made plans to try and sneak away to Tijuana this weekend.

"Go ahead and finish what you have to do. I'll wait and walk you out to your car."

She swallowed the lump in her throat. "That's not necessary."

"I think it is."

Instead of arguing with him she slid behind her small desk and began going over the paperwork she needed to give John in the morning. Out of the corner of her eye she saw Ethan had moved away from the door to straddle one of the chairs.

The air-conditioning system was working but she was beginning to feel hot. She was also feeling his eyes on her, singeing her flesh. In the quiet, she couldn't help but be aware of him. He'd been in the trailer with her lots of times while she'd applied his makeup, and because of where they were, things had always been professional between them. But she'd always been tempted with him reclining in one of her chairs and her over him and breathing in his scent.

Deciding the trailer was too quiet, she opted to share Charlene's good news with him. "Isn't that wonderful?"

"Yeah, I think it's great," he replied. "I hear they have a good outfit over there."

Rachel continued working, going through John's requests for the season finale. Out of the corner of her eye, she saw that Ethan had moved again. This time he'd gone over to the watercooler to get something to drink. She turned to look at him at the exact time he tilted the cup up to his lips to take a swallow.

The way his throat moved as water trickled down it did something to her. And when he licked his lips as if the drink had been one of the most refreshing things to go into his mouth, she actually began envying the water.

"How much longer before you're done?"

She blinked and realized he had spoken to her. In that case, he'd probably caught her staring. She drew in a deep breath as she looked down at the papers. "Not long. If you need to leave then I—"

"No, I don't need to leave. But I do need you."

Now *that* she heard. And upon doing so, she couldn't smother the heated sensations taking root in the pit of her stomach or the hot tingle between her legs. This was where she worked, her business sanctuary. Actors came and went and usually she was too busy, too involved to connect the insides of this trailer to any one particular person. But for some reason, she had a feeling that was about to change.

Deciding not to respond to what he'd said, she turned her attention back to the papers in front of her. Ten minutes later, she was signing off on the last sheet. She opened the top drawer to slide them inside.

"Finished now?"

She glanced over at him and met his gaze. He had gone back to straddling one of the chairs. "Yes."

"Good." He stood. "Come here, Rachel."

She continued to hold his gaze, felt the heat zinging between the two of them. She didn't have to ask what he wanted; the look on his face told her what he needed. It was there in his expression, in the chiseled and handsome features. Not to mention those beautiful eyes staring back at her.

Instead of putting up any fuss, not that she would have, she crossed the room without a word and walked straight into his arms. He pulled her to him and she felt it all. His heat, the pounding of his heart against her chest and the engorged erection pressing at the juncture of her thighs.

"It's been hell these seven days without you," he whispered against her lips.

"Actually, it's been eight but who's counting?" she said as her arms automatically went around his waist and she rested her head against his chest. She had to fight hard to keep from being overwhelmed by him.

When she felt his erection throb against her thigh, she pulled back and glanced up at him.

"We'll be together Saturday," she reminded him.

He smiled down at her but she still saw the tension in his features. "I can't wait. I need you now."

As he spoke, he backed her against the wall. Already his hands at her waist were lifting her up. Instead of wearing jeans today she had decided to wear a skirt. *How convenient for him,* she thought.

And for her.

Her legs automatically wrapped around him and his hands were busy under her skirt, pushing her panties aside before unzipping his pants and freeing himself. By mutual consent, he had stopped using condoms when she'd told him she was on the pill.

His finger slid inside her as if to test her readiness, and the feel of his touch had her moaning.

"Shh," he whispered in her ear. "There's no need to bring the guard in here to check out things."

No, there was no reason, which meant she couldn't let go and scream. How was she going to stop it? He always made her scream.

His finger inside her was driving her to the brink. He'd said he needed her and he was taking his time to make sure that she also needed him. She should tell him doing so wasn't necessary. She did need him. She did need this.

"Baby, you're hot and your scent is driving me insane," he whispered before taking her mouth in a kiss that told her this was just the beginning.

He covered her lips, captured her mouth in a combination of hunger and tenderness that zapped her senses. And when his tongue began doing its thing, exploring her mouth as if it were conquering unfamiliar territory, she went weak in the knees. But he held her, making sure she didn't go anywhere. She had detected his hunger the minute he'd entered the trailer, and now she was experiencing it firsthand.

Her body was responding to him as it always did and as it always would. Whenever it came to this kind of mutual satisfaction, they were always in accord. A deep, throbbing ache within her intensified and, of its own will, the lower part of her body rocked against his. She clung to him as his mouth clung to hers, plundering it, stirring sensations all the way down to the soles of her feet.

For one fleeting moment she felt the silky head of his erection probe her womanly core, then he entered her in one smooth stroke. She wrapped her legs around him to take him in fully.

She moaned into his mouth and gripped tightly to his shoulders, surrendering to the feel of him being embedded within her, stretching her wide. He deepened the kiss and at the same time he began to move, thrusting back and forth inside of her, feeding her hunger while making her skin tingle all over. Her breasts felt heavy, full and sensitive to the chest rubbing against them.

He was deep inside her and with each thrust he was going deeper still. As he rocked his hips against her, he used his hands to cushion her back from the wall.

He pulled his mouth away and whispered against her lips, "Come for me, baby. I need to feel you come."

As if his words were a command for her body to obey, she felt herself begin to shatter into a million pieces. She clenched her teeth to hold back her scream, and when his mouth came down on hers she gave in and felt every part of her body explode in a climax so intense she trembled all over.

"That's it, baby. Now I'm yours," he uttered huskily right before his body ignited in an explosion as well. She felt the hot, thick essence of him shoot all the way inside of her in the most primitive way, and she called out his name.

He responded in kind, and the sound of her name on his lips sent everything within her throbbing for more. She only knew this kind of pleasure with him. She only wanted this kind of pleasure from him.

Sensation spiraled inside of her and she knew at that moment that Ethan Chambers had captured her heart.

Chapter 16

"Ethan, wait. I need to see you for a moment."

Ethan looked over his shoulder and turned around. "I was on my way out, Paige. What's up?"

Joe Connors had finally stopped being his shadow, but that didn't mean he and Rachel could let their guard down. They'd been careful since that amazing night in the trailer, not hooking up until last weekend in Tijuana. Their Mexican rendezvous had been special, and they'd made up for the time they'd lost. Now they would be spending the night at *their* place and Ethan couldn't wait. He didn't need Paige Stiles delaying him.

"Evidently you're up, big boy," she said in that flirty voice that annoyed the hell out of him. "I need a date to the wrap party."

He chuckled softly. "And?"

"And you're going to take me."

He was surprised by her bold statement. He had finally gotten Tae'Shawna out of his hair by his persistence in letting her know he wasn't interested. Paige, on the other hand, was not getting the message. He'd just have to be more explicit. "I'm not taking you anywhere."

"Yes, you are. At least, you will if you want me to keep your secret."

He felt the hair stand up on the back of his neck. "And just what secret is that?"

"You banging Rachel Wellesley. She never fooled me. I figured she had the hots for you just as bad as the next woman, and I was wondering how long it would take for you to be lured by her bait." The woman then chuckled. "Seriously, Ethan, are you *that* hard up? You couldn't do better than Rachel? If I was picking some-one that you'd want to mess around with, it wouldn't be her. And don't deny the two of you are involved be-cause I can prove it."

He drew in a deep breath, not sure if she could prove it but truly not caring. "No, I seriously don't think I can do better than Rachel. Now if you will excuse me, I—"

"I mean it, Ethan. You make plans to get something going with me or else."

"Or else what?"

She smiled sweetly. "Or else everyone, especially Frasier and John, will know that Rachel isn't the sweetie pie they think she is."

Now that pushed his anger to the top. "I don't know what game you're playing, Paige, but keep Rachel out of this."

"Sure, I'll keep her out of this, but only if you give me what I want. My name connected to yours will open doors. I not only want those doors opened, I want to walk through them."

"It won't happen."

She wiped the smile from her face. "Then I suggest that you make sure it does."

She walked away.

On the drive home, Ethan tried to figure out the best way to handle Paige. Reasoning with her was out of the question since the woman was vindictive and obviously intent on hurting Rachel. He had detected her dislike and jealousy from the first.

The one thing he'd learned growing up as a Chambers was to not let anyone bully, or in this case blackmail, you into doing something you did not want to do. He had no intention of taking Paige or any other woman to the wrap party. The only woman he would take was the woman he wanted and would always want. Rachel.

He thought about telling Rachel about Paige's threats, but he could just imagine what her reaction would be. He wanted to save her from that worry. And he wanted to save himself from seeing it. No, he would simply ignore Paige as he had Tae'Shawna and hopefully she would forget about her foolish threat.

He had no problems with his and Rachel's relationship going public and he'd pushed for that several times with Rachel—only to meet a brick wall. For some reason she thought news of their involvement would diminish the professional career she had created, and then there was her intense desire not to be in the spotlight.

There was no one who could say his and Rachel's relationship on the set had been anything other than professional. And as far as her being in the spotlight, he thought she didn't give herself enough credit for handling things. He knew the media could sometimes be relentless, but because of their families, he and Rachel had been born into the spotlight anyway and the key was not avoiding it but dealing with it.

As he continued on the drive home, he finally admitted something else. Something he'd known for a while but just hadn't acknowledged. He had fallen in love with Rachel. And because he loved her, he didn't want to sneak around to be with her. He wanted everyone to know the woman he loved and adored, the woman who could make him smile just by being close to him. The woman he wanted to bring home to meet his family.

The woman he wanted to marry.

He wanted Rachel, and only Rachel, to become Mrs. Ethan Chambers. He wanted her to be the mother of his children. To walk by his side for always.

He gripped the steering wheel, knowing those thoughts were true. Every single one of them. But they were thoughts he could not share with Rachel. She didn't love him, and she didn't want to share a future with him.

Two days later Paige was back in his face again, reiterating her demands.

Ethan gave her his total attention, squaring off and looking her right in the eyes with an adamant expression. "Look, Paige, I told you once before that I'm not taking you to the wrap party and I meant it. My feelings haven't changed."

He saw the anger build in her features. Her jaw clenched and her eyes narrowed. "Then you leave me no choice. Now everyone will know what you and Rachel have been doing behind their backs."

Then she walked off.

Ethan got into his car, pissed but still positive he was handling the nagging woman the only way he could. He decided to forgo the air-conditioning on the ride home, preferring the warm breeze against his face. He imagined the stench of Paige Stiles being blown off him.

As if he'd warded it away, any thought of the encounter dared not enter his mind. Until the next night when his cell phone rang.

How Joe Connors, of all people, had gotten his cell phone number, Ethan didn't know and didn't waste his time asking.

"What do you want, Connors?" he asked instead.

"I like you, Chambers. You're different from most of the stars out there who can be anal, so I'm giving you a heads-up. You and your lady have been exposed. Not by me, but by a tip we received. And there are pictures, nothing sleazy, but pictures that will substantiate this person's claim. They are pretty damn excited over here, and I understand the article, pictures and all, hits tomorrow's paper."

Ethan felt his heart drop to his feet. He drew in a deep breath, knowing he had to get in touch with Rachel. She had volunteered to be a chaperone to Disneyland for a group of kids who attended the school where Charlene worked as a voice coach. She wasn't scheduled to return until late tonight.

When Ethan didn't say anything, Joe Connors continued, "I can't give you details but I can tell you the headline of the article isn't pretty."

Dread turned to anger, and it raced through Ethan. "Thanks for the heads-up."

Ending the call, he tried to reach Rachel. He had to prepare her for whatever the article said and assure her they would handle it, work through it and deal with it.

He only hoped she'd believe him.

Rachel finished taking her shower and was about to settle in for the night when she checked her messages on her cell phone. She lifted a brow. She had several missed calls from Ethan and just as many text messages and they all said the same thing: "Call ASAP."

Wondering at the urgency, she was about to punch in his phone number when there was loud knock at her door. After running downstairs she took a quick look through her peephole and saw Ethan. She quickly opened her door.

"Ethan, what is—"

He suddenly pulled her into his arms and kissed her, kicking the door closed behind him as he continued kissing her and sweeping her off her feet, into his arms.

She always enjoyed being kissed by him and today was no exception. His lips moved hungrily over hers and instinctively she melted against him, loving the feel of being in his arms. She whimpered his name when moments later he pulled his mouth away.

"Rachel, sweetheart, we need to talk."

She saw they were no longer at the door, but he had carried her across the room and had taken a seat on the sofa with her cradled in his arms. She had been so wrapped up in their kiss she hadn't noticed the movement.

It was then that she remembered the missed calls and text messages. "What about?" Her voice sounded wobbly from the impact of his kiss.

He continued to hold her tightly against him and when he didn't answer her, she glanced up into his eyes. She had been with Ethan long enough to know when he was deeply troubled. She pulled herself up. "What is it, Ethan?"

"I need to prepare you for something."

"What?"

"The tabloids know about us, thanks to Paige, and

The Wagging Tongue is breaking the story tomorrow. Someone I know on the inside called and gave me a heads-up."

Rachel felt as if someone had just doused her with a pail of cold water right in her face. She jumped out of his lap. "What?"

"Yes, baby, I know. This is not how you wanted things, but together we'll deal with it."

She backed away from him. "No, no, this can't be happening…" Shaking her head as if to get her thoughts in order, she asked, "What does Paige have to do with it?"

Ethan rubbed his hand over his face. "Earlier in the week she approached me claiming she knew about us and threatening to go to Frasier and John if I didn't begin dating her. She figured her name connected to mine would take her places. I flatly refused and two days ago, when she approached me again and I refused again, she got mad. I guess this is her way of getting retaliation."

Rachel's head began pounding. "She approached you earlier in the week and you didn't mention it to me?"

He came to his feet and faced her. "I didn't want to upset you and I was hoping she would drop it."

Rachel pulled in a deep breath. "Paige is like a sore that only festers. She's never cared for me, Ethan. Jealousy is deeply embedded in any decision she makes about me. She's always wanted you, and for her to find out you and I have been involved in an affair, there's no way she would have dropped it. You should have told me."

"Maybe I should have, but I didn't want you upset."

"Well, now I am upset. I am livid. I am mad as hell."

He reached out for her. "The truth is out, baby, and we'll deal with it."

She pulled away from him. "It's not that easy, Ethan. It's my privacy and professionalism being threatened."

"And I still say we will deal with it, Rachel. When we're approached we'll tell them the truth."

"No, we won't! We will deny everything. They can't prove anything."

"I'm not sure about that. The person I talked to claims there are pictures."

"Pictures! Oh my God!" She dropped down on the sofa and covered her face with her hands.

Ethan went to her and pulled her into his arms. He'd never seen her this upset. "Rachel, the best thing to do is not to deny anything. We're two consenting adults who—"

"Should not have let things get out of hand. We should not have gotten involved in the first place since we knew what was at risk."

"But we did and we need to own up to it and not let the tabloids or anyone else control our lives or our relationship."

She jerked out of his arms. "No! You make it sound so easy and it's not. Don't you understand what I'll be going through, Ethan? Don't you understand? You like this sort of stuff. It makes you who you are, but it can only destroy me."

"Rachel, we can deal with it. Together."

"No! That's just it. We can't be together. That will just be more fuel for their fire. We have to end things between us now."

"That's not going to happen, Rachel. I won't give you up because of any damn tabloid," he said angrily.

She glared up at him. "You don't have a choice because I'm ending things between us, Ethan. I can't sacrifice a professional career I've worked hard to build or a private life I've tried hard to preserve. Besides, our affair was about nothing but sex anyway."

Her words were like a backhanded slap to Ethan's face and he felt the pain in the depths of his heart. "You don't mean that, Rachel," he said softly.

He refused to believe all the time they'd spent together had been about nothing but sex. Maybe that had been the case the first few times, but there was no way he would believe she didn't care for him the way he cared for her. No way.

"I love you, Rachel. Our times together weren't just about sex for me and I refuse to believe that's the way it was for you. And I won't deny what we shared to anyone. I won't make it into some backstreet, sleazy affair. I've never loved a woman before you, and I hope that you'll realize that our love—yes, our love—will be able to deal with anything. Together. You know how to reach me when you do."

He then turned and left.

Chapter 17

By noon on Saturday, Rachel was ready to have a stiff drink. The entire bottle, if necessary. Her phone hadn't stopped ringing. Some calls she had answered and some she had not.

Ethan's calls were some of the ones she had not.

It seemed everyone was shocked by the tabloid's allegations that she'd been having a secret affair with Ethan, but they were happy if she had. Uncle Jacob and Aunt Lily told her not to be bothered by the accusations. Sofia inquired as to how she was holding up but didn't ask any specifics about the affair. So far no one believed the tabloid's headline that she only got involved with Ethan to further her career. That was so far from the truth. She had already had an up-and-coming career before Ethan appeared on the scene. But the goal of the tabloids was to sell papers, and with those kinds of accusations and the photos of them kissing in the studio lot, they created the sensationalism they craved.

Thanks to Charlene, who'd shown up for breakfast with a copy of *The Wagging Tongue* in her hand, she'd been forced to see the article. She wished she could claim the picture plastered on the front page had been doctored, but it hadn't.

Evidently, Paige had been around that night Ethan had shown up in the trailer unexpectedly. After they'd made love, he had walked her to her parked car. Since it was late, they assumed everyone had left and, before getting in her car, Ethan had pulled her into his arms and given her a very heated kiss. What she considered a special moment between them had been reduced to something sleazy, thanks to Paige and her cell phone camera.

She looked up from the book she'd been trying unsuccessfully to read when her house phone rang. She hoped the caller wasn't Ethan again. She couldn't help but smile when she heard the voice of Carmen Aiken on her answering machine.

"Rachel, I know you're there, so pick up this phone!"

Carmen was an Oscar-winning actress who was married to director/producer Matthew Birmingham. She and Carmen had become good friends when Carmen, new to Hollywood at the time, had been cast in one of Matt's movies. Rachel had been the makeup artist on the set.

She reached for the phone and answered, "Okay, so you knew I was here."

"You've been holding back on me, girl. Ethan Chambers! Why did you keep that hunk a secret?"

Rachel wished it had been a secret she could have shared, but the only people who'd known about her affair with Ethan had been Charlene and Livia. "You know why, Carmen."

"Yes, I know how brutal the tabloids can be. Remember, I was a victim of their gossip for a while. Even after Matt and I remarried, they claimed we did it as a way to get publicity for his next movie."

Rachel was aware of that lie. Carmen and Matt had been divorced for a little over a year and had remarried last month. Rachel was glad they had worked out their differences and had gotten back together. She didn't know of any couple who deserved each other more.

"It really doesn't matter what those reporters think. It's how you feel, Rachel. I can tell from the photo that was one hell of a kiss he gave you. You're probably the envy of a lot of women today."

Rachel drew in a deep breath. Charlene had said the same thing, but it really didn't matter. She wanted no part of the tabloids and no part of Ethan.

She couldn't help but remember what he'd said before leaving and in the messages he'd left on her answering machine and cell. He said he loved her.

Well, she loved him, too, but in this case love would not be enough.

Carmen breached her silence. "I don't want you to make the same mistake I made, Rachel, by letting the tabloids rule your life."

Moments later when Rachel ended her call with Carmen, she knew it was too late. The tabloids were already ruling her life.

"What do you want, Curtis?"

"I like the publicity, Ethan, but you could have hooked up with another woman. It would have benefited your career a lot more had she been a model or an actress. She's a makeup artist, for crying out loud, regardless of the fact her last name is Wellesley."

An angry Ethan slouched back against the sofa with a beer bottle in one hand and his cell phone in the other. He didn't give a royal damn whether Curtis liked the publicity or not. That last comment alone meant the man's days as his agent were numbered.

When Ethan didn't say anything, Curtis continued, "Now what we need to do is to play our cards right with this publicity and keep it moving. But you need to get rid of the broad in that picture and get someone more newsworthy. Someone like Rayon Stewart. We can work the angle that Rachel Wellesley was just someone you were sleeping with while waiting for Rayon Stewart to end things with Artis Lomax."

"Go to hell, Curtis."

"Excuse me?"

"I said, go to hell. By the way, as of now, you're no longer my agent. You're fired."

He then hung up the phone and took a swig of his beer. He refused to let anyone put Rachel down. She was the best thing to ever happen to him, and he loved *her* and not some model or Hollywood actress.

He reached for his cell phone and punched in her number. He knew she was at her condo hiding out. He'd tried calling her all day but she refused to take any of his calls.

Joe Connors had been right. The article hadn't been pretty and had made Rachel look like a schemer who had used their affair to build her career. No doubt that was the story Paige had told the tabloids and they had run with it. If anyone would have bothered to check, they would have known it was all lies fabricated by a jealous woman.

When Rachel didn't answer, Ethan clicked off the phone before standing and moving to the window. The paparazzi was out there and had been all day, waiting for him to come out with a story. Well, he didn't have one. At the moment, the only thing he had was heartache.

Rachel braced herself for work Monday, knowing everyone had probably seen the tabloid's article. She had decided the best thing to do was to deal with it and move on. She had worked too hard to build her career to do otherwise.

Ethan had continued to call her through late last night and had called her again this morning. By her not answering his calls, she hoped he now realized she hadn't changed her mind. Ending things between them had been the best thing to do. It was important that anyone expecting drama would get the professional she had always been.

She appreciated that the studio lot was private. But that didn't stop the paparazzi from being crowded out front with their cameras ready to get a shot of her when she arrived at work. A few even tried blocking her car from going through the gate.

From the way everything got quiet when she walked onto the set, it was obvious she had been the topic of conversation. She gave everyone her cheery hello as usual while heading toward the trailer, but she didn't miss Paige's comment, which was intentionally loud enough for anyone to hear. "And she actually thought someone like Ethan Chambers could be interested in *her?*"

Rachel refused to turn and comment, but she couldn't help the smile when she heard Livia speak up. "Evidently he was interested in her, since she's the one with him in that photo, Paige."

Livia's words had no doubt hit a nerve with Paige, since everyone on set had seen her flirting outrageously with Ethan. Tae'Shawna had been just as bad. Some people on set had placed bets on which of the two— Paige or Tae'Shawna—would finally get his attention. Neither had.

Rachel kept walking to her trailer, intent on not being around when Ethan arrived. It would be bad enough having to work with him on the set knowing they would be the subject of everyone's attention. She needed to get herself together before seeing him.

She appreciated her two assistants giving their support with words of encouragement and letting her know if she and Ethan were an item, that meant he had good taste.

For the next hour or so she went about her day as usual, and when it was time for her to go out on the set she left her trailer. The last thing she wanted was to give the impression she was hiding out.

Ethan and Livia were in the middle of a scene where Dr. Duncan was explaining to Dr. Perry why they couldn't be together and why they needed to end things. Boy, that sounded familiar.

Several people turned to look at her, including Frasier and John, who both gave her nods. If they believed the tabloid story, then they knew she and Ethan had broken the show's rule. In which case, she knew her job was in jeopardy. If they had to choose which of them to keep, no doubt Ethan would stay, since he was their star.

"Freeze! Rachel, kill that shine on Ethan."

At Frasier's command, she moved forward. The set got quiet and she knew everyone was looking at her.

At them. She greeted him only with his name when she stopped in front of him.

He did the same.

Their greeting sounded stiff. Being the professional she was, Rachel was determined to do her job. She took her makeup brush and swept across the bridge of his nose. She tried to ignore his scent, something she'd gotten used to, and the sound of his heavy breathing.

But she couldn't ignore the blue-gray eyes that seemed to watch her every moment. Emotions stirred within Rachel but she fought hard to keep them at bay. Making sure she didn't take any more time than necessary, she gave him a smile and said, "All done." And then she quickly walked away.

"Unfreeze!"

They resumed shooting the scene, and when she glanced over at Paige, there was a malicious smirk on the woman's face. Paige doubtless assumed it was Ethan who ended things between them and not the other way around. She was probably also thinking that although she might not be his date at the wrap party, neither would Rachel.

She didn't want to be the object of discussion and speculation. But since she was, she would do everything she could to stay professional and put her and Ethan's affair behind her.

No matter how much it hurt.

"Ethan, wait up."

He glanced around and saw Tae'Shawna approach with a smile on her face. Out of the corner of his eye, he saw Paige watching. She'd had the good sense to avoid him today.

"What is it, Tae'Shawna?"

"I see you're scheduled for makeup with Rachel tomorrow."

"And what of it?"

"If you're uncomfortable about it, I'll speak to John for you to have one of her assistants do it."

He didn't need Tae'Shawna to tell him of his schedule. He knew Rachel would be doing his makeup, which meant they would be alone in the trailer for a short while. But he figured to keep talk down, Rachel had already arranged for one of her assistants either to do his makeup or be there with her when she did it. He doubted very seriously they would be alone.

He looked at Tae'Shawna. "Why would I be uncomfortable with Rachel doing my makeup?"

She shrugged. "I just assumed since the news is out about how she came on to you to boost her career that you are leery of her now. Coming on to you was unprofessional on her part."

Ethan put his hands in the pockets of his jeans and he didn't care one iota about the fierce frown that settled on his face. He was sick and tired of people assuming the worst of Rachel. Bottom line was he had pursued her, he had wanted her. He still wanted her.

"First of all," he told Tae'Shawna, "anyone with good sense knows most of what's printed in those tabloids isn't true. Second of all, Rachel is one of the most professional women I know. She didn't have to come on to me because I found her attractive from day one. I saw in her something I haven't seen in a lot of woman lately."

Tae'Shawna lifted her chin and he could tell his words had hit a nerve. "And what is that?"

"Unselfishness. She is not self-absorbed and I doubt

that she has a shallow bone in her body. In fact, she never came on to me, but *you* did, many times, right here on the set. So who should I think is the professional one? Now if you'll excuse me, I need to call it a day."

A few hours later, in the privacy of his home, Ethan sank down on his sofa frustrated as hell. He hadn't tried making any type of contact with Rachel while on the set but he had called her several times since getting home, and she still would not accept his calls. If the paparazzi were on her tail like they were on his, he could imagine what she was going through, but that was no reason to block him out of her life.

Considering everything, he had expected her to withdraw for a day or so, but he hadn't expected her to put up an emotional wall that he could not penetrate.

For the last three days on the set she had been cordial yet distant, as if to prove to everyone that they were not together. When she looked at him, it was as if she was looking straight through him. He knew she was trying hard to maintain a mask of nonchalance where he was concerned, determined to avoid any situation that would compromise her professionalism.

He had tried not to be angered by her actions but a part of him couldn't help it. And now in the comfort of his home, lonely as it was, his anger was turning into intense hurt.

Why was he letting her do this to him?

Because, as he had told her, he loved her and a part of him believed she loved him back. And he believed that one day she would realize that nothing, not the paparazzi and not the threat of jeopardizing her career, was worth sacrificing their love.

* * *

Rachel cuddled on her sofa and pressed the replay button to pick up her last call.

"Rachel, this is Ethan. I know what you're going through but I wish you would let us go through it together. When you hurt, I hurt. I love you and I know you love me. Baby, please don't do this to us."

She glanced over at the beautiful bouquet of flowers that had been delivered to her from Ethan by way of Charlene. Her best friend had dropped by with the flowers earlier that evening. The card attached simply said:

I love you.

Ethan

Tears rolled from her eyes. She didn't think it would be so hard giving him up. She hadn't counted on the agony and the pain, the feeling of loneliness and heartbreak. It was hard during the day to see him and try to ignore him. Alone in her trailer, she would feel alienated. Even after three days, everyone on the set was still abuzz about her and Ethan breaking the rules, but so far neither Frasier nor John had approached her or Ethan. She figured they were probably waiting for one of them to approach them first, so tomorrow she would.

Tomorrow... Tomorrow she was scheduled to do Ethan's makeup. Typically they would be alone in her trailer, but she didn't want everyone speculating about what they were doing or saying behind closed doors. To have one of her assistants fill in for her would indicate she wasn't professional enough to handle a controversial situation. So in a way it was a "damned if you do and damned if you don't" situation.

Livia had come to her rescue. She volunteered to be the buffer by being in the trailer at the same time Ethan was there, on the pretext of repairing a broken nail or something. Rachel hoped the ploy worked.

Ethan knew all eyes were on him as he headed for Rachel's trailer. No doubt there were some who had their watch set to see how long he stayed inside alone with her.

"Ethan, wait up." He stopped and glanced around. Livia was walking toward him. She was one of the few women on set who hadn't tried coming on to him. Like Rachel, she was a specialist in her craft. Even with all those love scenes they'd done, they had still maintained professionalism.

"I need to see Rachel a minute myself," she said, smiling. "Broken nail."

He smiled, seeing through her ploy. Rachel was her friend and she was making an attempt to avoid gossip and speculation.

From the look on Rachel's face when they entered her trailer, Ethan knew for certain that Livia's appearance had been planned. Rachel showed no surprise at seeing them both walk in.

"Hello, Ethan, you can take my chair. And Livia, I'll fix that nail in a minute, just as soon as I finish with Ethan."

"No problem," Livia said, smiling. "I'll just sit over here."

"You can go ahead and take care of Livia and then do me," Ethan suggested. Only after the words had left his mouth did he realize their double meaning.

"No, Livia can wait until I finish with you," Rachel insisted.

"And I don't have a problem with you doing her first."

Before Rachel could open her mouth to retort, Livia spoke up. "Look, guys, evidently you two need time alone to clear up a few things."

"No, we don't."

"Yes, we do."

Livia shook her head. "Since the two of you can't agree, I'll make the decision for you," she said. "Rachel, you can work on Ethan while I excuse myself a minute to go to the ladies' room." Livia then headed toward the back of the trailer, where the dressing room and bathroom were located.

Rachel watched her friend's retreating back.

"You can take care of me now, Rachel."

Rachel turned and glared at Ethan. "Do you not care about my career?"

His face rigid, he returned her glare. "And do you not care about my heart? Or yours?"

Her stomach twisted with his question, and she forced herself to ignore the stab of pain that ripped through her. "I care, but there's nothing I can do about it, Ethan. Please just let me make you up so I can be ready for the next person."

"Fine, get to it then."

He reclined in the chair and she stood over him. She hesitated a moment and looked into the eyes staring back at her. Just like always when she looked at them, she was in awe of their beauty, but this time she saw the anger and pain in their depths.

Drawing in a deep breath, she brushed foundation across his cheekbones, then around his mouth, and she couldn't help but focus on his lips. Lips she had kissed so many times. Lips she wanted to kiss again. But she fought doing so.

Those lips moved and she heard the husky but low tone of his voice. "I love you, Rachel."

She dropped the brush from her hand and took a step back. "I'm finished, Ethan."

He eased out of the chair, his long legs bringing him to stand directly in front of her. "You might be finished but I'm not, Rachel. At least not where you're concerned. What we've shared is too precious and I won't give up on us. Admit that you love me as much as I love you."

She looked up at him, her heart full, but was unable to say the words he wanted to hear. "Ethan, I—I can't say it."

He reached out and gently pulled her into his arms and she could not have pulled out of them even if she wanted to. He lowered his head and, of their own accord, her lips parted as she sighed his name. The moment his lips touched hers she felt soothed by something she had missed for the past couple of days, something her body had gotten used to having.

A sensuous shudder passed through her as his tongue reinstated its rights to her mouth, letting her know that no matter how she continued to deny them, put distance between them, there would always be this—a passion so intense and forceful, it would take more than negative publicity to destroy it.

When he angled his head to deepen the kiss, she stretched up on tiptoes to get the full Ethan Chambers effect. And it was worth every effort. He was kissing her like a starving man, and in kind, she was kissing him like a starving woman. Her heart swelled with every stroke of his tongue, and she knew in her heart what she refused to speak out loud.

He finally pulled his mouth away and tenderly touched her cheek. "One day you will tell me that you love me and I'll be ready to hear it when you do." His tone was raw and husky and sent sensuous shivers all down her spine.

He leaned down and brushed a kiss across her lips before turning to walk out of the trailer.

Chapter 18

Rachel's lips twitched in a smile when the limousine pulled up behind Amaury's, an exclusive restaurant in Hollywood whose doors usually were closed until eight every night. Only Sofia, with a list of connections and contacts a mile long, could make the impossible happen.

For the past week, other than leaving for work, Rachel had pretty much stayed in and not ventured out with the paparazzi breathing down her neck. Although the breakup between Rayon Stewart and Artis Lomax and rumors of another adoption by Brad and Angelina now dominated the headlines, there were a few reporters who just didn't know when to quit.

"We're here, Ms. Rachel."

"Thanks, Martin," she said to the man who'd been the limo driver for Limelight Entertainment for years. She could recall sitting in the backseat of the huge car, with him behind the wheel, while being transported to and from private school as a child of no more than eight or nine. During those days, he kept her entertained with his own rendition of the animated voices of Bugs Bunny and Daffy Duck. He used to be so good at it.

Moments later, he was holding the door open for her as she got out. Amaury Gaston met her at the door and gave her a big hug.

"Sofia is already seated and waiting on you, Rachel," he said in a heavy French accent.

"Thanks."

"I've prepared your favorite," he added.

Rachel licked her lips. Chicken cordon bleu, she guessed, and Amaury's was the best. "You like spoiling me and Sofia," she said, smiling.

"Yes, just like I used to enjoy spoiling your parents. They were two of my first customers, and your father proposed to your mother right here one night. It was very special."

Rachel had heard the story before but didn't mind hearing it again. According to everyone who knew them, her parents had been very much in love.

"And I know if they were alive, they would want me to treat their girls just as special as I thought they were," Amaury added.

Moments later, Rachel made her way toward the table where her sister sat waiting. Sofia saw her approach and smiled. With her beauty and tall, slender figure, Rachel thought Sofia could have easily been a model or actress. Instead, she had followed in their father's footsteps and had taken his place in the family business working alongside Uncle Jacob. Despite their age difference, she and Sofia had maintained a close relationship, especially now that Sofia wasn't as overprotective as she used to be.

Sofia stood and Rachel walked straight into her sister's outstretched arms. Then Sofia took a step back and studied her from head to toe. "Hmm, it doesn't look like the tabloids have beaten you up too badly, although I'm sure there are scars on the inside that I can't see."

Rachel felt a thickness in her throat. She hadn't intended to let Sofia know just how shaken up she really was. Ethan's kiss yesterday had done that enough. She had expected him to call last night, but he hadn't. She wasn't sure what she would have said if he had.

"Are you okay, Rach?" Sofia asked, looking into her eyes.

"Yes."

"You sure?"

Rachel forced a smile. "Yes, I'm fine. Come on, let's let Amaury know we're ready to be served. I'm starving," she said, moving to her chair and away from her sister's intense scrutiny.

"Okay, but don't think you're not going to tell me everything," Sofia said, taking her own seat again.

"Everything like what?"

Sofia held her gaze with that "let's get serious" expression on her face. "Everything like how you really feel about Ethan Chambers."

"Maybe we ought to buy stock in those tabloids since you seem to be in them quite a bit these days, Ethan."

Ethan closed his refrigerator after pulling out a cold beer. He juggled the phone as he twisted off the cap. His heart had begun pounding in his chest when the phone had rung, in hopes the caller was Rachel. Instead it was Hunter. "That's a possibility."

"So is any of it true?" his brother asked.

"The only thing I will admit to is an involvement with Rachel. Her motives were exploited falsely. Our being together was mutual and she didn't need me to advance her career. She did that on her own."

"Pretty defensive, aren't you?"

"Can't help but be where she's concerned. I love her."

There was silence on the other end, and Ethan was well aware that his brother was recovering from what he'd said. In all his twenty-eight years, he'd never admitted to loving any woman. While his brother was pondering what he'd said, Ethan took a swig of beer.

"This is serious," Hunter finally said.

"I hope she realizes that it is. She's tabloid shy."

"And you're just the opposite," Hunter pointed out. "For as long as I can recall, you enjoyed getting in front of a camera."

Ethan shrugged, remembering some of his wild escapades while in high school and college. "Not when they portray my woman in a bad light."

"Well, we're all looking forward to meeting her. And since things are that serious, don't forget the traditional Chambers vineyard weddings."

Ethan smiled. "I won't, but first I have to convince her that she loves me and that I will make her life with me worth anything the tabloids might put her through."

"Good luck."

Ethan drew in a deep breath. "Thanks." He knew he was going to need it.

Sofia took another sip of her wine. "And you think Livia Blake might be looking for another agent?" she asked.

"Yes," Rachel said, eager to keep her sister talking about something else other than her and Ethan. "Livia says at thirty her modeling days are coming to an end, and she wants an agent who will take her acting career to another level and run with it. Of course, she's heard about Limelight Entertainment and would love to talk to you, but she's heard how selective you are."

Sofia didn't deny what Rachel said. She *was* selective. "I've been keeping an eye on Livia Blake's modeling career for a while now and wondered if she planned on doing anything beyond that. Limelight is definitely interested, so have her give me a call."

Rachel looked at her sister and could tell she was bothered about something and that it was something other than what was going on with her and Ethan. "You've been working a lot lately, Sofia. When do you plan on taking another vacation?"

Sofia smiled. "Hmm, a vacation sounds nice but I won't be going back to the islands any time soon. My clientele has doubled, and I have to find work for a lot of people." She took another sip of her wine, leaned back in her chair and asked, "Did you know Uncle Jacob is thinking about retiring?"

Rachel's eyes widened. "No. I talked to him a few days ago and he said nothing about that. But I can see him wanting to just chill, take it easy and travel. He and Aunt Lily have been saying they want to build that house in Barbados for years."

"Yes, I'd love for him to retire and enjoy life, too, but not if the rumors I'm hearing are true."

Rachel lifted a brow. "What rumors?"

Although there weren't others in the restaurant, Sofia leaned over the table and said in a low tone, "I've heard that he's thinking about selling his interest in Limelight to Ramell Jordan at A.F.I."

Rachel's expression denoted her surprise. Artists Factory Inc. had been a rival talent agency of Limelight Entertainment for years. In fact, Ramell's father, Emmett, had been a close friend of her father's, but for some reason they were not on good terms at the time of her dad's death. And because of Sofia's close relationship with their father, Rachel was not surprised that her sister would not favor a possible merger.

"What you heard is probably just a rumor," Rachel said, hoping that would smooth her sister's ruffled feathers.

"I certainly hope so. I can't believe Uncle Jacob would consider doing such a thing."

Rachel could see why he would. Although her father and Emmett Jordan had ended on bad terms, Uncle Jacob and Emmett had remained somewhat friendly.

"Ramell Jordan is nothing more than the son of a backstabber after what Emmett did to Dad," Sofia said angrily.

Rachel lifted a brow. "And just what did he do to Dad?"

She'd always believed there was more to the story than either she or Sofia knew, but no one would ever say. In fact, Sofia was the only one who'd ever made such accusations about Emmett Jordan. All Uncle Jacob would say was that it had been a misunderstanding between the two men and that had her father lived, his and Emmett's relationship would have been restored to a close friendship.

"You're better off not knowing."

Rachel only shook her head. For years that had been the same response Sofia gave her whenever she asked. Maybe she was simply better off not knowing.

"And now that you've tried to get me to avoid talking about you and Ethan Chambers, I think that we need to finally get to the meat of your problem."

Rachel pushed away her plate. Dinner had been delicious and now she was ready for desert and coffee.

But she would wait awhile until after she answered the questions she knew her sister had for her.

"There's really nothing to tell, Sofia. You know how I detest being in the public eye and Ethan's popularity right now puts him there, as well as any woman he's involved with."

"So the two of you *are* involved?"

Pain rolled through Rachel. "We *were* involved."

Sofia studied her sister's features, saw the pain that settled in her face. "The two of you kept things between you a secret from everyone—including me—which evidently was working for a while. So what happened?"

Rachel took a deep breath, and then she told Sofia about what Paige had done.

A deep frown appeared on Sofia's face. "And this Paige person works on the set of *Paging the Doctor?*"

"Yes, she's a production assistant."

"Not for long," Sofia muttered under her breath. "Tell me something, Rachel. Did your affair with Ethan have substance or was it all about sex?"

Rachel met her sister's inquisitive gaze. It would be so easy to claim it had been nothing but sex, but this was Sofia and she'd always had a way of seeing through any lie Rachel told. Besides, she would tell Sofia what she hadn't told anyone, not even Ethan.

"I love him, Sofia. It wasn't all about sex."

Her sister stared at her for a long moment, and then a smile touched her lips when she said, "Then I can see no reason why the two of you can't be together."

Rachel rolled her eyes. In a way she was surprised at her sister's comment, since Sofia of all people knew how she guarded her privacy. "You know that's not possible, Sofia. Ethan is an up-and-coming star, and being the focus of a lot of attention is what will boost his career. I can't risk that kind of publicity with the career I tried so hard to build."

"And what else?"

Rachel gave her sister a confused look. "What do you mean what else?"

Sofia leaned in closer. "This is me, and I can read you like a book, Rachel. So level with me and tell me the real reason you and Ethan can't be together. Since I'm always on the lookout for potential clients, I'm well aware that Ethan Chambers is hot news. I'm also well aware that during the time the two of you were having your secret tryst, his name wasn't linked to any Hollywood starlet, which made the tabloids wonder exactly what he was doing and who he was doing it with. And when it seemed he had decided to just live a boring life, they backed off. When the news hit the papers about the two of you, the tabloids had basically given him a rest."

Sofia paused to take a sip of her wine and then asked, "And what's this I hear about you taking a temporary leave from the show?"

Rachel placed her wineglass down after taking her own sip. She didn't have to wonder where Sofia had gotten the news. Few people knew that Frasier considered himself as their godfather. "I thought it would be best, and I met with Frasier yesterday. He wasn't all that keen on the idea but said since there was only a week left for filming, he would go along with it. But he wanted me back on my job when they began the new season. I can handle that."

Sofia lifted a brow. "Can you? They aren't writing Ethan out of the script, so he'll be returning, too. Will you be able to handle that?"

"I don't have a choice."

"Yes, you do. For once you can fight for what you want, what you have every right to have."

Rachel was still surprised by her sister's attitude. She'd expected her to be the voice of reason and agree with her that the best thing was to put her career ahead of anything else. That was certainly what Sofia was doing these days. She couldn't recall a time when her sister had gotten serious about a man.

"You don't think my career is important, Sofia?"

Sofia waved off her words. "Of course I do, but your heart takes priority."

At Rachel's frown, Sofia reached out and captured her hand in hers. "Hear me out for a second, Rach." She paused and then said, "This is the first time I can truly say I believe you're in love. It shows on your face every time you say Ethan's name. You, little sister, are truly in love and I don't believe it's one-sided. I've been waiting to see how Ethan was going to respond to the tabloids. He hasn't denied the two of you are having an affair. In fact, he's gone on record with Joe Connors to say that you were not using him to boost your career. Other than that, he's been low-key about everything, which shows me he's doing whatever he can to protect you, and I like him for that. He could take all this publicity and run with it, but he hasn't. He's trying to fade to black."

Rachel had to agree with Sofia on that. Ethan was keeping a low profile these days.

"A man like that is worth keeping, Rach. And it's time you do what I haven't been able to do yet."

"And what is that?" Rachel asked, taking another sip of her wine.

"Stop hiding behind your career as an excuse to avoid falling in love. It's an unfortunate Wellesley trait. I'm guilty of it, too. We're both scared that if we love someone, they will abandon us like Mom and Dad did."

Rachel met her sister's gaze. Is that what she had been doing? Was that the reason she'd deliberately kept men at arm's length? Although she was barely out of diapers when her parents were killed, and her uncle and aunt had always been there for her, she had grown up feeling a tremendous loss. It had been hard during her early years when all her friends had had someone to call Mom and she had not. A part of her had always had that inner fear that to love also meant to lose. Wasn't it time for her to finally take a chance on love and believe she was deserving of a forever kind of love like everyone else? Did she want to live the rest of her life afraid of the unknown? Wasn't a life with Ethan better than a life without him? In her heart she knew that it was, and it was time for her to take a leap of faith and take control of her life.

A smile touched Rachel's face when she recalled the party planned for the cast and crew this weekend. "You're right. It's time for me to stop hiding."

Chapter 19

"You look simply beautiful, Rach," Charlene said, smiling as she gazed at her best friend from head to toe.

"And I feel beautiful," Rachel responded, looking at herself in a full-length mirror. She glanced over her shoulder at the woman who was smiling proudly at her handiwork. "Livia, I'm thinking that maybe I ought to be worried. You could take my job as a makeup artist."

Livia chuckled as she waved off her words. "You don't have to worry about that, and thanks to your sister I won't either. I appreciate you putting in a good word for me. It's a dream come true to be represented by Limelight Entertainment."

Rachel smiled as she looked at herself in the mirror again. Sofia had gone shopping with her and helped her pick out her dress, Charlene had selected the accessories and Livia had done her makeup and hair. She felt like Cinderella about to go to the most important ball of her life. And her Prince Charming was waiting.

At least she hoped he was waiting.

She'd heard from Livia that Ethan had gone home to Napa Valley last weekend and that on the set for the season finale he had thrown himself into his work and pretty much kept to himself. More than once she was tempted to call him but decided to do things this way. Now nerves were setting in and all those "what-ifs" were stirring through her mind.

She turned to her two friends. "Are you sure he's coming to the wrap party tonight, Livia?"

Livia smiled. "I heard him assure Frasier that he'll be there to walk the red carpet."

Rachel nodded. "What if he brings a date?"

"I doubt that, and I even heard him tell Frasier that he's coming alone," Livia responded. "And just so you know, Paige was dropped from the show. All I know is that she got called to John's office and he told her she was no longer needed. So the only thing she gained by stirring up that mess with the tabloids is an unemployment check." Livia smiled and added, "And I heard she's having trouble finding a job. Seems like someone put the word out around town about her."

Rachel didn't have to guess who. Her sister was that influential.

"I think it's time for you to leave now," Charlene said, glancing out the window. "Martin just pulled up."

Nervous flutters raced through Rachel's stomach. Sofia had called her from London, where she'd gone to meet with a client, and given her another pep talk. Then Uncle Jacob and Aunt Lily had called and told her to follow her heart, and since they would be at the wrap party, they would see her later.

Rachel knew she was doing the right thing. Ethan had said he wanted her to tell him that she loved him and she was prepared to do that. And it no longer mattered who would be listening. She did love him, and she needed him in her life more than anything. It was about time that he knew it.

* * *

Ethan drew in a deep breath when the limo he was riding in alone pulled to a stop in front of the red carpet. The crowd was massive and, as usual, reporters were out in droves. People were standing behind the roped areas, and cameras were flashing from just about every angle.

More than anything, he wished Rachel would have been there with him, by his side, to bask in the moment of his accomplishments. He had worked hard to reach this point in his career and, more than anything, he wanted the woman he loved to be with him.

He had told her that he loved her and now the next step would have to be hers. And he could only hope that sooner or later she'd make it.

He had to believe that one day she would realize that together their love was strong enough to withstand anything. Even this, he thought, glancing out the car window at the crowd that seemed to be getting larger by the minute.

As soon as he stepped out of the car, flashbulbs went off, momentarily blinding him, and he was immediately pulled center stage to be interviewed. The cheering crowd made him feel good, but nothing could heal his broken heart.

"Everyone, we have Ethan Chambers, who this season became known as Dr. Tyrell Perry on *Paging the Doctor.* And how are you doing tonight, Ethan?"

Ethan smiled for the camera while giving his attention to the red-carpet host for the evening, Neill Carter. "I'm doing great, Neill, and looking forward to a wonderful evening."

Neill laughed. "I can believe that, but you came by

yourself, man. Surely there was a special lady who would have loved to make this walk down the red carpet with you."

It was Saturday night and, more than likely, millions of people were sitting in front of their television sets watching the festivities, including his family. He hoped Rachel was one of those watching because he intended to give her a shout-out. Even if no one else knew whom his message was meant for, she would.

"Yes," he said, looking directly into the camera. "There is a special lady for me and I want her to know that I…"

He stopped talking when he glanced over Neill's shoulder and saw a woman strolling toward them. He blinked. She was beautiful, from the way her hair was styled on her head to the gorgeous red gown she wore—down to the silver shoes that sparkled on her feet.

His gaze returned to her face and for a moment he didn't believe what he was seeing. Rachel was here, in the spotlight, and it was obvious she wasn't there to make anyone up behind the scenes tonight. She was standing out and she was walking toward him.

All eyes were on her, including his. When she reached his side, she smiled and leaned closer and whispered in his ear, "I love you, Ethan. Thanks for waiting on me."

He couldn't help the smile that touched his lips. He had waited on her. And that wait had not been in vain. He pulled her into his arms and lowered his mouth to hers, kissing her right there in front of everyone. It was a move that caused the crowd to roar with excitement. Photographers snapped pictures, taking it all in. When

Ethan finally released Rachel's mouth, he grinned down at her as flashes continued to go off around them.

"I take it you two know each other," Neill said with a teasing grin.

"Yes, we know each other," Ethan said, pulling her closer to his side. "This is my special lady, and she has something I've never given another female."

"And what's that?" Neill asked.

"My heart."

Later that night, Ethan opened the door to *their* place and swept Rachel into his arms. The party had been great. He'd made more contacts and had gotten numerous offers from new agents looking to fill Curtis Fairgate's place.

But the highlight of the entire evening was the woman in his arms, the star of his heart.

He tried to maintain control as he carried her to the bed. His hands began shaking as he slowly undressed her, hoping and praying this wasn't a dream and he wouldn't wake up to an empty room.

It was only after he'd gotten them both undressed and eased on the bed with her, right into her outstretched arms, that he finally accepted this was the real deal. He took her face in his hands and stared into the darkness of her eyes as his heart swelled even more. "I love you, Rachel."

Her smile brightened his whole world, and her voice was filled with sincerity when she said, "And I love you, Ethan."

For a suspended moment in time they stared at each other, and then he captured her lips with his as joy bubbled within him. He knew at that moment that he'd been made to love her, to be her shelter from the storm, to protect her, to honor her for always.

He deepened the kiss and felt her body tremble. When he settled his body over hers, he knew he was almost home.

He had wanted to take things slow with her, but it had been too long since they'd been together like this and his body was craving to get inside of her. When she moaned his name he knew he couldn't wait any longer.

He broke off the kiss to gaze down into her eyes at the same time he thrust inside of her, entering her with a hunger that shook every part of his body. As her scent swept through his nostrils and her inner muscles gripped him for everything they could get, he threw his head back and surrendered to her.

"Rachel!"

His sexy pixie was making her mark, and each time she lifted her hips to meet his thrusts, stroke for stroke, he was pushed even more over the edge. When he felt a mind-blowing explosion on the horizon, he glanced back down into her face and saw his passion mirrored in her eyes.

When the climax hit, he could swear bells and whistles went off. Their bodies exploded together, escalating them to the stars and beyond. They shuddered together as the power of love drenched them in an orgasm so potent he wondered if they would ever be able to recover.

But deep down he knew they would—only to take the journey over and over again, for an entire lifetime.

When their bodies ceased shuddering, he rolled to the side, pulled her into his arms and held her close to his heart. Just where she would always be.

* * *

Rachel lay contented in Ethan's arms. She hadn't realized how much she'd missed coming here, being here with him, until they'd stopped being together. But never again.

They had made love several times, and she kept telling him how much she loved him because she loved hearing herself say it and he seemed to enjoy hearing it. And he told her how much he loved her as well. She knew now that together they could face anything. She was no longer afraid of what the tabloids might print or how her career could be affected.

Tonight Frasier had congratulated everyone and indicated that he expected them all back for the new season. Everyone except Paige, of course, who ironically wasn't invited to the wrap party she'd been dying to attend with Ethan. And Tae'Shawna Miller. Apparently she had whined one time too many, because rumor had it she'd been released from the show as well.

Rachel shifted her body to glance up at Ethan. "You're quiet. What are you thinking?" she asked him.

He smiled down at her. "I was thinking about how surprised I was to see you tonight. Surprised and happy. What made you come?"

She reached up and her fingers touched his cheek. "You. I knew I loved you and you kept telling me that you loved me, breaking down my barriers." She paused a moment and then said, "And I also realized Sofia was right. I was hiding my love on the pretense of protecting my career when I was really afraid to admit loving you. I was afraid I wouldn't be able to handle it if you were to leave me the way my parents did."

Ethan held her gaze. "I'll never leave you, sweetheart. And by the way, while you were talking to Frasier tonight, I got a call on my cell phone. It was my mother. She was watching the whole thing on television and heard me when I said you had my heart. So she wants to know when's the wedding."

Rachel laughed. "The wedding?"

"Yes. I told her I hadn't gotten around to asking you yet." He pulled her closer into his arms. "So, baby, will you marry me?"

She smiled up at him. "For better or for worse?"

He nodded. "And richer or poorer."

"In sickness and in health?"

He chuckled. "Until death do us part."

She leaned up and threw her arms around his neck. "In that case, I accept!"

He wrapped her in his arms and kissed her, sealing what he knew would be a Hollywood marriage that would last forever.

* * * * *

SING YOUR PLEASURE
A.C. Arthur

To Julian Hawkins—for having the strength to just be you.

Chapter 1

Moving from her closet to the bed where her suitcase was opened wide, Charlene Quinn sang the lyrics to "Finally" while folding and carefully packing clothes for her trip to Miami. The song was an oldie but goodie in her mind. The classic single by CeCe Peniston, released in 1991, hitting the number-one spot on music's *Billboard* charts, was a great dance tune that didn't quite give CeCe the credit her vocal abilities deserved.

Charlene couldn't stop playing the song. She had been since receiving the phone call two days ago from her agent, Sofia Wellesley of Limelight Entertainment. And while CeCe was actually singing about finally finding Mr. Right and falling in love, Charlene's rendition of the lyrics was something else entirely.

She definitely wasn't looking for love. Granted, she wasn't running from it either, like some people she knew, but it wasn't high up on her list of priorities. For Charlene, working as a vocal coach at the local community college was both challenging and rewarding because everybody who thought they could sing couldn't.

Her parents hadn't seemed thrilled with her career choice. They wanted her to be more like her older sister. Candis Quinn's illustrious career began with her debut as a Dainty Diaper Baby at the tender age of one. From that moment on, Candis had been in front of a camera, gracing the pages of magazines and then finally graduating to commercials in her high school years. Candis was three years Charlene's senior, and it was expected that Charlene would follow in Candis's footsteps.

It was usually around age three to four that most babies dropped the baby fat due to their increased mobility. Charlene's stuck like old gum to a shoe sole. While there were some ads that especially requested plump child models, the ones that wanted the cute, perfect look clearly outnumbered them. So Candis was the child star of the family.

Her father, Randall Quinn, had been the executive producer of over twenty hit sitcoms in the last thirty years. That made him the adult star of the family. Her mother, Marjorie, was the perfect wife, mother and overall female in Charlene's life. She supported her husband, went to all the photo shoots and commercial callbacks with Candis and tried her damnedest to make Charlene into something she just couldn't possibly be.

Marjorie had finally had enough of Charlene's diet failures when she turned sixteen. She took her daughter to a doctor, who quickly diagnosed Charlene with hypothyroidism, a condition described as a lack of functioning thyroid tissue and thyroid hormone. Early symptoms of this condition included fatigue, weight gain and water retention, all things that had plagued Charlene since she was a little girl. The strange thing was that this condition usually hit women during the first year after they'd given birth. Charlene's was a unique case, the doctor had said.

His diagnosis hadn't changed the stigma of growing up in Beverly Hills among models and actresses and a sister who was a goddess at five feet nine inches, boasting a teeny-tiny waist and sizable breasts. Even now, holding her own bit of height at five feet five and a half inches with a buttery complexion and slightly slanted brown eyes, Charlene felt a little uneasy about her looks. She was better than she had been but still the memory of being constantly ridiculed in school stuck with her. That's where her best friend, Rachel, had entered the picture.

Only three weeks ago Rachel Wellesley, the younger sister of Charlene's agent, Sofia, had been dealt a heavy blow. One of the things both she and Charlene feared had happened—Rachel had found herself in the limelight of the tabloids. Charlene met Rachel when they were both in the third grade attending the Beverly Vista School. It was there in the cafeteria, over a carton of warm chocolate milk and sticky, tasteless mac 'n' cheese, that a true friendship had been forged.

Like Charlene, Rachel came from a famous family— the Wellesleys, known for their budding new agency Limelight Entertainment. That, coupled with living in Beverly Hills, California, put the two girls in a position they dreaded. Paparazzi and reporters were always abuzz either around their homes or the school yard. Everybody wanted a glance into their personal lives, or at the time, the personal lives of their famous families. It was sickening and both girls swore they'd keep a low profile in their adult lives, which for Charlene wasn't going to be a problem since she didn't fit the profile of your average Beverly Hills female.

But the night she'd dragged Rachel to the karaoke

bar in an effort to cheer her best friend up, Charlene's plans had changed.

"Why don't you sing something?" Rachel had said after the man with the beer belly and nappy-looking beard had shuffled off the stage. He'd attempted to sing "Flying Without Wings" by Ruben Studdard, but his rendition had been more than bad. Horrendous probably said it best.

"Oh, no," Charlene had answered quickly, taking a sip of her water with lemon slices. "You're the one on hiatus, you get up there. It'll do you good to get the whole situation with Ethan and the show off your mind."

Rachel was already shaking her head. "Now you know I can't hold a tune any better than I can hold hot coals in my hand. And the last thing I want to do is give the press any more ammunition against me."

Feeling the wave of sadness emanating from her friend made Charlene frown. She hated seeing the normally vibrant and cheerful Rachel this way. Reaching a hand across the table, she covered Rachel's. "It'll die down. You know those vultures find new targets every fifteen minutes. Besides, Ethan's love life is really old news."

Shrugging, Rachel tried for a smile. Unfortunately, the act was dismal and the smile never reached her eyes. "C'mon, Rach, I'm trying to cheer you up here. If you keep looking like that I'm going to get a complex. Being stuck with me can't really be that bad."

"You know what would really cheer me up?" Rachel asked, this time her smile seeming a bit more enthusiastic.

Feeling the twinges of dread, Charlene responded, "What?"

"If you'd get up there and sing."

Her lips had been about to form the answer "no." Of all people in the world, Rachel knew how much Charlene loved to sing. She also knew all the insecurities Charlene kept from everybody else.

It was no secret that Charlene's passion was singing. She'd been singing any and every song she heard since she was four years old. It had been the only thing she was good at that Candis couldn't do. The best part about it was that Charlene could really sing. But once she had graduated from high school and went on to study music at The Herb Alpert School of Music at CalArts, furthering her musical knowledge, Charlene's focus had turned to training other people with musical talent.

But tonight wasn't about her, it was about the friend who'd been there for her through all her trials and tribulations. After all, that's what friends were for.

"If I do this, you'd better smile for the rest of the night. No more sulking, no more regretting, nothing. Deal?"

Rachel, knowing she'd won this not-so-small battle, smiled happily, turning her hand over to grip Charlene's. "I promise. C'mon, let's look through the catalog to see what songs they have."

Before Charlene could say another word, they were facing the computerized jukebox, pressing buttons that allowed the display of songs to change quickly. After about four screen changes, Rachel pointed to a song and proclaimed, "That one."

Reading the selection, Charlene couldn't help but smile. It had been one of her favorite songs in high school.

So without further hesitation she'd selected the song

and headed up to the stage while Rachel hurried back to her seat. It was Friday night, a little after ten, and the bar was just starting to pick up more customers. Karaoke night was huge here and the hot wings and beer weren't bad either. So as she adjusted the microphone to fit her height—the man with the huge belly had been taller by a few inches—she experienced a slight case of the butterflies after noticing the amount of people sitting at tables waiting for her performance.

Crowds bothered Charlene only to the extent that she didn't like people staring at her. As for performing, once she began singing she was often so lost in the music and the lyrics that all else ceased to exist. So her fingers trembled slightly when she lifted her enclosed fist to cover her mouth, clearing her throat.

Applause had already begun from a few of the customers sitting right up front.

"Sing, baby! Sing!" a partially inebriated man with a cigarette stuck to his lower lip yelled. How did he keep that thing on his lip? she wondered absently. Then she nodded to the older lady operating the karaoke machine.

She didn't need the words that appeared on the prompter, she knew the song by heart. The already dim room grew just a tad darker until there was only a spotlight on her. She couldn't see the faces of the people in the audience but could make out the outline of their heads. The first chords of music started and she felt that familiar stirring inside.

It began in the pit of her stomach, swirling around until warmth filled her entire body. That's what happened when she sang, her entire soul was filled.

Then right on cue, with her eyes staring out into the

darkness, she began to sing the lyrics to Mariah Carey's "Hero."

"There's a hero, if you look inside your heart. You don't have to be afraid of what you are." This had been her theme song all throughout high school. Of course it had been out for a while by that time, but it didn't matter. She loved the lyrics, loved what they meant and how empowered they made her feel.

Loved them so much that they were all she could focus on while singing and she didn't see the tall, slender man watching her from a table in the far corner of the room.

Ten minutes and a roomful of applause later, Charlene had stepped down from the stage, only to be stopped just as she approached the table where Rachel was still clapping gleefully.

"Jason Burton from Playascape Records. And you are?"

For a second she'd only stared at him, not even acknowledging the business card he held out to her with one hand or his charming smile. Had he said he was from a record company?

Then Rachel was by her side. "She's Charlene Quinn and I'm Rachel Wellesley from Limelight Entertainment Agency. How can we help you, Mr. Burton?"

The conversation had gone on from that moment but Charlene was so flabbergasted at the actual thought of this man thinking she'd sounded good enough to record that she barely remembered it all.

The next day Charlene and Sofia were in downtown Los Angeles riding the elevator to the executive offices of Sahari Davenport, CEO of Empire Music, the music conglomerate that distributed Playascape Records. Charlene had officially been signed as a Limelight client and with Sofia's smooth expertise had left that office two hours later with her first record deal.

And now, as if she hadn't been on a fast enough roller coaster of emotions, she was heading out to Miami to work with superproducer Akil Hutton, the man who was going to make all her secret dreams come true.

Something was wrong.

It just couldn't be, Akil Hutton thought for the millionth time since he'd received the package from Jason early yesterday morning.

"She's gonna be the next Whitney Houston, Ace. I'm tellin' you, wait till you meet her."

Jason had called him Ace since their early days interning at Empire. Over the last ten years he and Jason had worked their butts off to build this company into the hip-hop and R&B powerhouse it was today. They'd both started out as interns for Empire Music, knowing that one day they wanted a piece of that pie for themselves. Since Jason was a people person with a distinct ear for what was hot and what was not, he'd been a shoo-in for the A&R spot, "Artists and Repertoire" was like his middle name.

And since Akil had been more of a beats-and-lyrics man himself, he'd taken his seat in the studio, working alongside the engineers and the artists to get the perfect sound for each recording.

Nineteen number-one hits, seven platinum CDs, three gold, five Grammy Awards ranging from R&B Single to Producer of the Year and millions of dollars later, Akil and Jason were still hanging tight. Akil could say that Jason was the closest thing to a friend he had in this world.

And that was a sorry shame.

But back to this latest dilemma.

In one hand Akil held a picture, an eight-and-a-half-by-eleven glossy print of a pretty woman, with butter-toned skin and root-beer brown eyes. Her smile was fun, touching the soft dimples in each cheek and the edges of her eyes. Her dark hair was pulled away from her face in some sort of updo that didn't really flatter her other features. But that was the least of his worries.

Although her face had captured him, sent a little tinge to his chest, the rest of her made him pause. She wasn't a rail-thin woman—after being in the business for years he knew this was the look, slim and trim, almost emaciated—on the contrary; she was full-figured with more curves than the law should possibly allow. Her clothes, however, left a lot to be desired. She wore slacks, nice enough, in a navy blue color and a button-down blouse, high heels and light makeup. An outfit that didn't scream "sexy" and barely whispered "diva."

It yelled "average, nondescript, forgettable" from the business standpoint. On the personal, well, he didn't even want to think about that.

All those words were deadly in his line of work.

Then he closed his eyes, shut out the visual and simply listened to the voice bellowing from the speakers in his home studio just outside of Miami.

The throaty, rich sound of a mezzo-soprano voice filtered throughout the room. He'd listened to this demo CD more than a dozen times in twenty-four hours, had become addicted to the smooth, melodious notes. There was no doubt she had a voice, a good strong one at that, just right for singing R&B ballads and dance tunes. Ten minutes into the first listen he'd known Jason had picked a winning voice.

As for the rest, the whole package, which was what he was responsible for, that was going to be a problem.

She just didn't fit the bill. This Charlene Quinn did not look like a "diva." Hell, she didn't even look like a nightclub singer. She looked like what she was, a voice instructor at the local college. Now he did have a little more information on her, she was the daughter of a television-and-movie producer and best friends with one of the owners of Limelight Entertainment Agency. That told him two things. One, she was rich and privileged and probably thought the world was supposed to treat her exactly that way. And two, she had high connections. Limelight was a contender in the business, representing a lot of the heavy hitters in the movie as well as music industries. Still, Akil focused on the talent; connections and money meant nothing to him if his artist had no talent to work with.

On the demo she'd recorded three tracks. The first was an old Tina Turner hit, "Shake a Tail Feather," that had him bopping his head and feeling the emotional energy that up until now, only Tina had been able to infuse into her songs. The next was the song Jason heard her sing in the karaoke bar, "Hero" by Mariah Carey. Again, a tune that is probably not advised to be tried by another vocalist, but Charlene had done it amazingly well. Her vocal range was outstanding as she hit the higher notes just as easily as she rocked the lower ones.

The last tune was an unknown, the beat was slow, jazzlike, and the lyrics were sultry. More suited to the Billie Holiday and Lena Horne types. Charlene had begun with a slow steady intro that immediately caught his attention. "The first time we made love," were the lyrics and from the way she belted them out you'd think she was experiencing her first time all over again. From the verse to the chorus to the bridge, which could have been instrumentally arranged better, to the killer climax of the ballad, Akil had been transfixed, pulled into the very heart of the song and the soul of the singer.

The contradiction between her look and her sound was astounding.

Akil was a music producer and as such he was responsible for all stages of the audio development, working with the artist, studio musicians, engineers and related staff. That's what his generic duties were. But Akil hadn't risen to the spot of being one of the most sought-after producers of the decade by being generic. When he took on a new artist, he took on every aspect, from the audio to the performance to the overall image that was presented to the public. His goal was to give the listeners what they wanted, to produce the best music, to give the best images. That's what made him unique in this business, it's what made him better than most of the rest. He was known as a perfectionist, a slave driver, some had said. But in the end it was all for the best; ninety-five percent of his songs debuted in the top five on *Billboard*. Eleven of the twelve entertainers he'd been responsible for introducing to the world were top charters and now multimillionaires sought after for performances on the Grammys, the BET Awards, the MTV Awards and so on. The twelfth didn't fall into that category only because Nichelle Dante had decided after her first R&B album that she wanted to sing gospel instead. Akil had hooked her up with a great producer at Footprints Gospel Records and she was now topping the charts there.

He had an impressive record, a great reputation and money in the bank to back it up. That all started with a confidence and heartfelt belief in his artist.

Looking down into the smiling face on the picture once more, he shook his head, not sure he felt that way about Charlene Quinn.

Chapter 2

Some men went for breasts, others big booties. Akil was a thigh man, through and through. So it was no wonder that when Charlene Quinn walked into his studio, where he was seated at the mixing console, and he'd turned around in the swivel chair and was face-to-thigh with her, his pulse quickened.

He'd seen her before, her photo and in person the day they'd met at the offices of Empire Music. So he wasn't totally shocked at how pretty she actually was up close. Still, the effect of those voluptuous thighs wrapped so succulently in soft denim slacks made the rise to his feet a little slower than he'd anticipated.

A smile a mile long—no kidding, she had a beautiful, wide smile that made her eyes twinkle slightly, if one was looking at such things. Anyway, she smiled when he extended his hand and he felt the frown before he knew better to stop it.

"Ms. Quinn, I'm glad you made it safely," he said. Shaking hands was customary in business. Feeling tugs of something indescribable when his flesh touched hers was not. So he pulled away quickly and acted as if the mixing console needed more of his attention than she did.

"Ah, yes, I did get here safely. The private jet you sent helped a lot."

Her voice was deeper than he remembered, throatier, kind of like when she sang. And whatever fragrance she was wearing was playing with his senses. Luckily Akil was a big boy, he knew how to handle his urges. He also knew that urges in the direction of one of his artists was a no-no. Besides, this was Charlene Quinn, the woman who was supposed to be Playascape's next diva. He would have his hands full with this transformation without adding the sticky strings of sex to the mix.

"So, I've got a few songs from a great writer I've worked with before. I'd like you to read over them tonight, get a feel for the flow, then we'll get started first thing tomorrow morning."

He was sitting again, not really looking at her but knowing she was there.

"I thought we were having dinner tonight," she said, then cleared her throat. "I mean, Jason said I'd meet the team tonight at dinner. Doesn't that include you?"

Akil nodded. "Yes, I'll be there. But I don't want you getting it confused with a night on the town in Miami. We're here to work. I brought you out here because I can focus better in my own space. And for this CD we have a lot to focus on."

She didn't like the way he'd said that.

As a matter of fact, Charlene hadn't liked a thing about Mr. Akil Hutton since the first time she'd met him. Could anybody be as rude and arrogant as him? Probably, but she hadn't met them yet—which was saying a lot considering her background in L.A. She was finding it hard to swallow these traits from Akil.

She should have expected it, though, she'd told herself repeatedly. He was one of the most sought-after producers on the scene today. She'd been shocked when Jason told her that's who she'd be working with. Truth be told, this entire situation was still a shock to her.

While she'd always loved to sing, Charlene had never really considered a career in music. Okay, well, that wasn't exactly true. Else why would she have had a demo CD all ready when Jason asked for one? The recording had taken place more than a year ago when one of her students had written a song and asked her to sing it. When she did he'd offered to record the demo for her. But Charlene had taken those CDs and stuffed them in her dresser drawer, realizing that she'd never have the guts to send them to anyone. As much as she portrayed a strong black woman, with confidence and intelligence, Charlene knew her limitations, her weaknesses, and the main one was her appearance.

She'd never been skinny like Candis, or even petite and curvy like Rachel. That wasn't who God had meant for her to be, she accepted that. Still, some days she actually did plead with the man upstairs to just reduce her waistline by about five inches, shave off some of her thighs so she could fit in a size fourteen without busting the inner seams. As it stood, today, taking her daily supplements of Levoxyl to help increase the levels of thyroid hormones her body produced, she wore a size sixteen comfortably. And barring any flare-ups she held steady at that size.

So she hadn't pursued a singing career, hadn't wanted people staring and gawking at her, possibly talking about her. Teaching was an ideal job because she got the chance to do what she loved and still keep a low profile. However, Rachel and Sofia had convinced her that this was an opportunity she couldn't pass up, and a small part of her knew they were right. With all her reservations, Charlene knew the smart decision was to at least give it a try. Not every singer received this chance: she'd be awfully ungrateful if she turned it down.

And now here she was, in Miami, standing in the home studio of the famous Akil Hutton wanting nothing more than to either walk out on his rude behind or sink into the floor where he couldn't notice her—both options held equal appeal at the moment.

Instead, she steeled herself, took a deep breath and pressed on. "We didn't get a chance to talk a lot about the project in L.A. I'm wondering what type of CD you have in mind."

Akil didn't even look up at her as he flicked his hand in her direction and said impatiently, "We'll get to that later. Just take the songs with you, have Nannette show you to your room and get changed for dinner."

She'd been dismissed, she was absolutely certain of that fact, and yet she still stood there. Just looking at him.

He wasn't bad on the eyes, that was also a fact. Smooth tree bark–toned skin, close-cut dark hair and clean-shaven face. He wore slacks and a long-sleeved shirt that melded around taut bicep muscles and, from what she could see, a trim stomach. His hands, she noticed as he continued to work the controls on the board, were medium-size, with long fingers, like a piano player's. He wore a gold watch but other than that no jewelry, which was outside the norm since most producers were just as jeweled-down as their artists these days.

"Is there something else?" he asked, yanking her out of her "he's damned good-looking" reverie.

"No," she said in a clipped tone. "There's nothing else. See you at dinner."

And with that she did finally turn, thanking her feet for getting the message, and stalked out of the room.

If this was any indication of how their time working together was going to be, Charlene feared this CD would never see the light of day.

The house was gorgeous, there was absolutely no doubt about that. On the ride in the limo from the airport Charlene had already assumed it would be. They'd only driven on the highway for about forty-five minutes before turning off on a road that seemed to be paved right through a forest. The stately mansion was all white with black bases around each window and a brick-colored shingled roof. It sat nestled between a scenic backdrop of even more trees. It was big and palatial, definitely a home for the enigmatic Akil Hutton.

Nervousness had swamped her as she'd stepped out of the car. The chauffeur, who'd told her at the airport his name was Cliff, had moved quickly to the trunk, unloading the two suitcases she'd brought along with her.

Now, two hours later, in the room Nannette—the pretty Latina housekeeper—had directed her to, she was standing at the window wondering what on earth she was doing. This room faced the back of the house so she had a view of the tennis courts and the corner of the pool where river rocks were piled into a small fountain.

She wasn't overwhelmed by the space. Her family home in L.A. was just about the size of this one and the homes of some of the people her family had associated with were even bigger. So it wasn't her surroundings that made her nervous. She attributed that to the man who could make or break her newfound singing career with the snap of a finger.

The low chime of her cell phone disturbed her thoughts and she moved from the window, where she'd probably been standing too long anyway, to get her purse.

"Hello?"

"Hey, Char, thanks for calling to let me know you got to Miami safely."

Sitting on the bed, Charlene used one hand to smooth down the smoke-gray skirt she planned on wearing to dinner while holding the phone in the other. "Hi, Candis. Sorry, I was sort of caught up the minute I got here."

"Really?" her older sister, with the sense of humor that skipped Charlene upon her birth, chuckled. "Caught up in what? In the arms of that fine ass Akil Hutton? I still can't believe he's going to produce your CD. You have no idea how lucky you are."

Charlene didn't even need to close her eyes to see his face again. With a little moan she said, "Girl, please. Akil Hutton isn't concerned about anything but work. Which is just fine with me because I'd just as soon get this over with."

"Get it over with? You don't sound like you're too happy about this opportunity. Which is plain crazy since you've been singing since Mama had you."

"I know, but I was happy teaching."

"No. You're happy singing."

Charlene really couldn't argue with that statement. "But I was okay just doing it in the classroom. I don't know about performing in front of people, Candis. What will they think of me? What if they don't like my music?"

"And what if the world were struck by a nuclear bomb tomorrow? What if after I flew all the way to Paris for a photo shoot I woke up the next day with a zit the size of Texas on my forehead? What if? What if?" She sighed. "Char, you can't live your life wondering 'what if.' You've got a God-given gift, it's only right that you use it and share it with the world."

"But—"

"But nothing. Just stop worrying for a minute and go with the flow. Obviously the record execs thought enough of you to sign you to a contract and hook you up with Akil. They don't do that for just anybody."

Charlene nodded: Candis was right. The thing was, it wasn't only about talent. There were lots of talented singers out there; take the ones seen on that reality show *American Idol*. Many of the most talented singers on that show were kicked out before the final rounds. And one of the most consistent things the judges on that show—most of whom were record industry profession-als in their own right—said was that it wasn't just about the voice, it was about the total package. A package Charlene wasn't so sure she had.

"I know they don't. And I'm not ungrateful for the opportunity. I'm just not a hundred percent sure about it all."

"Then it's a good thing you're not the one who has to be sure. The record execs think you're good and want to put your CD out, and Akil has to think you're worth his time. So you just open your mouth and sing."

Leave it to Candis to be candid and honest with her, almost to the point of hurting her feelings. But if there was one thing Charlene knew it was that her sister had her back. When the girls in the neighborhood—the skinny, pretty ones who came to the house to hang out with Candis—made fun of the chubby younger sister with fat, too-thick braids, Candis had rounded them all up and kicked them out. She was fiercely protective of Charlene, even though Charlene had spent most of her teenage years both envying and hating her older sister.

"You're right," she said finally, smiling because she knew on the other end of the phone Candis was probably doing the same. "I'll just do what I know how to do and pray that what's meant will be."

"What's meant is already happening," Candis said. "Now you get to work. I've got me a hot date tonight that I need to go and get ready for."

Her words reminded Charlene that Candis was on the other side of the world in Paris. "I'm sorry you're up so late checking on me. I know how you enjoy your sleep."

Candis chuckled. "You've got that right. But I had to make sure you were all right."

"I'm fine. Go ahead and get your beauty rest."

"If you didn't think to call me I know you haven't called Mama or Daddy. Give them a call when you get a minute just so they won't worry."

"I'm not you. They won't bother to worry."

"That's not true. You're their daughter just the same."

Not wanting to go into this years-old battle, Charlene cut it short. "Okay, I'll call them when I get back from dinner. You go back to sleep."

"All right. Love you, kiddo."

"Love you, too, big sis."

Clicking off the phone, Charlene knew she did love her big sister. For all that seemed different between them they were connected by a sisterly bond. As for her parents, well, that was another story entirely. But, as promised, she would call them later. After all, she was the responsible and mature sister, the one always expected to do the right thing.

She only prayed the right thing was going to dinner with Akil and the rest of the team when what she really wanted to do was teach the superproducer a thing or two about basic hospitality.

Chapter 3

Shula's Steak House wasn't exactly what Charlene had envisioned for a dinner to meet the team that would work on her CD. Something a little fancier had been her thought. But this was just as well. The dark wood floors and contemporary dining room she'd been escorted to made her feel a lot more comfortable than a dimly lit place with candles and lots of clinking crystal would have.

Not that Shula's was slacking any, no, not at all. Located in the Miami Lakes district, it had topped the list on the *Miami Herald*'s Best of South Florida, easily defeating the trendy Prime 112 and Manny's Steakhouse. All places Charlene had been to in her trips to Florida and a ranking she happened to agree with.

Another surprise to her was that Akil had driven his own car to the restaurant, arriving just a few minutes after her with a tall, slim lady by his side. His bodyguards, two tall, beefy men she'd seen at the house when she was leaving, walked in looking all around the room right behind him. While her reaction to the fact that there was a gorgeous woman with Akil shouldn't have been mentionable, the momentary envy toward the woman for her small waist and long legs gave her a jolt. This wasn't new, she reminded herself. The supermodel look was more than popular where she came from and even more so in the music industry. And this woman fit the bill.

She had to be close to six feet with Akil only surpassing her height by about three or four inches. The dress she wore—or more aptly the swatch of material that covered her small, pert breasts and hugged every other inch of her from her shoulders to the upper part of her thighs, was fire-engine red and whispered sex with every step she took. Her skin was fair and coupled with her long dark hair gave her an exotic look.

Self-consciously Charlene brushed her hand over much heavier breasts and down past her thicker waist and meatier thighs. Taking slow, deep breaths, she tried not to acknowledge how much of a cliché this woman really was. She was exactly the type you'd expect to see on the arms of an NBA or NFL player, a rapper or, yes, even a superproducer like Akil.

She was so absorbed in the couple walking toward the table in the private dining room she hadn't even heard the door behind her open and close or the people who had obviously entered approach.

"Hi, Charlene. It's great seeing you again."

She turned at the touch of his hand on her shoulder and stared up happily into the smiling face of Jason Burton, the A&R rep who had first heard her sing in the karaoke bar.

"Hi, Jason. I'm glad to see you," she said with more enthusiasm than she probably should have. But it was true, she was glad to see him. Glad and hopeful that he'd be a buffer between her and Akil and his arm candy.

"Ace, my man. You made it," Jason said, standing and gripping Akil's hand in a shake.

He hadn't changed much from when she'd seen him earlier this afternoon. Well, his clothes were different. He now wore black pleated slacks and a matching jacket. The gray silk shirt that molded against his muscled chest and abs almost matched the color of her skirt. He looked cool and comfortable, yet still powerful and important. Something about the air around him, the ambience of control, made her shift uncomfortably in her seat.

After the handshake Akil reached for his date, pushing her closer to the chair where Charlene sat as if to tell her to sit there so he didn't have to. On the inside Charlene bristled but on the outside she found the strength to smile. "Good evening, Akil."

"Charlene," he said curtly, with a simple nod. "This is Serene Kravitz, head of Artist Development. Serene, meet Playascape's newest R&B artist, Charlene Quinn."

Reaching her hand up and shaking the other woman's wasn't as hard as Charlene thought it would be. Once she got over the fact that the other woman seemed to be drinking in the sight of her much like a lion would its next meal.

"Nice to meet you," Charlene said with a polite smile.

"Likewise," was Serene's response before she dropped Charlene's hand and walked around to the back of her, then to the front again. "Okay, I see what you mean, Akil. We do have our work cut out for us."

What was she talking about? The calm that Charlene had fought to obtain was quickly slipping.

"Yeah," Akil said, clearing his throat. "Let's take our seats, then we can get started."

Serene sat to one side of Charlene while Jason sat on the other. Akil sat directly across from her. They were in a private dining room so there was no one around them beside the waiters who had come out to fill their water glasses and set up buckets of ice with bottles of champagne sticking out of them.

"Where's Five and Seth?" Jason asked.

Akil shook his head, picked up a napkin and sat it in his lap. "I told them we'd see them in the morning. We don't want to overwhelm her tonight."

"But I wanted Seth to see her and maybe get an idea of her range tonight." Jason looked as perplexed as Charlene felt.

"Her voice is all right. I don't think we have to work much in that area."

Akil looked at her then, his dark eyes piercing as they found hers and held. Charlene wanted to squirm under his scrutiny, felt like slipping right out of that chair and running from that room. What was it about his glare, the intense edge to his looks, that stirred her?

"It's the other that we need to work on right away."

His words were like icicles scraping over her skin. "The other?" she asked before she could think of whether or not it was wise.

"Image and presentation, dear," Serene said, extending a long, diamond-clad hand to pat Charlene's. "That's what I do. My job is to plan your career, spearhead promotion and publicity. I create the best image for Playascape's artists and present them to the world long before the CD even hits the shelves, unlike other record labels that have downsized Artist Development to Product Development, which promotes artists heavily in the beginning of their career then stops abruptly. At Playascape we're more interested in the long-term planning."

So she wasn't *his* woman. Charlene could breathe a sigh of relief on that one. This little aspect of the business that she'd explained was new to Charlene. While she knew the ins and outs of singing and a little about recording, the workings of the back end of the music industry wasn't her forte. So Serene was like a publicist and stylist all rolled into one? Charlene had a feeling she wasn't going to like her.

"We're doing that now?" Jason asked.

"I think that's the priority," Akil responded tightly.

"The priority's always been the music."

"You know we work with the complete package at Playascape. And we don't take any shortcuts."

Suddenly she could see exactly what Akil meant. The "big picture" was her. Her appearance, to be specific. He didn't seem worried about her voice because he'd already heard that, no doubt. What he was worried about was her look. Did she look like the singing stars hogging the charts these days? To that the answer was a resounding no.

Glancing down at her gray pencil skirt and white blouse, cinched at the waist with a thick black patent leather belt, she didn't see Beyoncé's tightly honed curves and blatant sex appeal. Lifting a hand to her thick hair lying on her shoulders in heavy curls didn't bring to mind the short, sexy cuts of Rihanna or Keri Hilson. She just wasn't in the same class as those acts. But she could sing. That was not a question.

"I see what he's saying, Jason. We have to make sure every aspect of this CD is top-notch. Not just the vocals but everything that comes before and after the listener hears the music. Is that right, Akil?"

His gut clenched the moment he heard his name on her lips. She was looking right at him, one smoothly arched brow lifting over her hazel eyes.

He'd been trying to keep his composure. And to do that he found he needed to look at her directly as infrequently as possible. From her picture he'd thought she was pretty. Earlier today in the studio he'd felt a powerful thrust of lust at being so close to her voluptuous frame. Now, tonight, when he was supposed to be on his A game as her producer, he found it almost impossible to avoid the subtle hints of sexuality pouring from her.

Did she know what she was doing to him? Did she have any idea how the moment she'd touched her hand to her chest, smoothed down her clothes to her thighs, he'd wanted to clear the room of everybody but the two of them? When her fingers had grazed her hair he'd sighed inwardly, wondering how the soft strands would feel between his fingers. And her scent, it wafted through the air, covering even the mouthwatering aroma of perfectly seasoned and cooked steaks throughout the restaurant.

No, he answered himself as he found the courage to look into her eyes once more. She didn't know. Had no idea how she was turning him on. He'd know if she did because there'd be some semblance of triumph that she was getting to him. Akil had seen it a million times with groupies and other industry females. Charlene didn't have that, the look of a hunter, he'd called it. And that angered him just a little more because that meant she didn't easily fit into any mold.

"That's correct. Listeners today are much more interested in the personal lives and the looks of an artist than they've ever been before. Twenty years ago the R&B reins were held by such heavy hitters as Whitney Houston and Anita Baker, where voices carried you to another plateau. Today's listeners are much more materialistic. Everybody wants the bling, the high life, but most can only get it living vicariously through entertainers," Akil affirmed.

"That's why Beyoncé's bootylicious persona sells records," Charlene added.

"And once we get you into shape, yours will, too," Serene said with a smile. "I think I'll have Carlo come down for a look-see, Akil. You know he can work wonders with anybody. She may have to go to the spa for a week or so. I'd like to introduce her to the public at the Vibe Awards in two months."

"No!" Akil said so loudly Charlene jumped.

"Man, what's up with you tonight?" Jason asked. "First you say appearance is priority now you're axing Serene's plan."

He shook his head, unable to keep his thoughts straight. But he knew what Serene was saying, knew what she was thinking as far as Charlene went, and had to put a stop to it. Sure, he'd thought the same thing initially, but that was before Charlene had arrived in Miami. Before she'd stood close enough for him to smell her or looked so enticing he could imagine tasting her.

"That's not what I have in mind," he said finally, motioning for the waiter to come over and open the bottle of champagne. "I want her polished and ready to go at Vibe." He took a sip of his bubbly and managed to look at Charlene again. He'd thought about her all afternoon but wasn't entirely sure of this new direction until this very moment. "But I don't want her dieting down to a size two. I think the best way to present her is to be different. To take R&B back to its roots."

To his surprise, Charlene lifted her glass to the waiter, watched as the chilled liquid filled to the top then licked her lips before taking a sip. "You mean you're going to let me sing like Tina Turner and Gladys Knight did and not worry about the highly commercialized packages gracing the airwaves today?"

Akil nodded, inwardly applauding her intelligence. He had a feeling that there was much more to Charlene Quinn then he'd originally thought.

"That's exactly what we're going to do."

Chapter 4

Music soothed his soul. Always had and Akil suspected always would.

Sitting back in the chair, pushing the springs as far as they would go, he folded his hands behind his head and stared up at the ceiling. He was in his Miami home, past the personal rooms to the back where his studio was located. In the background a slow beat played. The piano solo was coming up in a few minutes, after the tight strain of violin notes. It was a riveting beat, an emotional ballad that he'd composed but had yet to find the words to accompany.

Be better than me, Akil. Promise me you'll be better.

The familiar words echoed in his mind. That's where they lived now, twelve years later. They were a whisper on swollen and ashen lips, a plea from the one person he'd loved the most at the time.

He'd made the promise. And he'd kept it. He was better than her. His life, because of hers, had gone down a similar path with an entirely different mind-set, one that brought him fame and fortune, everything he'd ever wished for.

But also one that had cost him much.

It was times like these, times when it was quiet except for the music of his heart, that he thought of his past, of the life he had left behind.

Of the one person he'd wanted so desperately to help but who was completely unreachable to him.

"Akil."

At the sound of his name he was jolted out of the past.

"I'm sorry. I didn't mean to disturb you," Charlene was saying, already backing out of the room.

"No," he said, halting her instantly with the single word. "It's okay. Stay."

She'd changed into lounge pants and a T-shirt that brushed just above her knees. On her feet she wore slippers and on her face a look of confusion that scraped over his already tense nerves. How did she do that? How did she look so naive and so innocent one minute, then open her mouth to talk and sound older and much wiser than he could ever be the next?

"I went to the kitchen for some water and heard the music."

"I'm sorry. I should have closed the outer doors to block out the sound. I didn't mean to wake you."

She was shaking her head, the long hair she'd pulled up into a ponytail swaying behind her.

"You didn't wake me. I can never sleep the first night I'm away from home." She was shrugging the words off as if she were embarrassed by them. "This is nice. Did you write it?" she asked about the music.

He nodded.

"What's it called?"

"Nothing right now. The music was in my head one day so I composed it. But I haven't come up with the words or theme for it yet."

It was her turn to nod as if she understood exactly what he was saying. "It's kind of sad," she commented.

Pushing the button, he looped the song, let the slow, heated beginning start.

"Kind of."

They remained quiet, letting the music move around them.

"But kind of inspiring, encouraging."

Leaning forward, he rested his elbows on his knees. "She's growing. Learning."

"She?"

"I always call songs 'she.' Females have a lot more emotion, empathy, compassion, triumph, in their souls than men."

She smiled. "You think so, huh? I guess I can relate to that."

"Being a female, I figured you could."

After a few more beats she said, "He's giving her something."

"Something that moves her to another level."

"It moves them both. See right here," she said, lifting a finger in the air just as the piano solo picked up the beat and drowned out the keyboard and percussions. "Right here is where it changes from just her song to their song. To their journey."

For a moment he was quiet, letting her words and the music sink in. "You're right," he said finally, almost incredulously. "You have a good ear."

"I studied instrumental composition in college."

He sat back, let his eyes gaze at her once more. Each time he looked at her he could swear he saw something else. This time she looked vulnerable, yet capable. Weak only in that she was new to this scenery, but strong in that she was determined to make the best of her situation. He admired that.

And in that instant he feared her.

"You should get some rest. We're starting early tomorrow and will probably work all day. Did you look at the songs I gave you?" Turning his attention back to the board, he cut off the music and began shutting down the rest of the power.

She hesitated and Akil almost turned to see if she was still there. But then she answered him in a voice just a tad smaller, a hint less enthusiastic than it had been a moment before.

"I'll be ready for tomorrow's session. You don't have to worry, Akil. I teach my students how to sing and probably know just as much about vocals, if not more, than you do. So I won't let you down."

Before he had a chance to say that wasn't what he meant, that he'd just wanted to make sure she was prepared, she was gone.

Cursing, Akil slammed his palms down on the mixing console, standing and pushing the chair away from him so hard it slammed into the wall a few feet away. "Dammit!" he cursed, then flicked the light off and left the studio himself.

Why did it always seem like he said the wrong thing to her?

Felix "Five Minute" Hernendez was one of the best sound technicians in the business. He'd also been known for the number-one hit he'd written for Lady X two years ago in about five minutes, hence his nickname.

Seth Dante was the sound engineer. Charlene knew because Jason had told her all about Seth and Five last night during dinner. Right about the time Serene had been giving Akil scathing looks because of the direction he wanted to take with her image. It was comforting to know now that Akil had plans to work her career around the real her.

There was a guitar player whom she hadn't been introduced to yet but could see was already set up and touching the strings on his guitar in the soundproof isolation booth. She'd figured the music had already been digitally recorded by using a gobo panel to keep the sound from bleeding into the other microphones as she sang. But, of course, Akil knew what he was doing. She was sure he had as much control of each instrument channel at the mixing board as he planned to have of her and her voice.

This is it, Charlene told herself, standing in the doorway of the studio. She must have spent the better part of four or five hours reading over the songs Akil had given her, practically memorizing the musical arrangements, the high notes, the lows, the climax of each song. And she was ready, she knew she was ready.

With her bottled water in hand, she moved into the studio full of people, taking a deep breath before saying, "Good morning."

All eyes immediately turned to her and a small nip of fear touched her. Stamping it down, she smiled even brighter and walked right between the huddled group of men.

"Good morning, sunshine," Jason said in his always playful voice. Leaning forward, he kissed her on the cheek. "Somebody call the police. It has got to be a crime for someone to be as beautiful as you are this early in the morning."

Charlene chuckled. "One, eleven o'clock is not that early. And two, that was one weak-ass line."

Jason laughed right along with her. "Yeah, you're right. You're right. C'mon, let's get started."

A tall guy with spiked raven-black hair and a touch of gold in front of his mouth reached out a bony arm toward her. He was dressed in jeans and a Pittsburgh Steelers jersey and she couldn't help but smile. "If I'd known we were showing our teams I would have worn my Raiders shirt," she said.

His smile spread and she was thankful to see there was really only one gold tooth in his mouth and not a row full like some of the acts in the industry these days. Still, he looked young enough to be one of her students.

"You got jokes," he said. "You're on the East Coast now. You can't come in here with that West Coast nonsense."

"Whatever," she said, letting him clasp her hand.

"I'm Five," he introduced himself.

Charlene liked him instantly and knew they were going to work well together.

"And I'm Seth. And that's T-Rock on the bass. He's going to be in the booth with you because his sound is crisper in there."

A shorter man with caramel-toned skin and green eyes stepped up to her then, pointing to the tall Caucasian guitarist she'd already noted in the isolation booth. She was about to take his offered hand when Akil interrupted.

"If you're all finished gaping over her like you've never seen a female before, we can get started."

His voice was like a blast of arctic air, chilling the room instantly and snapping her spine straight.

"Let's start with 'Never Before Like This.'" He continued to bark orders and she watched as Five took his place, moving into the control room with Akil.

Seth went to stand near the DAW, the digital audio workstation, which usually took the place of mixing consoles, recorders, synthesizers, samplers and sound-effects devices. She noted Akil still had a mixing console that he liked to control on his own. Seth was probably the backup he needed to complete the full sound. Meanwhile, Jason walked her over to the booth and attempted to help her with the headphones.

"She knows how to do it, Jase," Akil snapped. "Come on, we've got a lot to get done."

He was in his desired spot in the control room with what she could see was his game face on. He was all about business today. Whereas last night when she'd seen him in that very same position he'd looked, for just that short amount of time, human.

"I've got it, Jason. Thanks." Picking up the headphones, she moved to the stand, dropped her music down onto it and took her place in front of the mic.

She liked this song a lot. Its tempo began slowly but then picked up with the verse. It was good old-fashioned R&B, just what she loved to sing. So if Mr. Superproducer was all about business this morning then she could be, too. She was going to sing this song and every other song he put in front of her like her very life depended on it. Because Akil Hutton was not going to beat her. Not here, not today.

"Never like this before. No, never like this. I never loved like this. Never kissed like this. Never felt like this before."

This was the fifth time she'd sung this song, the fifth time he'd listened to her take the verse written on that song sheet apart only to put it back together in her own special way again.

Her voice rocketed through the air, tore through the speakers and rubbed along the contours of his heart. It was strong, practiced, professional. She hit every note and then hit it again even better the next time around. His palms had begun to sweat, his pulse quickening with the music.

They'd been at it for hours, stopped for about forty-five minutes for lunch, and went at it some more. She never faltered. He'd worked with a lot of artists in his time, had seen a lot of commercial acts. Females who could sing well enough in their church choir or in a talent contest and looked hotter than a house full of strippers. But they weren't serious. He'd known it then, but he'd worked his magic, got enough recorded to make their CD one of the hottest out there. All the while knowing, deep down inside, they weren't real singers. They didn't have real talent. Sure, they were commercial and they were still selling lots of records, selling out concerts and making him and Playascape a boatload of money.

But at the end of the day, at night when he lay down to sleep, he felt like a sellout.

He wasn't producing music anymore, he was making money. But now, listening to Charlene Quinn, he felt that old surge inside, that old feeling when he listened to such greats as Aretha and Ella, Gladys and Dionne. He felt like Charlene could be the one.

"Let's do it again and tape it this time. Get it right

and you're done for the night. We can remix after you're gone."

He knew his tone was clipped, cold, distant. But that's what it had to be. The way he needed it to stay. Or he'd lose more than just the chance to work with this new talent—he'd lose himself.

Chapter 5

"Okay, tell me what's going on?" Jason asked Akil the moment they were alone in the sound booth. Seth and Five were working on remixing the track they'd just finished with Charlene in the live room and Serene had gone home for the day. Serene made some remark about getting Carlo here as soon as possible and Akil had made sure to correct her, just as he had last night.

"No dieting. I want what she's already got spruced up, build her image from there. Got it?"

No, Serene didn't get it and neither did he, that's why Jason was questioning his partner and longtime friend now.

"What? We're making this CD. What do you think is going on?"

"I think you've got something else on your mind than this music, something that might interfere with us getting this CD done."

"C'mon, Jason. You know me better than that. Nothing interferes with my music."

Jason folded his arms over his chest and leaned against the wall. "Tell me what you have in mind for her."

Akil didn't answer as quickly as he normally would have. Another fact that concerned Jason.

"Like I said last night, I think we should go old-school with her. Back to the roots of R&B and steer clear of the commercial BS."

Jason nodded. "The commercial BS is what's made us rich over the last ten years."

"I don't deny that."

"It's built our reputation, made this label a number-one contender with anything Sony, Arista, Columbia or the rest of them have. We're the hottest thing in the game right now. Why would you want to mess with that?"

Akil sighed, sat back in his chair and glared at Jason. "Because I'm tired of it. I'm tired of putting out average CDs and calling it music. Tired of the gimmicky groups and half-assed singers we reform and glamorize then slap a label on them and put them on the shelves. I want to make real music, to listen to the real sound of R&B again. Can you relate to that?"

Jason had to pause a moment at the words and the amount of money they stood to lose if this didn't work. "You're serious?"

"As a heart attack after years of fast-food burgers." He ran a hand over his face. "I think Charlene's got real talent, Jase. I think she has longevity to make it in this business. But I also think that Playascape needs something fresh, something different. I don't want us to be typecast, putting out the same product year after year. I want us to grow."

Jason nodded. "I see what you're saying. And I hear you about Charlene, she's not like the others we've worked with. But you know Empire's got a lot of money invested in this. I don't know that going against the grain right at this moment is financially feasible for us."

"It is," Akil said adamantly. "Empire's been distributing us for years. They know we're perfectionists and that we bring the money to the table when it counts. They trust us. The question is, do you trust me?"

It was a moment of truth, one of those times when friendship had to be the glue to hold things together. Jason had doubts but they were minimal compared to all the times Akil had come through. Just like he'd trusted his gut when he first heard Charlene sing and rushed to get her signed, he trusted that Akil's vision was going to work. That they were going to make Charlene a success, a different kind of success.

"Yeah, man. You know I trust you," Jason said finally, reaching out to shake Akil's hand.

Akil stood, shaking Jason's hand then pulling him in for a hug. "It's going to be big. The biggest thing we've ever done, Jase. Watch and see."

He picked up the phone again. Alone in his bedroom in the wee hours of the morning, Akil knew he should be asleep, gearing up for tomorrow's session. But he couldn't rest.

Charlene's powerful voice had brought back memories. Some painful and some happy—some that just need to be addressed once and for all.

Dialing the number, he sat back on his bed, leaning forward so that his elbows rested against his knees. Looking down to the floor as he held the phone to his ear waiting for the call to connect, he wiggled his toes in the ultra-soft dark blue carpet. It lined the entire length of his master suite until it opened up to the deck, which was tiled with black marble speckled with a blue similar to the carpet. His walls were painted a subtle gray, his furniture, sparse, sleek and expensive. The entertainment center that spanned the entire left wall was state-of-the-art with Dolby sound and a sixty-inch mounted plasma. Music was his life and so it surrounded him wherever he went. Even in his bathroom there was a sound system, designed to match the black-and-blue color scheme in there, as well.

He'd arrived, he thought as the overseas connection had finally been made and the line rang in his ear. He'd arrived at rich and famous, just as he'd always planned. And he liked it here, or so he thought.

His childhood hadn't been easy and neither had hers. But he'd made them both a promise, to get them out and to make them both happy. He succeeded in one area and drastically failed in the other.

She hated him, had told him as much more times than he could count. Yet, he still loved her, still held a place for her in his heart.

Charlene reminded him of that place. She reminded him of Lauren.

"Centro di riabilitazione del Seminary di buona mattina," a female voice answered, speaking quick Italian that Akil struggled to understand.

"Ah, *buona mattina*," he said, clearing his throat and sitting up straight as if the person on the other end of the phone could see him. "Lauren Jackson, please?"

He hated that name, hated the way it rolled off his tongue with complete bitterness and contempt.

"Chi è questo?"

"Akil Hutton."

The line went quiet and he waited, heart pounding against his chest, palms sweating. He hadn't spoken to her in more than three years. Not necessarily all his fault. He'd written to her a couple of times but had only recently found a number where she could be reached.

"Ms. Jackson non è disponibile. Non denomini ancora," she said and hung up without another word.

From traveling all over the world on business Akil had picked up a basic understanding of most languages like Italian, French, hell, he even knew a little German because one of his artists was a big hit in Germany. From the woman's clipped words he gathered two things: (1) that Lauren was definitely a patient at the Seminary Rehabilitation Hospital and (2) that she did not want to speak to him. The words not available and the stern do not call again sort of tipped him off.

Lauren was in Milan and she was in a rehab center. That meant she was safe and she was getting the help she so desperately needed. That should have been enough for him.

And he shouldn't still be plagued with guilt. Yet he was and there was nothing he could do about it.

Chapter 6

"So how's it going?" Rachel asked the moment Charlene answered her cell phone at a little after ten the next morning.

"It's going," she replied, falling back onto the bed. She'd already showered and was dressed. They were starting at ten-thirty this morning and every other morning unless Akil said otherwise, that's what Jason had told her yesterday. She'd had another restless night, unable to get the contrary man and his beguiling eyes out of her mind. But with the rising of the sun she'd tried to shield herself from that negativity, embracing the new day ahead. Hopefully it would work.

"Uh-oh, that doesn't sound good."

Rachel knew her too well, just as well as Candis did, and that was too well for both of them, Charlene thought suddenly.

"What's going on? You don't like the songs? You know, if you call Sofia she can pull some strings, maybe get you another producer or something."

"No, it's not that. I just mean that we got right down to business. Akil's every bit as focused as we'd heard. I got a firsthand look at how much of a perfectionist he really is."

"Again, that doesn't sound good. You don't like him?"

Afraid that the answer to that question was the real problem, Charlene closed her eyes and took a deep breath. "I didn't say that. He's just different."

"Okay," Rachel said, exaggerating the word. "So he's different from all the other superproducers who wanted to work with you on your debut CD?"

"No. I didn't say it like that. You know I'm grateful for this opportunity. Hell, I wouldn't even be in this position without your pushing me up onto that stage."

Rachel chuckled. "Now why doesn't that sound grateful to me?"

"I am grateful, really. Jeez, you and Candis are really ganging up on me this week."

"You talked to Candis? Where is she this week?"

"Paris."

"Lucky girl."

"You're sort of lucky yourself with that hunky actor you've got feelin' you," Charlene countered.

"I so do not want to talk about Ethan right now. This call is about you and how you're making out. I think I might need to fly out there."

Charlene was shaking her head as she sat straight up on the bed. She knew that Rachel was in Hollywood on the set of *Paging the Doctor,* where she was makeup artist and wardrobe designer. The show was in its final weeks of taping for the season but Rachel had already taken a two-week hiatus when the story of her affair with Ethan Chambers had hit the press. She was almost positive her friend couldn't just hop on a plane and come to Miami. But that wasn't saying much. When

Rachel put her mind to doing something there was usually no stopping her.

"You definitely do not need to do that. I'm fine. The situation is fine. I don't need you or Sofia getting involved."

"Good, because Sofia's got enough on her plate. I swear, if that girl doesn't slow down and start to enjoy life I don't know what's going to happen to her."

Sofia was Rachel's older sister and Charlene's agent. She'd known Sofia for as long as she'd known Rachel, but since Sofia was older by nine years they'd rarely hung out together. But the moment Rachel heard of Jason's interest she'd volunteered Sofia as her agent. Sofia hadn't minded at all; she loved her job as an entertainment agent and was waiting for the day she could take full charge of Limelight Entertainment. At the moment she was second in charge to Jacob Wellesley, the uncle who had raised her and Sofia after their parents' untimely deaths.

"She's still working twenty-five hours a day, eight days a week." That was a joke between her and Rachel. Sofia worked so much they'd started to believe that there were extra hours and days created just for her hectic schedule.

"Is she? I'm almost ready to run in that house and tie her to the bed for a full month."

They both chuckled but Charlene could hear the concern in Rachel's voice. She knew her friend was really worried about her sister. For that matter, so was she. Besides being her agent, Sofia was just like family to Charlene. "Let's pray she comes to her senses soon. I definitely don't want to see you and her going at it as you try to tie her down."

"You know you're coming along for backup so don't even try to get out of it."

Again Charlene found herself laughing, which was a good thing. She needed to be in as positive a mood as possible to deal with Akil today. Oh, dang it, Akil!

"Girl, I am so late. I've gotta get going. Akil's going to have a fit."

"Damn, he's clocking you?"

"Not like that. You know this is a job. I was supposed to be in the studio at ten-thirty. Talking to you, it's now ten minutes to eleven."

Rachel was laughing. "Okay, go on. But I really don't think he's going to dock your pay."

"It's about professionalism, Rachel."

"Girl, you don't have to tell me. You know I live by those same rules. Tell Akil it was my fault and apologize profusely on my behalf. If that doesn't work then maybe I really will have to fly out there."

"No, you stay right where you are. I'll handle Mr. Akil just fine on my own."

Clicking off the call and tossing the phone on the bed, Charlene made a hasty retreat out of the room hoping she really could handle Akil, the superproducer with his manic mood swings, on her own.

"Do you need a personal wake-up call, Ms. Quinn?" was the first thing Akil said to her.

A hot retort simmered at the back of her throat just itching to be released. However, she *was* late. And she'd anticipated his reaction all the way down the steps and the long foyer that took her to the west end of the house where the studio was located. He had reason to be angry, she knew, so she'd suck up her own attitude at his tart words and take it. "I apologize. I was on a call and—"

He held up a hand to halt her words. "You will learn in this industry that time is money. And it's usually somebody else's money. So make this the last late appearance and we'll remain on a good note."

What? Had they ever been on a good note?

Charlene only shook her head, bypassed the live room and headed straight for the isolation booth. She wasn't sure what song they were working on this morning but it didn't matter, she'd read over the song sheets so many times she probably knew all of them by heart. Stepping inside the booth, she noted she was alone today. The music tracks had apparently already been laid for whatever they were working on.

"Since you were wasting your voice talking on the phone, let's go through some warm-ups," Akil said through the speakers in the room.

Casting a quick glance toward the live room, she tried not to frown or show that he was getting on her nerves. A fact that only aggravated the new conflict roiling through her. Despite all his negative traits she thought Akil Hutton was attractive. There, she'd admitted it to herself finally. Even now she found herself honing in on the dark tint of his skin, the rich brown color of his eyes. Eyes that held her captive each time she dared look at them.

"You do know about vocal exercises, I presume."

She did. She taught them to her students every day. Taking a deep breath, she vowed to bite her traitorous tongue and squelch what she hoped was a minor attraction—or temporary bout of insanity.

She simply nodded in his direction, attempted a stiff

smile, then straightened her posture. Steady and sure of herself, she began to breathe. Slowly she inhaled and exhaled using her diaphragm, making sure she wasn't forcing any air. This was a common error with novice singers, forcing their voice by breathing incorrectly. An experienced singer did not need to force their voice to produce a good strong sound; that caused too much pressure against the cords and could damage the voice permanently.

She was in full work mood and nothing, not even the fine temperamental producer, was going to stop her.

She is perfect, Akil thought with alarm.

A perfectly trained singer, he amended but still didn't feel that was quite adequate.

Even now as he watched her he felt there was something else—something more to her that seemed to touch him. That touch was both alarming and unwanted, new and familiar in a way that again scared him. Akil wasn't afraid of anything. He'd grown up on the drug-infested streets of east Baltimore and didn't flinch at the sight or thought of death. How could he when it was an everyday possibility where he'd lived? Those streets had made him the man he was today—the one who wasn't afraid to take risks, to reach for what he wanted then hold on tight when he got it. Nothing tripped him up, nothing made him think twice about his goals, his aspirations. For as long as he could remember it had been that way, for better or for worse.

Until now.

Until Charlene.

He had realized that the moment she began to sing yesterday. She'd rehearsed the song, that was the first thing that surprised him. For a woman who had buried herself in a school, surrounded herself with aspiring singers but hadn't chased the dream for herself, she was surprisingly professional and on cue.

She'd known the exact pitches to hit, even though this was her first time singing the song with music. Normally he had to rehearse a song with an artist for at least a day before they could begin recording anything, but at midnight last night he and Jason were remixing her voice over the music, blending the two together until they almost had a perfect recording.

Her talent was amazing and Akil wished his attraction to her stopped there.

Unfortunately for him, the rest of Charlene Quinn was even harder to resist. From her infectious smile that reminded him of the few happier moments in his life to the fire he saw in her eyes when she sang, she was gorgeous. And while she seemed completely oblivious to it, she was sexy as hell. Take right now, for instance; here they were in the studio supposedly working. He'd given her the simple task of vocal warm-ups. He'd assumed this would be painless; of course a vocal teacher could do vocal warm-ups. He'd really just wanted to get her reaction to the order. Wanted to see if she would tell him she didn't need to warm up, that she knew what she was doing. Instead she'd just done what he'd asked and now he was paying the price.

His gaze was locked on her lips as she sang the scale up and then back down again.

Her voice rose when needed, dipped when expected, flawlessly working the scale in a way he'd rarely seen or heard done.

Her lips were a little shiny, both from the gloss he

noted she'd worn when she came in and from the water she'd sipped just before starting the warm-ups. They looked soft and warm and he couldn't help but wonder how they'd taste.

At her waist her arms lifted until one hand centered on her belly. Her back was straight and he watched the rise and fall of her breasts as she sang. Voluptuous wasn't exactly the right word for Charlene's body— mouthwatering described it much better in his mind. Her jeans were fitting thighs he'd watched for the last two days and imagined were as soft as her mouth. The shirt she wore today wasn't formfitting—a fact he had noted with most of her clothes—yet the soft fabric draped over the curve of her breasts in a way that had him growing hard the moment she had entered the studio. That was most likely the reason he'd snapped at her.

Maybe if this were a different time or if he were at a different place in his life, wanting her physically wouldn't bother him so much. But he wasn't. Lately, memories had been haunting him, a sense of dread that he hadn't felt since he was a teenager looking over his shoulder on the dark city streets crept down his spine. Something was about to happen, he just had no idea what.

Ms. Charlene Quinn might be that something.

Chapter 7

Twelve hours. That's how long they'd been in the studio. Today's session moved a lot more slowly than yesterday's. Charlene attributed that to the surly attitude of her star producer.

On the one hand, she couldn't dismiss Akil's talent or his keen sense of knowing what worked and what didn't. On the other, his personality sucked!

All day she'd been singing, taking his direction and starting over and over again. This song, "Break You Down," had a dance rhythm, it was fast and sexy and hip. There was even a rap part that Jason said they were trying to get Young Jeezy, Drake or Ludacris to do. Her personal preference would have been Ludacris but from the way Akil looked at Jason when he'd told her this, she figured she'd best keep that opinion to herself.

Now it was just past midnight, she was tired and hungry and cranky.

"Okay, let's try this—" Akil began saying.

But Jason, who had just come into the isolation booth with her to see how she was doing, pushed the intercom button and interrupted him.

"I think it's a wrap for today, Akil. She needs to get some rest."

Akil's frown was instant, his dark gaze seeking hers. And her eyes found his just like she knew they would. It was as if she knew the exact moment he was going to look at her, like they were drawn together like magnets. It was eerie and stirring all at the same time.

She didn't open her mouth although she desperately wanted to agree with Jason. Instead she waited for Akil's response. But he didn't say a thing, only continued to stare at her as if she were the only person in the room.

"Fine," was his tight reply.

She released the breath she hadn't been aware she was holding the moment he looked away from her.

"Listen, I'm sorry about that. I don't know what's going on with him. He's usually not this bad."

Charlene had already slipped off the stool she'd been sitting on and stretched. "You mean he's not always a mean SOB?"

Jason chuckled. "Yeah, that's exactly what I mean. He's a perfectionist and he gets the job done. I just don't know what's up with the attitude lately."

She nodded. "Maybe it's just me," she said, absently moving toward the door to let them both out.

"You know, I think you're right."

Stopping abruptly at his words, she turned to face him and asked, "Really? You think I did something to piss him off?"

"Oh, no," he replied quickly. "Nothing like that. You're doing a great job. I mean, I've worked with a lot of singers and you've got them beat by a long shot. Don't worry about it," he said, putting an arm around her and walking toward the main door of the studio.

"Okay, well, I'm off to bed. I'll see you two in the

morning," she said, deciding quickly that Akil Hutton's bad attitude was taking too much of her energy for one day. But just as she was nearing the door, now a few feet away from Jason, Akil stepped out of the live room.

"You know this is serious business, Charlene. If you can't hang, just let me know."

The professional in her said to smile, say good-night and keep going, but the other part of her, the one that lived by the motto I Am Woman, Hear Me Roar, spun around so quickly she could have snapped her neck.

"I understand this is serious business, Mr. Hutton. I'm doing my job. If you have a problem with it, just let me know."

Folding his arms over his chest only made him look angrier—not intimidating the way she figured he'd meant.

"My problem is with your carefree attitude. Despite the impression others may have given," he said, cutting an evil eye at Jason, "we don't play all day. This is about working hard to achieve a finished product we're all happy with. A CD that will sell. A product we can market."

Her hand was sliding to her hip before she could stop it and she'd taken a step closer to Akil. "And you don't think I want the same thing?"

"I don't think you know how serious this all is."

"I flew down here, didn't I? I studied the songs like you told me. I sang for eleven hours yesterday and almost twelve and a half today. I did the warm-ups you requested although you and I both know it was unnecessary. I've adhered to all the changes you've made in the song when again, we both know, they weren't necessary. What else would you have me do to show I'm serious about this business, as you call it? Jump through hoops singing nursery rhymes backward?"

Jason stuffed his hands into his pockets, looking like he didn't know what to say to either of them. And Akil just stood there. Not saying anything and not budging.

"Good night, Charlene," was all he finally managed.

Biting back the rest of what she wanted to say to him she looked directly at Jason. "Good night, Jason."

He was an idiot.

Ten times an idiot, he'd told himself with each step he took upstairs.

"You're trippin'," was all Jason had said to him the moment Charlene left them alone. Akil had to admit his longtime friend was absolutely right.

He was trippin'. Over the fact that Charlene reminded him of Lauren and over the fact that he was attracted to her. This was not how he usually handled women and it was certainly not how he handled clients. What the hell was wrong with him?

Akil didn't have a clear answer to that question, but had decided to put an end to at least one of his mistakes. He'd been wrong to treat Charlene the way he did and Akil always admitted when he was wrong.

Just apologize and say good-night, he told himself when he finally stood in front of her door. *Tomorrow's a fresh start,* he recited in his mind while lifting a hand and knocking softly.

It seemed like an eternity standing there in the hallway, his fingers clenching and unclenching at his sides. He was about to give up, figuring she was already asleep and turning to leave, when she opened the door.

"Akil?" Even the sound of his name in her voice was

alluring. He was so busted. "Did you have something else to say to me?" she asked in a frostier tone.

He deserved it.

"Yes, I did." Taking a deep breath, he looked right into her eyes. No, more like fell into the complete compassion and honesty he saw there. Damn, could he feel like more of a fool?

"Look, I apologize for acting like an ass today."

She raised one of those thick, arched eyebrows and he sighed.

"Okay, I apologize for acting like an ass since you've arrived. I've been rude and harsh and it was totally uncalled for."

She nodded her head slowly and his gaze slipped from her eyes to what she was wearing.

"I accept your apology," she said, taking a step back like she was retreating into the room to leave him standing out there.

But that was a no-no.

In the time it had taken him to curse himself, shut down the studio and walk upstairs, she'd changed from the jeans and shirt she was wearing to a floor-length nightgown. It shouldn't have been sexy because it showed nothing but her bare arms. Every other inch of her was covered all the way up to the shoelace-type tie at the base of her neck. Whatever, it made her butter-toned skin appear even more radiant, her eyes just a tad exotic.

He felt himself stiffen as his eyes raked over her, up and down and down and up. The moment she moved he reached for her, grabbed her by the elbow and took a step closer so that they were face-to-face.

She opened her mouth to speak and he knew there

would be an argument. She'd tell him to get off of her and he'd refuse, it would go nowhere. So instead he simply lowered his head, let his lips touch hers lightly and shivered at the connection.

Releasing her arm and pretty certain that she wasn't going to run, Akil lifted both hands and cupped her perfect face, tilting her mouth so that it was easier for his taking. He'd meant to move slow, to sort of sip on her sweetness, but the moment his tongue touched hers, slow and sweet withered away.

Instead the kiss turned into a firestorm, bolts of lightning probably fizzled above them as he moved closer, sank deeper into her taste. Somewhere in the distance he thought he heard her moan, then her palms flattened on his chest. Something feral and distinct rose in his chest and he took more and more.

She sighed. Or was it him?

Her hands slipped downward, wrapped around his waist.

He moaned, but then again, it could have been her.

His thumbs brushed over her cheekbones as his teeth bit lightly on her bottom lip.

"Damn."

Somebody said it, he just didn't know who.

Her tongue traced his top lip and he shook, right down to his toes, his entire body vibrated. He took her lower lip, suckled for a moment before diving back into the warmth of her mouth. It was fevered and hurried, urgent and dire. He wanted so much more, needed this to last just a little bit longer.

At the same time warning bells echoed in his head, chiming and all but chanting for him to stop, to take this slow, to be sure. He pulled back, tore his lips from hers, but couldn't bear to stop touching her. Breathing like he'd just run a marathon, he rested his forehead on hers, felt her trying to steady herself, as well.

"I didn't do that because I like you," he said gruffly, his hand still cupping her face.

"Then you must lie as good as you produce music," she replied, pulling out of his embrace, stepping back into her room and closing the door quietly.

Chapter 8

Akil Hutton liked her.

The superproducer with the volatile dark brown eyes, multimillion-dollar bank account and cranky attitude liked her. The not-so-skinny woman who loved to sing but didn't want the spotlight.

Rolling over in the king-size bed with mauve satin sheets in a room she'd only been in for three days but already felt comfortable in, Charlene smothered a smile with the back of her hand.

He'd come to apologize and she'd accepted. She hadn't a moment to digest that little bit of information before he was in her face, touching her arm, his lips moving against hers.

It had been strange to kiss him. To kiss Akil.

She'd kissed men before, no way was she inexperienced in that area. She'd kissed men and had sex. Yet the three experiences she'd had were just a reaction to the attraction of male and female.

Clutching a pillow in her arms, she relaxed to the notion that she was attracted to Akil. Hadn't she already accepted that fact yesterday? Yeah, but that was before he'd been, in his own words, "an ass" after their recording session.

And before he'd kissed her.

As she lifted a hand back to her mouth, one finger slid slowly over lips that still tingled from his touch. Hours later it felt like he'd just pulled away, just stopped giving her the best kiss she'd ever had.

Then he'd pulled away and said something else stupid. She'd swear that man invented the concept of not knowing what to say out of his mouth. Sitting up in the bed abruptly, she craned her neck to look at the clock on the nightstand. The last thing she wanted was to be late for another session. Only Akil hadn't said what time today's session was going to start. *Forget it,* she thought, moving her legs and letting her feet hit the floor. She'd be early if that were the case.

Twenty minutes later, after her shower and slipping into a turquoise-and-white sundress that hugged her breasts, tied around the neck and hung loose to her ankles, she moved to the closet and surveyed herself in the floor-length mirror. She loved this dress because besides the curve of her breasts that were lifted high in her super-supportive bustier, no other aspect of her figure was decipherable. She'd fussed for a few minutes with her hair, adding some curl to the normally plain ponytail she wore.

Not because of Akil's kiss, but because the dress made her feel more feminine than jeans and a shirt. She figured her hairstyle should support that feeling. When she was satisfied with her overall look she picked up her music from the table right by the door, reached for the knob and pulled it open.

"Good morning," Akil said, an unfamiliar, yet sexy, smile pulling at his lips.

Her heart leaped; the hand that was on the doorknob

quickly went to her chest as if that action would stop the now-rapid beating. "Mornin'," she finally managed. "What are you doing here?"

In addition to the uncustomary smile he was wearing, his light blue jeans and royal blue sneakers that matched the royal blue T-shirt he wore were casual and unlike anything she'd seen him wear thus far. He looked different, relaxed, and she was trying to figure out why.

"Truce," he said, pulling a hand from behind his back and offering her one long-stemmed pink rose.

Her smile was instant and probably as big as the proverbial Cheshire Cat's, but she couldn't tone it down. Not while reaching for the perfectly simple, perfectly beautiful rose.

"I was just coming to meet you in the studio." As soon as the words were out she figured they weren't what he'd probably expected to hear. "I mean, thanks. I hope I'm not late for the session again."

All of a sudden she felt shy and more than a little nervous. What happened to the woman who was so sure he liked her and was just a bit proud of that fact? She'd apparently stayed somewhere in that bed, probably hiding under the sheets. Because right now she was plagued once again with the question, why?

Akil shook his head. "Nah. I figured we'd start a little later today. Give us time to get a good breakfast first. Join me?"

His extended hand stood between them and looked a little out of place since before last night he'd never touched her and she hadn't thought of touching him. Those butterflies were back, performing a whole choreographed number probably for the benefit of telling her to take his hand and go.

With a mental shrug she dropped the music she'd held in one hand onto the table by the door. Taking his hand, she put the rose to her nose and inhaled. "Breakfast sounds good."

The terrace was located on the south side of the house, so in the morning it received lots of sun. One long glass-topped table with white, high-backed chairs was shaded by the deck covering above. Still, the light morning breeze trickled inside, lifting the tips of her hair just slightly.

Akil wasn't surprised. He'd been noticing little things like that about Charlene since he'd first seen her photo. All those little things were adding up to something, he knew. Last night after she'd closed the door in his face, again, he'd felt even more disturbed. What was it about her that had him acting like a confused teenager?

Bottom line, they had two things going on here— his budding attraction to her and this CD. There needed to be boundaries so things wouldn't get out of control.

She was sitting across from him, had set the rose he gave her right beside her place setting. She kept looking at it, like it meant a lot to her. Actually, it had been an afterthought for him to bring it to her. Mrs. Williamson, for some reason, loved to have fresh flowers around the house. It didn't bother him and he was used to seeing or smelling them all around whenever he was here.

"About the last few days," he started, never being one to beat around the bush. "Again, I want to apologize. I'm not usually that hard to work with."

"Should I consider myself special?" she asked with that smile that had warmth beginning to spread from somewhere in the southerly region of his body.

"Let's just say I needed to get a handle on a few things." She looked away from him and he wondered if once again he'd said the wrong thing. "That doesn't make you any less special. It's just that the problem was mine, not yours."

She shrugged. "So you've fixed the problem?"

Mrs. Williamson, with the young housekeeper, Nannette, following behind her with a big pitcher of orange juice, approached the table.

"Good morning. Breakfast will be served in a few minutes," she said, moving her sixty-four-year-old body as if she weren't a day over twenty-one. She was a tall woman with a thick build and a scowl that could burn a hole right through you. Delores Williamson also possessed a laugh that could touch the deepest recesses of a person's heart and the compassion to save the world if she could. She was a great woman, a great find on Akil's part. He loved her like a mother and she treated him like a son.

"Thank you," Charlene murmured as Mrs. Williamson placed a glass in front of her and Nannette quickly filled it with orange juice. She smiled at them both then lifted the glass to her mouth for a sip.

Akil nodded his head and waited until they were once again alone. "I've come to grips with a few things that were bothering me." He picked up the conversation where he'd left off.

"Oh, the fact that you didn't want to like me, for instance?"

She was smart and to the point. He liked that about her.

"I never said I didn't want to like you."

"No. You just said you didn't like me." Her head

tilted a bit to the side and her eyes squinted. He couldn't tell if it was because she was studying him so hard or that the sun was getting in her eyes.

"But do you normally kiss women you don't like?" she asked.

He'd known he wasn't going to be able to avoid that question or what he'd done last night. And for the record he hadn't regretted the kiss. In fact, it had played an intricate part in the sultry dreams he'd had about her throughout the night. The ones he wasn't about to mention to her.

Clearing his throat, he replied, "I don't normally kiss women that I don't like. And I never kiss singers that I'm working with."

"Oh." She sat back in her chair as if the picture was just now clearing for her. "So, clarify something for me. Are you upset that you're attracted to someone like me or because you're attracted to a singer?"

Saying she'd hit the nail right on the head would be a cliché, but no less true. "Can I first get a clarification for the statement 'someone like me'?"

"You know, a big-boned woman. Even though I really hate that saying. Bones have nothing to do with your weight. Anyway, is that why you're upset?"

Her statement left him incredulous. He hadn't figured her for a woman with self-esteem issues surrounding her weight. Although he could see where they stemmed from. She'd grown up in L.A., where gorgeous, thin bodies seemed to fall from the sky. A woman who was outside those parameters was not the norm. Plus her own sister was a model. Yet, here on the East Coast, especially in the South, women with a little meat on their bones was the preference. Or was that a cultural thing? Did only black men appreciate a shapely woman? Maybe? Probably? But right at this moment he wasn't concerned about the generalities. He was more concerned with her and squashing any misconceptions she might be having.

"First, let me start by saying I'm a thigh man. Silicone breasts and twenty-inch waists aren't my style. So the answer is no, your physique has nothing to do with my sour attitude."

She looked as if she'd released a held breath and he was surprised to realize that's exactly what she'd assumed. He wondered if some other jackass man had made comments about her weight.

"Then it must be my singing. You don't think I can do this CD? I'm not what you want on your label? If that's the case then I don't see why you'd bring me all the way out here. I mean, if you want someone else I can easily go back to L.A., to my teaching job."

She was talking faster, pushing her chair back and standing, about to leave.

"Hold on," he said quickly, getting up himself and coming around the table to grab her arm. "Wait a second, that's not what I was thinking at all. I love your voice."

That stopped her cold and she looked up at him. "You do?"

He nodded. "Your voice is perfect. Especially for this project. I wasn't so sure at first, but that was my being shortsighted for thinking about the commercialism and the bottom lines instead of focusing on the music the way I should have."

She was shaking her head, trying to pull out of his grasp. "I don't understand."

He only moved his hands to her shoulders, holding her still and close. "When the execs at Empire called me to talk about you and what they envisioned it didn't match with what I saw in the pictures or heard on the demo. Jason was so excited after he'd heard you at the karaoke bar, he'd only told me that we'd hit it big scooping you up before any other companies could hear you. So I went into this project with one thought. Then I saw you and you were different. I didn't know how to handle it."

"And now?"

"Now I've got my focus back. I know what I want."

And Lordamercy, so did she.

She wanted Akil to kiss her again.

Instead he guided her back to her chair, where she sat and tried to rein in her tumultuous hormones. She'd brought up the kiss and he'd neatly waltzed around that conversation. Instead he'd focused on explaining why he'd been so nasty to her the last few days. And while she understood what he'd said she still felt he could have handled it differently. At any rate, she was cool with letting bygones be just that.

By the time Akil had returned to his side of the table and taken his seat, Mrs. Williamson and Nannette were back with trays of food. When they were finished, after two trips to the kitchen and back, it looked like a buffet for about fifteen people.

"Does she always cook this much?" Charlene whispered to Akil when Mrs. Williamson was gone.

He grinned. "She's got it in her head that I don't eat enough while I'm away. So when I'm home she cooks enough to feed an NFL team."

Charlene nodded her agreement. "I see."

"Well, shall we?"

"Ah, just a sec," she said then bowed her head, about to bless her food.

"My mother used to do that," he said sort of absently.

Charlene paused and looked back up at him. "What? Say grace before she ate?"

"Yes."

"And you don't?"

He shrugged and looked sort of embarrassed, then said, "Not usually."

"Well, you should always give thanks for what you have. Others aren't as fortunate." When she was about to lower her head again she saw that he looked a little perplexed. So she extended her arm across the table, wiggling her fingers to signal that she wanted his hand. He gave it to her and their fingers entwined.

"Now bow your head and close your eyes."

"I know that part, Charlene."

"Oh, okay. Lord, we humbly thank You for this food that You have given. We thank and bless the hands that have prepared this meal and pray Your strength for those less fortunate. Amen."

"Amen," he said quietly, looking at her with that same puzzled expression.

"Why are you looking at me like that?"

He shook his head, then turned his attention to the fork next to the platter of bacon. "Nothing. I mean, you're just different, like I said before."

Charlene filled her plate with fluffy scrambled eggs, a few slices of melon and two spoonfuls of grits. "You make different sound bad. My mother used to do that."

His plate was overflowing by this time with eggs,

French toast, bacon, sausage and a biscuit that he was now slathering with grape jelly.

"Not bad. Just different." He shrugged. "So, I take it you and your mother aren't close."

She finished chewing the bite of eggs she'd taken. "Quite the contrary, my family's pretty tight. We just don't agree all the time."

"Most people don't, family or not."

"I guess you're right. She just wanted something different for me."

"Different from teaching?"

"Yes. She wanted me to model like my older sister or get into acting since my dad was a movie and television producer."

"But you preferred singing."

"I preferred being out of the spotlight. Doing what I love in a place that's comfortable to me."

He stopped chewing and stared at her. "So this making a CD isn't what you want to do?"

"Oh, no. It is. I just never told anybody that it was a goal. I think I was afraid of the rejection or something." She stared down at her plate, kept on eating because she knew he was looking at her and it was making her nervous.

"So, you've been hiding?"

"So to speak."

"What made you come out of hiding?"

"My best friend was feeling down. I wanted to cheer her up."

"And you got a record deal out of it. How'd your best friend fare?"

The thought alone made Charlene smile. "She's getting married next month to a man she thought wasn't her type but ended up being the love of her life."

"You think that's sweet, don't you?"

"Of course. Don't you? I mean, just because I've never personally experienced romance and falling in love doesn't mean I don't believe in it and can't rejoice when someone else finds it."

She'd said a mouthful, giving him more information than he'd asked. But he was glad. Now he knew what she needed. Only problem was, he wasn't sure he was the one who should be giving it to her.

"You've never been in love?"

"Nope." She licked her lips after taking a sip of juice and Akil felt his groin tighten.

"Never been romanced?"

"Let's see," she said, holding a forkful of melon midway to her mouth. "I've been taken to dinner, which we both paid for. Taken to a family cookout, where I was asked to cook and help clean up. Oh, and this was the best one, I've been asked to wear dark glasses and a trench coat when coming to visit at his apartment."

"What? Don't tell me you did that." Anger bubbled low in his gut at the mere thought of some dude asking her to camouflage herself to come and see him.

She hurried to finish chewing. "Of course not. I knew he wasn't worth my time when I noticed he had two cell phones. The only people who should have two phones on their hips are doctors or drug dealers. And there was no M.D. after his name."

Akil's entire body tensed at her words but he hoped she didn't see. "Good. You were too good for him anyway," he said in what he hoped was a steady voice.

For a minute she looked as if she wasn't going to say

anything else, as if she was almost hating what she'd admitted to him so far. That could be true since it was his perception that Charlene Quinn was very guarded about her personal life. Still, she took a deep breath and continued. It was that strength in her that he was beginning to admire immensely.

"I was too big for him is what I really think. But I'll settle for your opinion, too."

She smiled and he'd swear that action actually touched his heart. He liked talking to her, liked sitting here like this having a meal with her. He'd never shared a meal with a female in his home. Ever.

"Does it bother you? Your size, I mean."

She put her fork down and stared at him seriously. "I guess. Sometimes. Not all the time. Does it bother you?"

"No," he answered quickly.

She smiled. "Good."

"Real good," he said, lifting her hand from the table and kissing the back of it.

So, she'd never had romance, always had cornball dudes in her life. Akil decided he would fix that because she deserved it. And he wanted to be the one to give it to her.

Chapter 9

Charlene had no clue whose idea it was to have a barbecue. But on a Thursday afternoon, two weeks after the first day she'd stepped into Akil's house, once they'd finished recording for the day, they'd all headed out to the pool. She was shocked to see that the area had been transformed into what looked like an outside club.

Mrs. Williamson and the crew must have worked all day getting this set up. The thing that really shocked her was that it was a little after nine in the evening, past time for a barbecue to have started. Then again, since being in Miami and watching the way Akil worked, she was starting to think nothing was impossible.

He just had that type of presence. The one that said "I'm here now, the job can be done right." His household staff respected him and his studio staff were in awe of him. His directions were very rarely challenged—everyone just trusted what he did or said would produce a hit.

Today's session had gone fairly well. They now had four recorded tracks for the CD—three ballads and one dance tune. As for the dance tune that had the rap portion, Akil still hadn't decided which rapper would provide the flow.

Stepping out into the humid September night, Charlene saw a few celebrity faces that included some of Akil's top contenders for the spot.

Drake, who was steadily climbing the charts with his latest hit, "Successful," featuring Trey Songz, stood near one of the two lighted bars that had been set up. He was chatting it up with none other than another super-producer, Sean "Diddy" Combs, and a scantily dressed, half-shaved-headed Cassie, who looked as if she were bored already. Young Jeezy was also there, fresh off the release of the track he'd done with Rihanna. And one of her favorites, an old-school hip-hopper who had blazed her own trails in the late eighties and early nineties, MC Lyte was there looking as classy as ever.

So while the guest list made this look like a star-studded event, the atmosphere seemed laid-back and relaxed. Just a barbecue on a fall night in Miami.

"You planning on hiding out here all night?" Jason asked, coming to stand beside her.

"No," she replied quickly. "I'm a little tired so I might just head up to bed."

But Jason was already shaking his head, grasping her hand and pulling her out of the little alcove she'd found near the entrance back into the house. "Oh, no, you don't. We're gonna kick back and relax tonight. We've been working hard, every day for two weeks now. We've earned this break."

"Yeah, but you know we still have an early session tomorrow. If I stay down here relaxing too long I'll be no good in the morning."

"Relax, Charlene. Akil wouldn't have okayed this get-together if he didn't think we all needed a break."

"Well, he's not even here," she commented, looking around and noticing that she had yet to see him out here.

"He'll be here, don't worry. Akil loves a barbecue and he loves to have company."

"He does?" She wondered at his words. "I wouldn't have guessed that."

"Akil's not the all-work-and-no-play guy you've seen so far. He can party with the best of us when he's not stressing about work. Which, unfortunately, is most of the time."

She had to chuckle at that. "Yeah, I'm definitely getting the all-work side." Except for the morning meals they'd been sharing. It was then, she thought, that she got a glimpse of the real Akil Hutton.

The Akil Hutton she was beginning to like beyond the walls of the recording studio.

He'd been watching her all night. As she smiled and shook hands, danced and laughed, he'd watched. Two hours after his little get-together had started Akil felt like a stalker standing to the side, watching Charlene as if he were obsessed.

Truth be told, he sort of was.

Not since that first day seeing her in the Empire offices had he been able to get her out of his mind. Her voice echoed in his head when he was alone, her scent hovered in his senses, keeping him awake when it was rest that he needed. This entire project had begun to revolve solely around her. He'd sent back two songs that didn't match the woman. In his eyes she was pure, radiant, terrific.

It was crazy, he knew. These feelings he had for her coming from out of nowhere. All these years he'd kept his heart under lock and key. And now, in the span of two weeks, he was afraid someone—Charlene Quinn—had effortlessly picked that lock.

But it wasn't leading anywhere, his feelings for her, his desire for her. It couldn't. Hadn't he just admitted her purity? Hadn't he seen from the very start that she was different than anyone he'd ever met? No way would she be able to live with his past, with the darkness that still haunted him on a daily basis.

Still, he couldn't stand there another minute and watch another man touch her. Jason had stuck close to her most of the night, introducing her around, convincing her to dance with him. Then Five had taken a turn, bringing her a drink, talking to her while Jason escaped for a while. That was what had really pissed Akil off. While he liked Five, they'd worked together on a lot of projects and he respected the man's talent, he knew he was a dog when it came to women. That was as nicely as Akil could put it.

He'd danced with Charlene, some rap song Akil couldn't even remember now. All he remembered were Charlene's movements. The gyration of her body as she felt the rhythm. The salacious smile on Five's face as he watched and danced up close on her. Only by great strength did he manage to keep from running across the yard and driving his fist into Five's jaw. He'd actually seen red, wanted to physically remove the man from his house, from Charlene's path.

It was insane. He knew it but couldn't control it.

That's what he was telling himself as he started toward her. He couldn't control this hunger he had for her any more than he could control the weathermen predicting they'd be hit sometime tomorrow by Hurricane

Viola. Couldn't control the urge to touch her, taste her, be with her. For as long as it could last.

"I need to speak to you alone," he heard himself saying as his fingers closed around her forearm.

She turned to him in shock, probably because he'd come from behind. Jason, Five, Jax and Steve—Akil's bodyguards—were sitting at the table with her talking. He'd had no clue what they were talking about, had only seen her once again surrounded by men tonight and had lost it.

He'd walked fast, wanting to get her alone as soon as humanly possible. That meant the pool house. Sure, it was kind of cheesy, sort of juvenile, especially when he had this huge house he could drag her into instead. But he didn't care and he couldn't wait. Pushing the door open, he pulled her inside. Then he slammed the door shut and backed her up against it.

She gasped, her lips falling open as she looked like she was about to say something. But his gaze had settled on her lips and heat soared through his body at a rapid pace that blurred his thinking. The next thing he knew his lips were on hers, his tongue plunging deep into her mouth.

Charlene was still reeling from the way Akil had grabbed her, all but pulling her up from her seat and dragging her across the lawn. She'd wanted to pull away, to scream at him that he was out of his mind, but something in his stance had stopped her. This wasn't the same Akil. It wasn't the man she'd watched discreetly throughout the evening, mingling with his guests, smiling here and there. It was the serious music expert she'd seen in the studio.

And more. When she'd looked up at him his eyes

had been different. Those eyes that had first drawn her attention that day in the Empire offices. They seemed darker, more intense, with an edginess that almost frightened her. Her heart had immediately beat faster. She probably should have pulled away from him. Hell, maybe she should have run from him. That's how freaked out the look in his eyes made her. But she didn't.

She let him pull her along, desperately wanting to know what was on his mind. What could have put that look in his eyes? It was probably more foolish than she cared to accept, but she couldn't turn away from him. Not now.

So they were going to the pool house. Maybe he wanted to talk.

No. She swallowed that thought the moment he pushed her back to the door and his lips crashed down on hers.

Like a firestorm, heat poured into her with his touch. She struggled to breathe but realized it wasn't worth it. This kiss was all-consuming. Akil was overwhelming. Their tongues dueled as if their very lives depended on this moment. His hands were everywhere, dragging past her breasts, touching her waist, sliding over her hips, reaching around and gripping her bottom. His fingers dug into her like he was fighting to hold on, to keep her in his grasp.

His teeth raked over her swollen lips, dragged a heated path down her neck where he bit none too gently. Her head fell back, banging lightly against the door. She inhaled and exhaled frantically, her own hands roaming from his taut shoulders down his muscled back. His touch was heated, the feel of his body beneath her fingertips electric. She whispered his name, over and over, because she was so full of him. No questions, no recriminations, just him.

He was moving downward, his tongue scraping along her chest, nipping at her nipples through her blouse. Her fingers clenched in the material of his shirt, trying to pull him back. She wanted his lips again, his tongue, everything.

But he had other ideas. Down farther, his face buried in her midsection. He mumbled something; it sounded like her name. His hands were still gripping her bottom, pulling and squeezing until heat waves floated to her center, the pulsating dampening her panties.

He moved farther down until he just passed the zipper of her slacks. He stopped there, extended his tongue and licked. His tongue moved over the linen material but she felt it as if it were her bare skin. Instinctively her legs parted.

He groaned again.

She sighed as he licked once more.

Her thighs were shaking now, her center lips throbbing incessantly. His face burrowed deeper between her legs and she thought he'd suffocate. But his breathing continued, just as ragged and frustratingly fast as her own. He continued licking as his fingers moved to the center of her bottom in a scintillating motion, up and down.

Her entire body trembled. "Akil," she cried raggedly.

She heard her voice, could barely recognize the wanton tone and was about to speak when she heard something.

It was music. No, more like a jingle. A cell phone jingle?

Akil cursed, letting his forehead rest on her thigh.

Yep, it was a cell phone jingle. It was Akil's phone ringing.

With another long string of curses, he stood up, reached in his back pocket and pulled the phone out. His eyes locked with hers and she saw his lips, too, were swollen. Lifting a finger, she touched his bottom lip and felt herself moving closer, wanting—no, needing—another taste.

She kissed his bottom lip gingerly, then licked its plump surface. He groaned and leaned in closer to her, pressing his obvious arousal into her.

And that damned jingle kept playing.

"Dammit!" Akil roared. He tore his mouth away from hers and looked down at the phone.

And just like that the heat that had engulfed them just seconds ago stalled. Replacing it was a frigid breeze that came the moment he stepped away from her.

He gave her his back, pressed Talk and said, "Hello?"

When he turned back around that look in his eyes had changed and Charlene felt ten times a fool. What the hell had she been thinking, letting him paw at her, kiss on her, arouse her the way he had?

He didn't say anything. He didn't have to. Their moment was over. Whoever that was on the other end of the phone had shattered it, effectively taking all his attention.

Well, the last thing she intended to do was beg. Instead she moved away from the door, giving him the out she knew he sought.

Seconds later he'd unlocked it, walked through it and left her.

Alone.
Aroused.
And pissed the hell off!

Chapter 10

"First." She started talking the moment she stepped onto the terrace. Akil was sitting in the seat at the head of the table. He'd long since stopped sitting across from her in the morning when they shared breakfast. He sat at the head and she sat right on the end beside him.

She'd enjoyed those breakfasts. After their rocky start, these last two weeks had brought new hope for her and Akil. He was no longer acting like a year-round Scrooge and had actually smiled a time or two when Jason and his interminable silliness got out of hand. Excitement about the project was steadily brewing, within her and the rest of the Playascape staff. She was beginning to believe it was really going to happen.

The memory of last night played brightly in her mind. She'd thought about it for hours while tossing and turning. Part of her wanted to be supremely pissed off at Akil. Another part was pissed off at herself for letting things go too far.

This morning she'd awakened determined to get some things off her chest.

"Let me just clear the air," she continued. "I am not now nor will I ever be an opportunist. I'm not a groupie or some right-here-right-now chick. I don't care what impression I may have given you last night but I don't jump into bed with just anybody, even if they're about to give my music career a head start. And I don't appreciate being toyed with as if I do."

He sat back in the chair, lifting both his hands as if to say he was calling a truce. "Charlene."

She shook her head, afraid that if she didn't get it all out at once she'd chicken out. "No." Cutting him off was rude but that was nothing in comparison to what he'd done to her last night. "I'm talking. I appreciate all you're doing for me career-wise. But everything else, if you're not serious in throwing your attention my way, then I'd prefer you back off altogether. I didn't come out here for these head games you insist on playing. Truth be told, I'm tired of them."

He stood and reached for her hand but she backed up.

"Don't touch me, Akil. I'm telling you that now is definitely not the time."

Dropping his hands to his sides, he sighed in frustration. "Fine. Then would you just sit down and listen to me for a moment? I totally respect what you've said, but I have something to say, too."

She thought about it a moment. She shouldn't. Her speech had been delivered, and very well if she could say so herself. Walking away from him now would prove her point. She was just about to go when she made a fatal mistake.

She looked into his eyes.

And everything she'd been thinking, feeling, fell to the side. He didn't look angry or intense. He looked confused, broken-down almost.

Now, that could be what she'd wanted to see but she wasn't willing to let it slide.

"Well, I do have to eat breakfast," she said finally and took her seat.

He sat down, too. The morning was a little overcast with huge gray clouds moving fiercely through the sky. It unnerved Charlene a bit since the local weather forecasters had been tracking Hurricane Viola's path through the Caribbean Islands.

"Worried about the storm?" he asked and she realized she must have been looking up at the dismal sky. "It'll be fine, don't worry about it. I didn't buy a beachfront property for just that reason. We're fairly secluded out here so a heavy rain and some wind is usually all we get." Obviously she didn't look convinced because he reached out to take her hand. She pulled out of his reach. "I promise not to let anything happen to you."

"Forgive me for not putting a lot of stock in your promises," she quipped.

"I apologize for last night," he said, looking directly at her. "Not for touching you or kissing you. Not for anything that happened between you and me. Because I meant that. I wanted that." He inhaled, then exhaled slowly. "But I apologize for the phone call and for leaving the way I did. It was rude."

"It was hurtful," she amended.

He nodded in agreement. "I'm sorry. That wasn't my intention at all."

"Who was on the phone?" She asked the question she'd sworn a million times she wasn't going to ask.

And he hesitated just like she knew he would.

"It was an old friend. One that I haven't heard from in a long time and one I'm not thrilled about hearing from now."

"I see," she said, nodding.

He immediately started shaking his head. "No. You don't. It wasn't a female friend."

"Oh."

"Anyway, let's just forget about it. The phone call had nothing to do with you and I shouldn't have left the way I did. So I'm apologizing." He reached his hand out to her again. "Forgive me?"

Looking down at his upturned hand she thought of all the reasons why she shouldn't. Because he's arrogant, and more often than not rude and disconcerting, and if he really wanted her why hadn't he come back for her and...

Then the reasons why she should interrupted. He was awfully cute when he was being apologetic. Beyond the fact that he'd run out on her, he didn't really need to explain about the phone call or the friend, and she was dying to touch him, to feel the energy produced by her skin against his once more.

"I don't know why I'm doing this," she began.

She hadn't extended her hand that far before he reached out the extra length and took her hand in his. "Because you know there's something going on between us. Something you want to explore as much as I do."

"Akil, what I said before about not jumping into bed with just anybody is true."

"I know it is and despite what you might think, it's true for me, too."

She chuckled. "Then we make some pair, huh?"

"Yeah, that's what I keep thinking. Listen, I cancelled recording for today. With the weather worsening I didn't want the guys coming all the way out here and getting stuck."

He reached for his hot chocolate and took a sip. He

didn't drink coffee, said it made him too jumpy and he liked to always be alert. She thought the reason was more the fact that Mrs. Williamson made it herself with whole milk and three kinds of chocolate, topped off with whipped cream and chocolate shavings, but she didn't dare say that to him.

She was a tea drinker herself, green tea or black decaffeinated with honey tasted better to her and also massaged her vocal cords. Charlene was beginning to get used to the not-so-subtle mothering of Mrs. Williamson and the other household staff.

"So what are we going to do today?" she asked, trying not to focus on the weather but instead on the platters Mrs. Williamson had already put on the table.

He shrugged. "Figured we'd just hang out, watch some movies. I don't get a lot of downtime. I should probably take advantage when I can."

"I agree. It doesn't seem like you enjoy your success much."

Still rubbing a thumb over the back of her hand, he looked at her seriously. "I'm enjoying being with you."

Seconds ticked by and she was speechless. And just when she'd thought she could talk without blabbering she heard the click of heels on the tiled floor from the direction of the kitchen.

Charlene silently cursed the end of her alone time with Akil. And from the look on his face he was doing the same thing.

"Good morning, good people. Charlene, I've got a surprise for you," Serene's high-pitched voice was already talking the moment she stepped onto the terrace.

"Darling," she said, leaning over and kissing Akil on the cheek. He didn't look too happy to see her.

"Good morning, Serene."

"Look who I've brought with me," she said with a flourish of her long, gold bangle–covered arm. "Carlo, you remember Akil. And this is Charlene Quinn—our next project."

Charlene didn't like being referred to as a "project" but smiled through the discomfort and extended her hand to shake Carlo's.

"Mmm-hmm," he said, his fake gray eyes assessing her. "Stand up, dear." He'd taken her hand and was stepping aside so she could stand.

With a fleeting glance to Akil, who only nodded for her to comply, Charlene stood.

Carlo was almost as tall as Serene, a rail-thin man with long arms and an even longer nose. He looked either Puerto Rican or Mexican, she couldn't really tell, but his hair was slicked back with enough mousse or other hair product to shellac one of Akil's hardwood floors. He held her arm up in the air and twirled her around.

"Mmm. No. No. No." He was grumbling and mumbling some other stuff that Charlene couldn't understand before he finally let her arm down to her side.

He stood in front of her then, one arm folded over his chest, the other propped up so that his hand rested on his chin. He wore skinny jeans that accentuated the fact that he was indeed skinny and a button-down striped shirt that made her dizzy if she stared at it for too long.

"This is definitely no good," he said, lifting the edge of her ruffled blouse, which she'd worn tucked into denim capris. "Ruffles are for little girls, which you definitely are not."

Charlene tried not to bristle at his comment. He was

doing his job, she told herself. But then he touched her. His long pale fingers gripped her waist, just beneath her breastbone, moving around one way and then another.

"This is the problem area. We've got to focus our work here. I think everything below this area we can work with. Pencil skirts, definitely. Leggings with long tops. Empire waists. Serene, are you writing this down?"

A glance in her direction said she hadn't been. She'd been too busy staring at Akil, who didn't look thrilled with the situation. In that moment Charlene wondered what was really between the two of them. Because while from their first meeting Serene had been what she probably considered pleasant to Charlene, in the past couple of days in the studio Serene had hovered a lot closer to Akil. Charlene hadn't yet figured out how she felt about that. No, that was wrong, she knew she didn't like it. It was crazy, she had no reason feeling territorial about Akil. They were just working together, or more like cordial friends. Even though each time she saw him she desperately wanted another one of his soul-searing kisses, she couldn't afford to fool herself into thinking they meant anything.

"I'm getting it," Serene said, hustling over to the table where she'd dropped her huge purse and pulling out a notepad and pen. "What do you think of the hair? I'm not really feeling it. A funky cut might work," she suggested.

Carlo was already shaking his head. "No. Won't work. Too round of a face, not flattering."

Now at that, Charlene did bristle. "Now, wait just a minute," she began to protest. At her sides her fists clenched but still they continued to talk. Maybe she should just be quiet, take the bitter with the sweet. After all, wasn't this a part of the job? She'd known this would happen sooner or later. She'd just have to deal with it. Besides, Akil hadn't said a word yet. Did that mean he was backing this little assessment of Carlo's?

Embarrassment bubbled inside her. She fought against the urge to turn and run from the room or grab one of these skinny idiots by the neck and squeeze. Akil had never looked at her like some of the men she met back home. He seemed to see past the physical to something else that she was beginning to think made him happy. Last night certainly should have proved that there was something about her body he liked. Now, with Carlo's words, she wondered if that were truly the case.

"We'll keep it long, feather it. Maybe add some highlights. Definitely need to work on the makeup." He lifted one of her arms, looked down at her nails. "I think two weeks at the spa will do. Thirty to fifty pounds off is our goal. By then she'll be trimmer and we can get started on the clothes. What are we doing for choreography? PJ or Simon? Catsuits will work with thick belts at the waist just in case we can't streamline all this right away."

Charlene had heard of the spa they were referring to; it was nestled in the pretty scenic city of Monterey in California. For a small fortune, celebrities could check in, receive a handful of laxatives on a daily basis and shed the pounds they needed to act in roles they were either too old or obviously too fat to play. Or, in her instance, to create an image that wasn't her at all. That was the absolute last place she wanted to be. The thought alone made her nauseous.

Then her head was swimming, her skin heated from

the combination of rage and mortification. She took one retreating step and felt light-headed.

"Hold still," she heard Carlo say.

"Copper highlights, you think?" Serene was saying.

The room was spinning, the French toast and cottage cheese she'd taken only a few bites of for breakfast flip-flopping in her stomach, threatening to backtrack. Carlo was no longer touching her but his words vibrated in her ears. Her eyes blinked but she couldn't see, everything had become blurry. She felt herself moving but couldn't tell if she were backing up on her own or if the over-the-top Carlo and Serene were pushing her.

"Enough!" Akil roared.

Silence fell quickly, as if a stripper had waltzed into a church sanctuary with her pole in hand ready to dance.

She felt a hand on her cheek. "Charlene, are you okay?"

She heard his voice and instantly began to calm down. "I...I think I need to sit down."

"Take it easy," he was saying, helping her to a chair and easing her down. Kneeling at her side, he took her hand and rubbed it gently. "Just breathe. It's okay. Just breathe."

He sounded so sure, so soothing, so she did as he said, breathing slowly in and out until her surroundings were much clearer.

"With all due respect, Akil. This has to be taken care of. The Vibe Awards are only four weeks away. We have to get started now." Serene was talking but Akil was still staring at her.

"I know when Vibe is," Akil said tightly.

"Then you know we don't have a lot of time to work with. And Carlo has other clients. We were lucky he could come by today. He's on his way to New York to work with Fantasia tomorrow."

Through clenched teeth Akil said, "He can leave now."

"What?"

Akil stood quickly, turning to face both Serene and Carlo. "Both of you can leave now. I don't need your help."

Carlo fanned a hand in front of himself as if he were about to have a heatstroke or was highly offended. Serene ran to Akil's side, lowering her voice as she said, "Akil, you know what has to be done. She's going to be a lot of work. We talked about this already."

"Yeah, Serene." Akil spoke loud enough for Charlene to hear him. "We did talk about this, on numerous occasions, and I thought I made myself perfectly clear. We're not changing Charlene's physical look. I told you maybe hair and makeup. Pick out a wardrobe that compliments, not exaggerates and not demeans. I want her image to project her as is. It's the voice we want to focus on, the music, the sound that will be different. That will sell. All this other BS is for somebody else. Not her."

Serene was shaking her head. "You've bumped your head if you think that's going to work. Maybe I need to call Sahari for further direction because you're apparently blinded by something personal."

Akil let out a small chuckle. "I'm not blinded and you can call Sahari all you want. Playascape is *my* label. Charlene is *my* artist. The final call is *mine* to make and I've just made it. Now, if you don't agree, *you* can walk. You and the beanpole over there."

At that Carlo let out something like a yelp that had Charlene jumping in her chair. She was still light-headed, but now she knew why. It wasn't Serene's or Carlo's comments but her own stupidity.

Lifting a hand, she touched Akil's arm. "It's okay. I'm fine, Akil."

"Is that what you were worried about?" Serene asked in an incredulous voice. "That she was upset by what we were saying? Come on, Akil. This isn't like you. Since when does the artist have any say in how we package them? They don't know the stats we know, the pressure we're under to make back the money we invest. She's gonna have to toughen up if she's going to be in this industry."

Akil took a step closer to Serene, one that had enough tension in it that Charlene found herself struggling to stand, to hold on to his arm.

"I'm only going to tell you one more time that any decisions regarding Charlene's image will come from me. I was giving you the benefit of the doubt, thinking you had enough professionalism in you to do the job you were told to do. But I see that's not going to work. Now I want you and Carlo out of my house."

His body was trembling, with anger, she supposed. He seemed oblivious to her gentle urgings, her touch. She didn't want this to get out of hand, not because of her.

"Akil, come on, let's go into the other room. Give them a few moments."

"Oh, no, I don't need any time. You and your chubby friend can stay right here and do what you want," Carlo said in a huff. "I don't have time for the drama. I'm out."

When he was gone Serene stood looking as if steam were going to pour out of her ears at any moment. Then her glare settled on Charlene. "You won't make it past the first CD looking like that. Don't let him and his high-minded delusions of grandeur fool you. This industry will chew you up and spit you all the way back to that little vocal class in L.A. And if you're thinking that by sleeping with him you're a guaranteed success, think again. That only works for the pretty slim girls, not your kind."

Akil had reached out and grabbed Serene's arm at that point. "Goodbye, Serene."

"Don't touch me," she said tersely, pulling her arm from his grasp.

Charlene had endured lots of insults in her lifetime. She'd dealt with the mean girls in school, the boys who'd rather throw dodgeballs at her than steal kisses from her behind the bleachers in the gym. She'd listened to her mother complain about her weight, about her being the only one in the family not on the fast track to a great career. She'd watched her father's sadness when her mother spoke about her that way and also listened to Candis and Rachel as they'd told her she was a good person.

None of that seemed to matter now. All of it swirled into a funnel, slipping away in the wind, compared to the mean insults out of Serene's mouth. The main one being that Charlene wasn't even good enough to sleep her way to the top.

There was no hole in the floor that would graciously open and swallow her up. No glittering red shoes that she could click and instantaneously be transported back home. No, there was nothing she could do to hide her humiliation at what had just transpired. And even worse, nothing she could do to stop her knees from buckling and Akil's sympathetic arms from catching her before she could make contact with the floor.

Chapter 11

"She's gonna be just fine, Akil. Stop pacing or you'll run a path in the carpet," Mrs. Williamson quipped.

But he couldn't stop. He heard her words, trusted what she was saying, but still his heart pounded as he worried about the unknown. One minute they'd been having a nice peaceful breakfast, the ones he'd come to enjoy so much in the past few days. And the next Serene and her sidekick had barged in running their mouths until he'd felt bad for Charlene and wanted to murder them both.

Then she looked ill, not agitated or hurt or angry, but sick. Her skin had paled and she'd become unsteady, wobbling until he was sure she was going to fall on the floor. Rushing to her side had been late on his part. He should have stopped Carlo and Serene the moment they came in. He knew how they both could be, especially together, using their combined half-witted brainpower.

His fists clenched, he wanted to hit somebody or something. He could have beat the feminine nature out of Carlo for the nasty things he'd said to Charlene because, after all, he was a male on the surface. As for Serene, this wasn't the first time he'd wanted to ignore the teachings about not hitting a woman just to shut her the hell up. But to hell with both of them. His only concern now was Charlene and the way she still looked too pale, and too vulnerable, sitting on the couch in the living room.

That's where he'd carried her when she'd been unable to stand on her own a moment longer. He'd called for Mrs. Williamson, who'd quickly called for Nannette, sending the younger girl up to Charlene's room. She'd brought back a pill bottle and Mrs. Williamson had continued to wipe Charlene's forehead with a wet cloth. "Get the other bottle out of the first-aid kit in the kitchen, the smelling salts."

He'd frowned at that, thinking smelling salts were only used in the movies and weren't real. But he'd known better than to correct Mrs. Williamson.

"But she's not unconscious," Akil said, slightly confused.

"It's all right, the salts will bring her around. She's still a bit dazed. And she's tired. Aren't you, baby?" she asked Charlene, rubbing a thick cocoa-brown hand over Charlene's smaller, lighter one.

"Here you go," Nannette said upon her return, offering Mrs. Williamson a brown bottle with no label on it.

"How do you know that's the right one?"

"Because I make it myself," she answered tightly, unscrewing the top from the bottle and pouring the liquid onto a dry cloth.

Akil wasn't sure he'd heard correctly. "You make drugs in my house?"

She cut an angry look at him. "I'm from the South, Akil. I've been making my own remedies since I was a young'un working at my grandma's side. It's nothing but ammonium carbonate and perfume. When the ammonium is mixed with either water or salt it creates fumes," she said, passing the cloth right beneath Charlene's nose.

"The fumes irritate the lining of the nose, throat and lungs. That's what makes them wake up from a dead faint."

On the chair Charlene yanked her head back, frowning from the smell.

"There you go. That's a good girl," she said, passing Nannette the cloth and rubbing Charlene's cheek.

"I'm fine. Really, none of this is necessary, I just need to—" Charlene was trying to talk but Mrs. Williamson wasn't trying to hear it.

"I've got your medication," Mrs. Williamson said, opening the pill bottle Nannette had brought down from Charlene's room. "You forgot to take it this morning, didn't you?"

Looking away from Akil, Charlene answered quietly, "Yeah."

Mrs. Williamson nodded knowingly. "I thought so. You know you have to eat and you have to take this every day. Hypothyroidism is nothing to play with."

"Hypo-what?" Akil asked, not knowing what either of them was talking about. "You're on medication?"

He didn't know how he felt about that but Charlene's frantic look said she had no intention of ever telling him about the meds or whatever her condition was. That pissed him off to no end.

"Why didn't you tell me?"

"Hush, Akil. That's too many questions for this girl right now. Here, sit up," Mrs. Williamson instructed Charlene. "Nannette, give me that water. Now, I want you to take this and lie here for a bit and get some rest.

You've been working nonstop since you got here. A shame you're pushin' this girl like this. She needs to rest, Akil, not be yelled at or questioned to death."

With Mrs. Williamson's words, Akil dropped Charlene's hand and backed away.

She didn't need him. Mrs. Williamson was taking care of her and obviously knew more about Charlene than he did. Even though he'd thought they were growing closer with each day they spent together, he'd been wrong. She hadn't trusted him with this one detail.

He continued to back out of the room. The similarities were too eerie, too strong for him to dismiss. Panic ripped at his chest as he remembered the outcome of Lauren and her lies and omissions. The same could happen to Charlene. In this industry anything was possible. History could repeat itself.

He was sweating, his brow was damp and so were his palms as he walked into the foyer, stopping at the steps and trying to figure out where he wanted to go.

Fears from the past engulfed him, wrapping securely around a face from the present, around Charlene. He couldn't handle it. Couldn't breathe here. Couldn't stand the possibilities.

Not again. Not ever again is what he'd promised himself. Looks like he'd failed once more.

Enough is enough, Charlene thought hours later. She'd been closed up in her bedroom by Mrs. Williamson, who had brought her lunch and a snack and warned her that dinner was coming soon. Charlene wanted to tell her it wasn't food she needed, but hadn't had the heart. She got the impression the older woman didn't get enough chance to fuss over people with Akil not living here most of the year. So she'd sat back and let her go at it. Truth be told, she had been just a little tired. The long hours in the studio were beginning to take their toll. She was actually glad when Akil said he'd cancelled today's session.

But that was before the scene on the terrace. Before she was embarrassed out of her mind, then swept off her feet by her own idiocy. She'd been in such a hurry to get down to breakfast this morning she hadn't taken her medication. All the time she'd sat with Akil eating and talking she hadn't felt any different. Apparently the stress of Serene and Carlo's appearance coupled with her normal bouts of fatigue was just too much to bear. Mrs. Williamson had an auntie in North Carolina who suffered with thyroid problems, she'd told Charlene. That's how she knew what the medication was the first time she'd seen it in Charlene's room, and that's how she knew just what to do to take care of Charlene.

Admittedly it had felt good to just rest and wait for her meals. Charlene wasn't a lazy person and the staff at home was usually so busy running around at her mother's every command that they'd barely paid any attention to her.

So the day had passed quietly, night sneaking over them with just a light drizzle beginning to fall. The wind blew hard; she could tell because if she got close to the window she'd hear the whistling sound. The water in the pool rippled but Nannette, Cliff, the driver, and Yucatan, the yardman, had gathered all the lounge chairs and tables and brought them into the house. She suspected the terrace had been cleared, too, although she hadn't been back downstairs since earlier today.

But none of that kept her mind off Akil. They really

were a pair. Since the day they'd met, one of them was always storming off, angry at the other. It was beginning to be their routine.

He'd seemed so upset with her when he'd left this morning. Upset that she hadn't told him about her medication. Truth be told, she hadn't seen a reason to. Her illness was *her* business. Akil was just her producer. If she was singing and giving the performance he wanted, why did he need to know? Right?

Then why did she still feel the need to explain? Climbing out of bed, she grabbed the beige silk robe that matched her nightgown and tied it around herself. Pushing her feet into her slippers, she headed straight to the door. There was no way she'd be able to sleep with this unresolved situation between them.

It was a little after ten and she'd assumed he would be in the studio, but as she stepped into the hallway she could hear music coming from the other end of the hall. The end where Akil's suite was located. Taking a deep breath, she moved in that direction, pausing at the door to knock.

After two additional knocks and no answer she figured he couldn't hear over the music so she tried the doorknob. It was open so she walked inside.

His space was twice the size of her room. Upon entering she figured she was in what should have been the sitting room. Instead of a chaise longue, coffee table and maybe a bookcase, Akil had gym equipment in this space. A weight bench, free weights, elliptical, treadmill, you name it, he had it. Walking through the room, she touched a hand to the elliptical, picturing him using the machine. She lifted a free weight and almost sank to the floor herself, it was so heavy. No wonder his arms were so muscled, if he was lifting these every day.

The music playing was that instrumental piece he'd been listening to that night in the studio, the one she had said was the journey between man and woman, the journey to falling in love. She hadn't shared the latter with him, but after hearing the song in her mind the rest of the night instead of being able to sleep, that's what she'd finally settled on.

Two steps separated the sitting room from Akil's bedroom and as she took them she immediately felt nervous. She was in his bedroom, in his personal space without permission. She didn't know how he would feel about that but assumed he would be no more upset with her than he already appeared. The room was dim but her gaze couldn't miss the king-size four-poster bed sitting on a platform to the far left. It was huge, clearly large enough for more than one person. And it was formidable, so much so that she couldn't really picture Akil sleeping there. A week ago she'd have never doubted this was where he slept, but after getting to know him better, all this, the house, the private jet, the cars, seemed beyond Akil the man. There was only the music, that was the one thing that she knew suited him perfectly.

"I see you're feeling better," he said and she jumped at the sound of his voice behind her.

Spinning around, she saw that he was sitting in one of two black leather recliners that faced the wall, which was actually an entertainment center. There was a table between the recliners, where the only lamp was perched.

"Ah, yeah, I'm feeling much better," she said, taking a tentative step toward him.

"Good. We'll get back to work maybe Sunday. I want to give this storm a chance to blow over."

So they were back to the cool formal tones again. Her need to talk to him faltered a bit. This was ground she'd assumed they already covered. Well, she'd just say what she had to say and leave. She wasn't in the mood for Akil's roller-coaster moods.

"I have hypothyroidism. It's when there's insufficient production of thyroid hormone by the thyroid gland. A couple of the symptoms are fatigue and weight gain. I have to take a medication called Levoxyl every day to help keep the levels up. If I skip a dose I'm really light-headed and even more tired than usual. That's what happened today. I forgot to take my medication."

He remained quiet and she kept her hands folded together in front of her. Suddenly she felt very vulnerable and almost foolish. What was she thinking coming into his bedroom, dressed in her nightclothes and giving him a lesson in the thyroid glands? Foolish, that's what she was.

"So anyway, I just figured I owed you an explanation. I guess I'll stay out of your way until Sunday."

She had already turned to go when his voice stopped her.

"Why didn't you tell me before?"

She didn't turn back to him but answered anyway. "I didn't think it was important."

"It is. Important, I mean," he said.

Her palms had begun sweating, which was unusual for her. Usually her skin was really dry. That was another effect of her illness.

"I didn't know. I guess I didn't think about it. I'm just so used to dealing with it that I don't talk about it much."

"How long have you had this condition?"

Refusing to continue this conversation with her back facing him, Charlene turned. He was still sitting in the chair, still staring at the wall.

"We found out when I was sixteen. When my mother was tired of me failing on every diet she could come up with."

"She wanted you to lose weight, too?" he asked, a hint of incredulity in his voice.

"I've always been overweight, even as a baby. She thought it would change with time, but when it didn't she tried other ways. Until the doctor told her there was no use. The most common symptom to hypothyroidism is weight gain and water retention. So even if I starved, which was never in my nature, I would most likely be overweight."

"I thought a couple times at breakfast that you didn't eat a lot. I wondered if you were dieting but didn't want to bring it up."

"Oh, no. I'm not dieting. I just try to watch what I'm eating before I sing. Some foods just aren't good for the voice at any time. And others just make singing for long periods of time uncomfortable and most often cause missed notes. Believe me, I eat." She smiled.

He chuckled. "I'm glad to hear that."

He looked up at her then. "I wouldn't want you to starve or diet. Like I told Serene, I like you just the way you are."

Her throat was dry. Did it seem hot in here? "You didn't tell Serene that. You told her your plan for my image had changed."

Nodding his head, he finally stood and walked toward her. "My plan for your image did change. But I've always liked the way you looked. From the picture you sent with the demo CD and the first day I met you in L.A. with your agent hovering about and Jason and Sahari seeing dollar signs. I liked the way you looked."

"Really?" It wasn't possible. Well, it could be. She didn't believe it. The great Akil Hutton liked the way she looked.

He smiled. "You sound surprised."

"I am. I mean, most men, even ones not in the business, have a certain vision of the women they like."

"That's true. And you happen to fit my vision."

Yeah, it was hot. Charlene was warm all over and when he took her hands in his she thought she'd just melt at his feet. He led her to the recliner where he'd been sitting and eased her down. "Mrs. Williamson would kill me if she knew I had you standing up all this time."

"I understand I'm no Beyoncé or Ciara. And it's fine if you can't market me and this CD doesn't become a hit. I'm just glad for the opportunity to work with you and to actually live a part of a dream I've held close for so long."

He was shaking his head, holding both her hands in his. "Have you seen Beyoncé lately? She's not all skin and bones. The public really appreciates a bootylicious figure and they're going to love you." He chuckled. "I don't want you to be like anybody but Charlene Quinn. That's the singer I'm working with and that's the woman I'm going to market. End of story."

Charlene sighed with relief and sat back in the chair. "Serene's not going to be happy to hear that."

"Serene's fired so it doesn't really matter what she likes."

"Oh, no. You're firing her? Because of me? I don't want to cause that type of trouble."

"You didn't cause it. You just brought it to a head. Things have been brewing with us for a while. She's blinded by the dollar signs and notoriety."

"And what are you doing? You know what the trend is now, you know what the listeners want. Why are you so sure it'll work if you take a chance and do something different with me?"

"Because when you sing I can feel it here." He'd taken her hand and guided it to his chest, rested it over his heart. "No singer has affected me that way in years. What you have is true and it's pure. It's the soul of music and that's what I want to record."

Charlene didn't know what to say or how to react. She tried to take a deep breath, licked her lips and gave a nervous smile. "I'm flattered," she said honestly.

His smile was different than any she'd ever seen on him before. It touched his eyes until he looked like he could really be happy for once. "I'm honored to be working with you on this project."

With that he lifted her hand from his chest, brought it to his lips and kissed the tip of each one of her fingers.

"I'm thankful to have finally met someone as honest and real as you. In this business that's hard to find."

She could relate to what he was saying. She was thankful for Rachel for that very reason. True friends, sincere connections, were hard to come by when you had money, fame, prestige or all three.

"More importantly," he was saying, his kisses having moved to the center of her hand, where his tongue swirled over her skin until tingles of pleasure soared through her body, resting quite suddenly in her center,

"I just cannot seem to get you out of my mind. And since the first time I kissed you, you've become like a drug. My own personal addiction. Damn, I'm dying to kiss you." He finished with his tongue scraping over her wrist, kissing up her arm as the wide-armed material of the sleeve on her robe slid downward.

"Oh," was all she could manage. Had he been reading her mind? Sure, she'd come here to talk to him, to explain what had happened, but she'd wanted him. For days now she'd known she wanted Akil, and last night had only brought that need to a head.

The aggressor in sexual encounters she was not. And so she'd resigned herself to wait until he'd made a move like he was interested in her in *that* way. Well, coupled with last night in the pool house and now watching the swirl of his tongue on the heated skin of her inner arm, she could safely say that he was.

"I apologize for being so harsh and behaving like a greedy teenager last night. I can be better," he said, giving her just the barest hint of a smile. "Can I kiss you, Charlene?"

Hell, yeah! her mind screamed even as the slow melodic tune still blared from his speakers. Luckily she had a little bit of control left. She would not act like a desperate, horny female aching for his touch.

However, considering she hadn't had sex in over a year and her hormones had been racing at the simplest thought of Akil since the time he'd kissed her, that's exactly what she was.

"Yes, you ca—"

Her words were cut off, her breath stolen and the world as she'd known it officially shaken as Akil's lips descended upon hers in an action that was not soft and not slow, but was full of as much passion and energy as the first roars of thunder crackling outside his bedroom window.

Chapter 12

From the steady thumping water against the window she'd say the light drizzle had picked up. Winds were still blowing as Miami sat waiting to go through round one with Hurricane Viola.

While inside Akil's bedroom Charlene waited for something else.

His kisses had the effect of a drug, making her limbs weak, her body compliant and her sex hot with anticipation. Her hands had gripped his taut shoulders as he'd slanted his head, deepening the kiss until it felt as if their mouths had been fused together. His tongue persistently stroked hers, his hands cupping her face with a gentle touch that didn't match the intensity of the kiss.

Her mind whirled as sensations poured into her. On the one hand she wanted nothing more than to continue kissing Akil. The feel of his lips, the taste of his tongue, the touch of his hands so soft on her face, all of this was pleasurable. Enough so that her knees quaked, closing as her thighs squeezed tight to tamp down on the growing pressure in her center.

On the other hand, she wanted more than she'd ever wanted before. This need that burned inside of her was new and intense, causing her entire body to tremble, her breath to come in erratic spurts.

"Akil," she managed a whisper when he'd pulled back slightly to suckle her bottom lip.

On a ragged moan, he murmured, "I can't stop wanting you."

"You don't have to stop," she heard a voice say but wasn't sure it was her own.

His hands moved down her neck to cup each of her breasts. It was her turn to moan and to squirm once more against the force of need boiling inside. Her body was hot, like liquid fire ran through her veins. When he flicked his fingers over the tight nipples of her breasts she almost screamed. Between her legs her clit throbbed and her head fell back on the chair as she tried to swallow, tried to get a grip on these raging emotions.

"No," he said adamantly. "I want you to look at me when I touch you."

At his words her head snapped up, her eyes wide open. He was beautiful with his eyes half-closed, his long fingers gripping and squeezing her full breasts. Leaning forward, he breathed over one taut nipple that she felt puckering even more through the thin material of her robe and gown. As if the material weren't there at all his tongue extended, rubbed over the nipple once, twice, until the material was damp and so were her panties.

His name tore from her lips as she gripped his shoulders, her chest heaving, legs holding tighter together.

"Tell me what you want," he said, moving to the other nipple, taking it between his teeth and biting lightly.

"Oh. My." She couldn't even finish the thought, let alone do what he'd asked of her.

"Do you want me to take your clothes off?" he asked, flattening his body against her the best he could, considering she was sitting in the recliner.

His broad chest brought a new heat against her midsection. His strength pressing into her thighs ignited the fire already brewing in that region and she felt herself pressing into him desperately.

"Do you want to be naked?" His voice was more urgent, strained with what she could only assume was desire. "You naked? Me naked? Me touching you, tasting you? Tell me, Charlene. What do you want?"

"Yes," she almost screamed but ended with a guttural moan that sounded more animalistic than human.

Akil didn't waste a second after her answer. His hands worked quickly, untying the robe, pulling it from her shoulders. Then he lifted the hem of her gown and waited as she lifted slightly from the chair so he could pull it over her head. She never slept in a bra, so her panties were next to go. Feeling a wave of self-consciousness hit, she regretted her emotion-filled answer to becoming naked. The table with the lamp on it wasn't quite four feet away. The balmy gold light poured into the room, placing her and her body on unfettered display for Akil.

As her heart continued to pound and she wondered how she could maneuver herself to the bed, to the sheet she could use to camouflage some of her not-so-alluring body parts, she caught Akil's gaze.

He was standing, looking down at her as she lay sprawled naked on the recliner. Only he wasn't looking at her body, his eyes were fastened on hers. "You're beautiful, Charlene. Don't ever let anybody tell you or make you feel differently."

Even through the heavy haze of sexual tension she felt the softness of his words, the tenderness of sincerity prick her heart. She didn't answer because his eyes had moved from hers to venture down her torso. In the dimness she could still see the shift. His normally dark, intense eye color had darkened even more, shading with a haze of lust and something else she couldn't decipher.

Not knowing what else to do and unnerved by his concentrated examination, she lifted her arms to him. If he was kissing her she wouldn't be nervous. When he touched her she felt safe, wanted. And if she could only have this moment, this night as a storm raged outside, if this was the only time she'd have Akil to herself, then she wouldn't waste a moment.

"Take off your clothes and come to me," she said and knew it was the arousal talking. Never in her life had she been this open and willing with a man. Then again, she'd never been with a man like Akil before. A man whose sheer presence spoke of power and strength and at the same time compassion. Yes, there was a part of Akil that she'd seen on occasions when they were together that said he had a softer side, a side he didn't show often. What would it be like if she were the one he chose to open up to?

He was already doing as she'd asked. Removing his clothes in a slow and precise manner, all the while keeping his eyes on her. It was kind of erotic, especially since at that moment she remembered the music playing in the background. It had changed from the first instrumental piece to another one that didn't sound familiar but cast an oddly sensual vibe around the room. So they had music, they had a stormy night and two almost naked adults. This was a perfect combination.

His thumbs were on the rim of his sweatpants, his chest already bare, when he paused and asked, "What are you thinking?"

Hmm, was this a trick question? She was definitely thinking he had one banging set of abs. Ripped didn't quite describe him as her gaze roamed over his succulent chest. She'd known his arms were tight, probably could be considered cannons for a man of exactly six feet and medium build. His pectorals were tight, the nipples erect. Her mouth watered.

"Um, I'm thinking what's taking you so long?" That was an honest enough answer, she figured.

He smiled. "Okay. Just making sure we're on the same page here."

"What page is that?"

"The one where we spend the entire night making each other feel real damn good." As he spoke he'd pushed the pants down, simultaneously stepping out of the tennis shoes he wore.

She swallowed hard, almost lost the little bit of courage she'd garnered from his earlier words. If she thought the top half of him looked good, then the bottom was definitely a prizewinner. Long muscled legs sprinkled with black hair. He turned to the side, kicking his clothes out of the way. His butt was absolutely to die for, tight and just handful-size. She thought of Will Smith in the early scenes of *I, Robot.* Akil had him beat by about a million more sweat glands reacting in her body. He turned back to face her and she heard herself gasp and wanted to crawl beneath the chair instead of sitting in it.

The phrase "he was hung like a horse" was crass, so she chased it out of her mind. Still, he was no lightweight in the size department and her body wanted more.

"I'm glad we both like what we see," he said in that cocky, arrogant tone he used more often than not. Usually it rubbed her the wrong way. Tonight it massaged every horny inch of her.

She could only lick her lips in response. Nervousness was coming back, claiming a spot right in the center of her chest. Was she in over her head with Akil? Surely he was more experienced in the sex department than she was. While both of them admitted to not just sleeping with anyone she was almost positive Akil Hutton had had more than three lovers in his whole life. His every movement spoke of sex, like he was advertising the ride of a lifetime a woman could expect from him. She wondered if she were really ready for all this.

"You wanna know what I really like about you, Charlene?" he asked, coming closer to her, going down on his knees in front of her once more.

"What?" Her voice seemed smaller or was the music in the background, the wind outside, louder?

"These," he said, his palms resting softly on her thighs.

That wasn't possible. The most hated part of her body was his favorite? She couldn't even speak.

"I knew the moment I saw you they'd be soft. I like a woman with real legs, not twigs."

At his words said legs quivered and his smile grew even wider. "Oh, yeah, that's what I'm talking about."

With his palms sliding down to her inner thighs, he pushed her legs apart, as far as they would go within the confines of the chair. Even that was far enough as she felt air over the damp skin of her center. On display for him suddenly had a new meaning.

"And I'll bet you're even softer there." His hands moved up higher, his fingers touching her swollen lips softly. "I've dreamt of touching you here, tasting you here." He looked up at her and while her eyes were dangerously close to shutting his heated glare kept them open.

"Do you taste good, Charlene?"

She couldn't even think of an answer to that question. Instead her fingers clenched the arm of the chair, her teeth sinking into her lower lip as anticipation tore through her.

Up and down his fingers stroked until she shivered. His hands were between her legs, touching her more intimately and openly than she'd ever been touched before. A fingertip grazed the tightened bud of her center and she sucked air in through her teeth. For seconds he played there, stroking her now-drenched lips, tweaking her tight and puckered clit. She squirmed and lifted her hips in request for more.

"Yeah," he moaned, his gaze fixed between her legs. "You're gonna taste damn good, baby girl."

Charlene couldn't think, her mind was so completely wrapped around the pleasure he was evoking. She'd thought momentarily about how wickedly wanton she must look, naked in a chair, legs gaping open, greedy hips moving incessantly. But she couldn't stop, didn't want to stop.

When she thought she couldn't take anymore, his fingers slipped into her entrance, stroked, found a particularly sensitive spot and worked there until she was panting and writhing beneath him.

"Not yet," he whispered, his warm breath fanning over her thighs as he kissed his way up to her center. "Not yet."

When he arrived, his tongue took over the steady stroking of his fingers, licking up and down her lips with an efficiency that should be patented. It wasn't long before his tongue found the nub he'd touched with such perfection. Heat swirled through Charlene until she felt like she was outside in the twisting, surging wind of the brewing hurricane. If this continued she was going to explode, she knew it with certainty.

And with all her sighing and moaning, Akil probably knew it, too.

While his fingers worked her, pumped deep inside of her, his touch tortured the outer realm. She was delirious with pleasure.

"Come for me, baby girl. Now," his voice rasped over her sensitive skin, sending off a rocket-like explosion deep inside her body.

She trembled from her head to her toes, her fingernails dug into the arms of the chair and his name tore from her throat in lyrical notes not registered on any scale.

She was wrapped tightly around him as Akil moved from the chair to the bed. Her arms held him unyieldingly, like he was the only one in her world. He relished that feeling, held it as close to his heart as he could.

She sang his name and it had been the sweetest song he'd ever heard. Even the sweet taste of her orgasm, the swelling of his ego the moment she took that final plunge, none of that compared to the sweet sound of her voice, the high pitch of his name echoing throughout his bedroom. He'd kissed her then, after the last tremors of pleasure had torn through her body, after he'd felt steady enough himself to move. His lips had captured hers in a slow dance of sorts, a promise of more, an agreement of forever.

Laying her on his bed as gently as possible, Akil took a few moments just to stare down at her. This woman who he'd known for less than a month, who'd come into his life with a powerhouse voice, a mouthwatering body and the persona of a simple, naive schoolteacher. This woman who in such a short period had turned out to be so much more.

As he stood at the side of the bed she rolled over toward him, reached for his heavy erection and stroked him. His breath caught and not even the ever-growing storm outside could make him tell her to stop.

The softness of her hands produced a steady heat against his shaft and soon he was moving to her rhythm. When she looked up at him, her eyes seeking permission, he knew he had to do something. Leaning over, he reached into his nightstand, pulled out a condom and passed it to her. Intelligence was something he'd immediately known she possessed. Her fingers moved swiftly, opening the packet, removing the condom then smoothing the latex down his rigid length.

"Lie back," he whispered when he knew she would continue stroking him.

She did as he asked and he climbed on the bed, using his knees to spread her legs wide. Touching two fingers to her already wet center he stifled a moan and looked into her face as he spread her juices over the latex. Her gaze followed his fingers. He swore he grew harder just knowing she watched so intently.

Slipping his arms under her knees, he lifted her legs until her feet were planted firmly on the bed. Reaching up, he grabbed one of the pillows from beside her head and tucked it securely under the base of her back.

He positioned the thick head of his arousal at her center, but looked up at her before pressing forward.

"Thank you," he whispered.

She looked momentarily perplexed. "For what?"

"For choosing me."

As the soft smile touched her lips Akil pressed slowly inside her. Tight muscles gripped him just like her arms had wrapped around his neck. She pulled him in, deeper and deeper, until he felt like they'd been fused together.

Being inside her felt so good he had to grit his teeth. Then he kissed her lips, sucked her tongue into his mouth and moaned. "You taste good. You feel good. So damn good, baby girl."

His kisses trailed down her neck, to her breasts, where he found a pert nipple and suckled like a baby. All the while his strokes grew deeper, her hips moved with his rhythm, music played in the background and for the first time in a long time, Akil also wanted to sing.

The emotion was dangerous; it was spreading in his chest like a cancer. He'd recognized it the moment he'd been alone with her. Had fought it like a boxer fighting for a title. But it wasn't working. He was falling for her and falling fast.

She wouldn't stay, he thought, even as his name again fell from her lips. She was grasping the sheets of the bed, thrashing against his brutally slow stroking. He liked it slow and deep, liked the feel of her muscles gripping him. He wouldn't go faster, wouldn't rush this moment.

Her hips moved, circled, jutted up to meet his stroke. To hurry him along. "Slow, baby girl. I like it nice and slow."

"I can't," she whimpered, her head thrashing about the pillows.

"Shhhh," he said, rising to her face, touching her lips with a light kiss. "You feel so good I don't want to stop. I don't want this to be over. Baby—"

His words drifted, his stroke deepened. He palmed her bottom, clutched the plush cheeks in his palm and thrust into her again and again. Her breasts moved with their motions, making his shaft harder, his arousal more intense. Her creamy thighs pillowed against his own and his spine tingled.

She watched him, watched them, her gaze sliding down to where they were joined. He pulled out slowly, let her look her fill. Then slid in with a little more speed, a lot more intensity and watched her eyes darken. Using his fingers he touched her plump lips, pulled them apart and slid inside of her once more. He liked to look himself, liked to see where their bodies met, joined, where he lost himself inside of her.

They both watched as the crescendo climbed. The storm outside raged a little harder, the wind rattling louder against the windows, the rain coming down in heavier sheets. The music had even changed, the song still instrumental but the tempo a little more fevered. His hips matched the moment, moving faster, riding on the impending waves of pleasure.

When he came, she came. When she came, she sang.

When they both came, the music mixed with the storm. It was a symphony of pleasure, a composition of delight.

It was all he'd ever wanted.

All he ever needed.

And it was probably going to end.

Soon.

Chapter 13

Charlene had never been on the receiving end of oral sex. Until Akil.

She'd never showered with a man. Until Akil.

And she'd never in her wildest dreams thought she'd desire a man the way she did him. They'd rested for a few minutes after the intense round of sex. She'd almost called it something else but was too afraid to hope. Then he'd rolled over, chuckling and grabbing her up in his arms. They'd ended here in this shower stall built for about six people. There were benches along two of the walls and two shower heads. The blue marble reminded her of the ocean, the flecks of silver of the stars in the evening sky. It would have been relaxing if Akil weren't in there with her, intent on bathing her.

"I've been bathing myself for quite some time," she'd said, trying to move out of his grasp.

"Yeah, but this is much more fun."

"No, really, I'd rather do it myself."

He grabbed one of the arms she'd put up to ward him off, his look a little more serious. "Why? What are you afraid of?"

"I'm not afraid of anything."

"Okay, so you're uncomfortable? Nervous? Why, after what we've just shared?"

A logical question, she thought. Unfortunately she didn't have a logical answer. Her feelings just were. "I normally shower alone."

He nodded. His skin looked like a root-beer soda, glossy, wet, tempting. His sex, even at half-mast, still very impressive. "So, I'm making you nervous by being in here with you, looking at you, wanting to touch you."

She crossed her arms over her breasts, shifted from one foot to the other. "I'm just not used to it."

"Okay. That's fair." He took a slow step toward her. "But listen to this, I like the way you look. I like the way you feel in my arms. You're a strong, confident woman who can do anything she puts her mind to. I think you can shower with me and I think you can like it."

She thought he was a damn good talker. Her heart warmed at his words and her body trembled at his glare. But old habits died hard.

"Take a deep breath and prepare yourself to be touched and looked at on a regular basis because I like it."

"You can be quite cocky, Akil Hutton," she said, silently admitting to herself that she did kind of enjoy him looking and touching.

He was up close now, pulling her arms from her chest, placing them at her sides. "I know, been like that since I was a kid."

"Then I'll bet you didn't have a lot of friends."

He was rubbing his fingers along the sides of her breasts. "Friends are overrated."

"Just regular friends or girlfriends?"

He smiled, dipped his head down to run his tongue

over her nipple. "You trying to ask if I've got a girl-friend, Charlene?"

"I'd like to think after what we just did and what you're currently doing that the answer is no."

He bit her nipple, then turned to adjust the spray of water. "I knew you were smart. Now can you wash my back."

She couldn't help but smile. This was the side of Akil she'd thought was there, lying just beneath the ruffled surface he displayed for everyone else. It was the part she wanted all to herself, she thought with a slap of honesty.

Reaching for the soap, she lathered it in her hands and proceeded to bathe him. Another first for her, but she was beginning to think that doing new things with this man wasn't so bad at all.

"I didn't have a lot of friends growing up because enemies came easier." Akil spoke into the darkness of his bedroom.

They'd finished their shower hours ago, the music had been turned off but the rain still beat against the windows. She was cuddled against him in his big bed, where they'd been lying just talking.

"I used to think the same thing," she admitted.

"We lived in a corner house on one of the worst streets in the city. The sound of gunshots lulled me to sleep and the smell of crack being smoked through a pipe woke me up."

She was quiet. Her childhood had been vastly different.

"I went to school every day, or at least tried to. Not too many kids on our block did. Their parents were too busy gettin' high, sticking somebody up or pimpin' their bodies for a hit to even care. But I knew it was my ticket out."

"When did you get into music?"

He sighed. "I was always into music, or should I say music was always in me? My dad was a trumpet player before he got shot up for not paying his dealer. My moms, she was a singer. Great voice. Sometimes I still hear it. So I guess it's in my blood."

"That's sad. I'm so sorry, Akil."

"Don't be. You didn't put the drugs in his hand, make him get high or make him let my mother do the same." She felt his shoulders shrug. "Anyway, I always knew what I wanted to do. I wanted to make music. So I went to school. I did what they told me to graduate. Then I stalked one of the reps at Empire until they gave me an internship. And now I'm here."

"And now you're only one of the five hottest producers on the scene. Very impressive."

"Yeah, but I wish Lauren was with me."

At the mention of a female's name Charlene stiffened.

"No, it's not like that. But I like that you'd get jealous so quick." He kissed her forehead and she settled down.

"Lauren's my younger sister. Younger by seven years. We have different fathers. Mine was dead and buried by the time my mother found Lauren's. And Lauren was cutting her first tooth by the time hers disappeared."

Wow, Charlene thought to herself, such sadness and despair all his life. No wonder he was cranky all the time.

"Lauren could sing. I mean really sing. You remind

me a lot of her, your range and clarity. She was going to be big."

"What happened to her?"

"Life happened, I guess. Lauren wanted to sing, she wanted to make it big, to have money and nice things. Since we didn't have that growing up, it was like a lifeline to her. She was impatient, always had been. Impulsive and reckless. I tried to keep her on the right track, or at least that's what I thought I was doing. When I went to work at Empire I kept her up-to-date on the trends on what they were looking for, but I wanted her to at least finish high school first. There's nothing out here worth ditching your education for. Lauren disagreed.

"She latched on to some neighborhood rapper who'd just inked a deal with Sony. His records climbed the charts and he kept Lauren on his arm. Overnight she went from a high school student with a smart-ass mouth to a certified rapper's girl with shiny cars, lots of bling and scanty clothes. Darian 'MacD' Jackson was going to put her on to a record deal, just as soon as he got established. But the more money he made the less time he had to work on her career. He wanted her right where she was, under his thumb. I tried to talk to her and she kicked me out of her apartment, said I was jealous, trying to bring her down. I shrugged it off, left her to make and clean up her own mess."

This sigh was deep and full of what Charlene could tell was regret.

"Six months later I heard she was getting high. I tracked her and MacD down in L.A. and could see for myself that she was heading down the same path as our parents. I begged her to come with me, to come home with me." His voice cracked.

Charlene ached for him. Wrapping her arms around him, she held him tightly.

"That was eight years ago. I haven't spoken to her since. She's been in and out of rehabs. Every time I try to get in touch she pushes me away. I don't know if I'm gonna try again."

"You will," she whispered. "You will because you love her and you want what's best for her. She's sick, Akil. You can't take anything she says seriously."

"I know all that. I try to convince myself of that every day. But it's all so textbook, so predictable. The child following in the parents' footsteps. But I didn't," he said adamantly. "I didn't. I wanted more and I got it."

"Yes, you did. There are more like you, only the statistics don't show the success stories."

"But what if more isn't enough, Charlene? What if everything I obtained isn't enough?"

She didn't know the answer to that, didn't really know what he was asking her. So instead of commenting she just held on to him, reaching up and kissing his lips lightly. "You're enough for me," she said and kissed him again.

His arms wrapped around her. He pulled her on top of him and words were no longer necessary.

He had to be kidding. There was no way they were heading to a shopping mall the day after a hurricane had ravaged the city.

"It's the best time to shop because people whose homes were hit are busy cleaning up. The malls aren't crowded," he'd told her as they climbed in the back of the limousine.

She could relate to what he was saying but thought it might have been a little insensitive. That probably wasn't Akil's intent, just his rationale. He could be very blunt, brutally honest and sometimes a bit unsympathetic, she'd come to realize in the weeks of spending time with him. But after hearing about his childhood, she couldn't really blame him. She didn't show him pity when he talked about his past, didn't mention how sorry she was for the boy who was forced to grow up too soon and for all the love he'd lost on the way. All through her own childhood she'd felt like an outcast, like the Lord surely had dropped her into the wrong family. But for all that her mother wanted to change her and her father working so much he barely knew what was going on in the household and her sister was traveling so much she rarely got to see her, Charlene always knew that she was loved. No matter what, she knew that at least one weekend out of the month she'd be in a room with both her parents and her sister and for at least a few moments they'd be together sharing a smile, a meal, a laugh, making a memory.

It took her a moment to realize Akil was already pulling her in the direction of Saks Fifth Avenue. The sign out front, just between tall looming palm trees, a koi fishpond full of beautiful koi and flowers, read the Bal Harbour Shops. Because shopping wasn't one of her favorite pastimes she couldn't say she'd ever been here. Akil, on the other hand, looked as if he knew his way around this mall and was headed directly where he wanted to be.

Once in the store he looked toward the women's section, to which she'd quickly replied, "This is your shopping spree, not mine."

He only laughed, held her hand a little tighter in his own and moved to the men's section. He took his time, she thought as she watched him go from rack to rack of jeans. In his mind he probably had an idea of what he wanted and he wasn't going to be pleased until he found it. That's sort of the way he worked in the studio, pushing until the sound was just right. She found she admired that about him.

"Try these on," she heard herself saying as she scooped a pair of pants from the rack and handed them to him.

He looked a little skeptical but reached for them. Taking a look at the size tag he glanced back up at her. "How do you know what size I wear? Have you been sneaking into my closet?" he asked in a tone that was obviously teasing.

Sleeping with him last night had translated to him moving all her stuff from the guest room to his. "You didn't leave me any space to hang my clothes so I had to move some of yours around. And let me say you have just as many clothes as the women I know combined."

He smiled. "I like to look good."

"Just try the pants on."

"Don't try to get me in those skinny jeans I see guys wearing now. That's not going to work with me."

"Yuck, no, I don't think that should work for any man. All these are regular bootcut," she told him, handing him yet another pair of jeans, this time darker than the ones he already had thrown over his arm.

An hour and five pairs of jeans—including the two pairs she'd selected—three dress shirts and a couple of jogging suits later they were headed to the women's department.

"I don't need anything," she said instantly.

"I didn't ask if you did."

"Then I don't want anything."

"I didn't ask you that, either."

She sent him a smoldering look at that remark, but he ignored her and kept moving toward the other side of the store. Where he finally stopped had her both gasping and turning to walk away.

Akil grabbed her by both elbows, turning her back around. "Come on, it's your turn."

"I told you I didn't need anything," she said, hastily looking around. "And I definitely don't need anything from this department."

Heat fused the back of her neck and freckled her cheeks as she stood in the middle of two aisles full of lingerie. From long silky nightgowns to skimpy little teddies to what looked like a bunch of straps and strings arranged neatly on a hanger, this was so out of her element. While she'd enjoyed shopping with Akil for himself, this was a little more personal than she'd ever imagined he'd want to do for or with her.

"I like this." He held up a black nightie that would probably stop along the middle part of her thigh. It wasn't bad-looking, it just wasn't for her.

She shook her head negatively. Akil simply tossed the garment into the shopping bag with the rest of his soon-to-be purchases. "Ooh, and this one is a definite," he was saying.

He'd left her in the first aisle and was now a short distance from her, picking up something else. Charlene raced around to the other aisle to see what he'd picked up this time. "No, Akil. Absolutely not!" she said, her voice elevated a bit. Looking around, she took a step closer to him and reached for the ruby-red sheer item he held.

Of course he held his arm up higher, keeping the piece out of her reach. "Are you kidding me? This is hot! I can visualize you in it now."

She made another reach for it but he simply took a step back. "No. No. No. Don't you visualize anything."

But when she looked at him she could tell he was doing just that. His eyes had grown darker and his tongue was stroking his lower lip.

"Akil, I'm not playing."

"C'mon, baby girl. You can see it, too," he said, holding the nightie in front of her.

Reluctantly Charlene looked down. It was sexy, she'd say that much. What she'd seen that was sheer was a jacket held together by one thin silk red string. Beneath it was what looked like a high-waisted one-piece bathing suit. It was strapless and of course red satin, with laces going from the breast cups down right to the crotch.

She swallowed and put a hand to her chest. "I can't visualize it," she said slowly, then turned away.

Coming up behind her, Akil placed a hand on her shoulder. "What's the matter, Charlene? Did I say something wrong?"

She shook her head. "No. It's not you, it's me." Then she chuckled. "That sounds so cliché."

"Actually, it sounds like a lie."

She turned to face him. "Look, Akil, I just don't want you to buy me that because then you'll expect me to wear it."

He nodded. "You're right, I would expect you to wear it. And I know you'll look terrific in it."

"No, I won't."

With a finger to her chin he lifted her face until she was looking directly into his eyes. "You look terrific absolutely naked. Adding this garment can only enhance that beauty. I don't want you to be shy around me or nervous that I won't like how you look. I'm telling you right now that I like everything about you, physical and mental. Okay?"

No, it wasn't okay, she thought with even more flames of embarrassment shooting through her body. Not to mention the instant arousal she always felt whenever he was touching her.

"Baby girl?" he whispered, then leaned forward and kissed the tip of her nose. "Did you hear what I said?" He kissed both of her eyes, her cheeks, then finally her lips.

She nodded. "I heard you."

"Do you believe me?"

And she had to tell the truth. What one man thought of her shouldn't have meant so much. She'd lived in this body with her feelings about it and her acceptance of it for far too long to still rely so heavily on words or opinions. Still, it felt good, it felt right. "Yes, Akil. I believe you."

"Good," he said with one last smacking kiss on her lips. "We're getting this red one and the black one. Now let's see what else we can buy in this store today."

And just like that, their shopping spree continued. As if it were the most natural thing in the world, like they'd been together for months and months, they moved through the mall, laughing and window-shopping, purchasing and laughing some more. It was maybe one of the best times of Akil's life.

He only hoped it could last.

Chapter 14

Mrs. Williamson fixed a spectacular dinner of ham, homemade baked macaroni and cheese, collard greens and apple pie. Charlene ate a full plate with a smile on her face.

Today had been perfect. Spending it entirely with Charlene, there was only one other thing that could top their day.

Music.

After dinner when she'd assumed they'd relax and prepare for bed he fooled her by going straight to the studio.

"You want to work now?" she was asking from behind him. "Aren't you tired?"

He chuckled. "No. And you shouldn't be. We didn't walk that much."

"Oh, yeah, tell that to my aching feet. Well, at least my stomach's full. But if you don't mind I'll just watch you work for a while."

"Whatever you want, baby girl."

Unable to keep his hands off her for long periods of time, Akil draped an arm over her shoulder as they went through the first door that led down a short hallway to another door. This second door was the soundproof entrance into the studio. Once inside they headed directly to the live room, where Charlene quickly pulled up a chair and sat down.

"Did you take your medicine today?" he asked, eyeing her suspiciously.

"Yes, I did," she replied. "But I didn't get much sleep last night. Remember?"

He nodded. "That's right, you were afraid of the wind and rain. Couldn't sleep."

Just as he'd expected and wanted to see, she smiled. "Yeah, that's exactly what happened."

Today had been a first for him. He sensed it was because of the woman, because of what he knew he was beginning to feel for her. Those feelings unnerved him because he knew they were headed in a direction of uncharted territory. He didn't fall in love with women, didn't allow himself the time or the energy to do so. He had sex, that was natural, a need that required slaking from time to time. Anything beyond that was a hassle and a danger to the man he'd become.

Switching on the power, he pulled up the recording he'd been aching to listen to all day. It was his favorite instrumental. He wanted to listen to it because lyrics had been bubbling around in his head all day long.

"You really like that arrangement, don't you?" Charlene asked from her seat a few feet away from him.

He nodded. "It speaks to me."

"I know what you mean."

And he knew that she did. From the very first time that she'd listened to it he knew she'd felt it.

"She's afraid to give him her love," Charlene began saying.

"But she has so much love to give. He'd be honored to have it."

Charlene began to hum with the music, he suspected because she was so used to the melody by now.

"And after all is said and done you're mine," she sang along with the rhythm that signaled the hook of the song was beginning.

To his own surprise, and he was sure hers, too, Akil joined in. "You belong to me and I belong to you."

The fact that he could sing only startled her for a minute. Most producers were multitalented when it came to music. They could definitely carry a tune and in today's market could most likely flow with the smooth ease of a practiced rapper. The music was in his mind, in his soul, the slick sound of his tenor voice said it reached a part of him that most singers only hoped for.

"You belong to me and I happily belong to you," she sang and closed her eyes, listening as the rhythm slowed again. "When I first met you I didn't believe— didn't want to consider the possibilities. But with the first touch, the first taste I was lost."

The lyrics just flowed and she sang. They were passing the time, letting their combined love of music entertain them for the evening. But when her eyes opened again it was to see Akil staring at her, a pencil in hand and piece of paper in front of him.

"Go on," he prompted when she stopped.

"Oh, no, I was just thinking out loud. I didn't mean—" she stammered.

"It's good. The lyrics are good. She was nervous about loving him in the beginning and then what?"

"She," not her, not Charlene. He wasn't thinking about her when he thought of this song. That was her thought and she sighed. If she weren't such a coward she'd just tell him that each time she heard this melody she thought of nothing but them. From that first night she'd heard it she'd felt his soul and hers in the very beat of the music. Last night they'd made love to this very rhythm in its extended version and then as it was stripped to one instrument at a time. The rhythm of their bodies matched this song from every up-tempo sweep to the straining piano solos.

But Akil didn't seem to know that.

"What about him?" she asked.

For a second he paused, then his head nodded in beat with the music. "Even I wasn't convinced. Something was there but was it true? Could it be what I've always wanted but never really knew existed?"

His voice sent chills down her spine, in a good way, of course. She felt the sincerity and wanted desperately to believe that it was coming from his heart and not just his creative mind.

"Could she be the one for me? Does she know I desperately want her to be?"

With that Charlene's gaze locked with his and the next thing she knew she was standing, moving toward him. Her heart hammered in her chest, her mind screaming questions that her body refused to hear. Her actions were purely emotional, purely physical at this moment, and that's just how she wanted them. To think about what she was doing, what she was risking, might cost her too much.

Cupping Akil's face in her hands, she stared deep into his eyes and sang with the hook once more, "You belong to me and I belong to you. You belong to me and I happily belong to you."

His hands had snaked up to her hips as she sang, his eyes shifting to that molten color, lust rising in him just as it was in her. But was that all? Not for her, she knew. For Akil, she could only hope.

Lowering her head, she touched her lips to his. Tentatively at first, then with more pressure, more persistence. He obliged, matching her movements and coaxing her tongue to join in the mix. Before long she was straddling him. Her arms wrapped around his neck, his around her back, moving up and down, and they struggled to breathe without breaking the connection of their mouths.

The music in the background was louder than last night but Charlene wasn't really listening. She was feeling every trickle of heat, every massage of his hands. Her body was on fire with need, a scorching storm building inside waiting, aching for release.

When she knew her lips were swollen from their kisses Akil stood, lifting her in his arms as if she weighed no more than a CD in its case. With one arm he pushed the pencil and paper on the control board aside before sitting her down.

"You belong to me," he sang, his fast-moving fingers going to the buckle of her jeans, pulling them apart and down.

She shimmied out of them, heard the jeans and her shoes fall to the floor. Next went her shirt and her bra. Akil bent forward, kissed each nipple, all the while humming along with the music.

Bracing herself back on her flattened palms, she offered herself to him, totally, completely. He was slow in removing her panties, his lyrics mumbled as he pulled them down her thighs with his teeth.

Charlene was wet and trembling, her desire for Akil quick and potent. With strong hands he grasped her thighs and pushed them apart.

"Could she be the one for me?" his voice sang and her body hummed along.

With one arm extended he touched the tender moist folds of her center, his eyes fastened on hers. His other hand made quick work of his own buckle and he pushed his pants and boxers down his thighs. "Could this belong to me and only me?"

That line shocked her, not just in the words but in the almost falsetto voice he'd used to sing them. At the sound her nipples tingled, her center clenching and juicing more along with his touch.

When his first finger entered her she wanted to scream but bit her bottom lip instead.

"Uh-uh, don't hold it in," he whispered, coming closer so that his thick erection brushed along her inner thigh teasingly. His lips were so close to hers, his warm breath fanned her face. "Nobody can hear you in here, baby girl. If this belongs to me," he said, then traced a heated path from her cheek to her lips and sang, "Say my name. Sing your pleasure and say my name."

She could feel the broad head of his sex pressing past her swollen folds and scooted a little closer, eager for him.

"Sing your pleasure," he repeated as just the head pressed forward.

Her body vibrated with anticipation and longing and she inhaled, exhaled.

"Say my name."

And she did, in a long note held in A minor she sang

his name so that there would be no question, no mystery, no denial. She was all his.

As she sang, her voice meshing with his. Akil pushed deeper inside her, feeling his own body convulse with the pleasure. His strokes were slow, measured, but the feel of her lush breasts against his chest even through the material of his shirt was too arousing to keep up that motion. In no time he was thrusting deeply and quickly, loving the sound of their arousal combined with the music and their voices.

Both of them were singing, gyrating, feeling, needing. It was like they were caught up in this funnel of emotion that was spun just for them. And as he felt himself nearing his climax her body shook against his.

Her lyrics changed, slowed until it was if she were just whispering in his ear, her body still shaking from her release. "I think I'm in love with you."

With those words his own release came. In a rush of feeling from his scrotum bursting through his engorged head, he let go. Poured everything he had directly into her.

The words tumbled out, as if they were expected—no, written in the lyrics of the song that Akil now knew belonged to them. "I think I'm in love with you, too."

It was back to business on Monday when Charlene walked into the studio. Akil had gotten up a little earlier, going for a run. He'd whispered in her ear as she continued to sleep in his bed. More and more Charlene was beginning to feel that was exactly where she belonged.

After their heated admissions about possibly being in love with each other she'd expected being together outside the bedroom would be awkward. The exact opposite had occurred. On Sunday Akil had been attentive, open about his past, his feelings, his future plans. It was perfect. So much so she was almost afraid to go back into the studio, to bring more people into their newfound bliss.

"There you go," Jason was saying, dropping an arm over Charlene's shoulders. "How'd you handle the storm?"

She must have looked a little startled at his question because then he said, "The hurricane? I see Viola did no damage to the house. Akil said you mostly had strong rain Friday night and most of Saturday morning. On Thursday you said you didn't like storms."

Oh, yeah, she'd forgotten all about the hurricane. With an inner smile she wondered why. "I did fine. It wasn't as bad as I'd anticipated," she said, trying to keep her gaze from Akil's.

He hadn't looked at her, either. He was at the control board, his fingers moving over the buttons, adjusting the sound, getting everything prepared. He was in business mode, so she assumed she'd better do the same thing.

"Listen, I've got some news. I was waiting until you came so I could tell you both together," Jason said.

Akil did look up then. "What news?"

Jason was rubbing his long fingers together, his caramel-toned skin almost gleaming as he smiled. Whatever it was he had to say must be good. "Seven Nights, you know that new club down in South Beach?" he said to Akil.

"Yeah? What about it?"

"Well, the club's promoter is dating my cousin. I saw him over the weekend at a family gathering and he mentioned they were looking for hot new talent to premiere at the club. Said the crowd on Friday nights is sick. They start packing in around nine. He wants acts to hit the stage around ten, ten-thirty. Like thirty-five grand per night," Jason finished with a slap of his hands together. "What do you say?"

Akil was already looking skeptical. "It's not about the money," he said first.

"I know that, man. It's the exposure. I think she's ready."

Charlene had no idea what club they were talking about but she was focused on Akil, on his reaction to what Jason was saying.

"It would be good exposure. Like a test run," Akil added finally.

Jason was nodding his agreement. "The buzz would already be underway before we even hit Vibe. It's good, Ace. So you want me to call him?"

Akil's gaze finally found hers as he nodded. "Yeah. Call him, tell him we've got a hot new singer who will blow his mind."

"Somebody want to clue me in on what's going on?" Charlene asked, not unnerved by Akil's gaze as much as she was curious.

"You're performing at a club on Friday," he said as simply as if he'd given her the time of day. "Get into the booth so we can go over what you're going to sing."

And just like that the day's work began. Later, Charlene thought, she'd have the meltdown about performing in public, but for right now, all she had to do was sing.

Chapter 15

"Were you busy?" Charlene asked Rachel, the cell phone pressed to her ear as she walked along the terrace.

Jason and Five were still in the studio with Akil re-mixing one of the tracks they'd finally gotten recorded. It was almost midnight and Akil had come into the booth personally to tell her she was finished for the night.

"You did good," he'd said with a smile. But hadn't touched her, hadn't made a move remotely intimate.

Charlene had tried not to be hurt by the nonaction. She'd been trying all day long. Singing love songs when you're about twelve feet away from the man you love and he's acting like you're just another employee isn't exactly an ideal working condition. Still, the butterflies that seemed to have moved back into her stomach kept her plenty occupied in the meantime.

Her first performance as Charlene Quinn, the singer, the R&B artist. She sighed.

"No. What's up? You don't sound so good."

Taking a seat in one of the high-backed white chairs, she let her muscles relax even though her mind still reeled with all that had gone on in the past few weeks. The fast track to a singing career had been the furthest thing from Charlene's mind, ever. And now here she was. To top it off she was in Miami, where the only people she knew she also worked for. Her friends, her family, were all on the West Coast.

"I'm trying," she said and knew it didn't sound convincing.

"Trying to what? Charlene, just tell me what's wrong."

Now Rachel's voice had hiked up a notch, which meant she was getting worried. Not Charlene's plan.

"I'm singing in a club on Friday. Akil and Jason think I'm ready."

"That's fantastic! Your first performance," she practically yelled and Charlene could tell she was smiling. "So wait, why do you sound like that's a bad thing?"

"Not necessarily a bad thing, but certainly a new thing."

"Well, that's part of being an entertainer. You sing, record the CD then you go out to promote it. That's how it works."

"Excuse me if I'm still trying to acclimate myself to this singing-as-a-career thing. It's been barely a month and I'm already recording my first CD and performing in clubs. That's not how it usually happens."

"But you're not usual," Rachel quipped.

"Gee, thanks." With two fingers Charlene rubbed her temple.

"You know that's not how I meant it. I'm just saying that you should be happy. Like you said, this is not how it usually happens. You've seen for yourself how many singers wish for this their whole lives and still never get it. You should be thankful for your talent and extremely encouraged that Akil and your record label have this type of confidence in you."

Leave it to Rachel to sound so logical. "And I am."

"But?"

"But—" Charlene hesitated, looked up at the indigo sky void of any stars that she could wish on "—I'm scared."

"Of?"

"What if they don't like me? What if I'm not good enough? What if all this was just a dream and I'm going to wake up the minute I step on that stage and all those people staring up at me start to laugh?"

Rachel chuckled. "I swear I've never known anyone who could 'what if' something to death like you."

"Ha-ha, very funny," Charlene quipped, even though Candis often told her the same thing. "You know what I'm trying to say."

"I do," Rachel said with a sigh. "And I get it. I know how you feel about performing in front of people, but, Char, I've got to tell you, for a long time I've thought that was all just in your mind. I mean, take the karaoke bar, for instance. You didn't want to do that but you did. There were about thirty or so people in the audience that night and you got right up there and sang. So good you landed a record deal."

"I did that for you."

"Partly, yes. But more so because you love it. You were born to sing."

Charlene smiled. "That's a movie, Rach."

"Is it?"

"I think so. Or is that *A Star Is Born?*"

"I don't know, you're the one into watching all those old movies. Anyway, what I'm trying to say is once you get on that stage you forget about all those reservations you've nursed since you were a kid. You forget how many people are staring at you and what they may or may not be thinking about your physical looks. You just sing. And when you do people are entranced by your voice."

"So what you're trying to say is don't worry, they're not really looking at me anyway."

"No," Rachel added quickly. "That's not what I'm trying to say. I'm saying that all this stuff about not looking good or not looking like other people is a complex that your mother created and you've nursed. It might be time to let it go, you know."

The words sounded so right. Rachel was honest and she cared. That's why she was her best friend. "I hear you."

"But are you listening to me, Charlene? You're twenty-five years old and in a position that a lot of people would die for. Do you really want to throw it all away because you don't think you look good enough? Because you know you can sang," she said with a giggle and that twang to her voice that always made Charlene laugh.

"I'm listening to you. I always do," she said truthfully. That's why she'd called Rachel first. While Candis was her older sister and Charlene valued her opinion, she and Rachel were not only closer in age, they were closer, period, had more in common. Charlene knew undoubtedly that she could always count on Rachel. That's why her next words came out as smoothly as if she were talking about the weather. "I'm in love with Akil."

"What? Wait a minute, you're confusing me. Weren't we just talking about you being nervous about singing onstage, in front of people? Now you're telling me you're in love with someone? *Akil?* As in your *producer?*"

"Okay. Okay. Slow down, maybe I should have given the conversation change a minute to sink in," Charlene said, unable to help herself from laughing. "Yes. I said I'm in love with Akil, my producer."

"And," Rachel said slowly, "when did you come to that conclusion and what brought you there? What happened?"

"At first he was an ass. I mean, honest and truly, there were days when I felt like knocking him right out."

"Obviously that changed," Rachel said.

"You wanna hear the story or not?"

Rachel chuckled. "Okay, sorry. Go ahead."

"Then he kissed me. And then we had breakfast, lots of breakfasts. You know he doesn't like coffee?"

"Ah, no, I didn't know that."

Of course she didn't, Charlene thought and smiled. She was babbling. She made a concerted effort to stop. "Anyway, we spent some time together and then we slept together and we talked. And we went shopping and we slept together again. And I just figured out that I'm in love with him."

"Okay," Rachel was saying in that slow voice again. "And how does he feel about you?"

"He said he thinks he's in love with me, too."

"Are you happy about that?"

"I think."

"But you're not sure?"

"Where Akil is concerned I can never be too sure."

"Girl, I need to get on a plane and get to Miami. You know I can't leave you on your own for too long."

"Hush, you know I can handle myself." She let out a long sigh. "I just needed to get some things off my chest. But really, I'm doing fine. Actually, I might be excited about performing on Friday if I hadn't gotten the stylist Akil hired fired."

"And how did you do that?"

"By being me," she answered with a chuckle.

"Yeah, right. And I'm sure this person didn't do anything to deserve getting fired. But never you fear, even though I'm across the country you know I've got your back."

"How? What are you going to do, Rachel?"

"Don't worry, I've got this."

"Rachel," Charlene said warningly.

"Oh, I've gotta go, Ethan's here."

"Uh-huh, don't even try it. Ethan is not there. Rachel, what are you going to do?"

"He is here and I have something to talk to him about. Girl, Sofia is having a fit."

"Oh, no. What's going on? I haven't spoken to her but I was going to call her to let her know about the show."

"Don't worry. I'll tell her. But she's still reeling from Uncle Jacob's decision to merge Limelight with A.F.I."

"Wait a minute. A.F.I., Artist's Factory Outlet, your rival talent agency?"

"Yes, that's the one. Apparently my family has a problem with the Jordans, who own A.F.I., or at least the previous generation did. So we're inclined to carry out the feud. Except Uncle Jacob doesn't want that anymore. He wants this merger."

Charlene knew what Rachel was going to say next. "And Sofia isn't trying to hear that."

"Girl, she's livid. You know Limelight is her life.

She wanted to take the helm after Uncle Jacob retired. It's always been her dream. And now she feels like he's taking that from her."

"But he's not firing her, right? That would be crazy. Sofia's the best at what she does."

"I agree and so does Uncle Jacob. That's why he's suggesting she and Ramell Jordan become partners. But you know how Sofia is about being the boss."

"I sure do. Not a good situation."

"Not at all. But look, you don't worry about a thing. I'm going to get off this phone, make a quick call and have you set for Friday. Just trust me."

A half hour later when Charlene was stepping out of the shower she had a funny feeling about Rachel's words. But she'd known her forever so she would trust her, this time.

The next day's session was cut short as Akil had some business meetings to attend. Charlene was left to entertain herself in the big house. Mrs. Williamson, of course, was around cooking and cleaning as usual. She'd even seen Nannette as she'd headed out to the terrace, which was quickly becoming her favorite spot.

She didn't know if it was the quiet rustle of the waterfall picturesquely situated toward the end of the pool or the beautiful skyline the back of the house afforded. Against the crystalline blue sky and sparkling sunshine the tips of trees spread into an expanse of deep green. Lower to eye level, palm trees swayed in the warm breeze, creating an almost tropical—without being on an island—feel. She loved it, which was probably due to the fact that she was from California and used to this summerlike scenery all year long.

Nannette had been a darling and purchased all the magazines she'd asked her for. So with a cup of warm tea with honey, Charlene made herself comfortable in one of the lounge chairs and settled in for the afternoon.

She had fashion magazines, which she was sure would have Candis on some of their pages, music and entertainment magazines. What she was looking for she had no clue. Actually, she did. She wanted to know what "the look" now was. Wanted to know if she was remotely close since Serene and her sidekick were now out of the picture.

Akil had come to bed late last night. Though she'd heard him in the shower, felt him climb in bed beside her, reach for her and hold her throughout the night, she hadn't awakened fully and they hadn't talked. This morning Jason was there for breakfast, so again, she didn't have the chance to ask him about the lack of a stylist or her having no clue what she was going to wear on Friday. He'd promised to spend the evening with her as he'd kissed her before leaving this afternoon. He'd seemed a little agitated but she figured maybe he just didn't want to deal with the meeting right now. He hated to be interrupted while working on a CD and since hers was on a fast track, meaning they hoped to at least drop the first single early next year, a day away from recording could really hurt them. The days lost due to the hurricane had been setback enough.

So she settled in, flipping the glossy pages and seeing some things that she could go for. Jill Scott had a nice, real look. She loved the woman's voice and admired her stance to sing only songs with lyrics she'd personally experienced. Her Neo-Soul sound was original and definitely had an audience. And she wasn't wafer thin, either. That made Charlene smile, boosting her ego just a bit.

A picture of the pretty but slim Keri Hilson was on another page, her hair in a longer, feathery style. Charlene liked the color—like a soft bronze, with some blond highlights. But she was a lighter complexion than Keri Hilson so she wasn't sure how that would look on her. Liya Kebede was in one of the fashion magazines. She was a gorgeous model from Ethiopia. Charlene had met her when she'd traveled to Italy with Candis last year for a photo shoot. She'd enjoyed spending the time with her sister and seeing all the hard work that went into modeling. It definitely wasn't always as glamorous as it looked. Both Liya and Tia St. Claire Donovan—another model whom Candis and Charlene had actually known for a couple of years and who had just a few months ago married the infamous Trent Donovan and given birth to her first son—had complexions just a shade darker than Charlene's. And both of them had eyes that weird shade of hazel and darker brown like she did. So Charlene concentrated on their hair color and their makeup, wondering if any of the tones could work for her.

"I don't need no help. Stop following me. I can find the pool."

She heard a high-pitched voice but didn't think it was exactly female. It was getting louder and she wondered who it could be.

"See, she's right here. I told you I didn't need any help."

Charlene looked up and had to do a double take.

"Following me around like a stalker. Or like I'm gonna steal something. She better recognize."

Not too tall, maybe five-seven, five-ten in the black silver-heeled stilettos he wore. Charlene had to strain her eyes because she could have sworn she was correct in assuming he. But…

"Charlene Quinn, girl, I know you betta get up off that chair and give me a hug. Don't make me come over there and yank your behind."

The face definitely looked familiar, caramel-toned, slim, pert lips, assessing eyes. Wait a minute, she began thinking, moving her legs to stand from the chair. Magazines fell to the ground but Charlene was too busy staring to care.

"What? I look good, don't I?"

He struck a pose and Charlene couldn't help but take in his full attire, skinny-legged black jeans, a slim-fit T-shirt tied into a knot just above a flat stomach and dangling navel piercing, black-and-silver bangles dancing up both arms and two diamond studs sparkling from the ears. The hair was a short, sleek asymmetrical bob that even Charlene had to admit was fierce. She thought she recognized him.

"Mark?" she finally gasped, taking a step closer. "Mark Hopkins?"

With a wave of his hand and a jingle of all the bracelets on that wrist, his lips turned and he sucked his teeth. "I'm Mia now," he said and emphasized that change by using both hands to cup his modest breasts.

Her gaze immediately dropped and rested there. "What? Who?"

"That's right, baby. I've got my own now. And you—" he actually reached out and flicked one of Charlene's breasts with one long finger "—you're going to be so jealous when I surpass your girls."

Shaking her head, Charlene was still trying to get a grasp of this situation. "What are you doing here? And when did you get these? When did you become *this?*" she asked for lack of a better word.

"'This,' as you so rudely put it, has always been me. You know how I used to always hang out with you and Rachel instead of the quote-unquote boys."

He was talking and Charlene couldn't help but recognize how his arm motions and facial expressions seemed a little over-the-top. Then again, this entire person standing in front of her was over-the-top.

"Mark, I mean, Mia," she corrected when one elegantly arched eyebrow on his face raised in question. "I just can't believe it. Does Rachel know? Wait a minute, what are you doing here? How did you know I was in Miami?" Charlene asked suspiciously.

"First, I want my hug," Mia pouted.

"Oh, boy-girl, get over here," Charlene said, grabbing her old friend in a hug. Mark had always been skinny and for a while Charlene had hated him because he ate like a hog and didn't gain an ounce. It felt a little funny hugging him now that he had the unmistakable curve of breasts. "It's been a long time since I've seen you. I see you've changed a lot in that time."

Mark pulled back, waving that hand again. "Girl, I started hormone therapy about nine months ago. I'm preparing for the full gender reassignment."

"A sex change? You're getting a sex change operation?"

"Chile, now you know that's déclassé. Talk like you've been brought up right. What would Mrs. Quinn say if she heard you? It's gender-reassignment surgery."

Yeah, whatever. It was weird in Charlene's book. "Are you sure this is what you want to do?"

He touched those breasts again. "It's a little too late to change my mind."

"Oh." Charlene shrugged. "I guess so. Now answer my question, what are you doing here?"

"Rachel called me last night going on and on about you getting a record deal and performing in a club. The first thing I asked was who was going to do your hair. Because, girl, you know you never get anything good done to your hair. And it's such a shame, you've got such a good grain."

Mark's—Mia's—fingers were already pulling the ponytail holder from her hair. He raked through the length, straightening it so that it lay limply on her shoulders.

"Ump, see, this is what I mean. Such great length and volume. You know people would kill for this kind of hair."

"Yeah, right. People like who?" Charlene snapped.

"People like Lynell Dennison. You remember her? Girl ain't never had more than three strands of hair and they were all nappy as hell."

Charlene laughed so hard at the memory and the way Mark said it she had to sit back down. "You haven't changed a bit. Well, you have, but, you know, you're still just like I remember you."

"I'm only improving the outside, there's no hope for the inside, honey. Now, we have to make you divalicious for Friday."

"What is divalicious?"

"It's a Mia Hopkins original, that's what it is. And when I'm finished with you everyone from here to L.A.

will be looking for me to reinvent them, too. Now, come on, let's go shopping."

Charlene didn't even argue, just got up and headed out the door with Mark—no, Mia. If he wanted to be a she, Charlene wasn't in any position to argue. Wasn't she about to make some changes to her appearance? It was the same and yet different, but she wasn't going to overanalyze the situation. No, today, Charlene Quinn was simply going to go with the flow.

In the mall again. Charlene almost sighed but this trip was full of laughing and chatting just as much as it was shopping. Some of the stuff Mia pulled out was just too off the hook for Charlene to even consider. And then there were the rare pieces that she actually thought she could like.

"Stop being so uptight. You've got good curves, you need to flaunt them," Mia was saying as they walked into yet another store.

Charlene was walking behind him, her hand absently touching the black dresses on the rack in front of her. "Serene and Carlo thought I should stick to empire waists to cover my problem area."

Mia spun around so quick he almost fell on top of her. "What problem area?"

With a sigh, Charlene ran her hands over her midsection. "This one."

Mia clucked his teeth and lifted a finger to tap on Charlene's head. "You mean this one. Because that's the only place you've got a problem."

Charlene swatted his hand away. "Stop playing, this is serious."

"It sure is. Rachel said you were still the same but I

couldn't believe it. I figured the years had to have given you some sense."

"Look, Mia, don't cross the line," Charlene warned.

"Oh. Oh." Mia was rolling his neck like a scared chicken, his voice getting louder and louder until two of the salespeople were now staring at them. "I know you're not going to get a backbone with me after you let Ozzie and Harriet tear you down about your size."

"What?" Charlene asked, confused, then sighed. "Lower your voice, we don't need an audience. And who the hell are Ozzie and Harriet?"

"Those two fools that told you all you could wear was empire waists," he said with a roll of his eyes and a toss of his neck, which made his perfectly styled hair sway.

"Serene and Carlo."

"Whatever. The bottom line is they must not have any style themselves, trying to tell you what not to wear."

"Well, it's their job. They're publicists and stylists."

Mia kept right on talking and walking, every now and then picking up a piece, looking at it, then putting it down. "Do they have their own show on a cable network?"

"What? No, they don't have a show."

"Then they don't know what they hell they're talkin' about."

Charlene just shook her head. And Mia said she was still the same. She remembered endless conversations like this during their high school years. Mia fussing about this or that, Rachel either agreeing or arguing with him and Charlene trailing behind the both of them, shaking her head and wondering why she even bothered.

"Okay, now that you've shared your opinion of them, what do you suggest?"

"Oh, now she wants my opinion?" He started looking around the store, a hand fluttering to his chest. "Little ole me? I'm not a publicist but—"

"Just shut up and tell me what to wear," she said in a huff. He was getting louder and sooner or later one of those salespeople was going to come over and put them out of the store. Then again, she thought looking at Mia, they probably weren't going to come near them no matter how much money they had to spend.

"Humph," was the next reply she received from him before he walked quickly to the back. Along the wall were black cocktail dresses, some simple and some with a little more sparkle.

"Friday is your debut, but it's a sneak peek, right? So you don't want to blast them with everything. You know, don't really give them the whole Charlene Quinn look. Just a glimpse is what'll keep them itching for more."

Charlene agreed.

Mia quickly picked three dresses. "Here, go try these on. Black is simple. And sexy as hell. Go!"

She didn't even bother to argue with him, just took the dresses and moved toward the dressing rooms. When one of the salespeople who had been staring them down since the moment they walked into the store approached with a key she asked, "Could I go in and try these on?"

For a minute the woman looked as if she wanted to say no. A part of Charlene hoped she wouldn't because then she'd have to curse the woman from here right to the courthouse for discrimination. Luckily, she just gave a tight smile and opened the door, ushering Charlene inside.

The first one was a quick no as Charlene's breasts were about to topple over the bodice. The second was just okay, nothing spectacular, according to Mia. The third, thankfully, hit the mark. It was a wraparound with gathers all across the bodice and a straight bottom that looked plain until she walked and her thick thigh peeked through.

"Hotter than hell," Mia had said the moment she walked out of the dressing room. "Simple and sexy. That's what you are, simply sexy."

He chattered on about earrings and shoes and how to style her hair, but Charlene just looked. Standing in the three-way mirror she was able to observe herself at every angle. Black was certainly slimming and she always wore good undergarments. She felt that was the problem with a lot of plus-size women; they refused to spend the money it took to keep their curves looking neat and precise. So there were no hanging rolls, nothing jiggling—that shouldn't be—and nothing about to burst out. She had to admit, this time Mia was right. It was simply sexy.

And Charlene immediately thought of Akil. What would he think of the dress and the way it made her look?

She didn't have ten more minutes to think further before Mia was pushing her back into the dressing room, yelling for her to take that dress off because they had much more shopping to do. Normally she didn't like shopping, but she had enjoyed the other day with Akil. This afternoon, with her old friend who was now sort of a new friend, was shaping up to be just as nice.

Until she heard Mia's loud voice once more.

"Miss, why are you following me around this store like I'm a shoplifter? Do I look like I'm broke?"

All Charlene could do was shake her head. And laugh.

Chapter 16

"Really, Mia. Did you have to threaten that woman at the salon?"

Mia looked totally appalled as they walked into the house after another six hours at the mall. It was after eight in the evening by the time they'd made it back and Charlene was tired. Her feet hurt from walking and her cheeks hurt from laughing so much.

"Are you crazy? That chick did not know me. As cute as I am people should not get it twisted, I will slice and dice anybody who crosses me. Go back to Big Sur and ask that little hoochie who worked in the spa. Tried to put a curly perm in my head." He was using both hands to smooth down his hair, which still wasn't out of place. "Shoot, you know how long it took to get my hair this straight and glossy. I don't know where people get their licenses from."

Charlene was laughing again. "That was like the third time you almost got us arrested."

"Oh, please, I am not afraid of jail."

Charlene dropped her bags as they made their way into the living room. "Well, I am."

"That's because you're uppity. Always have been," he said, waving his hands again and plopping down into the puffy white leather lounge. "Just because your daddy made all that money in movies and TV, you thought you were privileged."

Charlene feigned indignance. "I was."

"Honeychile, you were not. You were the second born and you weren't the model. You were just like me—close but no cigar."

"Shut up!" she said, tossing one of the colored pillows from the couch toward his head. "Your mother acted in just as many movies as my father produced and won just as many awards. And your daddy wasn't any slouch, either, with all the oil money he'd inherited. You're just as uppity as I am."

"But we weren't talking about me. We were talking about—oh...my...Lord." Mia sat up in the chair, staring off at something.

"What?" Charlene asked, following the direction of his gaze.

"Who is that? He is some kind of fine." Mia was getting up out of the chair, smoothing down her shirt and pushing up her breasts.

In the hallway Akil and Jason were talking. It looked as if Jason were leaving for the night.

"Oh, Akil," she called as she started walking toward them.

They both stopped talking and met her halfway. "Hey, you're back," Akil said, his smile making her warm all over.

"We thought you'd gotten lost. Ace here was about to call out the search posse."

"It wasn't like that," Akil said, looking a little awkward at Jason's words. "I was just wondering where you were."

"I should have left a note. It just happened so quick. Mia showed up and we just headed out to the mall, didn't think about anything else."

"Mia?" Akil asked.

Charlene turned, grabbed Mia's arm and pulled him forward. "My old friend from L.A., Mia Hopkins. Rachel couldn't come so she sent Mia out to help me get ready for Friday's show. That's where we've been, out shopping for my outfit."

Akil barely looked at Mia. "You got your hair done?" he asked.

She smiled and turned to the side and back. "I did. Do you like it?"

"It's nice," Jason said. "Sassy."

"They cut a few inches and feathered it a bit on the ends. I think it's sexy. She needed a little oomph," Mia spoke up.

Akil cut his eyes at him. "This was your idea?"

Mia poked her hormone-enhanced breasts out farther. "Of course. Do you like?"

Akil couldn't tell if she was asking if he liked Charlene's hair or Mia's breasts. Or seeing as she had an Adam's apple the size of a golf ball, he should probably say "his" breasts.

"I liked her before," was Akil's immediate reply. "But this is nice, soft. It fits you."

"I know it does. When I set out to make someone over that's what I do. And nobody knows Charlene like I do, so I know what's best for her," Mia was saying, moving so that she now stood closer to Akil.

Behind him he heard Jason stifle a chuckle.

"Have you had dinner?" Akil asked Charlene.

"We ate at the mall."

"Yes, we did. But if you'd like to go out for a night-cap?" Mia left the rest to linger in the air.

Akil was about to speak when Charlene grabbed Mia by the elbow. "Enough. It's not even that type of party so move along."

Mia shook his head, looking at her over his shoulder. "I was wondering how long it was going to take you to speak up. If I've told you once I've told you a thousand times—if it's yours stake your claim and make it known."

Turning back to Akil, he said, "Hurt her and I'll bust your kneecaps. Good night."

He walked past Jason, blowing a kiss in his direction. Akil didn't know what to say as they all watched the slim hips sashay out the front door.

However, as soon as the door was closed Jason let out a thunderous laugh that had Charlene following suit. Akil was not feeling the joke.

Actually, he wasn't feeling anything but paranoid right about now. He'd received another phone call, this time with a message. No, he knew this was no laughing matter.

This was it.

Charlene took one last look in the mirror. She and Mia had changed their minds several times in the last few days about what she was actually going to wear. But tonight was the night. The dress she wore was *the* one. And "the look" was all hers.

Her hair was flawless, flipped and feathered to fall softly around her face. Her natural brown color had been lightened just a bit with bronze highlights. Mia swore by MAC cosmetics, so he'd used the Shimpagne

Mineralize Skinfinish. The Play on Plums eye finish was a great accent, giving her eyes a bronze/peachy/pink look, and Roman Holiday Dazzleglass gave her lips just enough tinted shine she was sure would last the entire night. Never had Charlene seen her own face look so classically pretty.

The dress was simple and sexy, just "the look" she and Mia had decided would be her signature. A rich black sheath, modern square neck, cap sleeves and slim skirt was the simple. As for the sexy, the seven-inch split up the left leg played the part perfectly. Leopard-print sandals gave that little splash of "wow."

"You're gorgeous."

His voice was deep and sounded solemn as Charlene turned to face Akil. She hadn't known he'd come back upstairs into the room. He was dressed an hour ago and had gone downstairs to talk to Jason. All day he'd been with her, not talking about the show or her performance or the song or anything musical. She had laughed until her sides hurt, him right along with her. The afternoon had been relaxing and comfortable and made her think of their future together.

Akil never talked about their future as a couple. Actually, he never talked about them as a couple. He talked about the CD and how well he thought it would be received. He talked about other music he had in mind for her, appearances, et cetera. But never did he mention them maybe taking a trip together or just going out to dinner together as a couple. She was starting to wonder if this whole thing between them would be one of those celebrity secrets. The press could catch a shot of them together but if asked neither of them would comment, sort of like some popular celebrities were doing right now. People knew they were together but neither of them was actually admitting it. That wasn't something she wanted, wasn't a relationship she thought she could live with. While she had never wanted to be in the spotlight, never wanted to be in the tabloids for any reason, she also didn't want to feel like she was a secret.

"Thanks," she said finally, her hands moving nervously down the front of her dress.

"Don't fidget. You look great just standing there." He took a few steps closer until she could smell his cologne.

"You look really good, too." This was the first time she'd seen Akil dressed up in person. She'd seen pictures in magazines of him at award shows or other clubs, but face-to-face was a whole different story.

The black slacks and matching jacket were Ralph Lauren. His shirt had been delivered while they were watching movies earlier that day. The name on the box was Ace and she'd asked him about the unknown designer. He'd only smiled and said, "You're looking at him."

Now she had the chance to take in the entire ensemble—the wide-collared black shirt with what looked like a paisley print but was actually an array of microphones and long swirling cords in a pale gray color, black slacks and a single-breasted sports coat, with shined-to-perfection gray alligator-and-crocodile-print leather wingtips.

Even though he wore all black his dark complexion seemed to bask in the colors. His close-cropped hair sported rows of deep soft waves and his eyes held a sort of anticipation she'd never seen before. Her heart flip-flopped wildly in her chest just looking at him.

"I have something for you."

"What? Why?" She was already nervous. The fact

that he'd approached her with a hand behind his back and a somber expression wasn't working well to calm her down. She didn't want a gift, not from Akil. That would only add to the confusion she was already feeling about their relationship, which would only add to the anxiety she was feeling about singing at the club tonight, which would undoubtedly increase her chances of having a coronary right there on stage.

Dang, Charlene, can you be any more dramatic? She could almost hear Rachel, Candis and Mia all joined in together. *Okay, just calm down,* she told herself and took a steady breath.

"It's just a little something that I want you to have."

"For tonight?" Her voice squeaked a little with the question. She hadn't eaten a big lunch. Hot tea with honey had been her choice of drink, along with her daily eight glasses of water. So right about now she felt like the bathroom was going to be her second best friend this evening. But her voice would be flawless and that was all that really counted.

The left corner of his mouth lifted upward in a small smile. With his right hand he gripped her wrist and pulled it down to her side so she'd have no choice but to stop clasping and unclasping her fingers. "No. Not just for tonight," he said.

His left arm moved from around his back and he put the telltale blue box in front of her. "Just for you."

Now this was totally unfair. How was she supposed to accept a gift—from Tiffany's, no less—and not feel shaky? It was a medium-size box so she was sure it wasn't a ring. What she wasn't so sure of was why she even had the flicker of thought that it might be one. She was driving herself crazy with all these questions and no answers, which was the last thing she needed tonight. So with a nervous smile she resigned herself to simply deal with whatever it was and move on.

With one hand she took the box from him. With the other she removed the white bow and flipped the lid. Inside her heart all but stopped but on the outside she made a valiant effort to remain calm. Her slightly shaking fingers lifted the wide sterling silver bracelet with round diamonds marching in one single-file line across the width. "It's beautiful. Thank you, Akil," she managed to say without blubbering.

Akil took the box, put it down on the table near them, then slipped the bracelet from her fingers, unclasped it and put it on her right wrist. "You're very welcome."

His arms slipped slowly around her waist as he pulled her closer to him. It felt good to be in his arms. *Safe,* she thought all of a sudden. "You're going to be great tonight," he said, gazing into her eyes.

She nodded as a response.

"Trust yourself. Trust your voice."

She was nodding again then stopped because she felt like a mute. "I will."

"I love you," he said simply and kissed her lips lightly.

All the doubts, all the questions, all the reservations fell from her and she sighed in his arms. "I love you, too."

They'd come in a back door and she was taken directly to a dressing room. For a few minutes she was in there alone. Then Jason came in with a pep talk that left her laughing instead of worrying. She didn't see Akil again until she stepped out of the room to walk down the narrow hallway that would lead to the stage. Behind him was Jax and in front of them was Jason and Steve. He took her hand immediately.

Gripping her fingers tightly, he gave them a little shake. "Let's do this."

She smiled. "Let's do it."

A stage tech guided her onto the stage with its dark curtain drawn. Butterflies did more than dance in her stomach; it was like they were having some kind of festival complete with dancing and singing of their own. But her mind fought hard to calm them. She focused on the song, on feeling the lyrics, on making the audience feel the lyrics.

She barely heard her name, really didn't register the tentative applause. But the rustle of the curtain opening jolted her. Jason's directions from yesterday when they did a dry run of the performance replayed in her mind.

Stand still. Wait for the music, the first thumps of bass.

She heard it and her heart beat just a little faster.

The spotlight will go up, he told her. *It will move across the stage as if it's searching for you. Wait until it finds you.* She waited. Felt the heat of the light, saw the brilliant brightness in her eyes.

She took one step, then two. Then she leaned forward toward the mic and belted the first line of the song. It was slow, almost as if she were conversationally talking.

"Never like this before. No, never like this. I never loved like this. Never kissed like this. Never felt like this before."

Then the tempo picked up and she sang like she'd never sung before. Like nobody was there, it was just her and the band in the studio. The notes appeared in her mind, she could almost see the song sheet she'd practiced from on so many days. And she just sang.

Everybody was on their feet clapping and whistling as Charlene made her way off the stage. She'd been a hit. She looked absolutely beautiful and he'd never loved anyone more.

With his chest swelling with more emotion than he thought he could handle, he was making his way across the room, trying to get to the backstage door so he could see Charlene. A hand on his arm held him back.

Akil turned to see who'd stopped him and felt waves of dread clogging the air instead. With a nod of his head the guy who had been calling Akil, making outrageous demands and just recently very serious threats signaled they move toward a door near the restrooms. Akil followed him because there was no use making a scene. This was Charlene's night and there were bouncers all over this place. Not to mention Jax and Steve. If he did what he truly felt and knocked this dude the hell out there would surely be a huge fight, one that would definitely make it into every tabloid first thing tomorrow morning.

So he had to keep his cool. It was taking great effort but he did so, following the familiar face until they were closed in the small room alone.

"Well, well, well. Akil Hutton, superproducer," he drawled, a smirk spreading quickly over his face.

"T. K. Dupree," Akil said tightly as he turned, standing with his feet slightly spread, ready for anything.

"You look good, brotha. Glad to see you've been living well. Then again, I already knew that was the case."

"Let's cut the bull. I don't know why you wasted your time coming here. I told you on the phone how I felt about your little ultimatum."

T. K. Dupree, a six-foot-tall, half Puerto Rican, half African American man with short hair and two gold teeth stood in front of him. They were of similar build and similar backgrounds. T.K.'s mother, Rosita, spent many nights at Akil's house. Which meant T.K., also known as Thomas Keith after his father, spent many nights in the lower bunk in Akil's bedroom.

"And I told you I'm not stopping until I get what I want. You've come a long way, brotha. It's time you shared the wealth." T.K.'s hand moved to his waistband, where he no doubt had stashed his piece. Even though Akil had been out of the game for a long time, he still recognized the signs.

"Then you should have worked for it!" Akil spat. "You're a little too old to be a stick-up boy now, T.K."

T.K. just laughed. "You're right. I have outgrown sticking people up for five and ten dollars or whatever those poor junkies had in their pockets. I'm on to bigger and better gigs now. You should know what I mean."

"I know I'm not giving you a dime," Akil said, taking a step back and lifting his arms in the air. "So if shooting me is your final call, do your thing."

"Nah," T.K. said, stepping closer to Akil. "That's too easy. But I am going to give you one more chance. One million or the whole world finds out that the superproducer has a super secret, one that could land his ass in jail." He was about to walk away but as if he was having an afterthought he looked Akil directly in the eye. "And by the way, your new act, she's a hottie. Wonder what she'd say if—"

Akil reacted instantly, grabbing a handful of T.K.'s shirt and pushing him back until he slammed into the wall. "Don't even think about her. Don't say her name. Don't look her way. Or I swear, T.K., all that we've been through, all that we've seen together will seem like a day in the park compared to what I'll do to you."

Again T.K. laughed. "You know what to do, Akil." He pulled out of Akil's grip. "So do it."

Chapter 17

Now they were back to the silent treatment. For about fifteen minutes during the drive back to the house Charlene wondered why she even bothered. After all they'd shared Akil still had his moments.

The difference now was that she felt somehow compelled to dig deeper, to figure out what was really bothering him. Her performance had been a hit, Akil had said so himself. On top of that, Jason had said so, as had the applauding crowd. Hell, the manager wanted her to come back next Friday night. Akil quickly axed that offer, telling him he'd see her again after the CD release. The guy hadn't looked thrilled but he wasn't about to cross Akil. Just the promise that Akil would bring her back to perform seemed to be enough.

Everything had been going along perfectly until she'd gone to dance with Jason. When they'd come back to the table Akil looked as if he were about to overturn the table and everything on it. His eyes had gone dark and dangerous-looking, his shoulders were set, tension rolling off in thick heavy waves. She'd known the moment she stepped up to him that something had happened. She wondered if it had been another one of those phone calls.

They were about five minutes away from the house when Charlene started to get angry. With all they'd shared why couldn't Akil share this with her? Why couldn't he tell her what had happened to upset him? Why did she even bother?

The answer to that last question was the simplest one. She was in love with him.

Whether or not that was an intelligent decision on her part didn't really matter—it just was.

Cliff brought the car to a stop. Akil didn't even wait for him to come back and open the door for him, just jumped out. With a sigh Charlene slid across the seat and stepped out herself. Mild shock registered as Akil was still standing by the door waiting for her. His hand on the small of her back was comforting as they walked into the house together.

They headed straight for the stairs. Behind her Charlene could hear the beeps of the security system being deactivated and activated again. Jax and Steve were Akil's personal security detail so they'd stayed with him at all times. At the club there had been four more guys working security but they'd pretty much escorted them inside, then watched the doors and she presumed the car. Jax and Steve were the only two who stayed with them all the time.

In the club tonight he'd been her producer. In the studio he was the same. Only at night or when they were alone did it appear they were more. She sensed that Jason knew they were sleeping together and of course Jax and Steve knew and most likely his household staff. But nobody on the outside knew. Not even Sofia or Candis. With a start she wondered what they'd think. Would they approve? That, coupled with Akil's mood, had her turning in the opposite direction, heading toward the bedroom that had originally been assigned to her upon arriving in Miami.

Akil had been walking right behind her, his hand on her back, but when she veered away, he didn't follow. And he didn't try to stop her. With hurried footsteps she made her way into the other bedroom, closed the door and fell back against it, stifling a moan.

How could this be happening? How could she have come so far professionally and taken such a giant step backward personally? Never in her life had she allowed a man any type of power over her.

Until Akil.

He'd changed what she'd come to expect from a man, changed what she allowed herself to feel. He told her she was beautiful, that she was worth so much more than the label people around her wanted to slap on her. Things she'd tried to act like she believed on the outside, but had still haunted her on the inside. He'd pulled away the inner blinders and taught her how to feel emotion, passion, to revel in them both.

And yet she wasn't good enough to be allowed to do the same for him. There was something he was holding back, she felt it at times when they were together. He'd told her about his past, shared the emotional scars left by his parents' untimely and unnecessary deaths and his sister's traitorous departure. He shared his body with her unconditionally. But there was something else he was holding back. She knew it as surely as she knew her name.

The question was, what was she going to do about it?

Tonight wasn't the night to answer those questions. She shouldn't have to relinquish the joy of her success to the pain of his secrets. She wanted to call Rachel to tell her how things had gone but it was too late. Nearly three in the morning in Miami was just after midnight in L.A. She wouldn't disturb her by calling at this time, she'd wait until morning.

Stripping off her clothes, remembering how so many eyes had been on her tonight appreciating the way she looked, made her smile. Mia had done a fantastic job with her makeover, although she refused to call it that. Mia's exact words were "I'm simply providing the right accessories to accentuate God's given beauty." That had made her feel good, special, so she decided to hold on to that thought as she headed for the small bathroom and shower.

Staying in Akil's master suite was definitely different than being in this guest room. His shower alone was the size of this entire bathroom, but she wouldn't allow herself those thoughts a second longer. Stepping inside the stall, she turned on the spray of water, adjusting its temperature until the heated drops tingled as they hit her skin. Closing her eyes, she tilted her head and concentrated on the heat, the soothing rivulets of water washing over her. The day and evening's tensions rolled from her with the waves of water, falling to the floor and swirling down the drain. Mental signals moved throughout her body, to each tired or strained muscle so that her focus was on calm, serenity.

She was so engrossed in relaxing herself she hadn't heard the door open, hadn't felt the quick blast of cool air as Akil stepped into the shower stall with her.

Blood pounded at his temples as he remembered what had transpired at the club. T.K. was in Miami and was following his usual M.O. Everybody owed him something, money, opportunity, his very presence meant he should be important, known, recognized. Akil knew all this, remembered it from their time spent growing up. He hadn't liked it then and despised it even more now. This was a grown man, two years shy of being forty, and he was still living under the same BS philosophy of not working for anything but bullying his way to each and every meal. It was sickening and had Akil so angry that he'd almost punched his old friend right there in the middle of the club, on Charlene's big night.

He felt like scum for even having the thought and hadn't shaken the mood by the time she made it back to the table. He knew she saw the change in him and that only angered him more. The last thing he wanted to do was ruin this moment for her. Damn T.K. for showing up and damn him for falling right back into that old mentality that he needed to get rid of T.K. for good. That he should have done it a long time ago. Just the thought made him feel ashamed, evil, demented. It was part of what he'd run away from years and years ago, part of what he'd prayed would stay in his past. But sometimes—Akil knew this better than a lot of other people he associated with—sometimes, God didn't answer all prayers.

The look in Charlene's eyes as she watched him for the duration of the night had almost destroyed him. The mixture of pity, misunderstanding, question, anger, it all tore through him like a jagged-edged knife. He hadn't known what to say, how to shake the mood, how to fix things with her. The ride home had been tense and uncomfortable for them both. He'd fooled himself into believing they'd get home—his home, funny how he'd begun to think of it as theirs—go to bed and wake up to sunshine and a better day tomorrow.

She'd walked away from him.

He deserved it, he knew, but it stung just the same. And tonight of all nights he couldn't stomach another woman he loved walking out of his life.

So he'd come to her. Not knowing how to do anything else but what he was doing now. Reaching out, wrapping his arms around her waist and pulling her back against his naked body. For one brief second she was startled, then she settled a bit, her body stiff against his.

"I'm sorry, baby girl," he said, burying his face against the softness of her neck. "It seems like I'm always apologizing to you."

She didn't speak.

"I'm trying so hard to be the man you desire. Help me, please."

Her head lay back against his shoulder, one of her water-slick hands reaching up to cup the back of his head. At her touch every tense muscle in his body relaxed, every bad memory of the evening and his life before vanished. There was only the here and now. There was only Charlene.

He kissed her neck, his tongue mixing with the warm water along her silken skin. His hands moved upward, gripping her breasts and squeezing. Against her soft bottom his sex jutted and strained against the condom he'd donned before entering the bathroom. He needed to be inside of her, to feel her completely surrounding him. He needed that like he needed his next breath.

And she knew it.

Covering his hands with her own, they pushed her

breasts together, massaged, toyed with puckered nipples and moaned with delight. His mind was a thick haze of desire, like music if sound could be seen and not heard. One of her hands slipped down and back until her deft fingers were wrapping around his thick arousal. He gasped, stroked his tongue over her shoulder, then nipped lightly. Without preamble she guided him between her cheeks, into the dewy haven that he sought. With a ragged moan he slid into her like a moth to a flame, a key to a lock, a player into home base. He was there, safe, finally.

Lifting her hands, he flattened them on the wet tiles in front of them, gripped her hips and pushed deep inside her. Her head fell forward as she moaned, her body shaking with every stroke and retreat.

They didn't speak. Didn't need to because their bodies were totally in sync with their minds. She knew what he needed. He knew what he wanted. The hows and whys didn't really matter at this point.

She bucked against him, pressing her plump bottom into his groin, her sweet walls clasping his erection like a glove. He pulled out and slipped back in, loving the slick heat, the tight and precise fit as if she were made specifically for him.

In and out. Out and in. The timeless motion seemed to go on forever. Until her thighs began to quake, her arms shaking as they were extending above her head. His spine tingled, his scrotum tight and heavy with anticipated release. He closed his eyes, let the swirling vortex of pleasure engulf him. Two powerful strokes later and his release soared through his system, halting in the condom, yet connecting them on a higher, more emotional plane.

For endless moments he held her right there, against the tiles, the water growing tepid. Pulling back only enough so that he was not embedded inside her anymore but their bodies were still pressed tight, he whispered over and over again, "I love you, baby girl. Love you. Love you. Love you."

It had been a week since Charlene's performance at the club and Akil hadn't heard from T.K. He wanted to believe that was a good sign, but knew differently.

In addition to money, T.K. wanted a job at Playascape, something high-profile, he'd told Akil. He wanted to keep his money rolling in. And he expected Akil to oblige. Just like that he expected Akil to give part of what he'd worked for to a man who was determined to do anything with his life but work.

He and T.K. had grown up together, had been through some really tough times, had seen some pretty brutal things. They should have been as close as blood brothers. Instead they appeared to occupy space on two different planets. Akil's answer to their childhood struggle had been to study, to find a goal and work hard toward it.

T.K.'s mind-set was that he was owed by any and everyone, especially those who knew him best and had something. He'd grown up hating the black cop who'd picked his mother up for prostitution yet had her sleep with him for free to keep from going to jail. He hated that his mother had gotten pregnant with him that night in the back of the police cruiser and that she'd spent every day and night after that getting high and continuing to sell her body. Because that jackass cop hadn't looked at her again after throwing her limp body out of his car. For years he'd rolled through their neighborhood arresting some drug dealers, stealing from others, threatening the users and their kids. He knew who T.K. was, found out the first time he arrested him when T.K. was eleven years old. "You ain't nothing, just like your dirty-ass mother," he'd said, then opened the back door to the cruiser and kicked T.K. out after he'd driven him far from the city into Harford County and stripped him of all his clothes. A county cop had brought T.K. home that night but didn't believe his story. Rosita had smacked T.K. so hard when he told her, his bottom lip bled for hours. From that point on T.K. had sworn to kill Officer Thomas Keith Dupree, Sr.

The year they turned eighteen Officer Dupree's body was found in an old crack house two blocks from where Akil and his family lived. He'd been stripped of all his clothes and shot at close range in the head. His killer was never found.

But Akil knew who it was.

He had a secret on T.K. just like the one T.K. had on him. Only nobody would care about a half-assed drug dealer shooting a crooked cop almost eighteen years ago. However, the deeds of a famous music producer making more money than a lot of white men in the country would be made an example of if his past were ever revealed.

The deal he'd just worked out with Sony Electronics for a line of studio equipment would most certainly disappear. Ace, his new clothing line, would never make it to Fashion Week. And his artists, they would suffer, as well. The bad publicity would surely attack their sales.

Then there was Charlene.

He stood to lose the most with her. He loved her, had

admitted that to himself and to her. He'd never thought he'd have these feelings for a woman, especially not a woman in the industry—his mother and sister had really jaded him in that area. He wanted to be with her, wanted her to want to be with him.

If T.K. talked that would all change.

But he couldn't, *would not,* give in to blackmail. It went against everything he'd ever believed, ever fought for. He wouldn't be used by anyone, ever again.

"I'm ready," Charlene said as she entered the living room. "Are you okay, Akil?"

"I am now," he greeted her with a smile and a hug. With her in his arms, in his life, he was more than okay. He was perfect and he intended to keep it that way.

Chapter 18

Cine Citta Cafe was one of the trendy restaurants in the Miami Beach area. Akil said he liked the food here and the low-key atmosphere.

"This is nice," Charlene was saying as she opened up her menu. It was their first real date and she was excited. Cliff had driven them but he'd made Jax and Steve follow in another car. There had been a lot of whispering between Akil and Jax before he'd finally gotten in the car and she desperately wanted to ask what was going on but didn't want to spoil the evening.

Now they were seated and about to order and although he was sitting right across from her Charlene still felt like he was miles away. Deciding that enough was enough, she put her menu down. "Akil, what's going on?"

He looked at her strangely. "What? I'm looking at the menu to see what I want."

"You know that's not what I mean. You've been acting weird for a couple of days now. Actually, since the night at the club. What is it? Did I do something wrong?"

"No. No." His answer was quick. He reached a hand across the table to take hers. "You were great. The audience really loved you and the owner wants you to come back again. 'Never Before Like This' is definitely going to be the first single we release. The sound was just right and you looked fantastic up there."

And he was dancing around the real subject like Usher danced around on stage.

"Great. Now tell me what's going on with you. Not the producer. Not the songs on the CD or how I looked. I want to know what's bothering you."

He sighed heavily, released her hand and resumed looking at the menu. "Nothing's bothering me. I'm fine."

"You're not fine," she snapped. "You bounce from happy to sad to mad in ten minutes flat. I'd venture to say you might be bipolar but I don't think it's a chemical imbalance causing your mood swings. I think something is going on, something you don't want to talk to me about." He didn't say anything and she felt like she was losing this battle.

"Jason's worried about you, too. He says you're not focused and that's not like you. I tend to believe him."

Akil slammed the menu on the table. "So you and Jason have been cozying up talking about me?"

"No. Me and Jason care about you and we're concerned. If you gave a damn about us you wouldn't keep us in the dark about whatever it is that's bothering you."

"Don't do that," he said slowly, his dark eyes burning into hers. "You know how I feel about you, Charlene. Don't use it like that."

"I'm not using anything, Akil. I'm just trying to understand you. Ever since I met you you've been hot and cold, either toward me or just in general. I don't know how to take you from one minute to the next. It's crazy."

"So you want to leave, is that what you're saying?"

Well, where had that come from? This entire conversation was going in a direction Charlene hadn't anticipated and wasn't sure she could handle. But she'd come this far, she wasn't about to back down now.

"I love you, Akil. I came out here to make an album, not to fall in love. But I did and I'm okay with that. I enjoy being with you and working with you. But I feel like you're holding something back from me."

"I'm not seeing someone else, if that's what you think. I'd never do that."

"I didn't think it was another woman. But I know it's something. Something that's keeping you from being with me completely. I don't know what it is and that scares me."

"Don't," he said, reaching for both her hands this time. "You don't ever have to be afraid of me, Charlene. I would never hurt you."

"Well, isn't this cozy."

Akil froze the minute he heard the voice.

"Superproducer Akil Hutton and his new singer, Ms. Charlene Quinn." T.K. was pulling up a chair, sitting down between Akil and Charlene. "Or should I say Akil Hutton and his new honey having a nice romantic dinner? Yeah, that would be a better headline, don't you think, Akil?"

Charlene was looking from him to T.K. and back to him again. He released her hands and sat back in his chair. "What are you doing here?"

"Come on, man. Is that any way to introduce me to your lady friend?" He extended his hand to Charlene. "I'm T.K., an old friend of Akil's. Actually, we're more like brothers. I'm sure he's told you about me."

Shaking his hand, Charlene looked questioningly at Akil. "No, I'm sorry he didn't. You said you're old friends?"

Akil knew she was remembering back to that night in the pool house when he'd gotten that call and told her it was from an old friend. One of the things he loved about Charlene in the studio was that she was a quick study, she picked up the notes and rhythm after he'd gone over it one time. He could see that she was that way with every aspect of her life.

"Hell, yeah. We go way back. I mean we used to share bunk beds, that's how far back we go."

"That was a long time ago," Akil said tightly. "Why don't you get going, T.K.? You and I can hook up later."

T.K. was shaking his head. "Nah, I'm hungry. You haven't ordered yet, right? So let me get the menu."

"No!" Akil said quickly.

"It's okay," Charlene stated. "I don't mind having company for dinner, Akil."

"Well, I do."

"But we aim to please our women," T.K. said with a wicked gleam in his eyes.

Akil sighed and out of the corner of his eye saw Jax making his way to the table. He held up a hand, halting his bodyguard's approach. He could handle T.K. himself. He just needed to get him away from Charlene.

"How about we go outside and talk," Akil offered.

T.K. picked up a glass of water, drinking slowly. "No, thanks. We tried that and it didn't work. I figure it's time for phase two."

"T.K.," Akil warned.

Charlene put her napkin on the table. "Akil, what's going on?"

Her question echoed in his head, replaying as if she'd been asking him that for hours, days, weeks since they met. "Nothing. I'll take care of it," was his reply but he didn't know if he believed it.

"I hoped you would," T.K. said. "This place doesn't have any red meat, did you know that?" He acted as if he were engrossed in the menu.

Akil pushed back in his chair and stood. "Let's go outside, T.K."

"No," T.K. said simply, letting the menu drop to the table. "Let's not. I have other things to do so I'll make this quick." He looked up at Akil. "You can stand or sit, suit yourself."

"T.K." His voice was low, warning.

"So, Charlene, you're sleeping with Akil here? I guess you could do worse."

"What?" Charlene gasped.

Akil reached for T.K.'s arm and pulled him up. "Don't do this."

T.K. laughed. "Oh, now you're taking me seriously. Too late, bro. What's the matter? You were Mr. Tough Guy at the club the other night, standing me down, even threatening me not to go near your little lady."

"You were at the club last week?" Charlene asked, confusion clear in her voice.

Akil waved his other arm and signaled for Jax to come over; this was getting out of hand. Jax was at the table in seconds. "Get her out of here," he told him.

"You want her to leave before I tell her the news?" T.K. drawled.

Charlene had just pulled her arm from Jax's grip. "What news?"

"I knew he wouldn't tell you. The FBI, they're looking for him."

"I'm gonna kill you," Akil said through clenched teeth.

"Ah, there you go with those threats again. You know I'm scared one day he's really going to go through with it. It's said after a killer makes his first kill the others are like a walk in the park."

Everything around him froze. Jax didn't move. T.K. kept that stupid grin on his face. And Charlene's gaze fell on him, confused, hurt, still.

"A killer," she barely whispered the word.

"Yeah," T.K. lowered his tone to a whisper. "Akil killed his mother—that's why he had to leave Baltimore. And since she was a federal snitch and the Feds just got new info on her killer, they're looking for your boy here. You should probably distance yourself from him now. He'll kill your career." T.K. chuckled. "No pun intended."

"What…" She tried to swallow but her throat was dry, her tongue like a blob of cotton. "What's he talking about, Akil?" She wanted, no, desperately needed to hear a heated denial. Any minute now Akil was going to punch this man for lying. Then they would go home and Akil would explain it all.

"Akil?" she heard herself saying again.

But he wasn't speaking. Actually he looked like he couldn't speak. He looked from her to T.K. and his eyes gleamed. That's what she'd always seen in them, a lining of hate, a fierce violence just brimming under the surface.

Could that violence lead to killing? Did he kill his mother?

The room felt like it was spinning. Her legs began to buckle and Jax's strong arms around her waist were the closest thing to reality she could feel. "Tell me what's going on, Akil." She'd spoken again, a repeat of the question she'd been asking him all evening. "Tell me."

"I'll tell you," T.K. offered. "Betty was a junkie, strung out on that crack and heroin, whatever she could get her hands on. Everybody knew it and nobody cared. Especially not her do-gooder son, the one with his head always stuck in a book. So when she got some bad dope and lay in an alley dying, he looked down on her and left her there. Just walked away and let her die. Ain't that right, Akil?"

Charlene felt like she was choking. Her chest pounded, words died in her throat and she gasped for air. Akil was at her side quickly.

"Baby, just let Jax take you home. I'll explain it all when I get there. Just go home, baby. Please."

His voice was deep, flushed with anger as he whispered in her ear.

"No," she responded weakly. "Tell me now. Tell me right now! Did you do this?"

"Yeah, tell her right now, Akil. Tell her how I stood in that alley with you, watched you leave Betty to die in her own urine and filth. Tell her how when you got to the end of the alley you broke out into a run, leaving me behind." T.K. sat down. "Tell her." He laughed.

Jax hit him then, watched as he fell right off the chair onto the floor. T.K. got up, wiping the blood from his nose. "Now I'm gonna have to sue. Pity." He grabbed a napkin from the table. "You know where to find me, Akil. She was phase two. Don't make me go to the next phase. I promise you'll like it even less."

Akil was still pressed to Charlene's side, his forehead resting on the side of her head as he continued to whisper in her ear. "Baby girl, please. Let's go home so we can talk. Please, baby. Let's just go home."

Where the strength came from Charlene had no idea but she pulled away from him, stumbling a bit then righting herself. "No. I asked you for the truth, give it to me now."

"Charlene, we're not alone."

"No, we're not!" she yelled. "But I want to know right now what you've done. How could you do something like that? Who *are* you, Akil? Who are you?"

He straightened at that. His dark eyes going cold.

"I'll have Jax take you home," he said and walked away.

"Akil!" she yelled but he kept on walking. "Akil!" Her voice would grow hoarse, singing tomorrow would simply be out of the question, but she didn't give a damn. Everything she thought she knew, thought she felt, was a lie. He was a lie.

Chapter 19

There had been no sleeping, yet she crawled out of the bed in the room where she'd originally slept that first night in Akil's house. She showered and slipped on jeans and a T-shirt. She had one goal, one person she needed to see.

He would be in the studio, she knew that without a doubt and walked straight there. After letting herself in she didn't even go through polite formalities.

"You owe me the truth," she said, sitting in the chair across from the control board where he sat.

He wore jeans, too, and a wrinkled T-shirt, a sign that his night had been just as rough as hers.

"I owe you," he said with a smirk. "I owe everybody, huh?" He was shaking his head.

"I asked you for the truth long before your little friend entered the picture. You should have just given it to me then."

"Should I have?" he asked. "Why? Because you wanted me to? Because you asked me to? Let me ask you something, Charlene, do you get everything you ask for?"

She opened her mouth to speak but he held up a hand to stop her.

"Wait. Yes, you did. Whatever you wanted growing up you got. You didn't have to ask for shoes that had a new sole on them because you were tired of your toes sticking out in the winter. You didn't have to ask for a couple of dollars to go to the market to get milk and cereal because you and your sister had nothing else to eat. You didn't have to compete with a crack pipe or a needle full of heroin to get your mother's attention. So I guess when you ask me something I should bend over backwards to give it to you."

His words stung. The vehemence in his voice brushed coarsely over her skin. But she would not take the blame for this or anything else that had happened to him. "You can try to shift gears all you want but I gave you respect. From the first day I met you, Akil, I respected you. Even when you acted like an ass I still respected you enough to tell you. So yes, when I ask you a question—no, *correction*—when I ask the man I'm sleeping with a question, I expect an answer."

He sat quietly for a moment, his hands folded. He looked like he was thinking, possibly about a song or an arrangement. From first glance you couldn't tell the emotional battle going on inside him. But Charlene felt it, felt the deep-seated fury just itching to break free, and was afraid of what he would say next.

"What T.K. said was right. My mother was a junkie. She'd taken her first hit of cocaine straight from my father one night after he'd played at some nightclub and she'd sung. They were so excited when they came into the house late that night. I knew where they'd been so I stayed up to hear how it went. I heard their laughter and crept out of my bed into the living room. That's where I saw him dig into his pocket and pull out the little packet. He made two straight white lines on the coffee table, which was full of so much dust it was a wonder they didn't snort all that up, too.

"Every day after that she was high on something. Coke, crack, heroin, whatever she could get her hands on that could take her to the place she wanted to be. When my old man was killed I thought she'd finally have a chance to get clean, but she didn't, she just found another pusher who would keep her appropriately sexed, pregnant and of course high."

"Akil," she whispered.

He shook his head. "No. You wanted an answer, now you take it! I owe it to you, remember?"

She remained quiet, tears already burning her eyes.

"Lauren was thirteen. She needed her mother. She needed some guidance. I'd been working at this record store while I was volunteering at Empire so I was paying the bills in the house and making sure Lauren got up and went to school. While Betty was just doing her thing. I don't know where she got money to get high, probably stealing or selling herself. But I'd long since stopped putting money in her hand. I couldn't stop her from shooting up or snorting, but I didn't have to pay for it, either. She had a key to the house and a bed to sleep in every night. That was all I could do for her.

"One day the school called me, said Lauren hadn't shown up that day. I knew I'd gotten her out of the bed that morning and watched her go to the bus stop. So I left work, drove around the neighborhood looking for her, asking if anybody had seen her. Somebody said they saw her and Betty late that morning. I didn't like the sound of that so I started looking around at Betty's hangouts. I don't really remember how I ended up on

Oliver Street or why I started walking down that alley. It was dirty, full of trash and old needles, broken bottles, just a mess. But I kept right on walking down that alley. It was getting dark by then and I was going to leave but I heard something coming from behind a couple of the trashcans. I walked farther and there she was."

He dragged his hands down his face, rubbed his eyes.

"She was only skin and bones by then but I recognized her from her hair, it was matted but it was long, dark. Then she opened her eyes, brown eyes that used to have these tiny flecks of gold in them. I remember when she smiled they kind of sparkled." A muscle in his jaw twitched. "She was so high she couldn't even stand up. I tried to help her up twice, asking where Lauren was.

"'You're so much better than me, Akil. You always have been.' That's what she said. I ignored her, didn't want to hear anything unless it was about Lauren. We walked a couple feet before I finally picked her up and was carrying her. She pulled on my shirt and tried to yell but her voice was just about gone. 'Save my baby,' she whispered. 'He's got her and you need to give him this to save her.'"

Charlene stood then, walked over to the control board and took his hands. "It's okay, we don't have to talk about this if you don't want to."

He shook his head and pulled his hands from her grasp. "She gave me three hundred dollars. Told me I only had an hour left to get to her, to save her. To save my thirteen-year-old sister from the drug dealer she'd sold her to for a hit."

Tears poured from Charlene's eyes and she wanted to reach for him again but his entire body had gone rigid.

"I put her down because she'd started yelling that she

was in pain. 'Be better than me, Akil. Save my baby.' That's what she kept whispering while she rolled into the fetal position, pain from the bad drugs she'd been sold eating away her insides. Be better than me. She told me that. And I thought I was. So I went straight to the police station, told the desk sergeant everything Betty had told me. They packed me up and put me in the cruiser. We went to the house where the dealer was holding Lauren. They sent me in. I paid him and he pushed my sister out the door. Her clothes were ripped, her face streaked with tears. I carried her out, fighting back the need to find me a piece and kill that son of a bitch. The minute I got outside the police raided the house. Everyone inside was arrested."

"Oh, Akil," Charlene couldn't help saying. She knew he didn't want pity, knew he didn't want her tears, but she couldn't help them. The more he talked the more her heart broke for the child he'd been, the years he'd lost and all he'd tried to do.

"They just dropped us back off at home, told us to keep our mouths shut and we'd be safe. They never told us that I was the one who led them to the dealer who they'd been trying to get for years. Said they had an anonymous tip in court and watched him walk away with a life sentence for kidnapping, bartering a minor and drug charges based on what they found in the house. They knew that if word got out that I'd come to them I'd be labeled a snitch in the neighborhood and neither Lauren nor I would make it alive another year. So we all went on with our lives like nothing happened.

"Betty died, ten minutes after I left her in that alley. We buried her the next weekend. About two years after that I found out that the drugs that killed Betty and the dealer who supplied them to her were a part of a federal investigation. They were somehow connected to a senator and his Colombian connections. But by that time I didn't even care. I never looked back. Never regretted what I did," he said slowly, then looked up at her. "Until now."

"I'm so sorry," was all she could say. "I'm so, so sorry."

"Why? You were millions of miles away living a happy life in your mansion. What could you have done to prevent it?"

She hadn't thought she'd lived a happy life but it paled in comparison to his. Her battles with weight and her fight for her mother's unconditional love were nothing compared to his fight to save his mother's life and his burden to save his sister's.

"I don't understand what T.K. wants."

"T.K. wants what everybody who didn't make it out of the hood wants, Charlene. Money. Fame. Fortune. Purpose. The life they were denied. He expects me to give it to him because he's threatening to tell what he knows about my past. I don't do threats and I don't owe him a dime."

"What are you going to do?"

He stood abruptly then. "I answered your question." His voice was tight and Charlene felt like she was once again being dismissed. "We have a few more weeks to work on the CD but I think it would be better if you stayed in a hotel while we did. Cliff will drive you. I'll leave a message with the hotel with the date and time of our next session."

She blinked rapidly, confusion blanketing her. "What? Hotel? What are you talking about?"

"I'm talking about us taking care of business. That's what we should have been focused on in the first place."

"But, Akil, what about T.K.? What about the FBI looking for you?" *What about us?* she wanted to say but had too much pride to go there.

"I'll take care of me. All I need you to do is sing. Just sing."

Chapter 20

The sound of rain tapping against the hotel's window was dismal and monotonous.

Charlene turned over in the bed, burying her face deep in the pillow. Breathing was hard this way, but not as hard as it had been since she'd left Akil's house. A part of her was still there; miles away in that secluded mansion her heart remained.

It had been three days. He'd called off all recording sessions, probably so he didn't have to see her. The first day away from him she'd thought about how she could have handled the situation differently. But how did one act when they heard the man they were sleeping with had killed another person? And when that other person was their mother? After the initial shock she'd realized the man she was in love with could never take a human life, especially not his mother's.

She'd remembered that night he'd told her about his family and the hurt and despair in his voice when he'd spoken of his mother. He wanted her to get clean and to be healthy. He couldn't have killed her. And when she'd gone to him for a complete explanation, the one he'd given her had broken her heart.

How had he survived? How had he lived all these

years knowing the moment he'd walked away from his mother in that alley she'd died? But she understood, there was nothing else he could have done. Betty knew that, so she'd sent him away to save her daughter, to save both of them. And Akil had done that. He'd walked away from his mother to save Lauren. But now look where Lauren was.

Guilt must be a constant companion to him. Heartbreak like a close relative. She cried for him, for the way he blocked his heart to anyone else out of fear. She cried for his loss—his mother, his father, his sister. And she cried because she loved him too much to just walk away. She just didn't know how to stand beside him right now.

Steady knocking at the door meant she had to climb out of this bed, to move her body when her limbs were tired from not moving much the past few days. She didn't know who was at the door but they were persistent. So she climbed out of the bed, grabbed her robe and shuffled barefoot across the room.

"It's about time. You could answer your cell phone, you know. I've been calling and calling. And so has your sister."

Marjorie Quinn came into the room like a summer's breeze. Her salon-treated auburn hair was perfectly styled, her bronzed complexion highlighted just so with expensive cosmetics. On her arm was a Chanel bag—her mother only carried Chanel bags. She wore a cream linen pantsuit and taupe patent leather pumps. Her fragrance was light, breezy, sophisticated.

"Mother?" Charlene said, a little blurry-eyed and a lot confused. What was her mother doing here in Miami? The last time she'd spoken to her had been weeks ago. Or rather when she'd called home the day after she'd arrived here she'd spoken to the answering machine letting them know where she was and that she was fine. She hadn't received a callback, which made this impromptu visit all the more perplexing.

"What are you doing here?"

"Just like I said, you haven't been answering your cell phone."

Charlene shrugged. She hadn't answered it because it wasn't the number belonging to the person she most wanted to speak to.

"I've been busy," she lied. No way was she telling her mother she was screening her calls.

"And you're not staying at the address you gave me on the message."

So she'd been to Akil's house. "No. I'm not."

"And you look an absolute mess."

That was said in the normal Marjorie Quinn "I'm so tired of going through this with this girl" voice.

"Thanks, Mother. You look really nice."

Marjorie smoothed down her jacket and gave Charlene a weary stare. "You're about to be a big music star, Charlene. Please tell me you're going to do something about your wardrobe. Your appearance. Your father and I do not want to be embarrassed."

Her words stung. Charlene was so not in the mood for this. "Is that what I've always been? An embarrassment to you?"

Marjorie shook her head negatively. "No. That's the role you've elected to play."

"Maybe because of all the pressure you put on me to be like Candis. To lose weight, to model." She was walking back and forth now, her arms flailing, her frustration clearly misdirected.

"To make something of yourself. To follow your dreams. To not settle for just anything," Marjorie finished. "That's what I did, Charlene. I pushed you to reach your potential. I never asked you to be like Candis. That was all in your head."

"In my head! The diets, the exercise programs."

"So my daughter would be healthy. Do you know how many ailments start with obesity? I never once wanted you to be something you're not. But you created that story and you've lived by it so long you believe it."

Charlene finally plopped down on the bed, the little amount of energy she'd had already gone. "Why? Why are you here now? Why are we talking about this now after all this time?"

Marjorie sat beside her. "Because you brought it up."

Charlene sighed and Marjorie took her hand. "Why don't you tell me what's really bothering you?"

Truth be told, all the stuff she'd just mentioned had been bothering her for years. But her mother was right, it wasn't foremost on her mind right now. And while her mother wasn't her first choice of who she'd like to be discussing this with, right about now she was as close as Charlene was going to get.

"How do you help someone who doesn't want to be helped?"

Marjorie chuckled. "You've said a mouthful there. I've been trying to help you all your life and you've fought me every step of the way."

"Mom, I thought we weren't discussing 'us.'"

"Okay. Okay. Maybe we can finally discuss that later and put it behind us once and for all."

"Fine," Charlene agreed just to be done with it.

"Sometimes, Charlene, we think people need help. And if we care about that person then who better to offer that help but us? We never really think about whether or not we should help, or whether we should just leave well enough alone. You know, let the good Lord do His work, in His time."

Charlene thought about her words for a moment, wondering if they were talking about the situation with Akil or still the past disagreements between her and her mother.

"But what if you really love this person? If you only want what's best for them? If you just want them to know that you're there for them?"

Marjorie nodded with each of Charlene's statements. "But you may be the only one who believes you can help them. This person may need to find their own way, make their own mistakes or decisions."

Okay, this was paralleling too much with her issues with her mother. She was talking about Akil, trying to help him. But he didn't want her help. Would he want her love instead?

"How will he know I love him and I care?"

Her mother smiled as she tucked a strand of hair behind her ear. "Tell him."

Charlene looked at her mother, knowing definitely that what had just transpired between them was groundbreaking. It was taking their relationship to another level. "Thanks."

Marjorie held out her arms and Charlene went into her embrace. "I love you, Charlene. I love you because you're you and you were stubborn enough to fight me on everything I did or said that I thought was helping you. You were strong enough to stand your ground and become your own woman. I'm so proud of that woman. And if this man is worth a dime he'll love you for being there as well as wanting to help him."

"He's worth it," she whispered, her face resting on her mother's shoulder. Akil was worth fighting for. All these years people had been letting him down, walking out of his life, and he'd been fighting to keep them there in any way he could.

He deserved so much better. And for all that she was not model-thin or picture-perfect, she was good for him, she knew it with all her heart.

What she also knew with a major degree of certainty was that there was no way Marjorie Quinn was going to let her off that easily. The next hour was spent telling her all about Akil, about the man she loved.

Akil was pleased.

He'd just finished writing the lyrics to the song that had been in his head for much too long. Only yesterday afternoon had he figured out why the words hadn't come to him sooner.

Charlene.

It was that simple. Just as she'd said when she first heard the instrumental version of the song, it was a journey between this man and this woman, falling in love. He'd written a few songs in his career, none that he'd sold or had published, but just a few projects he'd done on his own. This one was totally different.

The woman was different and the timing was right. That's all he could figure.

He was tired of fighting demons, tired of carrying all this guilt. It was time for him to live and to love. That was basically what Mrs. Williamson had said when he'd been at the breakfast table alone yesterday morning.

"Akil, I've known you a long time. I know things about you that I don't think others know."

He'd only been able to nod, sure that whatever she was going to say would make him feel ten times worse then he already did.

"You're a good man and you deserve happiness. It's time for you to let go of all that old baggage and move on."

He'd steepled his fingers and rested his forehead against them. "That's what I was trying to do."

"Ha!" She'd yelled so loud he'd jumped. "That's not what you've been doing. You've been hiding behind work, snapping at anybody that dared to get closer than your music. It's a shame the way you treated that woman when all she wanted to do was love you."

"Are you talking about Charlene?"

"You know good and darn well who I'm talking about. She may have come here to make a record but I think it was more. I think the good Lord brought her here for something more. You're just too stubborn to see it."

He sighed. "I really don't want to talk about this right now."

"That's just fine with me," she'd huffed and sat down across from him. "Don't talk. Listen for a change. That's a strong black woman. Strong enough to handle her illness and rise above all this petty talk about skinny women being the only beautiful ones out there. I ain't never heard such foolishness. God created us all different. Beauty is in here." She had pounded against her chest with a closed fist, her light brown eyes staring fiercely at him.

"She has a lot to give and some man is going to take her up on that offer one day. It'd be a darned shame if it wasn't you."

Just the thought of Charlene being with someone else had him seeing red. His temples had throbbed with the headache he'd had since the day before when she'd packed her things and left for the hotel. He'd wanted to call her back, to tell her he was wrong and to beg her to stay.

But she would have turned and looked at him again, given him that look of pity he didn't want to see again. His past was his past, he didn't want pity for it, didn't want anybody's apologies because it wouldn't change a thing. He just wanted it to be forgotten.

Charlene wouldn't forget, she would remember and she would probably love him more because of what he'd gone through. Every day she was with him he'd wonder if it were out of pity or something else.

"She loves you," Mrs. Williamson had said quietly. "I think it's about time you stopped questioning that and just accept it. I believe you love her. Well past time you stopped running from that, too."

He couldn't speak, he only looked at her.

She had stood and gone to him, grabbing his face in her beefy hands and kissing his forehead. "Stop making me yell at you all the time. You're not a stupid boy, Akil. You're smart and talented and you should know a good thing when it's staring you right in the face. Now get up and do something about it."

All afternoon he'd thought about that conversation and admitted to himself that Mrs. Williamson was absolutely right. So he decided to do something. He'd finish the song that Charlene had given him some lyrics to and then he'd go to her, begging for her forgiveness.

But this morning there had seemed to be too many people in his house, so he'd gone to his yacht for some quiet time before going to see Charlene. That's what he was doing when he heard footsteps on the dock.

For just a minute he thought the footsteps would keep going. Then he expected his bodyguards to stop whoever was approaching. Of course that could only happen if he hadn't given them the day off. Yeah, he knew T.K. was still around and that he wasn't going to give up his quest for the money he thought was rightfully owed to him. But Akil didn't care. He'd never run scared before and he wasn't about to start now.

Besides, it was probably just Jason. He would know where Akil had gone to get some peace and quiet. So Akil hadn't moved to the upper level, just waited for him to come down the steps to where he was.

"See, this is what I'm talkin' 'bout. I'm gonna get me one of these real soon."

It wasn't Jason, Akil thought, standing from the couch, where he'd been sitting to glare at T.K.

"What are you doing here?"

"You keep asking me that question, man. But you already know the answer."

"I told you I'm not giving you a dime."

"Okay. You did say that. But I figured with our history I owed you one more chance to reconsider."

"There's nothing to reconsider," he said. T.K. stood about five feet away from him. He was wearing saggy blue jeans with a frayed hem over boots. His jean jacket matched his jeans, the Barack Obama shirt looking dismally out of place on a black man who refused to work for anything.

"It's simple, Akil, you cut me a check. Then I can even work for your company or something to keep the money rolling in. It's either that or I go to the FBI."

"Go where you want, but you won't be going with any of my money."

"You's a stingy, ungrateful, nig—"

Akil took a step closer to him. "Don't do it. Don't call me out of my name. I'm trying to deal with you like a man, T.K., but you don't want to go that route."

"I ain't gotta go your route to anything. Don't forget I saw you in that alley. I saw you leave her there. You knew she was dying, you could have saved her."

Akil's jaw twitched, the memories flashing back in his mind quick, like a trailer for a bad movie. "Yeah, you keep saying you saw me. But I didn't see you. Why is that? Huh? Why were you in that alley, T.K.? And when I left why didn't you help her?

"She fed you, washed your clothes. Hell, sometimes she had to do the same for your just-as-strung-out mother. So I'm confused. Why didn't you help her?"

T.K. was up in Akil's face now. "You don't have to bring Rosita into this. We're talking about you and what you did to your own mother. I took care of my mother until the day she died."

Akil nodded. "Yeah, you took care of her, all right. Probably put the needle in her arm for her."

"Oh, no, don't get it twisted. You're the killer, not me."

"But you were in that alley. Like you knew Betty was there, that she was high. How would you know that, T.K.? How would you know unless you were the one who sold her the bad dope?"

T.K. just laughed. "You can't prove that."

"You're right, I can't. But I know that's what happened and that's all that matters."

"But the Feds are going to get proof that says otherwise."

"You can't blackmail me, T.K."

"I can do whatever I want!"

"That's what you think. Just like you thought your no-good daddy was coming back for you. Until he picked your behind up, drove you out to the county and stripped you naked, leaving you like a piece of trash."

T.K.'s nostrils flared. His eyes grew darker as his fists balled at his sides.

"Yeah, you were real pissed off about that. He didn't want your mother, didn't even pick her up off the streets when he rode by and saw her nodding on the corners. And he sure as hell didn't want you. You were his half-breed son, half boy, half junkie—why would he want you? So you killed him. You stripped him and shot him and left him in that crack house. So which one of us is going to the Feds first, T.K.? You with your news about a junkie being left to die in an alley or me with my info on a dealer who killed a cop?"

T.K. growled in anger. With both hands he pushed Akil back. As Akil stumbled backward T.K. reached into the back of his jeans and pulled out a gun.

"I will kill you where you stand," he said, his voice deadly calm. Like a man who'd done this before.

Charlene had heard enough. When she'd stopped by Akil's house to see him Mrs. Williamson had hurriedly told her he was at the yacht and that he was probably waiting to see her. She didn't really believe that but was not going to be deterred.

At the dock she was directed to his yacht. She was walking slowly down the dock. Since she hadn't anticipated being out on the water, she'd worn a sundress and three-inch-heeled sandals. The last thing she wanted to do prior to taking a stand with Akil was to fall on one of these wooden planks and break a bone.

Then she'd heard the yelling. It was coming from Akil's vessel. She'd moved closer and recognized the second voice as T.K.'s. Wondering what he was doing there, she'd decided to eavesdrop for just a few minutes, then she'd let them know she was there.

The exchange was heated, with Akil verbally attacking T.K. for his transgressions as T.K. had tried to blackmail Akil for his. It was on the one hand disheartening to hear the tragedy of both their childhoods. When they should have banded together to rise above their situations, they'd been brutally torn apart. On the other hand, it was scary as hell to hear them yelling at each other like this and it just about stopped her heart to hear T.K. threaten Akil's life.

That was the final straw.

Using her cell phone as she made her way onto the boat and down the few steps, she alerted the police to their location.

She thought T.K.'s threat was just that. It didn't dawn on her that he might really have a weapon to carry out his plans. But the moment she stepped into the cabin his entire body, including the arm with the gun, turned and now pointed directly at her.

"I know you're not using her as your backup," he

snarled. "Get over there with your man, since you picked right now to show up."

"Don't move, Charlene," Akil said in a slow, venomous voice.

She didn't know what to do. All she knew was that her heart was racing and her palms were sweating.

"Fine. I ain't got no problem shooting her first, then taking your sorry ass out." Something clicked and Charlene thought it might have been him taking the safety off the gun.

But at that exact moment Akil pounced, knocking T.K. to the floor.

They tussled for a minute but T.K. was still holding on to the gun. Charlene took another step in their direction and stomped on his wrist, over and over until his fingers finally gave out and let the gun go. That pointy three-inch heel had come in handy. She didn't want to pick up the gun but didn't want T.K. to have the opportunity to pick it up either so she kicked it out of his reach.

Akil took that moment to plow his fist into T.K.'s face. Okay, he deserved that one, she thought. But then Akil didn't stop, he kept pounding and pounding on T.K. until she could see blood and didn't know where it was coming from.

"Stop it! Stop it, Akil! He's not worth it," she said as she heard the first police sirens pulling into the marina.

Stepping around them she tried to grab his shoulders, then his arm as he went to swing again. "He's not worth it and beating him to death won't bring your mother back."

Akil's chest was heaving as he sat back on his legs. She held the right arm but his left one fell to his side.

When his head turned and he looked at her she saw the weight of his world clearly in his face.

He'd felt guilty for leaving his mother to die. For years he'd lived with that guilt. He felt guilty that Lauren was on drugs and had lived with that, too. Now he felt rage, a tremendous amount of rage that she feared could lead him down the wrong path.

"It's okay, baby," she was saying, falling to her knees to kneel beside him. "It's okay now."

His head dropped, his chin hitting his chest, and he made a sound that she wasn't sure was crying or sighing. But she put her arms around him, hugged him tight and kept telling him that it was all right.

"You did what she asked you to do. You saved Lauren, that's all she wanted."

"But I didn't. I didn't save her."

"Yes, you did. Lauren grew up and made her own decisions. You can't blame yourself for that. You did your best."

"I should have done more. I should have been stronger, put my foot down, made her listen."

"No!" Charlene said adamantly, pulling back to look at him. He still had his head down so she cupped his chin and lifted it up. "She should have been stronger. Lauren should have fought harder to be different. That wasn't your battle and it's not your burden to carry now."

On the floor T.K. was moaning. Footsteps sounded on the dock and in seconds the police were busting into the cabin. Akil stood, then helped her to stand, holding her hand tightly.

The officers were cuffing T.K. and retrieving the gun Charlene told them she'd kicked to the side.

"I'm sorry," he said.

She was already shaking her head. "Don't. It's done."

"But I hurt you.'

She nodded. "You did. But I'm stronger than I look. I'll get over it because I know you were doing it out of self-preservation."

"No matter what you call it, I was wrong. And I apologize. I love you," he said simply.

And it was enough.

She picked up his bruised hand, kissed his knuckles. "And I love you."

Chapter 21

Two Weeks Later

Holding that last and final note-had felt good. The following applause felt even better.

She'd done it!

The song was titled "Journey." It was the one she and Akil had both written the lyrics to. After the episode on the yacht they'd returned to his house to be pampered by Mrs. Williamson and the staff. The FBI had come along with questions to which Akil openly provided answers. Even about his mother's death and his involvement in the impromptu sting to catch a drug dealer all those years ago.

He said he felt like he'd completely purged himself and she was happy for him. Heading back into the studio, the first song he wanted to work on was "Journey." It was a joint decision that she'd sing it tonight as she was in L.A. performing for the Pediatric AIDS Benefit Concert produced by Playascape.

There were no nerves when she'd stepped up on the stage this time. Well, okay, there were some, but they were quickly tamped down when she touched the bracelet on her wrist, the one Akil had given her. Just that action reminded her that he was in the room with her, that their hearts were now intertwined and their love strong. Singing the song, "their" song, seemed appropriate.

Afterward, the gang was all there, so to speak.

As Charlene walked off the stage, down some stairs and through a door that led to the seating area of the club, she saw them all sitting at a large table, already toasting glasses of champagne.

Jax was right beside her, helping her make her way through the crowd. A few people stopped her, gave their congratulations or comments, making her feel like all her hard work had paid off. Well, all *their* hard work, she should say.

At the table her parents were the first to hug her. She still couldn't believe they'd shown up, but as Marjorie had tried to tell her, all she'd done in the past had been out of love and concern for her child.

Candis was also back in the States, sitting a little close to Jason on the high-backed black leather couches that offered seating for one whole half of the table. After her parents, Candis had torn herself away from Jason to stand and give her a hug. "He's too young for you."

Candis only laughed. "Girl, didn't you know I was a cougar?" she said giving a mock growl.

Charlene was still laughing as Jason pulled her in for a tight hug. "You're doing the damn thing, girl! I'm proud of you."

"Thanks, Jason. It's all because of you."

"Yeah." He nodded. "I'll take some of the credit."

He was so goofy, maybe he and Candis did make a good couple after all.

"Hey, girl, you were fantastic up there." Rachel was next up, hugging her once, then again for good measure. "And you look great. Mia told me you were going to look good. I wish he was here, but he had to go to New York. You know how he is."

"I know you should have warned me about the hormone therapy before he showed up as a she," Charlene said, laughing.

"Oh, yeah, forgot about that one." Rachel laughed.

Charlene noticed the handsome man sitting right next to where Rachel had been and looked in his direction.

"Oh, almost forgot. This is Ethan Chambers."

The first thing Charlene noticed was that this brother was even finer in person. The tabloids didn't do him justice. The second thing she noticed was that he absolutely adored Rachel. The way he'd been watching her as they'd talked said it all.

"Hi. It's nice to finally meet you, Ethan."

He nodded and shook her outstretched hand. "Same here."

"And this—" Rachel took her hand from Ethan's and walked her a couple steps toward the end of the table "—is Olivia Blake. She worked on the set with us at *Paging the Doctor* and now she's signed up with Limelight."

Wow, was Charlene's first thought. Tall, mocha-skinned and gorgeous were the only words she could think of to describe Olivia.

"Livia, please. And you sounded great up there."

"Thanks," Charlene said, shaking her hand also.

"So, listen, Ethan and I are getting married at his brother's winery."

"What? Married? Did I miss something?"

Rachel looked from Livia to Charlene. "Oh, no! I told you. I know I told you, Char. I had to."

"You didn't, but we can talk about that later. So you're getting married at a winery?"

"Yes, his brother has this great winery in Napa Valley. The perfect setting, right? So, anyway, I want, no, I need, both of you to help me plan this thing because you know I don't have a clue."

"She's been talking like this for the last couple of days," Livia explained to Charlene.

Rachel was getting married? "Sure, you know I'm there for whatever you need."

"Okay, so how soon can you be in Napa Valley?" she asked.

"Who's going to Napa Valley?" Akil asked, stepping up behind Charlene and wrapping an arm around her waist.

"We are, to plan a wedding," Rachel said, practically beaming. "So you have to give my girl here some time off so she can come and help me."

Akil looked at Charlene and was all smiles. Since leaving his yacht that day and watching the police toss T.K.'s begging behind into the patrol car she and Akil had been inseparable. And their relationship—the personal one—was now common knowledge. Everybody who had eyes and were blessed to be in their presence knew they were in love and Charlene was ecstatic about it.

"A trip to Napa might be nice for both of us," he said, then dropped the sweetest kiss on her lips.

"Hmm, we might be hearing more wedding bells soon," Livia chimed in.

Everybody was talking and laughing and having a good time. Everybody except Sofia.

Charlene had talked to her briefly before going onstage but she had yet to see her since finishing her performance. She was curious to hear what she thought of the song and the sound of the CD, but she didn't see her.

She'd just left the table and was headed to the ladies' room when she spotted Sofia and the guy Rachel had told her earlier was Ramell Jordan, head of A.F.I. Ram, as Rachel said he liked to be called, who was also a good-looking man. Only Sofia probably wasn't thinking that right at this moment.

From Sofia's defensive stance and the sway of her neck as she was speaking, Charlene was guessing that whatever those two were discussing wasn't good. She figured she'd better get back to Rachel and let her know. It looked like they'd be planning some sort of intervention for Sofia and her workaholic status some time in the very near future.

Akil owned a penthouse in L.A.'s South Park district. Here, in stark contrast to his Miami home, was all about what money could buy. Spacious, decorated in sharp black, silver and gray tones, each room spoke of elegance.

Charlene didn't not like it, she just liked the Miami house better.

They'd been back from the concert for about an hour. She'd changed into her nightclothes as it was almost one in the morning. Akil still had on his slacks but had shed the jacket and button-down shirt he'd worn earlier. He was sitting at the piano that she hadn't known he could play. Going over to sit on the bench beside him, she noticed it was a Steinway grand piano and whistled.

"Really nice piano. I didn't know you could play," she said.

His fingers were moving idly over the keys and a quick melody echoed throughout the room.

"I can do a little somethin', somethin'." He smiled and she leaned against him.

"You're very talented, Mr. Hutton. I think that might be one of the reasons I love you so much."

"Oh, really?" He played a little more. "So it has nothing to do with my charismatic personality?"

"Nah," she said, playing along with his good, joking mood.

He nodded. "Good, because I thought it was more about the way you seem to hit all the high notes when you're with me."

That made her blush but she didn't back down. "That's certainly a high point. But that's not it, either."

He stopped playing and took her hands in his. "I can tell you why I love you so much."

No matter how many times he said the words her heart still fluttered at the sound. "Why?"

"Because you're you. Never once were you afraid to just be yourself. I had no choice but to fall in love with Charlene Quinn, the woman, the singer, the friend."

She smiled at that and he was rewarded. There was no need for her to say the words to him; he knew how she felt. And he was content just having her here with him. Finding Charlene was the best thing that had ever happened to Akil and he vowed never to mess that up.

The doorbell rang just as he was about to tell her they should retire for the night.

"Don't tell me you planned an after party?" she joked.

He was already standing and walking toward the door. "I didn't, because I wanted us to share this part of the celebration alone. So if it's Jason with more champagne I'm leavin' his butt right in the hallway."

But it wasn't Jason, as Akil saw quickly upon opening the door. She was about thirty pounds smaller than the last time he'd seen her, but he'd know her anywhere. They had the same eyes, the same strong chin. She fidgeted with her bag, looked down at her feet then up again at him.

"Hi, Akil," she said in a raspy voice. "Can I come home, I mean, can I come in?"

His heart was too full to speak. When he felt Charlene's hand on his shoulder he could only nod.

"You must be Lauren," Charlene said, extending a hand to the pretty young woman standing nervously in the doorway.

Lauren nodded and shook Charlene's hand.

Akil finally cleared his throat. "Of course you can come home, Lauren." When she had released Charlene's hand he took a step forward and pulled his sister gingerly into his arms and hugged her tight. "I've missed you so much," he whispered in her ear and felt his life was now more than complete.

He had his sister back and he had Charlene, the love of his life.

* * * * *

REQUEST YOUR FREE BOOKS!

2 FREE NOVELS PLUS 2 FREE GIFTS!

KIMANI™
ROMANCE

Love's ultimate destination!